W9-CMF-496

CARDINAL BLACK

ROBERT McCAMMON

CEMETERY DANCE PUBLICATIONS

Baltimore

❖ 2019 ❖

Cemetery Dance Publications special edition

Cemetery Dance Publications
132B Industry Lane, Unit #7
Forest Hill, MD 21050
www.cemeterydance.com

The characters and events in this book are fictitious. Any similarity to real persons, living or dead, is coincidental and not intended by the author.

First Cemetery Dance Printing

ISBN: 978-1-58767-704-5

ONE.

INTO THE STORM

ONE.

"Hear me well," said Gardner Lillehorne, resplendent in his overcoat of peacock blue with rolled cuffs of pigeon's-blood crimson. Atop his head was a selfsame blue color tricorn whose red band clasped a single white dove's feather. He was, as the popular saying of the day went, birded up.

His thin ebony mustache twitched upon an equally thin upper lip, while at the downward point of his chin the perfectly trimmed goatee was yet another point, downward. "*Well*," he repeated, his small black eyes aflame in the low light of a December's late afternoon. "I am the honorable assistant to the High Constable. As such I have the power to slam the law down upon you like a two-ton cannon upon a penny's-weight mouse if you fail to comply with what I have demanded. I have neither the time nor the patience to dally with you an instant longer, therefore I shall ask you only once again before I am compelled to move to action...will you, or will you *not*?"

"But...sir," said the ten-year-old boy, whose gray clothing was indeed mouse-colored and yet ample enough to withstand if not the weight of a heavy cannonfall the tremble of light snowflakes that were beginning to swirl down on the streets, alleyways, crossroads, courtyards, gardens and garrets of cold but bustling Londontown. "It's just five pence!" the young salesman went on, as snow dappled his black woolen cap. "Surely, sir, you can afford—"

"My ability to afford is not the issue. I—"

"Not the *issue*!" spewed the rough voice and flecks of spittle from the mouth of Lillehorne's florid-faced henchman and companion in chicanery by the name of Dippen Nack, who stood just behind his master as any good dog should.

"Nack! I shall speak for *myself*, thank you!" said the master to the hound in a tone of sharp rebuke, and the two-legged canine pulled his neck in a little tighter to his fur-trimmed fearnaught. Though short and squat by nature, Nack wore beneath his garish purple tricorn hat an ornately curled and powdered white wig that nearly towered over Lillehorne's shoulders.

Lillehorne returned his attention to the boy, who he determined was not going to get away with ignoring this demand, which seemed now more important than ever simply for the principle of it. Lillehorne lifted his ebony cane with its hand-grip of a silver lion's head and placed the tip against the boy's right shoulder, beneath which was the leather pouch that held the solitary object of his desire.

"Give me that last copy of *Lord Puffery's Pin*," Lillehorne said. "I command it."

"*Command* it!" barked Dippen Nack, who didn't realize he had purchased a coat advertised as being trimmed with beaver when in fact it was brown-dyed street cur. The cherub cheeks of his bully-boy's face seemed to pulse with excited blood stirred by the prospect of a street fight with a diminutive paperboy.

Nack's outburst, however rough it sounded, brought forth only a slow blink from the lad and a resigned sigh from the assistant to London's High Constable.

"I have determined," said Lillehorne in a calmer tone to the subject of his obsession, "that I have paid for my last copy of the *Pin*. That is to say, as befits my position of authority—and responsibility—I expect

some items in this city to be given to me *freely* and with good cheer. Your newssheet shall be one of them."

"And why exactly should that be, sir?" dared ask the boy, with a defiant forward jutting of his chin.

"Simply because," came the silkily spoken reply, "without the protection of the law to Lord Puffery's business—and indeed to all the businesses in this fair city—he should see his *Pins* snatched away by ruffians at the very door of the printshop...if the printshop itself is not burned to ashes on the ground. We—*I*—am the sturdy wall of order that stands between Lord Puffery's door—and every door you might look upon all along this street—and the evil tentacles of chaos. I assume you know the meaning of that—"

"Ah! At last I've found a *Pin*! Five pence here!" A round-bellied gent in a brown overcoat and a same-hued tricorn atop his own pile of wig-curlings had suddenly pushed his way onto the scene, namely the corner of Farringdon and Stonecutter streets a few blocks west of the Old Bailey, from which Lillehorne and Nack had emerged strutting and full of if not the flames of justice then the steady embers of avarice. The new arrival had silver pennies in one hand, offering them up, and was already reaching for the newssheet with the other.

"Hold! Hold!" Lillehorne nearly shouted, as if finding a *Pin* this day were like trying to pluck out a haystraw from a stack of needles.

"*Hold*, he says!" And to back up this statement came Nack's wicked ebony billyclub, his favorite fiend. Nack plunged forward past Lillehorne like the devil's pitchfork and put the pain-giving end of the club beneath the intruder's descending terraces of chins. "You'll not have it!" Nack snarled. "It's already *took*!"

The gent staggered back on his polished bootheels. "This is...this is an *outrage*!" he sputtered, looking back and forth from one man to another and finding them both as ugly as toenail soup. "You have no claim on the paper! Where is your money, sir?"

"Here's our roll a'dough!" Nack gave the man's chins a thrust of the billyclub. "It's good and solid, ya toad-faced warthog!"

"An *outrage* and an injury as well! I'm going for the law! There's a constable hereabouts, I'm sure!"

"To be sure, there is!" said Nack, with a crooked grin that displayed his unfortunate mouthful of jagged teeth. "You're lookin' at one! And right here's the assistant to the High Constable hisself, so bite on that apple and piss a prune!"

"You men are *mad*!" came the unsteady response. "Crude louts as constables? What's this world coming to?"

"I don't know 'bout the world, but you're comin' near to a ride in the gutter! Off with you!"

"Outrage! Outrage!" cried the man, and though he puffed steam amid the drifting snowflakes he gave up the battle as lost and retreated into the moving mass of London humanity at his back.

"No you don't!" Lillehorne reached out with his free hand to clutch the paperboy's shoulder, as the lad had made a move to dart away but it had been at first a twist of the head rather than a leap of the legs. "Take the sheet, Nack," Lillehorne said, and so it was done.

"My manager'll skin me for this! He counted all the copies out!" the boy protested.

"Some advice to you." Lillehorne released the shoulder and placed the cane's tip alongside the boy's cheek. "Tell your manager he miscounted by one. Look him directly in the eyes when you say this, and *believe* it yourself. Believe it so fervently that it becomes true. You'll have no trouble, if you believe it with enough ferocity."

The boy paused. Then, with a quizzical expression and a knotting of the eyebrows: "Thank you?"

"You are welcome. Now run along." Lillehorne gave the cheek a quick pat with the cane, the paperboy scurried away with his lesson on how to be an adept liar, Lillehorne snatched the *Pin* from Nack before Nack had a chance to read a word of it, and Lillehorne said with the air of the victor's satisfaction, "Let us retire to Mr. Chomley's coffeehouse. He already understands the importance of a cup of free coffee to a hard-working public servant."

"*Two* hard-workin' public servants!" said Nack, nearly adding a chortle.

"Um," Lillehorne replied with a frozen expression. Off they went, one following the other as had been their custom in New York for several years and now in London the same.

As the pair progressed westward along Stonecutter toward Chomley's establishment on Norwich Street, Lillehorne mused that on this day of the twelfth month of 1703 the entire six hundred thousand population of the city must be out on the streets, chattering and nattering, steaming the air with their breath and the noxious odors of their nags pulling coach, carriage and wagon. Most of them, it seemed to him, clutched copies of *Lord Puffery's Pin* in their gloved mitts. Oh, what a farce they played, these fancy prigs of London! he thought. Prancing to and fro to display their winter finery, their new hats and expensive powdered wigs, jostling and elbowing, crowding past each other for a look into the windows at some fresh geegaw or sugared dumpling, and they smiled and smiled their false smiles with eyes as hard as iron and teeth ready to bite the heads off their neighbors' children if it took that to prosper in this city.

He knew them. Knew what they were thinking of him, when they gave him those sideways glances that one might give a clump of horse figs in the street so as to avoid leaving a boot print upon it.

Yes, he knew them. And he hated them, for their thoughts and their looks.

Lately he'd realized he was a foreigner here. He was no longer a true citizen of England for he had the roughness of New York about him, he carried it wrapped around himself like a cloak of brine-soaked ropes, and no matter how he dressed or tried to cover it over, its essence—its phantom—was there to betray him. That last dinner party he'd been talked into attending turned into a nightmare of his ill-taken witticisms and botched choices of what fork to use for which dish of clotted grease. He feared he had lost his sophistication during his years across the Atlantic, and now what seemed to pass as sophistication here were caustic remarks aimed at belittling the colonists, delivered as if one were speaking through a clench of lockjaw. If it were up to him he would book passage on the next ship

leaving for the colonies, but...he had this prominent position, his wife the Princess had clutched upon this place like a mollusk on a sea-slimed rock, her oppressive—at least to him—mother and father had paid for their very fine living quarters, had bought their home furnishings and purchased for them two matched chestnut horses and a carriage, therefore...

Meet Gardner Lillehorne, assistant to the High Constable of London, oh-so-happy denizen of this great metropolis and ex-resident of the rustic town of New York, likely never to return there.

But the truth was...he felt he'd really been someone of importance there, with a job to do, and had earned the respect of all. Well...almost all. Here the title was grand, but he was naught but a bootscrape to the men above him. And above him were so many.

"Damn, what a mob!" he said to no one in particular, as he and Nack advanced against a stiffening and more frigid wind. The snowflakes were beginning to fly into their faces. In the sky the low gray clouds were interlaced with the black streamers of coal smoke rising from the industrial chimneys that stood tall over even the best parts of the city, as if reminding the population that one tumble and spate of bad luck could turn the finest of fashionables into a grime-streaked furnace stoker chained to the never-ending job of feeding power into London's massive maw.

Within a few minutes the blue-lettered sign of Chomley's Coffee Parlor came into view, and with great relief to remove himself from the swift currents of humanity Lillehorne entered the place with Nack at his heels. A coal-burning stove and a brick fireplace provided heat, and hanging lanterns cut the gloom. Though there were already too many patrons in the parlor for Lillehorne's complete satisfaction, he guided himself and his compatriot to a vacant table at the rear and, after doffing his overcoat, he settled his rump into a high-backed chair beneath a dusty oil portrait of a stern bewigged gent who seemed to be scowling at the new generation of Londoners from his current position in Eternity.

"Coffee, of course!" Lillehorne told the young girl who came to take their order. He was already spreading the *Pin* upon the table before him.

"Two!" he said, before Nack could open his fanged mouth and frighten the dame. "Black and medium-sweet," he went on, with no mind nor care as to what Nack desired. "Oh…and by the by," he said with silk in his voice, for this was not the same girl who had served him three days before on his last visit, "remind Mr. Chomley that this order is for Gardner Lillehorne, Esquire. He will know the name and the position, and that all shall be square with the bill." Then, with the maid's departure, he turned his attention to the news of the day, read beneath a flickering lantern and a dead man's disapproval.

"Lord God!" Lillehorne said, at his first sighting of the large print declaration across the top of the sheet.

"Read it, read it!" Nack was pressing forward over the table, his cheeks flushed with excitement.

Lillehorne did: "*Albion and the Monster Of Plymouth Still At Large.*" Beneath that was a declaration in smaller print but no less emphatic: "*Constables Fear Renewed Murder Spree.*" And tucked under that, a third: "*Beware Albion's Wicked Blade and the Evil Hand Of Matthew Corbett.*" Then Lillehorne repeated his first reaction, but with a quieter breath: "Lord God."

"I knew that damn Corbett was a rotten apple!" said Nack, with the smack of his palm against the tabletop. "Couldn't sit still in New York, he had to follow our tails over here! I shoulda brained him when I had the chance!" He frowned. "What's a *spree*? Sorta like a *squirt*?"

"In this instance, more like a puddle of piss." Lillehorne shook his head. "Zounds, what nonsense! As far as I know, we fear no renewed murder spree, or squirt, or whatever. At least not from Albion or Corbett. I have to say, Nack…this puts a sodden rag on my belief in the *Pin*. Of course many of these articles are fantastical—the item about the ape rampaging through Parliament, for one—but I had thought there was a fig of truth in most of it."

"*What*?" Nack sounded shaken to the soul. "Y'mean Lady Everlust didn't birth no two-headed child?"

"Entertaining, but doubtful. This thing about Albion and Corbett... well, it's true they're connected in some way, but..." Lillehorne let it trail off. The golden-masked killer and phantom of the night had indeed taken Corbett from a guarded coach bearing the New York ass-pain to Houndsditch prison nearly three weeks ago, and from there both Albion and Corbett had seemingly vanished from the face of the earth. Then Hudson Greathouse and that irritating Grigsby girl had come to the Old Bailey wanting to know where Corbett was, and what could be said? Nothing but the truth, and it be damned: somewhere, if he were still alive, Matthew Corbett was in the clutches of a masked maniac who had already dispatched six victims by the sword.

For that matter, what had happened to Greathouse and the girl, who evidently had accompanied that big oaf to London because she was in love with Corbett? Lillehorne had expected them to show back up at the Old Bailey to press their presence and oppress himself, but...no, they had not.

It was obvious to Lillehorne that Lord Puffery had decided the association of Albion and Corbett still warranted publication to a bloodthirsty audience. How Lord Puffery had gotten that story to begin with was no doubt easily explained by one of the coach's guards giving over the tale for a few coins. He might have done the same, had he been confronted by Albion that night. But larger questions remained: what need did Albion have of Corbett, and where were they?

The cups of hot coffee came. "Mr. Chomley says the bill is square," the serving-girl offered. "He says he wants no trouble with the law."

"There shall be none," Lillehorne replied, but he couldn't help giving the girl's ample bottom a push with his cane when she turned to walk away. In that instant of misdirected attention Nack grabbed up the *Pin* and squinted hard over its bounty of print in the yellow lamplight.

"This has been a strange time," said Lillehorne, who decided to sip his coffee and rest his eyes from any further inflammations of the names *Albion* and *Corbett*. "Judge Archer is still missing, you know. All that in the *Gazette* about him being kidnapped from the Cable Street Hospital in

Whitechapel, and him suffering from a gunshot wound. Well, what was he doing in Whitechapel and who has him? Somebody with a grudge against him, to be sure. And then the clerk—Steven Jessley—doesn't come in to work one morning and it seems the address he has given on his employment papers is false. No one can find him, either. It makes no sense! Nack, are you listening to me?"

Obviously he was not. "Says here a wall was busted down off Union Street and they found an old sea trunk with ten shrunken heads in it. Can you fathom such a thing?"

"It is beneath me," said Lillehorne. "I no longer can trust Lord Puffery."

"Can you trust *this*?" Nack began to haltingly read. "Word comes to us…that the missin' Italian opera star…Madam Alicia Candoleri…has been spirited away by her lover…the pirate Redjack Adams…taken to his secret hideout…Paradise Cove…more to come." Nack looked up and grinned, a frightening sight. "Ain't part of your job supposed to be findin' her?" His grin fractured as his brain came up with a thought. "Hey. Might be she run off with this pirate and don't *want* to be found."

"I'm not sure she wanted her escort and coach driver to be murdered, as they were," Lillehorne reminded the other. He took another sip of the strong black coffee. There were over two thousand coffee houses in the city; part of his mind was wondering where else he might get free cups. "The situation of Madam Candoleri concerns me, but until someone comes up with real news I and the street constables are equally at a loss to speculate."

"That brings me to some b'ness," said Nack. "I need ta'morra night off."

"Tomorrow night? What's the reason? I would bring it to your attention that you have worked only three nights this week, that you have a very short route and reasonable hours in a safe district and that I have pulled quite a few strings to get you a fair trial as a fledgling constable."

"Fledglin' or not, I'm in for a dice game at the Jackal and I mean to be there. So I need you to get me off ta'morra night." Nack cocked his head to one side, his ears awaiting an affirmative reply.

Lillehorne shifted uneasily in his chair. He mused that if this damn fool before him didn't know about the hundred pounds Lillehorne had skimmed from the New York treasury—and also about that certain lady of the town to whom most of the money had gone—then he would dismiss this request as much as he would've dismissed the demand for Nack to come with him to London. But there was the wife and her parents to consider, and God help the poor soul who crossed that bunch. Nack would certainly go running to them at the first opportunity to cause mischief, if he were not coddled in check.

"Very well," came the reluctant answer. "I suspect, however, that your association with those cretins at the Jackal tavern might be your undoing."

"I can handle m'self." Even sitting down, Nack managed to swell his chest in indignant pride. "Anyways, they all knows I'm a constable and I've got the power of the law at my backside. Ain't nobody givin' me no trouble over there." Nack took a drink of his coffee and continued scanning the *Pin*. "Ah!" he exclaimed, so loudly that two patrons at the next table nearly jumped out from under their wigs. "Here's somethin' for you! Lemme read it: *An Open Letter to the London Law, What There Is Of It*." He looked up and grinned again, while Lillehorne's face was a study in stone.

"Go ahead," Lillehorne prompted, when Nack decided to play out the silence with mischievous glee.

Nack read, haltingly again: "It has come to our atten…attention…that our so-called officers of the law in our great city…have turned a blind eye…to several local crimes of which…most would be…shock…ed. The latest being…the mass mur…murder…of—"

"Give that to me!" Lillehorne nearly ripped the sheet out from under Nack's paws. He positioned it to favorable lamplight and read aloud: "The mass murder in Whitechapel two weeks ago of the young men and women belonging to a group known as the 'Black-Eyed Broodies', a massacre upon which this publication has reported more thoroughly in our previous issues. While we certainly do not condone the activities of such groups, it is a crime upon itself that this particularly gruesome and demonically-inspired

mass murder seems to be overlooked by our so-called officers of the law. Indeed, the murders among these groups are becoming common, no thanks to our fine officials who appear to be as equally frightened of these organizations as they are of the denizens of the shadows who use them for their evil purposes." Lillehorne grimaced, but kept reading. "And yes, we dare to name names, among them Professor Fell, Colonel Phibes, and Maccabeus DeKay. Who can say what inhuman pestilence against society is being created even now, encouraged by the inattention—one might say the ineptitude—of our so-called officers of the law."

Nack chose that moment to make a rumbling in his throat that Lillehorne took as mocking humor, and when Lillehorne darted his own black eyes of brooding at Nack, the other man quickly pretended to be examining some small clean spot on his fingernails.

"Mind yourself," Lillehorne ordered, and then he returned to the last paragraph of this distasteful open letter: "Therefore this publication no longer aspires to encourage these absent lawmen to action, but instead aspires to encourage the average hardworking and lawful citizens of this great city to action, by storming the Old Bailey by force if need be to jolt these mindless sops from their paid sleep. We suggest that citizens band together to demand that justice be done, or else that our Parliament clean out every existing so-called officer of the law from their nooks, crannies, caves and hammocks and send them to the mattresses they may occupy in the quiet confines of their homes, where they will no longer be bothered by the demands of an occupation and no longer be rewarded with public funds for a job undone. Signed yours sincerely, Lord Puffery."

"How about that?" said a heavy-set gent at the next table, who had been leaning in Lillehorne's direction to overhear and whose own copy of the *Pin* was spread out before him. "Strong words, eh? And it's about time, I'd say! What's your opinion?"

Lillehorne's face quivered as if he'd been slapped. His teeth were clenched. He felt Nack watching him like a dirty cat watching a writhing mouse.

Lillehorne unclenched his teeth. "My opinion is…it's about time," he replied, and the man nodded, thumped a fist upon his *Pin* as if to drive the point even further home and returned to his coffee and the conversation he'd been having with his tablemate.

"Don't speak," Lillehorne said to Nack, before the other could get that mouth working. Nack consented to draw at his coffee, making a noise like the dragging of a chain across a wet stone floor.

"Well," Lillehorne went on, with a carefully lowered voice, after a pause in which he squared his shoulders and jutted his chin toward the ceiling, "now I know why Master Constable Patterson was in such a black mood this afternoon. He must've gotten hold of a *Pin* earlier on and been pricked by it. But the constables can't be everywhere! Anyway…they're hated in Whitechapel! The last one assigned there was found beaten to death and stuffed in a rain barrel, so what do the people expect? There can be no law when the people of a district don't wish it and actually fight *against* it! All right…yes, that gang massacre was a gruesome thing… those eyeballs gouged out, and put into a bottle…and the Devil's Cross carved into the foreheads…yes, one might say it was demonically-inspired, but we as men of the law don't fear grappling with these criminals! It is a matter of rooting them out of their holes! No, we don't fear them… not a bit, and it is unfair of Lord Puffery to make that false assertion!" His next swallow of coffee drained the cup. "*False*!" he hissed at Nack across the table. "Do you hear? Utterly false!"

"I hear," Nack replied, in a small voice. "But I sure as hell ain't gonna go 'round rootin' nobody outta no holes." And he added, for emphasis, "Me bein' just a fledglin'."

"To Hell with this!" Lillehorne started to crumple the sheet between his hands but saw something else that snagged his eye. "Here's the only item worth a damn in this paper! The weather prognosticator predicts we're in for a season of storms! Ha! Would you expect summery sunshine here on the eve of winter? Who *couldn't* make such a prediction? Lord Puffery must've taken that task upon himself as well as the job of stirring up Parliament against the High Constable…and against myself, who has to bear the weight of it! Oh, I also can be a prognosticator and see what the weather will be like tomorrow at that office!"

"I'm needin' ta'morra night off," said Nack, as if nothing else had been discussed since he'd first mentioned it. "You done vowed. You won't go back on your word, will you?"

Lillehorne didn't answer, but just sat glowering at Nack until the little red-faced bully picked up his club from the table, stood up and said, "I'm headin' to home. I'll walk my route tonight, good and proper."

"I'll count on it," came the terse reply.

"By your leave, then," said Nack, who turned the cur's-fur collar of his coat up around his neck, gave his master a quick and ungainly bow and headed for the door.

On the street, flurries of snow blew through the evening's gathering dark. As the dark had fallen, so had the temperature. The blue December eve was speckled with the lamps of passing coaches and carriages, and in the windows of shops that remained open late to catch the passing crowd, which had much dwindled since Nack had followed Lillehorne into Chomley's parlor.

Nack thrust his free left hand into a pocket, clenched his ever-present billyclub in his right, and began to trudge against the chill wind toward his cellar hovel a mile north on Errol Street. He kept his head down and his thoughts on how he was going to get through such a cold night on duty, even though his route took him only half a mile; all he had to do was walk a circle and swing his constable's lantern in an area that was mostly parkland, so what of it? It was fortunate for him that his six hours of work took him past two taverns that stayed open until the wee morning, and tonight he meant to make use of their fireplaces and mugs of warm ale.

Soon his mind drifted to the dice game tomorrow night at the Jackal, his favorite tavern and a place where everyone knew him and all were impressed by being in the presence of a constable, and so he failed to note

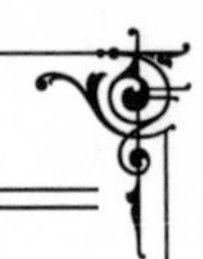

the coal wagon that had been steadily following him since he had walked out Chomley's door.

When he turned down the lonely length of Falstaff Alley to take his usual shortcut, he also failed to note the man who came up behind him and with one blow of a leather-wrapped piece of lead to the skull knocked Dippen Nack sprawling upon the rough stones. Nack's purple tricorn went spinning away and his ornate wig slid down upon one shoulder. He made a gurgling sound and tried to pull himself to his knees, but the assailant struck again and then most decisively Nack lay still.

"Aw shit!" said a second man, who had gotten down off the wagon and was holding the reins of his two horses at the mouth of Falstaff Alley. "Didja *kill* him?"

The first man knelt down to check for a heartbeat. "He ain't dead," was the verdict.

"He better not be! We're supposed to deliver two and God take us if we don't!"

"This one don't look like a fuckin' constable. You sure about him?"

"I'm sure. Like I said already, his name's Nack and he's been braggin' his ass off at the Jackal."

"All right, then. Let's get him in, we wasted too much time waitin' for him to come out of that damn coffee house. Somebody might come along here any minute."

"Somebody might," said the wagon's driver, "but what're they gonna do about it? Call for a *constable*?"

They both laughed at that one.

"Lucky I seen him comin' down the steps of the Bailey," said the driver as the two men hauled Nack's body up and carried him between them to the black pile of coal. "Figured I might see a constable I recognized. Anyhow, made our job one easier." They threw Nack into the pile and the man who'd done the striking climbed up and used a shovel to quickly cover the body with coal, being careful at the finish to leave a space of air around the nostrils.

When it was done he took his seat beside the driver and drew his coat collar up around his throat. He wore a gray woolen cap and had half of a nose. “Gettin’ colder,” he said, lifting his gaunt face toward the dark. “Snow’s comin’ down good and proper.”

“The *Pin* says storms ahead,” said the driver.

“Mark it, then,” the other answered. “All right. One down, one to go.”

The driver flicked the reins, the horses snorted steam and started off, the coal wagon’s tired wheels creaked as they turned, and beside the white wig and the purple tricorn a black billyclub lay untended on the snow-dusted stones of Falstaff Alley.

TWO.

"Yes," said Hudson Greathouse, "I do think I'd like another cup of tea, thank you."

"Surely, sir." She poured it for him from a white teapot painted with green and yellow flowers. "This is my favorite blend," she said. And then, with but an instant's cloud of shadow across her face: "I mean...I've been told it is."

"Told?"

"Yes sir. By my mother."

"Hm," said Hudson as he supported the dainty cup between hands more accustomed to holding rough-hewn wooden tankards of ale. He lifted his thick charcoal-gray eyebrows, the left of which was sliced by the jagged scar of a teacup thrown by a tempestuous ex-wife, which was one reason he abhorred teacups and the weak liquid they carried to the lips of the insipid. "You don't recall that it's your favorite?"

"Our daughter has always enjoyed that blend," said the man who sat in the room with them. His voice was perhaps a spike sharper than he'd intended. He had gray hair brushed back from his forehead, was heavily jowled and wore a dark blue suit with four silver buttons decorating the jacket. Up at his hairline on the right side was a plaster bandage, the flesh

around it puffed and ruddy. “And she enjoys a touch of extra lemon,” he added. “Don’t you, Mary Lynn?”

The response was a few seconds in coming, and again Hudson saw that cloud cross her face though it quickly cleared. “Yes, Father,” she said, “I do.”

“Ah.” Hudson gave her a smile; it was a tight smile, but he was doing the best he could. “Tell me what else you enjoy.”

The man said, “Mary Lynn likes to—”

“Pardon me, sir. I’d like to hear it from your charming daughter.” Hudson’s smile stayed fixed in place though the black tarpits of his eyes promised that violent destruction of this house could be achieved on a moment’s notice. He returned a softer gaze to the girl. “Go ahead,” he offered.

“Well,” she began, and she smiled brightly, “I do so enjoy—” She stopped suddenly, her smile faltered, and in her freckled face her blue eyes seemed to haze over as if they had become as ponds of ice. She looked to her counterfeit father, then back to Hudson, and then into her teacup as if her fortune—and the sense that was steadily leaving her mind—could be found there.

“Horseback riding,” Frederick Nash supplied. “You always enjoy that.”

“A notable endeavor,” Hudson replied, still staring at the girl. “Tell me…when was the last time you went riding?”

A silence followed. Berry Grigsby—now known in the Nash house and in this foul village of Professor Fell’s drug experiments as Mary Lynn Nash—took a sip of tea. Her hand trembled, just a fraction; her eyes, so usually sparkling with life, were now as dead as the doll’s face she had been painted and powdered to resemble. The sight of her like this—her body pushed into a pink gown too small for her, the brown wig of curly ringlets like a mudslide covering the coppery-red highlights of her own hair, her face whitened with powder and reddened with rouge and her eyes sunken down into purple hollows—made Hudson both saddened and enraged, and for a shilling and this pisspot of tea he would tear Nash limb from limb and then take this evil house apart at the joints. It had been explained to Hudson that Nash's wife—Mary Lynn's "mother"—was feeling poorly and had gone abed early, but Hudson thought it was a lie; he figured the woman simply didn't want to see anyone who had known Berry in a previous life. Hudson had had to display several violent temper fits to get this far, and after smashing the furniture in his own cottage and throwing it into the street the word had come that he was allowed to see "the girl", as his handler—a wiry and dangerous-looking man who called himself 'Stalker'—referred to Berry.

He wanted to beat them all to senseless pulps, including the woman in the other room. But there were so many questions he needed answers to, and up until now no one in this place—*Y Beautiful Bedd,* it was called—would give him satisfaction; therefore he needed to hold his seething anger and his fists until he could learn what exactly was going on, and where exactly was the young man he and Berry had crossed the Atlantic from New York to find.

"The last time?" Berry asked, her eyes still vacant. "I think…I think it was—"

"I had a very reliable horse once named Matthew Corbett," Hudson said. "I'm trying to locate where he might—"

"You were *warned,*" Nash interrupted, and he put his hand on the pistol that lay atop the table to his right. "None of your nonsense, sir."

"And all this is *sense*? Fuck that," Hudson said, with a snarl and a quick glance at the gun. "I would warn *you* that before you can level that little toy at me you'd go out through the front window, so take your hand away from it."

Nash didn't hesitate very long before he obeyed. "It matters not a whit," he said. "Our daughter is content as she is, with all the comforts we can give her. Isn't that right, Mary Lynn?"

Berry took another drink of tea as if none of this exchange had transpired. When she put her cup down into its saucer she frowned at her visitor. "That's a strange name for a horse," she said, with a faint and crooked smile upon her painted mouth.

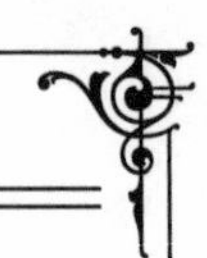

"More like an ass than a horse, but—" Hudson shrugged. He decided he could bear no more of this, and the situation was getting him nowhere except closer to another night without proper sleep. He stood up, noting that the motion made Nash flinch as if the man feared he might be attacked. "I thank you for your time...and for the tea," he said to Berry. Could he keep his throat from constricting to choke off the words? It was a difficult battle. "I'm sure I'll have the pleasure of your company again."

"*My* pleasure, sir." She stood up as well and gave him a curtsey that made Hudson think some invisible demon was actually floating above her, manipulating the marionette's strings.

Nash swept an arm toward the door. "I believe you can find your way out."

"That's exactly what I intend to find, and not just for myself." Hudson wrenched his brown corduroy coat off its wallhook so hard the hook came with it and fell to the floor's timbers with a ringing noise. He put it on over one of the flannel shirts that had been given to him, along with the coat and two pairs of breeches, since his own clothing had been removed during his first half hour in this damnable village and probably thrown into a fire; at least they'd returned his own boots to him, which was one positive thing. He braced himself for the chill outside, since Nash's house was so warmed by its fireplace, and without another glance at fictive father and delirious daughter he went through the door onto Conger Street, where four men with torches, pistols and swords were waiting for him in the blue twilight of evening.

One of them—a foolish man—reached out to grasp Hudson's shoulder and guide him on his way.

Hudson stopped short. Steam swirled from his nostrils. "If you want to keep that hand, you'll drop it to your side."

"We don't have to take any shit from you," another one said, and put the point of a rapier up under Hudson's unshaven chin.

Hudson Greathouse laughed. It was as much a release of tension as it was a reaction to this incredible scene of—as Frederick Nash, the so-called mayor of this town had said—nonsense. Around Hudson was a village of small houses and well-kept streets that could have been any charming locale in the country, except for the structures that for some reason had been reduced to ruins. So far Hudson had been denied explanation of what had caused such wreckage. The smoke of kitchen and parlor hearths curled from chimneys, lanterns glowed cheerfully in the windows, people in their winter clothing strolled about as if advancing to dinner or the theater in the finest neighborhoods of London, and indeed last night in the village square there'd been a concert by a fiddle-player and an accordionist, attended by perhaps forty citizens and warmed by a generous bonfire. Yet here in this midst of weird civility Hudson thought it absolutely absurd that he stood on the street with a blade to his throat while Berry Grigsby was a mindless puppet to Frederick and Pamela Nash…and also, he had noted the abundance of bloodstains in spaces between the square's stones, and whatever had recently taken place there had been gruesome indeed.

Hudson looked back toward Nash's house and caught sight of a figure standing at the front window with a candlestick and burning taper in hand. He thought it might be Berry but he couldn't tell because the glass had frosted over. Another figure—Nash? Or Nash's wife?—came into view and with an arm around the shoulder pulled the first figure into the darker recesses of the house.

"*Move*," said the man with the sword.

Hudson turned away from the house and began walking toward the cottage they'd afforded him, on Bluefish Lane. All the streets here were named after sea creatures…again, another ridiculous bow to the semblance of a real village, when in fact this was both a fort and a prison, as Hudson had determined in his walkabouts. Four strides further along Conger Street and the enormity—and tragedy—of what had befallen Berry hit Hudson like a ten-team lumber wagon. His broad-shouldered, six-foot-three-inch-tall frame trembled and staggered. His eyes burned with tears. He felt near fainting and devoid of strength, and when the man behind him gave him a shove he took it like a milksop. He had contained himself in Berry's presence, but now the shock of the situation emerged in the presence of a crawling upon his arms and hands, and when he held his hands up into the torchlight upon them were dozens of large black spiders scurrying over and between his fingers.

Sweat burst forth on his face. He nearly cried out…and would have, if he hadn't realized in a cooler part of his brain that this fearful hallucination was a remnant of the drug he'd been given on his arrival to this little corner of Hell. The torch flames themselves became horrors; like whips they flailed out at Hudson, and within them were the contorted and destroyed faces of the dead men he recalled on the field of battle, long ago when he was an English soldier in the last years of the Franco-Dutch war. The flames grew arms, as if to pluck him from this place and deposit him alongside the tormented souls on the shores from which no man returned.

Hudson squeezed his eyes shut and shouted "AWAY!" at the top of his lungs. The shout caused his guards to crash into each other as they retreated, their swords and pistols aimed for action but atremble so badly they couldn't have hit a wild bull at six paces, which at the moment would've been a tamer target than the man himself.

"*Hush*," said someone, in a quiet voice.

Hudson opened his eyes. There before him, as the fiery arms and the cinder-eyed faces crackled above and began to become simply torch flames again, was the wiry man who called himself Stalker.

"What's all this commotion?" Stalker asked, still quietly. He was about half the size of Hudson but there was something about his sharp-jawed face, the coldly intelligent eyes and the smooth economy of his movements that told Hudson this man had experience in killing people in the dark; an assassin by nature, is what Hudson suspected. Stalker was bundled up in a sheepskin coat and wore a black cap upon his bald head. His hands were lodged in his pockets and he had the easy demeanor of a man out taking the evening's air. "Ah!" he said, and then to the others: "He's had an incident. Don't be frightened, boys. He's coming out of it."

Hudson watched the last few spiders vanish from his hands like whirls of dark smoke. He ran a forearm across his sweating face. He said to Stalker, "Damn you."

"I presume you had a pleasant visit with the girl." It was a statement, not a question.

Hudson spat on the ground between Stalker's lizard-skin boots.

"Your opinion means nothing to me," Stalker said. "What becomes of you means nothing, either…but I've been told to find you and bring you to dinner."

"To dinner? *What*?"

"He wants you to join him."

Hudson knew exactly who was summoning him. "Tell the professor he can go to—"

"You have questions no one will answer," Stalker interrupted. "They have been forbidden to do so. The professor has instructed me to tell you that it's time you got your answers…from himself."

"I'm not hungry."

"Not for the knowledge you've been seeking? Oh come now, Hudson! You want to know where Corbett is, correct?"

Hudson didn't reply.

"It's dinnertime," said Stalker.

Hudson followed the man along Conger Street and was in turn followed by the other four. The wind had picked up, blowing in over the fort's ramparts and bringing with it the briny scent of the sea. At the end of the street stood a stone construction that looked nearly like a small castle, with many windows of stained glass and a balcony encircling the upper floor. Hudson had previously seen this house and had no doubt to whom it must belong. Lamplights glowed behind the green, blue and red patterns of the windows. The house stood on a slight incline beyond an open iron gate, the gravel pathway leading up to the front steps ornamented by small trees that had been blown into contorted shapes by the seawind.

"Wait here," Stalker told the other men, and then motioned Hudson on ahead.

In another few minutes Hudson and Stalker stood in a dining room with dark red wallpaper and heavy black drapes over the two windows. Hudson saw that the dining table had legs carved to resemble leaping dolphins, and suspended from the ceiling above it was a black wrought-iron wagonwheel chandelier holding six burning candles. On the table were four more burning tapers, two placed before the silver platter and utensils table setting at one end and two at the other. Hudson noted that both settings included knives, and both were very sharp-looking indeed. That particularly interested him, since he'd not been allowed a razor to shave with, and here were blades that could cut a man's throat as quick as a wish.

"I'll take your coat," Stalker said, and waited as Hudson shrugged out of it. "Sit there." Stalker tapped the high-backed chair that faced the other high-backed chair. Included with the setting at the other end was a small silver bell: the master's voice. As Hudson obeyed, Stalker used that same tapping finger to touch the knife. "You're already salivating over *this*. If I were you, I'd be a polite dinner guest. A blade won't get you answers any faster, and besides...you might need it for your food. Professor?" he called toward the staircase they'd passed on the way in. "Shall I stay?"

"No."

A shadow had moved not from the direction of the staircase, but from a far corner of the room draped in darkness.

As Hudson watched, the shadow became a man.

"Thank you, Stalker," said Professor Fell, "but I'm sure Mr. Greathouse *will* be a polite dinner guest. Just hang his coat in the hallway as you leave. And go get something to eat at the tavern, the catch was good today."

"Yes, sir."

Hudson didn't bother to watch Stalker leave the room; he was fixed upon his first sight of the notorious, powerful and infamous Professor Fell...

...who today looked like nothing more than a frail, weary and completely harmless man of sixty or so who happened to be up past his bedtime.

"Greetings," Fell said, with a slight nod. He wore a silk robe of purple trimmed in gold and a purple silk skullcap. "I am pleased to see you've recovered."

"Were you pleased to put me in that condition?" Upon arriving here by coach and under armed guard—how long ago?—he and Berry were separated, half-a-dozen men had held him down while a bitter-smelling cloth was held over his face, he recalled coming out of the fog to feel a needle jabbing him in the prominent vein of his right arm, and after that came the nightmares of excruciating terror. Among them was the sense that venomous spiders were not only crawling over him but growing inside him, and the feeling that his body continually burst into flame, burned him to a skeleton, and then charred him again when his flesh grew back. In that state, he remembered that hearing someone speak his own name was like the sound of a death sentence from a vengeful God.

"Experimentation is one of my passions," the professor replied. "Surely you won't hold that too much against me?"

"If I had my way, I'd hold *this* against your throat." Candlelight jumped off the blade as Hudson picked it up and aimed it in Fell's direction.

"Your way," said Fell, "has brought you and Miss Grigsby here. I think your way is not as successful as you would desire." He sat down, carefully unfolded the red napkin at his setting and placed it in his lap, and by the light of the tapers Hudson had the opportunity to study this man who had caused such death and destruction to the New World as well as to the Old.

Professor Fell was a mulatto, light of skin. His long-jawed and high-cheekboned face could have been described as gaunt, but that word might put too much flesh upon it. Hudson considered that the professor looked like a man whose misdeeds had caught up with him, and the violence of the storms within were contorting his bones just as the wind off the sea had blown the trees outside into grotesque shapes. On either side of the purple skullcap tight white curls of hair bloomed out like the wings of a snowy owl. Blue veins laced his hands; perhaps they trembled just the slightest with palsy, or mayhap it was a trick of the light.

Professor Fell smiled, and thereupon Hudson caught the glint of teeth. He saw in the deep hollows of the strangely luminous amber orbs of the man's eyes not a palsied and weary wisp but something of an animal—a king of beasts, as it were, who had gained his position of royalty with his intelligence and his cunning, and used the brute strength of lesser men for the jobs that involved blood and guts. It was in the way the professor was examining him, even as he examined the professor; Hudson had the impression that behind the lined face the wheels were turning so fast the friction might soon make Fell snort smoke, and it would drift slowly down the length of the table and wrap itself around Hudson's head like an envelope of fine spider webbing.

Fell placed his elbows on the table and steepled his fingers. Hudson thought that whatever the professor had been thinking, a decision had been made.

"I understand," said Fell, "that late last night you caused quite a scene by destroying most of the furnishings of your house and throwing the sticks into the street."

"Correct."

"Impatience does no one any good, Hudson. May I call you that?" He went on without waiting for a response. "You were going to be allowed to see Miss Grigsby today anyway. Now you'll be sleeping on a cold floor for your efforts."

"I've slept on cold floors before."

"I'm sure." The amber eyes were both piercing and entrancing. "You're not fearful of me in the least, are you?"

"I've worn my fear shirt to shreds," said Hudson. "Thanks to you, and whatever drug your people pricked me with."

"Hm!" Fell's head cocked slightly to one side. "Now wouldn't *that* be interesting? If after recovering from a drug that *intensifies* fear, the subject becomes immune to it. You see, Hudson, you may have delivered a service to mankind."

"What service is Berry supplying? How a young woman of intelligence can become a mindless doll?"

Fell gave no response. His face showed not a flicker of emotion. For a while he simply sat in silence and stared down the table into Hudson's eyes. At last he picked up the silver bell and rang it. "Let's get started, shall we?" he said.

A heavy-set woman with a tight bun of brown hair and wearing an apron entered through another door at the rear of the room. She carried a silver tray, and from it set down green ceramic bowls of cream-colored soup before first the professor and then Hudson. "Thank you, Noreen," Fell said to her. "We'll have the wine now, if you please."

When the woman had departed the room, Fell picked up his soup spoon and said in a quieter voice, "I have to say, Noreen is proficient but not as good an attendant as my last one, and also the gentleman who used to be my cook was injured in a little incident we recently had here, so the new man is still under evaluation. But go ahead and eat up, Hudson; you can be sure it's just cuttlefish chowder, and nothing more exotic."

Hudson dipped his spoon into the chowder and smelled it. Fresh enough, and no scent of drugs, but what would that matter? Maybe the professor was correct, and his sense of fear had evaporated. Anyway, he was hungry, and that finished the internal debate. He ate the first spoonful and found it very good indeed.

"I expected Mother Deare to be joining us for dinner," Hudson said.

"Two days ago Mother Deare *was* the dinner," Fell answered. "The sharks that prowl our harbor at the bottom of the cliff appreciated her body being fed to them in pieces."

Hudson paused with the spoon halfway to his mouth. He said, "I think I've missed a lot."

"Indeed you have. Oh good, here's our wine. A nice soft white, to go with our baked halibut." Noreen, carrying another tray, had emerged from what Hudson presumed was the kitchen; she placed a wine glass before Hudson and another before the professor, and then went about uncorking the bottle. She poured each of them about a half-glassful and left the bottle on the table as she returned to the kitchen. Fell took a drink and nodded.

"Very fine, as always. Unfortunately it's my last bottle of this, as recent vibrations to the house caused some breakage in my cellar."

"All right," Hudson said. He put his spoon into the soup and left it there. "I appreciate the dinner and the attempts at gentlemanly manners, but where the hell is Matthew Corbett?"

"Not here," came the reply. "He left three days ago with one of my men, Julian Devane by name. Matthew volunteered for a mission to be undertaken, and I sincerely hope he has not been by this time killed in trying to carry it out."

"Go on." Hudson felt a tightening in his gut that was definitely caused not by the chowder, but by the misadventures of a chowderhead.

"My village," said the professor as he continued to eat his soup, "was attacked from the sea by a ship armed with a mortar weapon. That would explain the destruction you obviously have seen. We were also attacked from within, by traitors under the command of Mother Deare, who was herself under the insane command of an individual who calls himself 'Cardinal Black'. They came for the book of potions created by my ex-chemist, Dr. Jonathan Gentry. You may have known him in New York?"

"Yes, and I understood from Matthew that he lost his head at one of your dinner parties."

"A more important thing has now been lost," Fell said. "The book that Gentry's head conceived. Without it—and without a chemist to decipher the formulas—there is no hope for the recovery of Miss Grigsby. By my estimation—and it could be quite faulty, but I do have some idea of the power of that particular concoction—she will continue to decline until the Nashes have an infant daughter to care for...if the antidote is not given to her in several doses, and I believe the threshold of recovery is now in the realm of...I would say, to be safe...twenty-one days."

Hudson sat very still. He didn't move even when Noreen came out with their platters of baked halibut, fried corncakes, applesauce and candied yams.

At last, Hudson unclenched his teeth. "What was the *point*," he said with an effort, "of giving her that drug? What had she done to *you*?"

"It was what Matthew *has* done. All that he has done, and all that he has cost me." Fell swirled the wine around in his glass and watched it, the candlelight glinting off the glass and into his amber-colored eyes. "I intended him to watch her decline into imbecility…and to watch you perish from the very force of fear itself." His gaze left the glass and aimed at Hudson. "I hope you intend to use that blade on the corncake," he said softly, "because the halibut needs only a fork."

Hudson realized he had picked up the knife and was holding it in a white-knuckled grip, the point upraised to stab not a fish but a foul.

"So," Fell continued, with a slight shrug as if the weapon Hudson held were no more than an apparition, "Matthew and Julian have ridden off to find Cardinal Black and bring back the book and a chemist. They are beginning at a village called Adderlane, six or seven miles northwest along the coast. We learned that Black's men were using it as their staging-point. We're in Wales, about twenty miles from Swansea, if you'd care to know."

Slowly, Hudson lowered the knife; there was no sense in stabbing the man in the heart for two reasons: Professor Fell had no heart, and his own death would be immediate and equally senseless. Anyway…he was still hungry, and he was going to force himself to eat. Keeping it down later might be a different kettle. "You mean to tell me," he said, his throat dry, "that only Matthew and one other man have gone on a *raid*? How many men does Black have?"

"Many. We killed a few and caught a few. But…many remain, I suspect."

"Gone *three days*? And not a word?"

"I wouldn't expect a letter anytime soon," said Fell. "The post out here is not dependable."

Hudson came so close to overturning the table that he broke out in a sweat and saw a few black spiders running across his hands.

"We made an agreement," said Fell. "If I let Matthew go to bring back the book, he agreed to find for me a man for whom I have been searching many years. I believe that man is somewhere in Italy. Who he is and what he has that I desire does not concern you." Fell's chin lifted a fraction, as if defying Hudson before the other man could object or question. "It is my sincere wish—*hope*—that Matthew does indeed find Cardinal Black, and that he and Julian can wrest that book from him and bring back a chemist to produce the antidote for Miss Grigsby. When—if—that happens, I have agreed to return you and the young lady to New York, and Matthew will be free to act on my accord."

"A great plan!" said Hudson, with a steaming dollop of sarcasm. "Well, what do you know about this Cardinal Black?"

"He's a demoniac and has so far murdered a score of people. His mark is leaving a Devil's Cross carved into the foreheads of his victims."

"Oh, is *that* all? Didn't Matthew take a Bible to beat his brains out with?" Hudson wrung his hands to make the spiders whirl away. "Lunacy!" he nearly shouted. "That boy's no match for a murderous demoniac!"

"*Really*?" Fell gave a short, sharp laugh, though his expression remained grimly solemn. "That *boy* has bested the gang of men I sent to New York to create a school for future talent, he caused the death of Tyranthus Slaughter, he finished off the Thacker brothers and destroyed my home and most of Pendulum Island, he stole from me the very valuable Minx Cutter, and the Devil only knows what else he's done...and you say the boy's no match for this Cardinal Black? Bite your tongue, sir! I say again...bite your tongue!"

Hudson had heard a quaver in Fell's voice. Perhaps it was as vitally important to him that Matthew return, as much as it was vitally important for Matthew to provide an antidote to Berry's decline. Hudson had the thought also that Berry was not the only one in decline; if this Cardinal Black had turned Mother Deare against the professor and dared to strike Fell so directly, then it seemed other sharks in the sea were smelling the blood of a weakened old man.

Hudson took a slug of his wine that emptied the glass. Weakened or not, right now Fell was in command. "What am I supposed to do while we're waiting for Matthew to come back?"

"You're to mind your manners. We'll put you to work rebuilding the structures that were damaged, if you're willing. Such effort will secure you a decent bed and some privileges that I have yet to decide upon."

"And what about Berry? How do I know those two won't...you know... take advantage of her condition?"

"Nash's wife needed a replacement for her unfortunately deceased daughter," Fell answered. "I understand it greatly benefits her own state of mind. I can also assure you that Frederick may be many things but he won't do what you're thinking. I've already broached that subject with him and told him that—mayor of this village or not—he is risking his head if I get a whiff of impropriety...and I have others checking on her, you may be sure."

"I don't think I can be sure of any damn thing," Hudson said, with as fierce a scowl as he could conjure.

"Well...I thought you might have that attitude." Fell reached into an inner pocket of his robe and brought out two small cards. He held them up so Hudson could see the fingerprint impressed in dried blood on each. "Do you know what these are? I'm sure you do, working with Katherine Herrald as you have. As I told Matthew, I have intended to send these to two people both you and he know—Gardiner Lillehorne and Minx Cutter—for their transgressions against me. The reality is that I presently have no messenger to spare to get these on their way, and I have—as you realize—more important matters on my plate. Therefore, as a gesture of good faith—" He didn't finish the sentence, but instead held first one card and then the other over the flame of the nearest taper. When the flames had consumed the blood cards nearly to his fingers he dropped the charred remnants into his soup bowl, where they hissed like little snakes.

"What say you?" Fell asked.

Hudson thought about it for a moment. God help Matthew out there in the wilds...and with one of Fell's killers at his side, too. Time was of the essence for Berry...but how the hell was the boy—no, the *man*—going to get that book of potions and a chemist away from a murderous demoniac—*Satanist*, to be exact—who had gathered a gang of probably like-minded deviates?

Damn, he thought. This was not just a pickle, it was the whole barrel.

But at the moment, in these circumstances, there was only one utterance that made sense.

Hudson held his glass up and said, "Pass the bottle down here."

THREE.

3 Days Previously…

In the distance, many miles away, stood a line of blue-hazed mountains. For several hundred yards around Fell's village the land was an unsightly morass of dark gray bogs streaked with brown and yellow, patches of knee-high grass likely hiding quicksand pits, and a few scraggly wind-sculpted trees reaching up as if for mercy from the brutal earth. The road that stretched from southeast to northwest was no more than a hardly recognizable track across the ground. Ahead, in the direction the two riders must travel, the track curved into forest.

They had gone only a short distance when Julian Devane reined his horse in and turned the animal to block Matthew's progress.

The purple knot above Devane's right eye had receded somewhat but the mottling of bruises had merged together to form a dark patch across his left cheekbone, both painful memories of the violence of Cardinal Black's raid on Y Beautiful Bedd. Devane's mouth curled when he said, "You're well aware that this is a suicide mission, are you not?"

"I'm aware it's a *mission*," Matthew replied. "I don't consider it suicidal."

"Then you're a bigger idiot than I suspected. And here you've dragged me into it!" He reached into his black cloak with an equally black-gloved

hand and brought out a pistol that had four short barrels, two atop two, and double triggers; obviously, Matthew thought, the sword that Devane wore in a scabbard at his side did not possess enough deadly power to suit him. "Should I kill you now or later, and tell the professor this was a fool's errand?" came the question.

"It should be later," Matthew said calmly. "The guards up on the parapets could likely hear the shot from this distance."

Devane urged his horse forward until he was side-by-side with Matthew. The sun faded;

the ironwork of clouds had arrived.

"Hear me well, Corbett," Devane said. "I don't like you, I don't like this damned circumstance you've gotten me into, and if I somehow survive it I will make you pay. But I will do this to the best of my ability, because I've given my word and I abide by that rule. I have killed many, and most of those deaths I enjoyed dealing out. If I have to kill you, I will...and you have my word on that. Understand?"

"Without question," said Matthew.

"I am the bad man," Devane said. "Just so you know."

Again without question, Matthew thought, but he remained silent.

Then Devane put his gun away and wheeled his horse toward the northwest. Matthew gave his mount a flick of the reins and followed behind, his resolve ready for both saving the woman he loved and meting out justice to the killer behind the deaths of his brother and sister Black-Eyed Broodies, as he'd vowed to a lost friend. He was wearing black leather gloves the professor had given him, but he was always aware of the tattoo of a stylized eye within a black circle, embossed between the thumb and forefinger of his right hand, reminding him that he was the last of the Broodies, and for the kindness they'd shown him—rough kindness, but kindness nonetheless when he needed shelter and friends—the loyalty oath he'd taken was not to be shrugged off and tossed aside like an old cloak.

They went on along the road, the good and the bad across the ugly landscape.

It was hard for Matthew to concentrate on the task ahead, because of Berry's condition, but concentrate he must *because* of her condition. If he had his druthers he would kick his horse into a gallop to get where they were going, but his sense of logic told him it might very well be galloping into a trap, and getting killed so soon on Cardinal Black's trail would not bring Berry back from the land of the lost.

It was equally difficult to keep his own heart from galloping. He knew their destination, from what Cardinal Black had said to Mother Deare before commending the souls of both Matthew and William Atherton Archer to the Devil: *I will meet you at the tower.* And then information was added by one of Black's men taken during the raid: he thought it was a medieval watchtower in the forest about a half-mile this side of Adderlane. A place, the man had said, where Black went to commune with Satan.

Matthew had to determine himself to relax in the saddle, because his mount was feeling his demons of demand and was jumpy under the bit. He pulled his gray cloak tighter around his neck and shoulders, for with the disappearance of the sun behind the vault of clouds the air had chilled. He knew it did no good for him to mentally pontificate about the future of this mission and the results of failure, and therefore he had to concentrate not on the moments ahead but upon the moment at hand.

Take Julian Devane, for instance. Matthew was curious about how any sane man wound up in the employ of Professor Danton Idris Fell. "What's your story?" Matthew asked, and waited for a reply that would seem as chilly as the wind.

It was a long time coming, and indeed was laced with ice: "None of your damned business."

"I thought it might be beneficial to know who I was teamed with."

"A fool teamed with a fool," Devane said. "Now shut your mouth and give me peace."

Peace, Matthew mused, was likely the one thing this man could never find. For all his criminal tendencies, Devane carried himself with an aristocratic air. One could tell a man's bearing—and education—by the way he sat astride and handled a horse, and Matthew was certain from his observations that Devane did not come from the school of the gutter. Under that rakishly tilted dark green tricorn was a brain, and not simply one that served as an automaton for the professor or had been for the recently deceased Mother Deare. No mere henchman was Julian Devane, and again Matthew wondered what the man's history was. He figured Devane to be maybe twenty-six or twenty-seven years of age, only two or three years elder than Matthew, who had turned twenty-four the previous May, which seemed eons ago here on the eve of 1704 and was not recalled as a very merry month. Since his adventure in the Carolina colony concerning the River Of Souls, time had been both a whirl and a disturbance. There was of course a period in which his memory had been lost until he had awakened on a ship bound for England as both a "servant" and a prisoner to that hideous Prussian swordsman, Count Anton Mannerheim Dahlgren, and the Devil must be lamenting that man's arrival to muddy up the pretty red walls of Hell. Then it was into Newgate prison for Matthew, his association with the Black-Eyed Broodies and the avenger Albion, and now…

Now this.

He watched the line of forest grow closer across the windswept, yellow-grassed moors. There was nothing to do but to allow his horse to move toward the future at what was for him a plodding pace. He was no stranger to the dangers of whatever the future might hold; as a member of the Herrald Agency and in New York a "problem-solver" he had already survived many dangers to arrive at this moment in time. Matthew was tall and slim, with a lean, long-jawed face and cool gray eyes that held hints of twilight blue. His thatch of thick black hair was protected from the wind and cold by a dark blue tricorn; other presents given to him by Professor Fell were a pistol and a powderflask in a holster at his waist, along with an ivory-handled dagger that had belonged to Albion. Matthew's pale countenance bespoke his intellectual qualities of reading and chess-playing, both of which had aided his educational progress from his upbringing in a New

York orphanage. One lasting mark of his journey through an uncertain and certainly demanding life was a crescent scar that curved from just above the right eyebrow into his hairline, the reminder of his nearly fatal encounter with a bear four years ago.

A few lengths ahead, Devane's horse moved at a steady walk. Matthew mused that the man wore his black cloak like an emperor's tunic, and his polished black boots were equipped with sharp little spurs. Devane was blonde-haired and handsome, with a chiseled and clean-cut face, and Matthew knew from their first meeting that Devane could be boyishly charming when he wasn't puffed up with the villainy that he seemed to like to wear as much as the green tricorn. There was a story in Devane, but whatever it was, Matthew thought that it was well-hidden and well-protected.

The horses went on. The wind shrilled around the riders. The road—such as it was, really a track through the grasses avoiding the belchy bogs—curved toward cliffs overlooking the turbulent sea, and then entered the darksome woods.

Beneath the gnarled branches of interlocked trees the two riders continued onward, the already-meager sunlight further cut to a gray haze. Crows cawed from a distance; that, the thump of the horses' hooves on the dirt, and the occasional keening of the wind were the only sounds. Devane trudged his horse forward, the gloomy forest closed in, and Matthew grappled again with the gnawing feeling that time was the enemy as much as was Cardinal Black.

After the passage of nearly two hours—enough to make Matthew's tailbone sore and move the sun like a smear across the sky—Devane suddenly reined his horse in and quietly said, "There." He pointed toward a narrow break between the trees. Matthew could see against the slice of solemn clouds a stone watchtower perhaps sixty feet tall, set upon a forested ridge another fifty feet up. "A mile or so to the base of the ridge, then maybe another half-mile," Devane calculated. Without a further word he urged his horse into a walk, and Matthew flicked his mount's reins and followed.

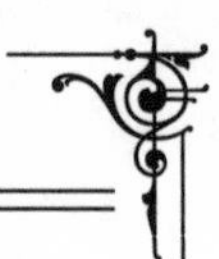

From time to time Matthew caught sight of the watchtower through the trees; the structure had a conical roof turned ebony by the elements, and set in the stone sides at different elevations were small loopholes from which could be fired arrows or ancient hand cannons. It looked to him like part of the roof had caved in and a section of stones had given way and fallen out about forty feet up, but otherwise it was still a formidable defense position. Of signs of life there were none…which worried Matthew more than seeing Black's soldiers manning the loops.

Their horses left the forest road for a rougher trail up the ridge. The watchtower loomed nearer. Matthew noted that Devane had brought his four-barrelled pistol out from the folds of his cloak and held it across the saddle in front of him, his hand upon the ugly weapon like the touch of a priest's blessing on a child's brow. Matthew had no doubt the gun had more than once been Julian Devane's salvation.

Further along they came to a wall of rough stones about five feet high, wracked by time and nearly enveloped by brown weeds and thorny thicket. They were nearly under the watchtower, and yet had seen no movement other than the scurrying of a hare and two deer bounding away side-by-side. An opening in the wall was wide enough for a single man to pass through, but not a horse.

Devane swung himself down, his hand still on the pistol. "We walk from here," he said, and reaching into his saddlebag that contained the supplies of ammunition, flints, pieces of dried and salted fish and beef wrapped up in waxed paper, he withdrew a spyglass. He opened the glass to its optimal position and aimed it up at the tower. After a moment of study he closed the glass but kept it in hand. "Tie your horse up," he directed. And then: "Ready your pistol, you might need—" He stopped, because Matthew already had it out, and readied.

They secured their horses in the thicket. With his pistol at his side Matthew followed Devane through the opening into another area of overgrown brush, yet there was a path of sorts through the tangle. Here and there stood piles of stone rubble and the occasional single slab that

A Victim of Cardinal Black

indicated the foundations of whatever had once stood here. "Quiet," Devane cautioned, though Matthew was making no noise. They wound their way through the ruins, still climbing. Presently the land straightened out at the top of the ridge and there before them, surrounded by chunks of stone that had fallen from the time-worn tower, was an open doorway.

"All right," said Devane, as if speaking to a spirit of protection Matthew could not see. He entered the tower, with Matthew two paces behind.

The dank interior offered a staircase, the risers worn thin and smooth by ancient medieval boots. Up and up Devane and Matthew climbed, passing several platforms from which the loopholes could be defended. The wind churned within through gaping holes in the walls, the one at forty feet large enough to fit a carriage if a carriage could be hauled by winged horses.

Near the peak of their ascent they could see the black beams of the roof and another huge hole where a portion of it had given way. Then they were at the top, in a circular room with more loopholes in the walls…and both Matthew and Devane were struck to silence because in this realm of Satan they were not the only bodies here.

The child was—had been—maybe six years old. A boy fair-haired, fair-skinned, now nude, the brown eyes still open in shock, the wrists and ankles bound by twine, the flesh around the gaping wound in the chest dark blue with the violence of the cutting. Upon the child's forehead was another cutting: the inverted Devil's Cross that Cardinal Black was so fond of inflicting upon his victims. On the floor there was a sheen of dried blood and a clay bowl with the charred remnants of what Matthew knew had to have been the child's heart. Around the bowl were several burned candle stubs stuck to the floor. And upon the walls…

"Hm," said Devane, a sound of judgement even from one so damned as himself.

Upon the walls were strange symbols scrawled in the child's blood. And not just a few, but an outpouring of communication to the cardinal's deity. Through his daze of revulsion and the sickness in his stomach Matthew recalled that Black was of a freakish frame, being extraordinarily thin and stretched to the height of six-five or thereabouts, his face and long-nailed hands also stretched to disturbing dimensions. With that height Black had been able to reach the top of the walls, and so there too were the symbols—thousands of them, it seemed, overlapping, bleeding together, running down in gory rivulets, a mad novel from a demoniac author, a paean of devotion to the father of Mother Deare's 'father'.

"Steel yourself," Devane said, when Matthew turned away to breathe cleaner air through a hole in the wall. Devane stood over the body. "Interesting," he said, as one might remark while looking at a crushed insect. "Human sacrifice to Satan," he continued. "Quite a fellow who's got that book of poisons."

"A *fellow*? Is that all you have to say?"

"I don't mourn the dead, Corbett. They have left a troubled world. And while this to you is a terrible sight, I have seen worse. You might also, before this is over. It might be your own heart cut from your chest while you're still alive."

Matthew was about to reply—to say what, he wasn't sure—when he realized that through the hole admitting cleaner air was also the sight of a village at the bottom of the cliffs, nestled against the sea. "I'm looking at Adderlane," he said.

Devane pushed him aside. The spyglass came up.

"Well?" Matthew prompted.

"A Welsh fishing village, a harbor, some fishing boats and poor hovels…not much else, and no activity I can see." He moved the glass's view further out toward the ocean. "No mortar ship in sight. Nothing out there. I think they're long gone."

Matthew had been afraid of this; he released the breath in a hiss between his teeth, biting down also on the flare of panic that jumped up within him.

Devane closed the spyglass with a sharp *pop.* "What's the plan?" When Matthew failed to respond: "You *do* have a plan, don't you?"

Matthew again did not answer, because he had none…neither answer nor plan.

"I see," said Devane, both silkily and flatly. "We have come this way—myself following your wishes, as I vowed to the professor—to find a dead end, and no further plan in mind. Which was *your* responsibility, I believe. And here I thought you cared enough about the girl to *really* help her…but I see I was mistaken, and—" He stopped, because Matthew had turned away from his view of Adderlane, his cheeks had reddened and he had heard as much as he could stand to hear.

"My *plan,*" Matthew said, grasping at whatever straws he might find in his windblown brain, "is to ride down to that village and find out exactly if they've gone or not, when they left and how they departed if indeed they *are* gone. You can't tell for certain by looking through that glass. I intend to *know*, not guess."

"You intend to ride down there to your death, is what," Devane retorted. "But I say Cardinal Black and his gang are gone. There are no boats in that harbor big enough to carry more than two or three men, and if you'll recall one of the men we captured told us that Black's people were soon to be moving out by coach, horse and *ship.* The ship has evidently already sailed, and with it I'm sure Cardinal Black and the book you're wanting."

For an instant Matthew thought he felt the entire watchtower swaying. In desperation he reached out to touch a bloodied wall and keep himself from pitching to his knees.

"A sad sight," said Julian Devane. "And I had assumed you were so *smart.*"

Matthew lifted his own cool gray eyes to Devane's colder gaze. "I'm going down to that village. Come with me or not. I release you from your vow."

"Oh, certainly! But you're not the professor, Corbett…so you *cannot* release me."

"Suit yourself. I'm going." Matthew dared not give another glance at the child's corpse, for he indeed did intend to steel himself for the task ahead and he felt his foundations turning to

wet paper. He got out of the circular room, down the series of staircases and out of the damned watchtower. They went to the horses in silence, untied the mounts from the thicket in silence still, and with Matthew in the lead they trotted toward Adderlane and whatever the fates held in store.

FOUR.

It was not much of a village, but it faced a decent harbor where seven or eight fishing boats were docked at a wharf, nets were hung up to dry and sails were stretched out in the process of being mended. Evidently, Matthew thought, Adderlane's fishing routines had been interrupted by the visitors and were yet stalled by the shock of having Cardinal Black in their presence.

As Matthew's and Devane's horses entered the single dirt road between the unpainted houses, first one and then another and another of the folk began to cautiously emerge, some holding axes, shovels, and whatever else could be used as weapons. A group of a half-dozen men came out of a larger structure that might have been a meeting hall. Two of them held muskets that took aim at the new arrivals, though one musketeer looked to be near eighty and the other a boy of about fourteen, both of them almost quivering in their boots.

"Hold your fire!" Devane commanded, in a voice that must've resonated from one side of the village to another. "We're friends, not enemies!" he said. And added: "Not like your last gang of visitors."

The boy's musket lowered a few inches but the elder's stayed fixed. "You say!" the codger growled. He had a face that made the stones of the watchtower appear smooth, and his wild white hair was a snowy forest in chaos. "Who the Devil are you and what are you wantin'?"

"Information only," Matthew spoke up. "May I dismount without being shot?"

"Watch 'em, Eurig!" said one of the other men who was armed with a pitchfork. There was a grumble of assent, and a brown-bearded man with huge shoulders stepped forward to take the musket from the boy and steady its aim at the horsemen.

"Step down!" Eurig decided after another few seconds. "Easy, like!"

Matthew did, and so too did Devane, who took up a position well behind the young—and in his estimation—idiot.

"Your village was raided in the last few days, yes?" Matthew prompted.

"Raided and ravaged. Those men…they weren't human, as we know humans to be."

"Especially not the tall one, the one in charge," said the bearded gent with the second musket. He had a voice like a saw on granite. "They called him Cardinal Black. It was a blasphemy, is what it was."

"Agreed, but they raided another village a few miles further down the coast last night," Matthew said. "We've come from there."

"The place that's sealed and guarded like a fort." It was a statement. Eurig's thick white eyebrows went up. "I suspect nothin' good goes on there."

"Point well taken, sir…but other matters are pressing. When did Cardinal Black leave, and by what means?"

"The early hours after midnight, by that big ship they come in. Twelve of 'em went with him. The other six left in two coaches."

"There was a second ship, anchored further out to sea?" Matthew asked.

Eurig nodded. "One just as big as the other. That one out to sea left last night and didn't come back. Black and most of the others rode out after dark but they left five men here with guns and everybody was herded into Caffrey's barn. Then we heard the thunder and I figured it to be cannonfire 'cause that ship looked to me like a man-o'-war. We all watched the other ship go, and thank God. Lord be praised they didn't kill more than three of our folk."

"Killed them? Why?"

"Chose three at gunpoint the night they got here: Brennan Owain, John Lyles the school teacher and Kendall Griffin, a goodly woman and mother to four children. Shot 'em down by the wharf and rolled their bodies on over. Rolled 'em over so we'd have to drag up what was left to have a Christian burial. That 'cardinal' said it was to show they would kill everybody here if we tried to fight 'em, or if any one of their men was hurt." Eurig at last lowered his musket. "Some couldn't watch it, but I did. Me and Gregor." He glanced at the bearded man. "Tell 'em what they done to the bodies 'fore they rolled 'em."

"I already know," said Matthew. "Cardinal Black cut a Devil's Cross in their foreheads and likely spoke some kind of a ritual over them. Is that correct?"

"*My boy*!" a woman suddenly screamed beyond the knot of onlookers. "*My boy! Lord God, my boy!*"

Through the group pushed a woman maybe in her late thirties, but gaunt and hardened by her way of life and circumstances, her hair already streaked with gray and her eyes swollen by tears. "My boy!" she cried out. "Where's my Gavin?"

Another man, about her age and just as time-worn, had been right at her heels and now he grasped at her arm but she shook free and cast a look of horrible imploring at Matthew and Devane. "They took my little one! My Gavin! Where's my boy? Please…can you find him for me?"

"Ariana, come on," the man said, trying to be of comfort, but she was having none of it.

"*My boy!*" she shrieked, and this time the fresh tears streamed down through the gullies of her face. "*Oh Lord my boy!*"

"SHUT HER UP!"

The voice behind Matthew was not Devane's…or, at least, it was not the Julian Devane he had known to this moment. His shout had been one

of an unnerved man calling out for something Matthew could not yet understand…whatever it was, it was much more than demanding a desperate woman cease screaming for her son.

"*My Gavin, my boy!*" she went on, a keening cry. "*Please help me—*"

Suddenly Devane shoved past Matthew. He had the four-barrelled pistol in his hand. "Shut her up or I will!" he shouted, his voice ragged and a look of sheer panic on his pallid face. She instantly went silent. "Put down that musket!" he told Gregor. "Do it *now*!"

Gregor hesitated. Matthew saw Devane's finger start to curl around one of the sets of triggers. Two balls at this range would be sheer murder.

Devane had put his sword back into the scabbard at his side. Matthew grasped the handle, drew it out and had no choice but to step between Devane and Gregor and, striding forward with absolute foolish bravado, place the point of the sword under Gregor's chin.

"You heard him," said Matthew.

The musket dropped to the earth.

"*Gavin!*" the woman shouted to the wind. "*My boy! Come home! Please come—*"

"Your boy's lying dead up there in the watchtower!" Devane shouted back. His voice cracked, and it was a few more seconds before he spoke again. In those seconds Matthew heard the woman draw a terrible breath and he thought he could drive this sword through Devane and sleep soundly for it. "Dead!" Devane went on. "They took him up there and killed him! So one of you fine men go get him and bring him home for the lady, won't you?"

No one moved or spoke. Matthew saw Gregor wanting to go for the musket so he kept the sword where it was. Eurig didn't try to raise his gun; he was slope-shouldered, weary and beaten.

"*What?*" Ariana's voice had become a ghost of a whisper. The wind moved her hair, and that was all that moved. And again, even more agonized: "*What?*"

"Take her away from here," Devane said to the man at Ariana's side, and this time she allowed him to lead her, stumbling and silent in her grief, off the street.

"You've seen the body?" Eurig asked after the woman had gone.

"We have. Now I'm asking some questions," Devane said, and he kept the pistol at his side as he walked past Matthew and stood almost face-to-face with the old man. He had quickly regained his composure, but Matthew still heard a strange weakened note in his voice. "The two ships. What flags did they fly?"

"Royal Navy. And sure I know the white St. George's ensign when I see it."

"What direction did the ship carrying the cardinal go?"

"South," said Eurig. "Hardly any lamps on her, but I marked it."

"Why did that bastard kill Gavin James?" another man in the group of villagers asked. "What were you doin' up at the tower, anyway?"

Devane ignored him and kept his focus on Eurig. "How many masts on the ship?"

"A three-master. Runnin' full sail when they set off."

Devane's gaze moved past the old man toward the wharf. He tapped his chin with the barrels of his pistol, and Matthew could see the gears working in his brain. Matthew already knew: Cardinal Black and twelve men, headed south in a triple-masted ship flying a Royal Navy ensign of the white fleet…it would be impossible to tell where they were headed, and yet…

Devane voiced it before he could: "I wonder where a stolen pair of large ships might find anchorage. And Black's not solely behind this. As incredible as I find it to be, he had to have help from within the shipyard to get those vessels. I'll wager someone with high authority is backing this entire enterprise."

"Little good that wager does us," said Matthew.

Devane turned upon him. "Are you a gambler?" He went on without waiting for a response. "Strike that. Of course you are, or you wouldn't

be standing here. Well, Corbett…if you wish to at least *try* to concoct a decent plan of action, we're to take a sea voyage." He stalked onward, parting the onlookers with a wave of his pistol. Matthew was torn whether or not to keep the sword at Gregor's throat; instead he picked up the man's musket and carried it with him to follow Devane to the wharf.

The dark sea sucked and gurgled around the old pilings and the boats tied there groaned in their sleep. Matthew could smell a generation of fish brought up in the nets that hung on their wooden drying racks. Some of the boats at rope were nothing more than oversized barrels outfitted with rowlocks. Two of them, though, were larger than the others, about twelve feet in length with a single mast, but both of those looked to have been beaten nearly to death by a sea insulted at their presence.

"Wreckage, one and all," said Devane. He gave a heavy sigh. "Can you sail? No matter, I can."

"I can hold my own. What are you thinking?"

"Black gave time for Mother Deare to meet him at the tower, as they'd planned, but when she didn't show he knew she wasn't coming. Therefore it was time to take his book and his men and leave. South takes him away from Wales. The only thing to do is set sail and follow."

Matthew nodded. He understood Devane's meaning. The two Royal Navy ships would be difficult to hide. Black must have a place already set for him…a secluded cove or harbor that could only be discovered by sea. The only course possible would be to try to find it. And there again was the pressure of time and Matthew's feeling that indeed in this gamble the cards were against both himself and Berry. But still…it had to be played out, for there was no turning back.

Devane spent a moment inspecting both of the decrepit single-masters. Matthew joined him when he returned to the group of men, who had advanced upon them but not raised their makeshift weapons. Devane walked past them and retrieved his saddlebag, and then he looked about in search of something. Seeing the village's well he took from the bag the small clay jug he had already uncorked several times during the journey but had not offered a drop of water to his companion. He said, “Fill this up,” and tossed it to Matthew. While Matthew reeled the well’s bucket up, Devane put the saddlebag over his shoulder and, pistol still in hand, walked back to face old Eurig.

“We’re taking the boat with the mummified pig’s snout nailed to the mast,” he announced. “I assume that’s someone’s idea of a good luck charm?”

“Nossir, you ain’t takin’ my boat!” cried out a slim and wiry fisherman with close-cropped gray hair and a face as dangerous as the axe he held. “That’s my livin’!”

“Consider the trade,” Devane said. “Our—”

“To Hell with you!” His eyes fierce, the man lifted the axe and stalked forward.

At the well Matthew jumped with the blast of the double pistol shot.

The man went down, the axe lost as he was grabbing for his right thigh. Blood had exploded from the wound and spattered some of the men who stood behind. Devane stood in the roiling blue smoke watching the man writhe on the ground, his face expressionless.

“Best tend to him,” Devane said to no one in particular. Then: “Matthew! You done?”

“Did you *have* to do that?” Eurig scowled, as Gregor and a couple of the villagers bent down to pick up the groaning man and carry him away. “It was a damnable thing!”

“I have no time to argue. He was too stupid to realize we’re leaving a pair of fine horses and tack as payment for his boat. And if anyone raises an axe to me,” said Devane, “he is as good as dead, so if that fool survives he can count himself lucky…even without the pig’s snout.”

“I think,” Eurig said, his seamed face as impassive as Devane’s, “that you’re a cursed man.”

“As you please. Matthew, I’m waiting!” Devane’s gaze scanned the villagers who remained on the street, most of them nearly huddled up in a knot behind Eurig. “*You*!” Devane said. “With the brown cap! Come here!”

“*Me*, sir?”

"*Here*!" Devane pointed at the ground before him with the pistol, and the young and terrified man came slouching like a dog expecting at the least to be kicked. "Do you have lice?" Devane asked.

"Sir?"

"*Lice*! Do you have *lice*?"

"No sir!"

"Good enough." Devane plucked the brown woolen cap from the man's head and held it toward Matthew as the water jug was brought back to its master. "Put that under your hat. You'll need it against the sea wind," Devane said, "which I intend to ride like a sonofabitch."

Matthew took it and saw a couple of small holes in the thin wool, but otherwise it was a welcome addition to his winter wardrobe. He immediately put it on to warm his ears, lice or not, and then topped himself with his tricorn. He was looking down at the scrawl of blood on the dirt where the wounded man had fallen when he realized Devane was already halfway to the chosen boat.

"Wherever you're goin'," said Eurig, "you're in bad company."

"I'll leave the musket on the wharf when we pull out," Matthew answered; he had the gun tucked up under his arm and Devane's sword still in his hand as protection. "The horses are worth that boat, believe me."

"Tell that to Ewan's wife and children," came the stone-faced reply.

Matthew could say nothing more. He backed away from Eurig and the others, fearing an *en masse* attack that his swordsmanship or pistolplay could not handle, but the wounding—maiming—of Devane's victim had done its work on the villagers of Adderlane; they had had enough of violence to last them a lifetime, and when Eurig turned away the others did as well. Matthew walked to the wharf, put the musket down upon the boards and obeyed Devane's order to first hand over the sword and then cast off. After he'd sheathed the weapon, Devane busied himself inspecting the mainsail, which was furled and not yet raised to the mast. Matthew tossed the lines onto the Pig's Snout, for want of a better boat title, and then stepped aboard.

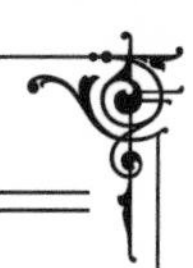

Matthew saw Devane sweep aside his cloak to secure the pistol on a hook that hung from a belt at his waist. "Put a pair of oars in the locks and start rowing," Devane said, motioning toward two pair of weatherbeaten sticks that lay in the bottom of the boat.

The locks, Matthew saw, were pieces of wood carved into U-shapes to steady the oars. He fixed the oars in position and then, settling himself upon the plank seat toward the stern, he began rowing them out of the protected harbor. It was not an easy task, and he was gratified when Devane took the remaining two oars and positioned them in a second set of locks amidships, then sat down on the other plank facing toward the bow. He began to row along with Matthew and the little craft cut through the waves, but about a hundred yards out was where the rougher water began. Matthew reasoned it was going to be very unkind to the Pig's Snout and its passengers.

After a few more strokes Matthew asked, "Did you really have to shoot him?"

"You know better than to pose that question."

"Maybe I do. But…did you?"

"Look at this craft. This was the most seaworthy boat in the harbor… which is not saying much. But if it wasn't this boat, we were finished. Is that answer enough for you? And for certain I would have shot that big bastard in the head. So you saved one life today. Congratulate yourself and keep rowing."

"It seemed extreme," Matthew said, keeping to the point he wished to hammer.

"*Extreme,*" Devane repeated, as if he'd bitten into a lemon. "You're a dreamer, aren't you? Live in your own fantasy world. Well…those people were one axe swing away from rushing us and ending your dream to save that girl's mind. Anyway, I did the little bastard a favor."

"Did you? How so?"

"He was the only one with enough courage to come at me. If he survives—and even if he loses his leg—they'll take care of him and his

family. Not that I give a shit, but they'll probably elect him mayor. So you see…I did a good deed today, too."

"I would clap my appreciation," said Matthew, "but I'm rowing."

"Yes, and put more of your back into it, I want to clear the headland before my next birthday."

The headland—the jutting cliffs on either side that protected the cove of Adderlane's harbor—was cleared in about fifteen minutes, which Matthew decided was not within the scope of Devane's day of birth. "Pull in your oars and let drift!" Devane commanded, as he did the same. Then: "Move up to the bow and stay out of my way."

Matthew obeyed without question, getting past the other man as best he could. Waves had begun to rock the craft. Devane hoisted the sail and secured it, and then he settled himself in the stern in a position where he was able to control the motion of the sail's boom with a line and also keep a hand on the tiller behind him.

Wind whipped at the patched-up sail, which for a few seconds whipped back until Devane made an adjustment with both line and tiller. The sail gave a *crack* like a gunshot as the wind filled it, and in response the Pig's Snout leapt forward like a hog with its ass on fire. Spray burst over the bow into Matthew's face, and he figured it wouldn't be long before he was both soaked and chilled to the bone.

The waves seemed to be coming at the boat from all angles. The Snout pitched up and down. There was nothing for Matthew to do but to huddle up, grasp hold of the plank beneath him and hope the bottom of the boat held firm against this aquatic assault. It was cold comfort to note that Devane was keeping them at most only two hundred yards off the shore, for to call this craft seaworthy was to call a pumpkin a carriage.

It did interest Matthew, however, to twist around not only to protect his face from the spit of the sea but to watch Devane work the sail and tiller. Obviously the man had sailing experience, not only from the way he handled the boat but from the way he gauged the wind; Matthew could see him watching the break of whitecaps across the gray expanse

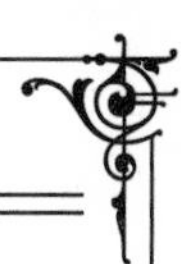

and then steering to take the most advantage of the wind's power. At no time did the sail flutter with failing exhaustion, for Devane seemed to be thinking ahead of the gusts and meeting them as they changed direction, even so minutely.

In little more than an hour they passed the harbor of Y Beautiful Bedd and the road leading up from it along the cliffs to Fell's domain. The upper balcony of the professor's small castle and the village's protective wall were clearly visible. Though there were better fishing boats in the harbor, Devane did not alter course in order to change craft; it seemed to Matthew that the man had decided this was the boat of destiny, as it were, and from the grim half-smile on Devane's face it appeared he enjoyed the challenge of besting the sea astride such a lowly mount.

The Snout swept on, its full sail defiant. Matthew wondered if this boat had ever seen the hand of a true captain; he doubted it, but Devane was in fact keeping them steady and fast-moving against a sea that smacked the hull in vain to slow their progress. They passed looming cliffs, gray stretches of beach and the occasional cove where there might be a few ramshackle houses and moored catboats or nothing but jagged rocks and tentacled trees. For certain there were no triple-masted ships of the Royal Navy in sight, and as the sun began to fade and sink toward the west the Snout kept going but to where Matthew was unsure.

"Come back here!" Devane called. "Mind your head!"

Matthew got past the sail's boom. He had begun to shiver with the cold and he could no longer feel his face; it was as if he were himself wearing the mask of Albion but it was made of ice instead of leather.

"Get some water." Devane motioned with a nod of his head toward the saddlebag at the bottom of the boat.

Matthew opened it, took out the small clay jug, uncorked it and drank. Devane let go the tiller to take the jug, which he too drank from, and then he quickly returned the jug and went back to steering. His eyes scanned the waves, while Matthew was still intent upon scanning for high masts in a hidden cove.

“They’re nowhere near, I’m thinking,” said Devane. “My opinion is… they are far and gone.”

“We can’t give up,” Matthew answered.

“I said nothing about surrender.” Devane attended to adjustment of the sail and tiller before he spoke again. “If you’re indeed a gambler, I have a game to propose.”

“A *game*? With Berry’s mind in the balance?”

“If we don’t play this game out her condition has no chance for recovery. Yet I do realize time is of the essence. Therefore the game involves time…and I see no way around playing it out.”

“I have no idea what you’re talking about.”

Devane once more was silent for a while. He looked at the setting sun, then at small lights that had begun to shine amid houses clustered along a beach: the glow of lanterns, and families preparing for the dark.

“About thirty more miles across this bay is the town of Bristol,” Devane said. “If the wind keeps up, we can make landfall sometime after midnight.”

“Why Bristol?” Matthew asked, because obviously the other man was leading up to something.

“We need information,” came the reply. “I have vowed to the professor that I will see this through to the best of my ability. As much as I despise the idea…as much as it sickens my gut…I do know one man living in Bristol who might help us.”

“One man? Who?”

“Rear Admiral Garrett Devane of the Royal Navy,” said the captain of the Snout. He looked into Matthew’s eyes and offered a crooked and horrifying half-grin, half-sneer. “My loving father.”

FIVE.

"The house on haunted hill," said Devane.

"Are there ghosts about?" Matthew asked.

"Oh yes." The dark green tricorn dipped in a nod. "Many." The breath that could be seen in the cold air might have been a specter, after all.

They stood at the end of the road they'd been following, two miles from the beach upon which the Pig's Snout had been left to wallow. It was dark, and Matthew reasoned the time was near three o'clock. But all was not quite impenetrable, for there was a glow on the low-hanging clouds over Bristol's harbor, which could be distantly seen from this hilltop as a forest of masts, lanterns moving back and forth on the wagons carrying cargo to be loaded, or carrying cargo that had just been unloaded. It seemed quite reasonable to Matthew that Devane's father would have his house situated so the man might have a view of the harbor, all its commerce and comings and goings, and of the sea beyond...which, of course, was the passage to the New World.

No lights showed in the house, which was an austere-looking gray stone manor of two levels, many shaded windows and multiple chimneys. The road became a gravel drive curving up to the estate on its spacious lawn. But getting to the house was a current problem that needed no solver

to deduce: the estate was guarded by a black wrought-iron fence at least seven feet tall and topped with a multitude of wicked spikes. Blocking entry was an iron gate secured with a lock the size of Magnus Muldoon's fist and that Matthew thought might've come directly from the none-so-gentle confines of Newgate Prison. He reasoned that climbing was out of the question; one slip and a spike in the stomach would not be a welcome accompaniment to the dried beef he and Devane had eaten from the saddlebag during the journey across Bristol Bay.

With the saddlebag slung over his right shoulder, Devane surveyed the locked gate. "Shall we announce our presence?" he asked. "Step back," he said, as he drew the deadly pistol and took aim not at flesh but at metal.

Matthew stepped way back.

Devane held the pistol at arm's length and put two of the barrels nearly against the lock. He lifted a hand to shield his face. Matthew knew better than to let his eyes be dazzled by the flame of the double shot; he looked away an instant before Devane fired.

In the stillness and silence of the night it sounded to Matthew as if people in London over a hundred miles away might be jarred from their sleep by such a conflagration. His ears felt almost torn from his head, or liable to leap free and go flopping down the road all bloodied and abuzz. He saw in the drifting smoke that the lock had been nearly torn asunder from the gate and turned into a mangled shape that hung by a blackened coil. Devane finished the task with a solid boot to the gate, which swung open with the *screech* of a protesting spirit awakened from the grave.

Matthew followed Devane through the opening and up the drive. In the distance several dogs were barking their heads off, but here no dogs thrived. The house remained dark…no, Matthew saw in another moment…a light had appeared in an upper-floor window, over on the left. It bloomed brighter as the wicks of the second and third candles were touched by flames.

Devane put the gun away as he walked, and he strode forward as if he owned the place. At his side the sword in its sheath made a rustling sound

against his cloak. Matthew watched lights move across the windows; definitely there would soon be a welcome, of some kind.

On the trip across Bristol Bay Devane had been mostly silent when Matthew had asked questions about Rear Admiral Garrett Devane; the only answer Matthew had gotten was that the elder Devane was a rear admiral in name only, having attained that rank many years ago but leaving the force to serve both as Bristol's harbormaster and to take up partnership in the Royal Atlantic Company to sell cargo to the New World. Still, the elder Devane kept in contact with companions in the navy and might know something about a missing mortar vessel, likely taken within the last few weeks from one of several naval dockyards. Other than that little bit, Devane had remained mute on the subject of his father.

It seemed now, though, that an introduction was imminent, for as the rear admiral's son and the New York problem-solver approached the house the front door opened and a figure holding a lantern and wearing a long white nightgown peered out. "Who's there?" the figure called: a man's thin voice, wavering and reedy.

"It's Julian," was the answer. And, more sarcastically: "Come home again."

"Young *Julian*? Why...I...young *Julian*?"

"The same. How are you, Windom?"

"I think...my eyes must be deceiving me...my ears also!"

Matthew and Julian were almost at the front steps. The old man in the white nightgown came down to meet them on age-stiffened legs, lifting his lantern up to catch their faces. He stopped, his wizened face open-mouthed, his halo of white hair being blown by the wind and his eyes widening. "My Lord!" he said, almost breathlessly. "Young Julian come home!"

"Hello, Windom." Julian reached out to quickly pat the old man's shoulder, a gesture of affection that surprised Matthew. "Best we get inside, out of this cold."

"Oh...yes, sir! Yes, of course! But...what was that awful noise?"

“Hell freezing over,” Julian said. “You’ll recall I said I’d return here when that event occurred.”

“Oh…I…I do recall such.” Windom, obviously the house servant or butler, still couldn’t seem to believe he was speaking to the young man upon whom the yellow lantern light fell. Perhaps, Matthew thought, Julian Devane was himself one of the ghosts who haunted this place. “Yes,” Windom said after a few more seconds. “Cold out here. Please…do come in.”

They entered the house, the door—with its large brass knocker in the shape of an anchor, Matthew noted—was closed behind them, and Windom set about lighting several other lanterns from the wick of his own. As the glows strengthened, Matthew saw they stood in a vestibule with a black-lacquered floor and a similar black-timbered staircase leading upward. Various colorful signal flags hung from hooks above, and foremost in this room was a marble-topped table upon which stood an intricately detailed model of a ship-of-the-line complete with its myriad of sails, lines and gunports, the entire construction being about three feet in length.

Julian was already moving onward; as seemed to be his nature, he waited for no man’s invitation. He shoved open a sliding oak door on the right and went into another room, with Windom close behind carrying two lanterns. Matthew heard a door open and shut with a solid-sounding *thunk* upstairs and he figured the rear admiral was soon to be sailing into view. He walked into the room after Julian and Windom and saw he had entered what might have been a combination library and office. The lantern lights spilled over many shelves of books and also a large desk with papers neatly stacked atop its blotter and an inkwell and a supply of feather pens near at hand. The room held several black leather chairs that all faced the desk and seemed to Matthew to look more forbidding than comfortable. On the floor was a navy-blue carpeting, the heavy drapes were of the same hue, there was a fireplace of gray tiles and a few little embers still glowing in the ashes, and on the walls were gilt-framed oil paintings of maritime scenes with the likes of huge sailing ships carving through tremendous waves as lightning-charged stormclouds bore down from the heavens.

"Dear bleeding Christ, what do we have here?"

It had not been a shout as much as it was a growl, brought up from the depths of a gravelly gut.

Julian turned toward the door with a frozen smile. "Good morning, Father," he said, and he removed his tricorn and flourished it in a mock salute, which Matthew would have told him was not the thing to do at the moment.

"With you in my presence," answered the older man, his face a square-chinned chunk of sea-weathered rock, "there can be *nothing* good."

Rear Admiral Garrett Devane wore his long coat of stature over his nightclothes and carried a ship's lantern in his right hand. Matthew figured he must've plucked the coat from a mannequin that stood beside his bed, because the item had not a single wrinkle or dimple in the fabric. It was dark blue, high-collared with a trim of gold and displayed detailed workings of gold across the breast area. The coat bore perhaps twenty large gold buttons down the front and four on each gold-striped cuff. On the left, over the heart that beat for England, were numerous gold and silver medals the size and shape of small starfish. Matthew thought that if all high-ranking officers commanded such coats there would be little left of gold in the treasury to build the ships and it would become a Pig's Snout navy.

It was clear to see that young Julian was his father's son—in appearance, at least—because their faces were similarly constructed, the color of the eyes was nearly the same, and the hairline and abundance of hair as well though Garrett—being what Matthew reasoned was in his later fifties—had gone all gray. The rear admiral's face, though his features so resembled his son's, showed the work of many years of wind and sea, both of which had conspired to whittle the flesh down to reveal the sharp juttings and angles of bone like the edges of dangerous shoals. The deep lines across his forehead and two between his fierce eyes bespoke a life of if not concern for his captains and crews then a continual worry over

the condition and upkeep of ships, which Matthew figured was enough to make any man cling to his glossy coat and medals when his day was done. Matthew thought that in any event this man had seen such storms of nature as the paintings on the walls depicted, and likely had lived through the storms of sea battles as well.

The elder Devane's eyes suddenly turned upon Matthew with the force of such a maelstrom. "Who is this? One of your sodomite friends? One of the male concubines you're so fond of entertaining?"

"His name is Matthew Corbett," Julian answered, calmly and evenly. "He is a business associate. And you must know, sir, that half the Royal Navy indulges at sea in the practice you so despise me for."

"Oh, of course!" The gaze he set upon his son might have burned holes through salt-crusted leather. "You would remake the world in your image, wouldn't you?"

"No, I would not," Julian said. "For if I did, who would there be for me to victimize?"

That hung in the air like a foul-weather flag for a few seconds, until the rear admiral swung upon Windom so suddenly Matthew feared an attack of violence. "How dare you let this creature into my house!" Garrett seethed. "You'll be docked a week's pay for this affront!"

All Windom could do was take a backward step, slump his shoulders in deference and stare at the floor.

"Well," said Julian, "we didn't come all this way just to destroy the lock on your gate, Father."

"My lock? Yes, I heard that shot! Are you carrying a cannon around with you now, the better to rob old women and infants?" His eyes narrowed. "What do you mean, 'come all this way'? Come from *where*?"

"Up the coast a distance. I have some questions to ask you, and—"

"The nerve of you! The audacity! Breaking in here at this hour to demand of me!"

Matthew thought the man was going to start foaming at the mouth, fall down and begin gnawing at the carpet, but before that could happen Julian

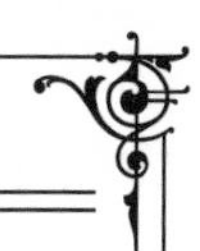

said firmly, "I want to know, first of all, if a mortar vessel and a ship-of-the-line have been stolen recently from any of the navy's dockyards."

That made Garrett's jaw drop. "Are you now *insane*, to boot?" His left arm came up and pointed into Matthew's face. "Does this 'associate' of yours not know to remove his tricorn in the house of a gentleman? Sir!" The fearsome face faced Matthew, striking him with fear. "Were you born amid *swine*?"

"As a matter of fact," Matthew replied, "yes sir, I was." He removed the tricorn and then the woolen cap that had so warmed his head on the cold voyage across the bay.

"God save us from such as these," said Garrett, speaking to Windom, who in response took another backward step toward the door. Then, to his son again: "A mortar vessel and ship-of-the-line stolen from a Royal Navy yard? You're jabbering an idiocy!"

"I would remind the rear admiral," Julian said, "that in the year 1667 the Dutch sailed a fleet into the Sheerness naval yard, captured the place and used it as a base to attack the English fleet anchored on the Medway river, so such an event might not be as idiotic as—"

"And I would present that of course all you could take away from your wasted naval education is a British *failure*, irrespective of the year or of the unfortified conditions of Sheerness at the time. So don't brandish that dulled sword at me, and again I say—"

His speech of indignation was interrupted by the high-pitched ringing of a bell…once…then once more, coming from further back in the manse.

"Now you've awakened Paul," said the rear admiral, with what Matthew thought was a wisp of a smirk upon his thin-lipped mouth. "Good for you. Of course Paul will want to come see his fine loyal brother. Windom, go fetch my son, please."

"Yes sir." Windom set one of the lanterns upon a small table between two of the chairs and left the room. Garrett placed the ship's lantern atop the center of the desk and opened its shutters to afford the most light

possible. "Mister…Corbett, is it?" he inquired. "What's all this about stolen Royal Navy ships?"

Matthew decided he must tread carefully upon this uncertain earth. "I can only say, sir, that we have reason to believe such a thing has happened."

"Then you are as much a fool as is the creature standing beside you. Don't you realize every naval shipyard on the island of England is guarded by a *fortress*? Oh yes, we suffered that calamity with the Dutch *thirty-six years ago*, but since then the yards have been strictly fortified. There are cannons a-plenty facing the seaward entrance to every shipyard, with flag codes also strictly followed. Guards walk the docks armed to the teeth. The roadway entrance is also heavily guarded, and any workman laboring on a ship must pass through the sentry's station. It would be utterly *impossible* for any human being to steal Royal Navy ships, and that is that!" He turned again his livid attention upon Julian. "What *insanity* is this, that has caused you to assault my home at such an hour—at *any* hour—with this kind of nonsense?"

"Oh," Julian said with a shrug, "I thought it might be a lark."

Someone was coming through the door. "Here's not a lark," said Garrett, "but a wounded eagle. Come in, Paul, and see your brother."

Windom was pushing a wheeled chair. In it was not a wounded eagle, but the wreckage of a man.

Paul Devane was wearing a nightgown similar to the one his father wore, but a dun-colored blanket was arranged across the lap and the legs. Matthew could instantly tell that the blanket had nothing to fill it from the knees down. The man—some ten or more years older than Julian, though it was difficult to tell because the bones seemed to be oddly and disturbingly misshapen in his face—had dark brown hair and the slate-colored eyes of his father; across the nose and covering the mouth and jaw was a black cloth mask held by laces around the back of the head. In Paul's lap was a blue bowl into which the saliva dripped from what was likely, Matthew surmised, the hole where the jaw and chin had been, and the mask—newly applied by Windom, Matthew thought—was already wet.

Even as Matthew thought that, Paul gave a convulsive shudder and made a noise of trying to swallow his own saliva and it sounded like someone drowning, going under for the third time.

Paul's hair was neatly combed; his eyes were bloodshot from the effort of living, but in them Matthew saw a rush of recognition. Paul wheeled himself forward, nearly up against Julian, and reaching out he grasped one of his brother's hands and pressed it against his own cheek.

"Now we shall have to wash your face before we put you to bed again," said Garrett.

There was a moment that seemed as if a storm had suddenly struck lightning in the room. Matthew felt it like the rumble of thunder in his bones, and the strong fishy aroma of the whale oil in the lanterns had taken on the rusted iron smell of disaster about to crash down from the clouds.

But…it passed. Matthew thought that they might be yet destined to brave many storms on this mission, but here in this room standing in Paul's feeble though touching and obviously heartfelt embrace, Julian was not going to allow the bad man to come out.

At least, not all the way out. Julian stroked his brother's hair with his other hand. "The warden treating you well in this somber prison, is he?" Julian asked.

Paul might have managed a laugh in his throat, but it became a terrible gurgling sound. He looked up at Julian and Matthew saw a sparkle of humor in the tortured eyes.

"May I offer the gentlemen tea, sir?" Windom asked his master.

"Heavens, no. They are on their way out. We have no use for sodomites and defilers of God's world in this house, do we, Paul?"

The older son did not answer or respond, other than to keep Julian's hand pressed against his cheek. His eyes closed, perhaps in memory of a younger and better time when both brothers had God's world ahead of them. Windom moved in, took up the blue bowl and emptied it into a larger clay pot attached to the rear of the chair by leather bindings, then quickly returned it to its more useful place. Matthew couldn't help but wonder how many times a day—and night—Windom performed that task, and how many times he turned the clay pot over to clear it out.

"You have the answer to your idiotic question about stolen mortar vessels and ships-of-the-line," Garrett rumbled on, a storm unto himself. "Now get out."

"A moment," said Julian. He tapped Paul lightly on the temple and Paul looked up at him. "I miss our sailing days," he said quietly. "But I have them still." He tapped his own head. "Don't you?"

Paul slurped and nodded and made something of a whine of assent.

"You are looking at a *hero*, Corbett," Garrett suddenly said in a great exhalation of breath, as if he had been carrying this in his throat for so long it had become lodged there. "A *patriot.* Unlike your *associate*, who has never cared for anything or anyone not seen in his shaving mirror. The man who sits before you gave *everything* for his country. Your associate can tell you, if you ask him. Oh yes, he knows the story very well…and that story is the nearest he'll ever get to being worth as much as a dog's turd on the street."

"Charming, Father," Julian said easily, still stroking his brother's hair. "You flatter me."

Paul convulsed and sounded as if he were strangling once more. Julian put a supporting hand on one of Paul's shoulders. Paul's other hand came up from the blanket to grasp Julian's wrist with what Matthew saw were only two fingers—the thumb and the index—as the remainder of the hand had been surgically sliced away.

"Easy, easy," Julian said, and his brother's body seemed to relax. In another few seconds the strangling sound ceased. Paul looked up at Julian and nodded, as the saliva continued to drip from the black cloth mask into the bowl.

"I want you out of this house, and never return here," said Garrett.

"Very well…for now." Julian offered his father the same charming smile that Matthew recalled receiving from him in London just before the trap had snapped shut on Matthew's neck. He patted his brother's shoulder

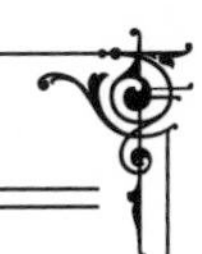

and smiled down into the ruined face. "I'll come back and take you sailing someday. I vow it. Would you—"

"Don't lie!" Garrett snapped. "And don't coddle him! He knows his condition!"

"A condition not helped by being held prisoner here, the same as it was last time. Get him out in the fresh air, for God's sake! Take him over to the harbor and let him—"

"Let him catch his death of cold in that fresh air and see men walking on two legs at the harbor, working and laughing and…and being *whole*? Oh, yes, that would be very helpful to him! Windom, return Paul to his room." Windom paused, a shade of indecision on his face as he looked from the rear admiral to Julian and back again. "*Take* him, this instant," Garrett commanded in a deadly-quiet voice, his gaze fixed upon his younger son.

"Yes sir," said the servant, and he took his position behind the chair to turn it and wheel it away. Paul made a noise like a grunt and his eyes narrowed with anger as he regarded his father; it was clear he wanted to remain in the room, but it was not to be.

Julian stepped toward his departing brother and, laying a hand upon his shoulder, walked beside the chair until Windom reached the door. At the door Paul grasped Julian's hand with both his whole right hand and the mangled left, and Matthew saw the knuckles whiten with the squeeze.

"I'll come back for you," Julian said, and then Paul released him and Windom pushed the chair onward, the wheels making small squeaking sounds on the lacquered black floorboards. The noise diminished as Windom guided his charge toward, Matthew presumed, Paul's chamber on the lower level at the back of the house.

"Our business is concluded," Garrett said. With a face of solid granite he motioned Julian and Matthew out of the room. He opened the front door to the cold winds that had begun to crisscross each other and blow through the naked trees on the far side of the road. Without another word Julian put on his tricorn, pulled his cloak up tighter around his shoulders and chin, readjusted the saddlebag across his shoulder, and strode out of

the house; Matthew put on the hopefully lice-free woolen cap, then his tricorn, and likewise situated his cloak tighter around his body, for winter had for sure and quite suddenly descended upon the land.

They walked through the blasted gate and along the road toward the harbor lights.

Matthew said quietly, "Do you want to—"

"*No*," came the answer, delivered like a blow to the jaw.

Matthew remained silent. They walked on, side-by-side for a few yards until Julian said sharply, "Don't walk beside me. Walk either in front or behind." This one was delivered through the gritted teeth of the bad man, returned from his visit home.

Matthew thought he could fling a curse into Julian's face but his teeth—which had already seen enough torment to last the rest of his days—might well wind up littering the road. He stalked onward, five or six paces in front, his head down and the need for sleep on this long day pressing in upon him, laboring his legs and fogging his thinking, but always the horrible clock that dictated Berry's fate ticking—always ticking—in his mind.

SIX.

"*Young Julian*! *Sir, please wait*!"

It was Windom's voice. Julian abruptly stopped and turned around, as did Matthew. They had not gotten quite a hundred yards from the house, and here came Windom carrying a lantern and wearing a heavy brown fearnaught coat over his nightgown and a white woolen cap with a brown tassel at its summit.

"Windom!" Julian said. "Christ, man! Get out of this cold!"

"A word, sir. Just a word and then I must get back. Your father went upstairs after you left, he doesn't know I've come after you."

"I should say not. What is it?"

"Well...your question about the two ships. The mortar vessel and the ship-of-the-line." He glanced quickly at Matthew, who had come to stand beside Julian whether he wanted the company or not. "It's peculiar, sir...I mean...well...what I overheard...that is—"

"Settle down," Julian told him. "All right, put your thoughts in order and start over again."

"Yes, sir. Well...a few days ago...three days, I think...yes, three days...a man came to visit Master Devane...and you know your father keeps his business office at the house. It was a business visit...but I saw the man in, and Master Devane told me to take the admiral's coat."

"So an admiral visited him? I'm sure that's not so—"

"Not so very uncommon, sir, because after all he is the harbormaster and has his…um…his history. But usually they are social calls when one of the gentlemen in blue is passing Bristol and perhaps puts into port for supplies. This one had a request. I overheard it when I brought in the teacart. He wanted to know if there would be any merchant traffic at sea between Bristol and Swansea on the date of last night. I mean…this being morning…it would have been the night *before* last."

"An unusual question," said Julian. "What was his reason?"

"He told Master Devane he was tasked with performing nighttime military maneuvers off the coast of Wales between here and Swansea, and they would be firing shells onto a stationary target at sea. Evidently the gentleman didn't wish merchant shipping to wander in range."

Matthew's ears had perked up. "*Shells*, you say? Not *cannonballs*?"

"No, sir. Shells was the term used, and he identified the vessel under his command as the mortar ship *Volcano*," Windom replied. "I thought it curious that you should arrive asking about the theft of a mortar ship, when—"

"Of course," Julian interrupted, his voice tense. "Father gave this admiral the all-clear?"

"He checked the bills of passage and the ledger. I assisted him in gathering the papers. The last merchant of the day from Bristol was scheduled to be docking in Swansea near six o'clock, and two from Swansea to Bristol well after midnight."

"Ah." Julian nodded. He looked at Matthew, raised his eyebrows and then returned his attention to Windom. "The admiral. What was his name?"

"I didn't catch that, sir, and of course I wasn't introduced to him."

"What did he look like?" Julian asked.

"A large man, sir. Bearlike, I would say. He had a heavy black beard down his chest and a long mane of black hair that hung about his shoulders. About his beard…he had applied streaks of crimson and orange dye to it, so that it took on the appearance of flames. I could tell Master Devane

didn't care for the man's grooming habits, as he feels the navy is becoming far too lax with such. But this gentleman spoke well and seemed to have excellent manners, which Master Devane holds in high regard. Also his uniform was well-decorated."

"I'm sure this admiral took pains to make certain his decorations were well-observed, too," said Julian. He frowned. "I don't know any admiral who fits that description…then again, I have long since foregone keeping up with the navy's officers."

"A question," Matthew said. "Windom, if you made the connection between what we were asking and the presence of the *Volcano,* why didn't your master?"

"We—*I*—didn't ask the right question," Julian answered before the servant could speak. "I asked about the *theft* of such a ship, not the presence of one that sailed right past Bristol with my father's approval and *aid*." He looked back toward the house on haunted hill, which had now gone completely dark once more. A gust of wind blew among the three, strong enough to stagger Windom and ruffle the fearnaught around his frail form. "My father is aware that my…shall we say…current occupation does not meet his standards," Julian went on, "I'm sure he doesn't want to explore that realm any further, and therefore he heard only the question and no more."

"And I, sir," said Windom to young Julian through lips that had begun to shiver, "am equally poor of knowledge about *why* you wish to know these things, and I believe it is to my benefit to remain uneducated. But…I did think you should hear about the admiral and his *Volcano*."

"Rightly so, and my thanks to you. Well…you'd best get to a warm place. Unfortunately you must return to Garrett Devane's house."

"It's not so bad, sir. Master Devane does what he thinks is correct, and I am in it for the—as the sailors say—long haul. I will ask you, though…do you need money? I have a bit saved up, I might spare you enough to—"

"Nonsense," Julian replied, with a shake of his head. "Corbett and I are fine on that account." He placed a firm hand on the servant's shoulder.

"Thank you for your consideration, and for the information as well. Get back to the house, now, and mind your footing."

"Yes, sir." Windom started to turn away and then paused. "Will you really return? I mean to say...Paul would be waiting for you."

"Tell him he won't have to wait very long."

"Yes, sir. Until that time, then. Goodbye, sir," Windom said to Matthew, and huddled up in his coat he turned toward the house and followed the yellow path of his lantern away from the two travellers.

Julian watched him go. After a moment he said, "Matthew, we're going to find a tavern that's open. If not, we'll open it up ourselves because I need a good strong drink. You with me?"

"All the way," said Matthew, who thought that if he could get a warm drink inside him on this blustery morning he would break the locked door down himself, and to the Devil with the Devil.

As befitted a town where work at the harbor was constant, there was a narrow street just past a grand cathedral of white stones where the dark water lapped up at old pilings and not one but three taverns showed lantern-light in their sea-grimed windows. "This one," Julian said, choosing the Flying Jib over the Wild Boar and the Checkered Horse. Inside the Jib, the place had the nautical trappings of hanging ropes, nets and the like that Matthew had expected; there were five other men in the tavern, two at one table and three at another, and a portly barkeep wearing an apron and the jaunty feathered and floppy-brimmed hat of a cavalier.

"Do you have coffee?" Julian asked, and received an affirmative. "Two coffees—black and strong—and a jug of mead. That suit you?" he asked Matthew, who nodded and figured the combination would either knock him out for a few hours or get his flagging jib flying again.

"You have money?" the barkeep inquired, before he got the goods.

Julian unhooked the sword and scabbard from his belt and placed it atop the bar, which immediately drew the attention of the other patrons and a look of dread from Matthew, in preparation to try to save the life of another hapless bystander. Julian drew the sword out, put it aside and

reached into the scabbard. His fingers came out with a leather belt in which eight notches were cut, holding eight golden guinea coins. He removed one of the coins and slid it across the bar to the open-mouthed cavalier.

"Sir," the man said, nearly stammering, "I don't have the change for such a coin!"

"No change needed, if you have a private place in the back…a table and two chairs and the desire to keep us undisturbed while we sleep for… say…two hours. And bear in mind that I sleep holding my scabbard, and I am a *very* light sleeper."

"Well…sir…there's just my own table back there, where the wife and I have our suppers."

"*Sold*," said Julian, returning the money belt to the scabbard and then sheathing the sword. He beckoned the barkeep closer and then leaned over the bar, and Matthew saw his eyes go as deadly as the barrels of his pistol. His voice, too, conveyed a dangerous promise. "Hear this, and heed it. If anyone tries to rob us, I will kill them on the spot. Even if you are innocent of such a scheme, I will kill you on the spot as well, after which I may just burn this fucking place to the ground. And if I *think* I taste something in the coffee or the mead that I don't like, you are a dead man. Are we clear?"

The barkeep nodded, his eyes huge. "Crystal," he croaked.

The back room did indeed contain a table with two chairs, crammed in amid various crates, boxes, broken chairs and other casualties of time at the *Jib.* A pair of lanterns hung from the rafters, emitting dirty yellow light. The barkeep showed them in and brought them the jug of mead and two clay cups while he brewed the coffee, and he closed the door between the room and the rest of the tavern.

"I didn't realize you were wealthy," said Matthew after they'd gotten settled at the table.

"A gift from the professor," Julian replied. "He had the thought that this endeavor might have a need for money. And that's for the coffee," he said when Matthew reached for the jug. "Mead alone will put you on the floor."

"I could sleep on a bed of nails right now."

"I predict you'll sleep with your head on the table for maybe two hours. Probably less. Then you'll be wanting to get on with the task at hand, because you and I both know we are far from done."

"Agreed," said Matthew. "I am *very* interested in finding this mysterious admiral, if at all possible."

"Nothing more can be done here. We'll have to go to London." Julian plowed on before Matthew could pose any questions. "I have contacts in London who can give me the man's name. You understand that the admiral was timing the *Volcano*'s attack, yes? He wanted to make sure no merchant vessel witnessed the mortar shells being fired at the professor's village. For sure that would have been reported in either Bristol or Swansea and led to an enquiry. What we have here, Matthew, is not the theft of a mortar vessel and a ship-of-the-line, but an admiral of the Royal Navy taking both ships out of the dock under the pretext of a military maneuver. Whoever this man is, he likely is the power behind Cardinal Black."

Matthew nodded. "It seems to me this operation was planned well in advance."

"Of course. Had to be. Months in advance, I'd say." Julian yawned and stretched. He took off his tricorn, rubbed his red-rimmed eyes and went about reloading his pistol with ammunition from the saddlebag, a leaden ball in each of the four firing chambers. "They didn't see this man in Adderlane," Julian said as he worked, "because he never left the ship. Cardinal Black was the face, but this man was the brain."

The barkeep brought their coffee, again in clay cups. He took a quick glance at the four-barrelled weapon from Hell and scurried out.

Julian poured a dash of mead into his coffee and Matthew did the same. "We'll need to hire a coach," said Julian after he'd taken a drink. "It's a two-day trip from here, but we'll pay the driver to keep going other than to change horses. I think we can make it in around thirty-six hours."

Matthew sipped at his coffee-and-mead, winced at the strength of it but knew he was so bone-weary it wasn't going to impede getting at least a

modicum of sleep. Julian was right, though; with time pressing upon him, sleep was the least of his concerns.

"Professor Fell has great confidence in you," Julian said as he finished reloading the pistol. He left it on the tabletop next to his sword and scabbard. "He wouldn't have allowed you to leave the village if he didn't."

"I promised I'd find Brazio Valeriani for him. I intend to keep that promise."

"And that's exactly why the professor allowed you to be here. He wants that man found. Why, I don't know, but I do know it's a matter of vital importance to him."

Matthew decided to go fishing in dark waters. "Why is Fell so interested in demonology?"

"Is he?"

"If he isn't, his purchase of every copy of *The Lesser Key of Solomon* is a waste of his time and money, and I doubt the professor wastes much of either." Matthew saw that Julian's face was an expressionless mask, meaning the man knew nothing about this or perhaps too much for his own good. "*The Lesser Key of Solomon* is a compendium of demons, their descriptions and powers," Matthew explained. "In case you really don't know."

Julian said nothing for a time. He drank again, his hand went out to caress the pistol with loving reverence, and then the cold slate-colored gaze returned to regard Matthew's face. "That scar on your forehead. How did you come by it?"

"I had a little encounter with a bear."

"Oh, really? You mean a bear *cub* did that?"

"No, the bear was big enough."

"You don't look the type to go out fighting bears."

"It was thrust upon me," Matthew said. "I can tell you that it nearly was my finish."

"But...you survived." Julian offered a faint half-smile. "Ah. That's what Professor Fell sees in you, then: the survival instinct. And the ability, evidently, to squeeze out of tight spots."

"Minus a tooth or two," Matthew answered, referring to his recent appointment with a deranged dentist in the employ of Mother Deare, who had been if not a competent member of his profession, then a more competent practitioner of torture.

"*But*," Julian repeated, "you survived. And here you are, hunting another bear with a beard done up like flames and wearing the uniform of a naval admiral. Interesting how these things come around."

"I don't look for trouble," Matthew said.

"Unlike *me*, you mean? Oh yes, some would say I do revel in the intoxicating musk of chaos and catastrophe. My father's opinion, in particular."

Matthew had not wished to pursue the matter, but the moment seemed right for a simple question. "What happened to your brother?"

Julian poured another quaff of mead into his coffee. He swirled the liquid around in the cup like God commanding the maelstrom.

"Paul," Julian said at last, "is proof of what a cannon broadside and a deck of flying oak planks can do to the human body. You know, it's not the cannonballs that kill the most in a sea battle…it's the oak of the ship itself. Those planks…ripped up, turned into jagged spears…those things…spinning through the air at tremendous speeds…and a small shard, enough to take off a man's head. A human body…the flesh and the muscle…it's no match for the violence of a ship coming apart under its crew…slicing through and maiming the men who have loved her." He took his drink. "Paul was an officer aboard the frigate *Newport*. On the fourteenth of July in the year 1696…the battle of the Bay of Fundy, two ships of our gallant navy against two ships of the French. The *Newport*…well, you have seen who got the worst of that encounter." He narrowed his eyes at Matthew. "Do you believe in God?"

"Yes."

"I don't. But I do believe in Fate. Take that date, for instance…the fourteenth of July."

"What of it?"

"Paul was destroyed on the fourteenth of July, 1696. I was *born* on the fourteenth of July, 1676, and my mother passed away four hours after my birth. Do you see Fate at work there?"

"I see terribly unfortunate circum—"

"*Fate*!" Julian shouted, and he slammed his fist down upon the table. Coffee jumped from both cups. Red whorls had surfaced in Julian's cheeks, and Matthew thought it was the better part of valor—and common sense—to keep his mouth shut. Julian's red-rimmed eyes had become nearly in themselves demonic. "Fate," he repeated quietly, looking away from Matthew as if pulling back into the hidden chambers of himself once more.

After a time, Matthew cleared his throat and said, "July...Julian. You were named for the month?"

"The nurses named me," he answered, and that was all.

There seemed nothing more to say. Matthew felt he was hanging onto this world by a bootstrap, and it was fraying fast. He took off his tricorn and the woolen cap and placed the cap upon the table as a makeshift pillow. Julian leaned back in his chair until he met the wall and with his legs stretched out before him he closed his eyes, but not before he first closed his hand around the scabbard.

Matthew put his cheek down upon the cap; it was not much, but better than nothing. As sleep came up to carry him away for a time the questions in his mind nettled him: it was more clear why Cardinal Black wanted to get his fingers around *The Lesser Key of Solomon* than it was why a Royal Navy admiral would want to join in such an attack on Fell's paradise. To steal Jonathan Gentry's book of potions and poisons? Why? Obviously the plan had been a long time in preparation, and for what purpose?

The answers would have to wait, for Matthew tumbled away into the darkness of sleep and for at least a while a blessed release.

He awakened—who knew how long it was—when Julian rasped out, "No!" and he lifted his head to see the man sitting upright, his eyes wild and staring at nothing. As Matthew watched, sleep-fogged, Julian settled

his chair against the wall once again, the tortured eyes closed and he was gone into the realm of Somnus, if he had ever really been awake.

Matthew slept again. The second time he was jarred to consciousness was when he heard a rattle and scrape and Julian was on his feet with the pistol in one hand and his drawn sword in the other, and the barkeep was peering in through the door he'd just opened. The barkeep looked nervously at the weapons and said, "Pardon, sirs…just seein' if you need anything."

"Privacy and silence," Julian answered, his voice as harsh as a horse-whip. The barkeep backed out, closed the door, and Julian returned to his chair with a muffled curse.

Matthew's cheek found the woolen cap once more and he drifted away, yet part of him remained on watch just as he knew Julian did. Precious time was moving, but the demands of rest had to be met.

It seemed no more than minutes later when Matthew felt a hand on his shoulder and instantly he surfaced from the depths.

"Let's go," said Julian, who already had his pistol holstered, his sword in its scabbard and the scabbard put away, the saddlebag over his shoulder and his tricorn on, tilted at its rakish angle. The dark hollows beneath his eyes said he had not rested well, if indeed he ever did. He took the last drink of cold coffee from his cup and said, "We need to find a ride to Londontown."

SEVEN.

The sun was just coming up, painting the town and the harbor a lighter shade of dull gray. Low clouds had settled in and cold wind blew through the streets. Seagulls flew amid the masts, and beneath them the workmen labored on with their crates and barrels, a never-ending task of loading and unloading.

Matthew and Julian, bundled up against the morning's chill and breathing out ghosts, were on their way toward the coach office the bar-keep had directed them to. The chalky and slightly bitter smell of old stones permeated the air. Here and there the rest of Bristol was awakening; horse-drawn wagons were trundling about and a few people were walking to their destinations still carrying lanterns to guide their paths. Further along, Matthew noted an office with the sign of an anchor centered within a gold coin. The signage read *Royal Atlantic Company*.

"Your father's business?" Matthew asked, motioning toward the sign.

"The same," said Julian, who gave it not a glance.

"Shipping what kind of cargo?" was Matthew's next question.

"Slaves," said Julian. "Every slave bound for the colonies passes through Bristol. Hundreds so far, I understand. Soon likely to be thousands."

They left Garrett Devane's slave company behind. Two more streets east of the harbor there stood a building of red bricks with a barn behind

it and at the side a fenced enclosure holding four horses. In front a coach was already hitched to a team of four sturdy-looking steeds, and a pair of workers were loading articles of luggage into a canvas-covered baggage compartment at the rear. Matthew followed Julian past the coach and through an oak door inset with squares of frosted glass. Within the office where a fireplace warmed the air a sharp-nosed clerk at his counter looked up from a ledger with an incurious gaze. "Help you gentlemen?"

"We want to hire a coach," said Julian. "London would be the destination."

"Ah." The clerk pushed aside his ledger and drew closer a leather-bound notebook. He opened it and dipped a quill pen into an inkwell. The pen was poised over the paper. "Passage for two, then? The next coach I have available will be going out tomorrow morning. Does that suit—"

"It does not." Julian angled a thumb toward the door. "Where's that coach going?"

"London, sir, but it's a private hire."

"Oh, dear." Julian gave the man the wicked smile that Matthew dreaded to witness. "Oh dear, dear me." He withdrew his sword, which caused the clerk's arm to jump. The pen made a scrawl across the pristine paper like a black wound. Julian set the sword atop the notebook, its tip pointed at the clerk, and produced the money belt from the scabbard. He slapped one of the guinea coins down upon the wood. "There's our fare, and I'm sure it's more than enough."

"Yes...well, sir...you see...Lord and Lady Turlentort are two of our best customers. I mean to say—"

"Say what?" Julian took hold of the sword's grip.

"I don't...think they would appreciate sharing a coach. In fact I know they would not."

"Are they already in the coach?"

"No, sir." He nodded toward the office's grandfather clock but Matthew noted he kept one nervous eye on the sword. "They'll be arriving within the hour, and due to leave as soon as they board."

"I think," said Julian to Matthew, "that we're talking to the wrong man." He retrieved the guinea and removed a second coin from the belt before the belt went back into the scabbard. Then he sheathed the sword and was going out the door so fast he seemed to Matthew to be naught but a blur.

"You the driver?" Julian asked one of the men, who was busy lacing up the canvas.

"Shooter," was the reply, meaning he was the armed guard. "Benson's the driver." He gave Julian a long hard look. "You ain't Lord Turlentort, so who the hell are—"

"Your new passengers," said Julian, holding the gold up under the man's hooked nose. "My friend and I want to go to London today, in *this* coach. I don't give a fuck about any lord and lady, they can come along if they want to, but we're riding in this coach today to London. Got that?" Before the man could answer, Julian called out, "Benson! Come over here!"

The shooter didn't have to think very long. He said, "Fuck if I care either, I don't run this damn shop." He snatched the coin from Julian's hand, while Matthew stood watching this endeavor with more than a little bemusement.

When Benson—an older gray-bearded and mustached gent who appeared to have quite the number of road miles on his stoop-shouldered shape—took the offered guinea it was explained to him that for both men to receive a second helping of gold coins they would not be stopping overnight at a coach inn, but just long enough to change horses, get something to eat and drink, piss and drop a fig or two if it was necessary, and then hell's blaze on toward London.

"Got that?" Julian asked, his face right up in the driver's.

The old man sucked his upper lip down and chewed on his mustache while he regarded the guinea, which seemed to shine even more brightly on this cold, grim and blustery morning. At last he gave a guttural grunt and rasped with dusty lungs, "Can be done." Then he stuck a black clay pipe in the wrinkle of his mouth, and when he went around to see to the horses he sauntered like the king of Siam.

Matthew and Julian climbed in and took one of the red-leather-covered bench seats that faced the other. The windows were protected from the elements by wooden shutters, and overhead in a rack was a dark blue horse blanket. On both sides of the interior, mounted on the wood in gimbals that kept them steady, were oil lamps with little red shades.

They didn't have long to wait. Within ten minutes there came the sound of clopping hooves and turning wheels. Julian opened the window shutters on his side and Matthew caught sight of an elaborately decorated carriage with a uniformed driver and being pulled by a team of white horses.

Julian removed his pistol and put it in his lap.

They could hear some inane pleasantries being exchanged between the male new arrival and Benson, who didn't let on about the present occupants. Then the door on the street side came open and a middle-aged woman in a white coat, a dress like a frosted cake and a high white wig was being helped into the coach by the shooter. Her heavily rouged and eyelined face took on the distortion of distress as she saw the two men within, but she was given a shove that was a little more than rude and she came tumbling in like a sack of the queen's laundry. Then the man in his white coat and attempt at the beribboned military uniform of some unknown force and country entered much the same way, and his heavily rouged and eyelined face under his high white wig took on the same expression. "What the devil!" he sputtered.

"Yes," said Julian. He put his hand upon the pistol and smiled. "Good morning to you both."

"This is a private coach!" said Lord Turlentort, the nostrils of his huge nose flared and his painted eyebrows lifted nearly to his false hairline. "Driver! Driver, come here!" he shouted.

Benson came, said, "On our way in a moment, sir," and shut the door with a flourish.

"I won't stand for this!" The lord reached for the door's handle but his hand stopped in midair when Julian lifted the pistol.

"Nice day for a trip to London," Julian said, and still smiling he scratched his unshaven chin with the four barrels.

"Heavens!" cried the lady. "They're ruffians bound to rob us!"

"Not at all, fair one," Julian answered. "We're simply in need of transportation to London. You're going there, so are we, and all is right with the world."

"The company shall hear of this, and mark it well!" Lord Turlentort threatened, but Matthew was sure that like so many others had been in Julian's career, the man's fearful eyes were fixed on that damned pistol.

"I'll mark it in my book of sins." Julian set the gun down again; Matthew thought that if that thing went off in here all that would be left of the Turlentorts would be wig curls and false eyelashes.

"Pullin' out!" Benson shouted, and then, the traditional coachman's cry for luck from the gods of safe travel: "*Tally ho*!"

With a jarring lurch the coach started off and quickly gained speed. Matthew mused that Benson might be a Jarvey—a regular, speed-conscious coachman—but the gold guinea and the promise of another had turned him into a Jehu, a coachman who drove the team with reckless abandon.

"Good Christ, we're moving fast!" said the lord as the wheels really started turning. There came the sound of the whip cracking the air. The coach itself began rocking back and forth, the weathered wood without and the varnished wood within making whines and pops of protest.

"Faster we move, faster we get there," said Julian. "Settle back and enjoy the ride." He touched his saddlebag. "I have some dried beef and fish I would share, if you'd like."

"We certainly would *not*!" said the lady. She looked near tears. "Travelling with two…two unkempt *criminals* is not my idea of a wonderful journey! You both smell *vile*!"

Matthew decided to try to ease the woman's fears. "I apologize for the aroma, but baths have not been on our recent agenda. May I ask why you're going to London?"

Neither one replied for a few seconds, and then the lady sniffed and said, "Shopping, of course! Everyone who is *anyone* does their shopping in London!"

"Little you'd know of that!" sneered the lord.

"True," said Julian. "I do prefer to rob for what I want. Also, killing is high on my list of pleasures. I've already sent a man to his grave this morning. It's what I do, just after breakfast." He glanced at Matthew. "Isn't that right, Scar?"

Matthew was taken aback, but he thought it best to go along. "Correct. I mean…right."

"Are they joking, Edgar?" the lady asked, newly stricken. "Tell me they're joking!"

"We never joke about murder," said Julian, grim-faced, and with a voice that would've made a professional assassin blanch.

The coach went on, rumbling and grumbling along the rutted road. Rain pelted the roof and Matthew envisioned the driver and shooter up there both curled up in their coats, under their hats with water dripping from the brims. In spite of the weather, Benson did not spare the speed, and Matthew figured the horses were being pushed to their limits, but Benson must have enough experience not to exhaust them entirely before they reached the next coaching inn.

Lady Turlentort had taken to opening a little white clamshell of a purse and dabbing her flabby throat from a bottle of perfume that smelled of roses, faintly rotten.

"Unshaven, unwashed beasts!" Edgar muttered. "I shall ruin this company!"

"Oh we're not so bad," said Julian. "You should have seen the men we've had to kill."

"Killing! Killing! Killing!" Edgar's nostrils flared wide again. "Is that all you live for?"

"No. I do like the occasional slice of chocolate cake."

"Madness! You two belong behind the bars of Newgate Prison!"

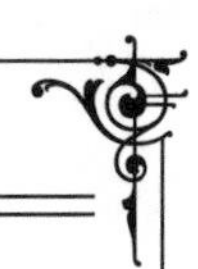

"I've been there," Matthew said, and realized at once that such a statement simply painted him a darker villain. The expression of renewed horror on the faces of the lord and lady spurred him on. "I broke out, of course." And then: "No prison can hold *me*."

Lady Turlentort stared at him as if he were a creature never seen before in the world...at least, not in her world. "You don't appear to have the face of a killer. I mean to say...I see that scar, but—"

"Tell them how you got that scar," Julian suggested.

"Well," Matthew began, "I was—"

"—about to be hanged by the neck for the murder of three men and a woman," Julian interrupted, his voice again as one nearly speaking from beyond the tomb. "Right there under the hangman's noose, he stood. About to go kick the very Devil in his ass. And then...his gang stormed the town square...swarmed over the gallows with their swords and pistols, cutting down every man of the law in sight." He nodded, looking back and forth from the two wide-eyed faces. "Yes. But...the executioner himself had a hook for a hand. Just as a pistol ball parted the rope that would send Scar to his maker...the executioner swung on him. Carved him, just as you see. And with the blood streaming from his face, Scar threw himself at the executioner and down they fell from the gallows to the gore-soaked ground below. They fought as animals do, down on that bloody battlefield, and—"

"But..." Edgar Turlentort's voice was a wisp. "Scar's hands were tied behind him, weren't they?"

"Yes, of course they were! I was about to say, they fought as animals do, though Scar's hands were tied behind him. And this executioner... well, he was viciously strong, and had been known to use his hook on unsuspecting victims late at night as they staggered drunk with rum from their taverns, though such could never be proven. That is to say, the executioner's soul was far from being lily-white."

"Quite far!" said the lady.

"Indeed," Julian replied. "As I was relating, Scar fought for his life. Kicking at his tormentor, you see, with his hands bound behind him. And

just as the executioner was about to slash his hook across Scar's throat…I shot him in the back of the head with this very pistol you see before you."

No one spoke, at first, as the coach creaked and squeaked, the wheels made a low thunder and the horses' hooves thudded on the earth, and then Lord Turlentort let go the breath he'd been holding.

"Zounds!" he said, so quietly it seemed he feared the wrath of a dead executioner.

The lady cleared her throat, fanned herself with a gloved hand, shifted her position on the seat and cleared her throat a second time. "Let me ask…a simple question, really…but out of curiosity…young man, did the four you murdered…how shall I put this?…did they in any way *deserve* such an end?"

"No doubt!" said Julian. "They were a ring of black-hearted villains brutalizing orphans."

Matthew lowered his head a fraction and stared down at the floorboards. Julian had no way of knowing that the pursuit of such a black-hearted villain who actually did brutalize orphans had brought him to New York from the Carolina colony in 1699, and had led to his recruitment into the Herrald Agency and in essence a new life and calling.

"I don't approve of taking justice into one's own hands," said the lord. "Yet…I imagine this ring of villains might have been operating beneath the attention of the law?"

"Absolutely so," said Matthew, who spoke the truth. "I had no choice but to try to trap him myself. I mean…trap *them*."

Julian was looking at him oddly, as if this tale had taken wings and flown away from him. He righted himself in an instant. "But, alas, simple trapping did not do the job nor save a single orphan. So…I won't go into the bloody details, but suffice to say the villains went to their rewards and Scar here was seized and a rope put about his neck."

"Hm," Lord Turlentort said after a moment's consideration, "the executioner might have been part of the ring. Do you think?"

"I have often thought as much," Julian answered. "You know…lord

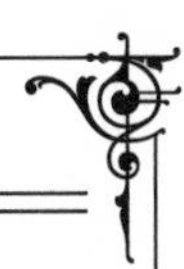

and lady…that if one is a villain, sometimes it is because villainy is the only open avenue when all others have closed. Then—by chance—one must wear his villain's cloak with a measure of *pride*, to best fight the darkest of evils. Thus Fate steps in and directs the course. What you see before you…myself and Scar…well, we are here to tell that tale."

"Oh, agreed!" the lady said. "I understand completely!"

"Somehow," said Julian with his most charming smile, "I knew you would."

Rain was still beating down, yet Benson still drove the horses hard. Lord Turlentort opened the window shutters to peer into the storm, then he snapped them tight again. Winter's light had turned gloomy. The lord reached into his coat, brought out a gold tinderbox, went about striking a flint and sparking the cotton and then he touched flame to the two oil lamps, which spread what Matthew considered a nice, comfortable and warming glow.

They had not gone much further when Lord Turlentort put his hand over his wife's and she seemed to settle against him. Cautiously, he said to the villain, "I must ask…since we are fellow travellers and are here in these confines…with time on our hands…do you have any further…um… episodes you might relate?"

"Oh, yes," Julian said. He again offered up the smooth smile. "Prepare to be amazed."

TWO.
LONDON CALLING

EIGHT.

It was a dark and stormy night. Truly it was. But with a difference, for the late-night lanterns of London taverns cut the dark, sending yellow beams out into the streets like lifelines to guide their patrons in from the storm, which had arrived over the city not as a howling horror but as a softer sigh of falling snow. Matthew mused that the snowfall—heavier within the last hour, and now blowing up flurries that swept through and nearly obscured those same tavern lights—was soon to completely cover the broken bricks and rude cobbles of the low city as well as the grand mansions and manicured parks of the high. All would be joined in white, in this town of many tones of gray.

Matthew and Julian trudged through the swirl, the former following the latter by several strides for it was clear Julian had another destination in mind in addition to the four taverns they'd already visited. The cold bit at Matthew's cheeks and nose, the snow beginning to dash him in the face with flakes that felt edged with ice. When a wagon or a coach passed, the sounds of the wheels and the horses' hooves were so muffled as to be nearly inaudible, and even the cries of a madman on a corner ahead were simply echoes within echoes, the snow imposing a quiet upon the most raucous of furies.

What part of the city they were in, Matthew had no clue. After Benson had let the exhausted couple of Lord and Lady Turlentort stagger from the coach in front of the majestic Mayfair Arms Inn and unloaded their baggage for the handlers to carry, he had agreed to take Matthew and Julian a mile or so further to the southeast, under Julian's direction to a locale called Pepperpot Alley. There Julian paid Benson and his shooter, Hedges, the other gold guineas and the coach—its driver and shooter ready for two days of solid sleep—trundled off, leaving its previous passengers staring through the flurries at what Matthew saw was indeed a narrow alley with red lanterns showing in the windows of several questionable establishments and a sign that announced this was the entrance to Howe's Cavern.

But the Cavern did not suit Julian. After one quick look around he was off again without a word, his cloak pulled up around his neck and his saddlebag across his shoulder. The next tavern they entered, further along the snow-dusted alley and named The Boggy Bottom, likewise held not a long interest from Julian, but here Matthew stood his ground and demanded to at least get a plate of the spinach pie that was advertised on the chalkboard, as well as a cup of hot chicken broth since the last meal he'd eaten—and quickly at that—was a bowl of stewed tomatoes and a slice of cornbread from the coaching inn they'd paused at six hours ago. Julian relented and they sat down in the corner with Julian's hand always on his pistol and his eyes ready for trouble from the surly-looking patrons. Matthew ordered his food and hoped for the best, Julian ordered a bowl of beef-and-rice soup that he said would likely be horsemeat, and they took a few moments of ease.

Then…off again.

The Black Grin Of Wisdom…one minute and out. "Who are we searching for?" Matthew asked as they left the odious place, which was the wisest thing to do.

"Someone important," was the answer. "He'll be out and about tonight, he always is."

Cat And Mouse...no once more, and then off to the east several streets to another bounty of bedlam, starting with a decrepit-looking hole that bore a sign identifying it as The Octopus Garden, a title which Matthew thought would meet with great interest from Professor Fell himself.

Before Julian pushed through the door he said, "I have hopes for this one."

"I have hopes to get next to a fireplace," Matthew muttered through lips as cold and stiff as metal.

They went in.

The trip from Bristol had taken thirty-eight hours, with several stops at various coaching inns along the route but only long enough for the necessities. Benson had crawled into the coach to get a few hours' sleep while Hedges drove the team, and then they switched up. Lord and Lady Turlentort would have been driven mad by the frenzied pace if Julian hadn't put on a performance that Matthew thought was masterful. In the pitching and swaying coach, Julian Devane took the Turlentorts away from their misery by the tales he spun, and whether they were true or not—and Matthew doubted any of them were true—the Turlentorts ate them up like sugar candies.

Julian was part of Queen Anne's bodyguard and saved her life from a foreign assassin bent on poisoning her afternoon tea. Julian had once been an assistant to a lion tamer at the Riggen Brothers' Circus—which Matthew doubted existed—and served in that position until, alas, Silkie the lion decided he was not getting enough meat and therefore the tamer's arm must suffice. Julian had sailed to South America in search of a shipwreck carrying a fabled emerald called the Green Goddess, and though he had not found the gemstone he was made an honorary member of the Tupinamba tribe for saving a young boy from drowning. Julian had once fought three duels in one day—before breakfast, after lunch and after dinner—and three men lay in the cemetery at Salisbury to prove it.

And on and on.

Listening to these yarns, Matthew thought Julian might well offer his services to *Lord Puffery's Pin* and be set for life.

Not once, however, did Julian mention Professor Danton Idris Fell, Mother Deare or any personage of that evil ilk; for the time spent entertaining the Turlentorts—and Benson and Hedges as well—he was simply an adventurer, or as Matthew believed, a young man dreaming of a life he might have had, and spinning his history from whole cloth much cleaner than the suit tailored for him by Fate.

Matthew had seized whatever sleep he could in the coach, and likewise had Julian. Matthew had seen that Julian never fully let himself go to sleep; the man slept so close to wakefulness that he just seemed to be resting with his eyes closed, and in truth his eyes were not closed that much, they were just glazed over and staring into space. Several times Julian had come up from his strange slumber with a start, on his lips a harsh whisper that in his dream—or nightmare?—must've been a shout, his eyes wide and red-rimmed with some private terror. And always his hand was either gripping that pistol or white-knuckled around the hilt of his sword, so that it seemed he was continually fighting duels in a Salisbury of his soul.

And that, Matthew thought, was the price the villain had to pay for his choices of profession and associates: unable to rest as normal people did, being constantly on guard, and shouting at phantoms that came reaching for him from the grave.

In that pitching coach, Matthew was fighting his own living nightmare of what he would do if Cardinal Black and the book of potions could not be found. Plus also a chemist to decipher Gentry's formulas had to be found and taken back to Y Beautiful Bedd in time to bring Berry back from her path to mindless imbecility. This entire journey to London might be a waste of time, and then where to go? He had to trust Julian because he had no choice; if Julian had any kind of connection in London to move them forward in this quest, then Julian was the master of the moment, and Matthew reduced to a tag-along.

But…what if this was all for nothing? The more Matthew let fact and logic enforce themselves in his brain the more he feared it was a delusion to think he could regain the book of potions—if it could even be *found*—and return it and a chemist to Y Beautiful Bedd in time. They still had something in the vicinity of twenty days before the potion became immobile, but if he failed in this quest how could he ever forgive himself? And to return to New York after he had found Brazio Valeriani…would he take Berry's broken shell back to her father, or would she be so far gone she imagined herself to be daughter to the Nashes and spend the rest of her life in that role?

Never in his life had he felt so helpless and so conflicted, for in exchange for this quest he had vowed to find Brazio Valeriani for Professor Fell and he was certain the professor did not want the man to discuss the weather in Italy. It had something to do with Fell's interest in demonology, Valeriani's dead father Ciro—a man of science who had for some reason lost his mind and hanged himself—and, strangely enough, a piece of furniture.

It sounded to Matthew like an evil mixture, to which Cardinal Black had become an added ingredient.

As the coach had gotten nearer to the city, Matthew could hear London calling. It was at first a low murmur or drone, felt more than heard, even through the noise of the wheels and the creaking of the coach. He recalled such a sound on his trip from Plymouth en route to his stay at Newgate Prison. It was the voice of London in all its life: the inhalation and exhalation of breath from human lungs, the thuddings of boots, the slamming of doors, the scrapings of wooden hulls against piers on the river, the noise of forks against plates, the clinking together of glasses, the music of taverns and street-singers, the beat of hooves on the streets and the squeak and crunch of innumerable wheels of wagons, coaches and carriages ever turning, all these and a thousand more elements to the voice of London and its six hundred thousand occupants…but in the depths of this voice Matthew heard only one question being

directed at him from whatever spirit ruled the sprawling city: *Will you succeed, or will you fail?*

And the observation, delivered like a blade to the heart: *I am the city that eats men alive. Once I almost consumed you. So come to me again, young Matthew, and test yourself against my age-old teeth of stone.*

He could not fail. Could not. But…how to succeed, when failure would mean such a torture he could not live beyond another twenty days, yet as a husk of a man he must find Brazio Valeriani for Professor Danton Idris Fell and in so doing have a hand in damning the world?

These things whirled through his mind as he followed Julian into The Octopus Garden. Within, the hanging lanterns cast greenish glows, there was a musty smell and many arms were reaching for tankards of ale, dice, cards and the like, but neither was there an octopus nor a garden. Over the hubbub of voices there bellowed the noise of excitement—hurrahing and shouting—toward the back of the place, where a dozen or more men were standing around a large table. "Ah!" said Julian over the tumult. "I believe I see our prize." He took a few more strides through the layers of swirling pipe smoke and then turned back to Matthew again. "He's there," Julian said. "Now: you stand silent while I speak to him. Make yourself invisible. Understand?"

"Yes."

"Come on, then."

They wound their way between the smaller tables to the larger. Under a brighter yellow lantern could be seen on the table a circular track lined with bricks placed end against end. On that track Matthew caught sight of four rather huge cockroaches scrabbling toward a piece of red twine stretched between two nails, the finish line for this insectile race.

The shouts of the gamblers merged together: *Go on, Goliath, go on!... Faster, Alfonzo, faster!...God blast you, Jimmy Jack, you're as slow as Christmas!...Move your damn ass, Brisket!*

And between shouts the men who were evidently the owners of such creatures were blowing puffs of air upon them with little miniature bellows, the better to speed their progress toward the red twine and the bowl

of silver coins held by a thin and unsmiling man wearing a white wig decorated with the dried bodies of what might have been former champions of this sport, or simply had been swept up from the floor. On closer inspection—and much closer he did not wish to get—Matthew saw that the shiny black backs of the struggling contestants were marked by dabs of paint: red, blue, white and yellow. It seemed not even its owner could tell Goliath from Brisket without a color cue.

Matthew noted that Julian had edged up beside a tall, slim man in his fifties who had a craggy but not unhandsome face with a long aquiline nose, flowing gray hair, voluminous gray eyebrows and a mostly-white mustache and beard waxed to such a sharp point it might have served as an icepick. This man appeared to be a gentleman of the upper class out for a night among the lowly, until one got a look at the patches on the elbows of the shabby dark blue suit and the unwashed collar and cuffs of his white—had it even been truly so?—shirt. A bright purple paisley cravat tucked around the throat did serve to detract the eye from this individual's wardrobe misfortunes, or rather it attempted to shock the eye into insensibility.

Julian leaned in closer to the man and over the noise of the race Matthew heard him say, "Hello, Britt."

The man turned, the copper-colored eyes took Julian in and the leathery face smiled. "Julian, my boy! How good to see you! Where have you been keeping yourself?"

"There and abouts. I have some questions for you."

"I am always at your disposal, but not now, please! Can't you see the drama unfolding before you?"

"I see the running of the roaches."

"You can't see that Alfonzo is about to overtake my Goliath with less than half a track to go? Blowwwww, winds, blowwwww!" Britt called to Goliath's owner, who was furiously manning his bellows. "Oh, you're blowing the wind up Alfonzo's ass!" Britt cried out as one in anguish. "Dear God, have you no mercy?"

"Which is Alfonzo?" Julian asked.

"The red-dotted demon from the pits of Hell!" Britt said. "Look at him scurry forward!"

Julian leaned toward the track.

His fist came down.

Slam! Upon Alfonzo.

And then Alfonzo was, like *Lord Puffery's Pin*, red all over. Or really rather a mushy kind of brown.

The silence of horror fell upon the crowd.

"Egad," said Britt, the huge bushy eyebrows up and twitching. But then: "And Goliath crosses the finish line! Right-o, chaps, right-o!"

At once a stocky bull-chested gent four inches short of Julian's height but with a mug like a meat cleaver was snarling up into his face. "Ya murdered my meal ticket, ya bastard! I'll take your head for—"

He stopped because four barrels did not exactly fit into two nostrils, but it was a near-run thing.

"I wouldn't cause a scene, Arthur," Britt cautioned. "And good advice to all my friends gathered here." He was already reaching for the money bowl. "This gentleman before you once fought three duels in one day in Salisbury, and you can see he's very much alive and kicking."

Julian was aiming that deadly stare into the eyes of the late Alfonzo's owner. Matthew saw Julian wipe his offending hand across the front of the other man's coat, leaving a streak of ill luck. "Give him a decent burial," Julian said.

There was some more muttering and a few half-hearted threats were thrown across the table, but Britt took it upon himself to give a coin each to the owners of Goliath, Jimmy Jack, Brisket, and even dead Alfonzo's owner, who brightened up considerably on his way to the bar.

"Next race in five minutes!" called the bug-wigged man in a sing-song voice that said this was not his first time around the track. "Masters, bring your contestants forward! Gamblers, get your bets on the table!"

Matthew stood nearby, close enough to hear but out of Britt's line-of-sight; he was just meandering around beside the table as if contemplating his next bet.

"So *good* to see you, dear boy!" said Britt. He cast his gaze upon the saddlebag. "Travelling far tonight? And still flirting with disaster, are we?"

"Yes, travelling far…and only flirting."

"It'll catch up with you! Mark it, and you know what I've told you if you keep up your dangerous walk upon the precipice! Every day you have the chance to start anew and afresh!"

"Yes, I recall," said Julian. "And as I recall, your own precipice is equally as dangerous as mine. Well, I'll start anew and afresh tomorrow. For now I have to ask you some questions."

"Oh?" Britt produced a red velvet purse from within his coat and began to put his winnings away. "Pertaining to what?"

"Pertaining to what Royal Navy admiral has decided to go into competition with Professor Fell."

Matthew saw the man's fingers pause in their deposit of the silver.

"You know who I mean," Julian went on. "I want a name."

"Dear *boy*," said Britt, who dropped the last shilling into his purse and closed the bag with its drawstring, "a question of that nature is best directed to Mother Deare. She should know far more than—"

"Mother Deare is dead. The admiral's name. What is it?"

"Mother Deare *dead*? Oh, my! That's certainly news for the street!"

"You know the news of the street twelve hours before it happens," said Julian. "And you know what street it's going to happen on. That's why I'm here looking into your face." Julian's hand came up to smooth one of Britt's sooty lapels. "You are the king of underworld knowledge. I don't have to tell you that, do I?"

"You flatter me. What can I say?"

"You can say the name, and please do it quickly because I really do *despise* roaches."

"Hm. Unfortunately I do not know the name of the personage you seek." From within the gentleman's well-worn jacket, Britt's fingers produced a pewter snuffbox. He opened it and took a whiff up each nostril as Julian waited for the next statement. Britt gave a polite little sneeze, wiped his nose with a cuff and then continued. "*But*, I do know of the professor's current predicament."

"Oh? What might that be?"

"The diminishment of his *power*. Dear boy, everyone knows it. Certainly you do. It seems a young stripling from the colonies has weakened Danton's hold on…well…his hold on *everything*. I am not aware of the name, but I have heard this upstart has not only upset the professor's business interests, but nearly destroyed that island of his he prizes so highly. Therefore the other sharks in this sea of ours smell blood and are gathering to consume the body. Isn't that correct?"

Matthew almost said *Yes it is*, but he kept his mouth shut and his eyes on the table as the next roaches were dabbed with paint for their race.

"No comment," said Julian.

"And that means *correct*," Britt answered with the sly slip of a smile. "I'm sure it will be common knowledge soon, and perhaps an item for all to read in the *Pin*."

"The only item that currently concerns me is the admiral's name, which I'm sure you have but which you for some reason refuse to reveal. All right then, what's your price?"

"My *price*? Oh Julian, not everything comes down to money."

"Ha!" It was a laugh without mirth from the slate-eyed face. "Now that's a lie for the ages."

"You hurt my heart, dear boy. And I thought I taught you such good manners." Britt's attention turned toward the man with the dead bugs in his wig. "Four shillings on…what's that little one's name?"

"Mongo," came the reply.

"Four shillings on Mongo. He looks quick out the gate." The coins went into the bowl along with the others being deposited there, and the

wigged bugateer wet a pencil's tip with his tongue and marked down the figure in a ratty-looking notebook. "Julian," said Britt, "you should go now unless you'd like to place a bet upon Mongo, who appears to me a worthy contestant to win the next round. And please, this time keep your fist to yourself."

"That's your final word?"

"Final unto finality."

Suddenly a thin figure slid up beside Matthew and a dirty face with a mass of black hair topping it grinned at him. "Drink a' ale, handsome? Then a ride on the pony?"

"The pony?" Matthew asked.

"Yep. My name's Pony."

"No, thank you," Matthew answered, and so moved away from the table while Julian and Britt traded a few further barbs that he was unable to hear. The crowd around the table was getting louder as the roaches were put into a wooden box, the box closed and shaken and then held over the track's starting point. Matthew figured the bottom of the box was hinged to allow the contestants to fall out upon the track, but he had no desire to see any further nor curiosity to watch the progress of Mongo.

In another moment Julian came up at his side and said, "We're done here."

Out in the cold, with the snow blowing around them, Julian said, "Cross the street. We'll stand in that doorway awhile."

"Why? Aren't we done here?"

"We are done in the Garden," Julian corrected. "Not with Britt. If I know him—and I do, very well—he has never turned down a coin unless it's for two more. Let's give him time to lose his shillings on Mongo and then see what he does. Or rather...where he *goes*."

They waited in the doorway's dark as the snow fell before them and the wind took on a high keening note.

In the next ten minutes a few men came into and went out of The Octopus Garden but Julian gave no reaction. At last a tall figure bundled up in a long greatcoat and wearing a floppy-brimmed hat pulled down low upon the head emerged and began striding westward. It was a man who obviously had somewhere important to go, and was sparing no speed even though the wind whipped his face.

"That's his stride. A bit gangly, like a roach running a race, isn't it?" Julian said. "Britt's on the move. So shall we be."

NINE.

Through the white curtains of night Julian and Matthew followed the man called Britt. They trailed at a distance, enough to keep their quarry in sight yet not close enough to trip the game. For block after block Britt went on, at one point his greatcoat seemingly losing its last button and spreading open with the wind like a pair of flapping wings. With one hand he kept the hat on his head, lest it too fly away.

The snow played tricks with measure, but Matthew figured they must've travelled half a mile before Britt crossed the street—quickly, in front of a coach whose driver obviously was in a hurry to get somewhere warm—and then descended a narrow set of steps.

"Move!" Julian said to rush Matthew along, but Matthew needed no urging. At the top of the steps they were looking down at an oak door, a pair of green-glassed oval windows and a sign that read The Green Spot. Britt had entered another of the tawdry taverns in what Matthew felt that, beyond the purity of the snow, was an area not so different from the dark bleakness of Whitechapel.

Julian grasped Matthew's shoulder. "Listen to me," he said. "You go in there and find out who he's meeting. Take a good look, come back out and describe him…or her. Britt didn't see you at the Garden, so you'll have a free moment, but *only* a moment. Understand?"

"I do."

"Go. I'll be around the corner."

Matthew nodded and went down the steps. Opening the Green Spot's door gave him a faceful of strong pipesmoke, the odors of spilled ale and wine and the smells of men who have gone a bit too long without a wash, but also the aroma and warmth of the fireplace that was brightly crackling wood opposite the door. Matthew entered, let the door close behind him, and walked between the tables and past the bar to stand before the fire. He turned around, the better to warm his backside and get a view of the room, which held perhaps ten or twelve patrons. There were no roach races running, so it was a quiet group intent on their drinking and their guarded conversations. The place was rather shadowy with stingy illumination, but quite suddenly Matthew realized he was standing about eight feet from a table where Britt had drawn up a chair to sit across from a second man.

By the fire's glow Matthew took stock of this individual: a slender man wearing a white suit—odd for this time of year, but there it was—and a white shirt with a black cravat around the thin neck. The man looked to be maybe in his late forties or early fifties. He had a stripe of gray hair down the middle of his head but the rest of his scalp was shaved bald. A small gray goatee was set in the center of his pointed chin, and he had a small hooked beak of a nose. But the most arresting thing about the man were his eyes; they were almost disturbingly large and slightly bulging as if they were being forced by pressure from the setting of the sockets. And their color: as golden and sparkling as the guineas in Julian's money belt.

Matthew saw Britt leaning forward, the man's face half in shadow and half painted orange by the fire.

Then, suddenly, it happened.

The man Britt was addressing turned his head to the left, the golden eyes still wide and quite strange-looking, and began to twist his head around in that direction. Matthew's heart jumped; in another few seconds the man was going to break his own neck, for the head was being twisted nearly back around to his shoulder blades.

Meet the Owl

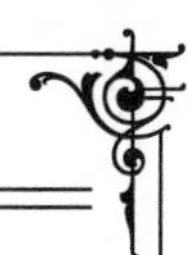

The man's head gave a slight jerk, Matthew saw the neck's muscles clench and relax, there was a quiet *pop* and to Matthew's amazement the twisting head continued to turn…to turn…to turn…until the freakish gent was looking behind himself…and yet the head still continued to swivel. Matthew almost stepped back and seared the heels of his boots on the burning logs, for this man in white with the golden eyes had turned his head only just short of all the way around on the neck, and now as Matthew watched the man's head began to slowly swivel back the other way…more and more…more and more…as the golden eyes glinted with firelight and Britt's shadowy face just kept talking as if this were the most natural sight in the world.

The man's head, turning to the right now, looked near breaking the neck once again until there was that jerking motion, the contracting and relaxing of neck muscles, and the *pop* of bizarre bones resetting into angles that defied the formality of the human skeleton.

And then…the weird golden eyes fixed upon Matthew and remained there, and to his horror Matthew found he could not look away.

"Help you, sir?"

Was someone's voice actually speaking? Or was it the strange man speaking from the depths of his mind?

"Somethin' to drink, sir?"

The golden eyes left him and the head began to swivel back to a normal degree. The man's full attention was being directed to Britt, and freed from that optic bondage Matthew looked to his side at the serving-girl who had come out from behind the bar.

"Sir?" the waif-like creature prompted.

"No," Matthew said. He was stunned and oddly enough his own neck felt strained to its limits. "No," he repeated. "I just…no." And then he was moving away from the fireplace, past the bar and between the tables, out the Green Spot's door and into the cold, up the crusty white steps and there stood Julian in a doorway around the corner.

"Well?" Julian asked.

For a few seconds Matthew could not speak.

"Who did he meet?" Julian prompted. "My God, what's wrong with you?"

"He met…it was…I mean to say…it was a man…*unbelievable*…I couldn't fathom such a thing…"

"All right, all right, it was a man! Now speak English instead of jabberguese!"

"A moment," said Matthew, to clear his mind. "Yes, a man," he continued. Snow blew into his face and clung to his eyelashes. "This man… he could twist his head around. I know it sounds insane, but he could—"

"Twist his head almost all the way around?" Julian asked. "So he can look behind himself? Ah. I know that man."

"Who *is* it?"

"It is the *Owl,*" said Julian. "Real name unknown. Pardon me but I could laugh at the expression on your face. I do understand how witnessing that particular talent of his could upset one's cart."

"My cart," Matthew answered, "has been turned upside-down."

"Well get it righted in a hurry because we're not here to dawdle and dance. I want to know why Britt stalked out in this weather to find the Owl. Did you see money being exchanged?"

"No. At least not that moment."

"I'll wager the Owl paid Britt for the information that I was asking questions," Julian said. He tapped his chin with a forefinger. "But…who is paying the Owl?"

"I don't…quite understand this." Matthew still felt brain-fogged, even in this cold. "Who is the Owl and why should he be paying Britt for information?"

"The Owl," said Julian, "is a security specialist. He takes care of…shall we say…keeping things buttoned up that need to be, and maintaining order. He's been working that angle for underworld gatherings for the last two years. Which means there's something cooking we should know about."

"Agreed, but how to find out?"

"We wait again. If Britt's information interests the Owl—and I think it will—our man of the twisted neck will be on the move himself very soon, and this time he might be reporting to someone we really do care to meet."

"The admiral?" said Matthew.

"We'll see. I'm going to cross the street and find a place to watch those steps. I want you across the street *there*," and Julian motioned toward the west, "so neither Britt nor the Owl run into you if they come up and turn this corner. Then settle back and try to warm yourself. We might be out here a while."

Matthew took up the position Julian had indicated, blending as well as possible into the darkness. Julian strode off to the north and became invisible. Then Matthew concentrated on watching the corner across the way and at the same time trying to envision himself standing before a bonfire that warmed every square inch of his body. He rubbed his hands together and was grateful for his gloves and the woolen cap under his tricorn that was keeping his ears from falling off. If the cap had any lice, by now they were only ice.

He had reached the point of dreaming not about standing before a bonfire but sitting in a hot bathtub with the fire in front of him and a warm cup of apple ale in his hand when Julian rushed around the corner and said, "Hurry! We can't lose him!"

"Who are we following? Britt or the Owl?" Matthew asked as they started off in a westerly direction.

"The Owl. He's wearing all white, a white greatcoat with a white hood up over his head. You can just barely see him up front half a block. He's walking fast. I don't trust getting much closer than this, with that swiveling head of his, but we've got to keep him in sight."

Matthew could indeed barely make out the white-clad figure against the snowfall, and even as he caught view of the freakish man the whirling flurries swept in and hid the Owl behind their veils. Julian picked up the speed of his stride and Matthew matched it; Matthew knew full well

that if they let this man get away they might lose whatever chance they had to find this mysterious admiral, if that's who the Owl was going to hoot to.

For block after block they continued, crossing street after street. At times Matthew feared they had lost the Owl because against all that white the white-hooded figure could not be seen, but then the flurries parted and there was just the glimpse of the man striding through the illumination from a tavern's window before he was again obscured. Matthew wondered if at some time during this pursuit the Owl might choose to swivel his head almost all the way around to check who might be following, but at least the hood would prevent such a sighting of his two trackers.

They were reaching an area of the city that was lit up by many oil lamps and had fewer staggering drunkards and raging maniacs upon the streets; here there were less tawdry taverns and more sophisticated music halls, theaters, coffee shops and restaurants. Still, it was the same falling snow. Suddenly Julian stopped and caught Matthew's arm, because on the next block the Owl had hailed a hackney carriage and was climbing into its enclosed space. The door closed, a whip cracked and the single horse started off with a steam-bellowing snort. Matthew realized the man had come to this more elegant district in order to catch a carriage, the likes of which did not roam very far into the darker and more dangerous territory he and Julian had just travelled across.

"Damn!" said Julian. "We've lost him!"

But not quite.

"*There*!" Matthew pointed at a second hackney carriage just pulling to the curb in front of the Sir Toddy's Music Hall and letting out two couples bundled up in woolens and furs. A woman laughed like the tinkling of chimes, and one of the gentlemen playfully swatted her ample rump as the group lurched toward the music hall's entrance.

"*Go*!" Julian said.

They ran for the carriage. "Hire a hack, sir?" the driver asked Matthew from the depths of his coat, muffler and well-worn beaverskin hat.

The carriage carrying the Owl was still in sight, about to swerve toward a roundabout.

Matthew pointed. "Follow that carriage!" he said, as Julian was already climbing in.

"Oh, zounds!" said the driver with a measure of glee. "An intrigue!"

Matthew was going to make certain the man followed the correct vehicle, so instead of climbing into the carriage he grabbed hold of the leather help-you-up grip and hauled himself up onto the seat beside the driver. The whip snapped the frigid air, the horse started moving and Matthew tensed forward like a greyhound on the trail of the fox...or in this case, an eagle on the flight of a lesser bird.

True enough, the roundabout led into a boulevard where many hackneys were converging. Even as the snow flew into his face Matthew fixed his eyes on the Owl's carriage, and he was aided in this by Julian, who opened the hackney's door wide enough to be able to lean out and keep watch.

The attitude was of a chase, but the mechanics were of a plod. Neither the Owl's hackney nor Matthew's could gain much speed in this weather, so it was more of a slow-motion ramble. At one point Matthew feared his driver was going to smash into the rear of the one ahead, which swerved to avoid another coming in from a street on the right, but with a hollered "*Whup, Hermes*!" from the driver which seemed to make some sense to the horse the steed slowed in its seeming intentions to crash through to where the Owl sat possibly twisting his head in all directions.

The hackney ahead turned north and so did Matthew's driver. Matthew thought he could hear the man giggling at this romp, which was likely a departure from his usual more staid nightly work. "Are we chasin' a jewel thief or an unfaithful wife?" the man called out, almost breaking Matthew's ear, and Julian shouted from below, "Both!" which made the driver hit the reins as if to make Hermes airborne.

In another few minutes they were entering an area of London that was so far removed from The Octopus Garden and The Green Spot as to be part of another world. The wheels crunched through snow on a road alongside a

large park where the whitened foliage was manicured into what appeared to be the whimsical shapes of horses. Pine trees surrounded a gazebo lit up with multi-colored lanterns to celebrate the Christmas season. Through the trees on the other side of the park could be seen the houses of the wealthy, also even at this late hour illuminated with many lanterns in their windows and on their sweeping porches as if time meant nothing but the accumulation of more money to that singular breed of men.

The Owl's hackney was curving around the park toward that grand row of stellar estates, and so followed Matthew's carriage.

"Slow down!" Julian advised from below, as it was apparent the vehicle carrying the Owl had begun to ease its pace as the road's curve straightened out before the abodes of what might have been the gods of London. Matthew saw the Owl's carriage stop in front of a high gate. Beyond the gate, another road led between more sculpted foliage perhaps twenty yards to the steps of a huge house of white stone whose array of slanted roofs were covered with snow, and whose windows of varied shapes were ablaze with lamplight. The entire estate was surrounded by an iron fence. At the gate stood a man wearing a long dark greatcoat, a tricorn and a woolen mask over his face as protection from the cold. Matthew saw the Owl hurriedly get out and approach the gate, and before Julian could voice it Matthew said, "Drive on past the house."

"Yessir, as you say."

Both Matthew and Julian looked back to see the Owl being admitted through the gate, which swung shut behind him, and the freakish man in the white-hooded coat strode rapidly toward the front steps.

"Pull over just ahead, on the park side," Julian instructed.

The driver did as he was told and reined Hermes to a stop.

Matthew saw that the Owl's hackney remained in front of the gate. He watched the Owl use a knocker on the door to announce his presence, and within a few seconds it was opened by a man in a dark blue uniform of some kind, but definitely not a bearlike man with a flame-painted beard. The Owl entered the house and the door was closed.

"Let's take a walk," said Julian. "Driver, we'll need you to stay here. An extra six shillings for you." One of the guineas had been made into change at a coaching inn, which Matthew was sure would meet with Professor Fell's approval since Julian was no longer throwing his money away.

Julian left his saddlebag and sword in the carriage, and he walked beside Matthew as they approached the man at the gate. The snow had abated though it was still blowing in flurries, but Matthew thought the temperature must be falling to bone-cracking lows. He figured the guard at the gate had been on duty for a while or was set to be there for a time, therefore the woolen mask to ward off the freeze. Julian reached out to rub his hand along the flank of the horse that had brought the Owl's hackney here, and then he faced the guard and said, "Pardon me, sir. I fear we're lost in all this weather. Whose house is this?"

The guard said nothing. The hard blue eyes in the mask's holes stared impassively at his questioner.

"We're to be guests at Lord Somerset's. Isn't this his house?"

Still the guard did not speak. But there *was* a response: a gloved hand moved a fold of his coat aside to show a holster and a pistol's grip.

"Oh!" said Julian, feigning both surprise and offense. "Pardon me again, we must have the wrong address! Come along, Samuel." He gave a tug at Matthew's sleeve and started walking back toward the Hermes carriage further up the road. Before he followed, Matthew cast another look at the mansion and saw at its highest roof a large crescent-shaped attic window lit by a lamp. On the other side of the glass a ship's spoked wheel stood on a pedestal presumably mounted to the floor.

The admiral's house, he thought. Bravo, Julian!

Then he turned away, the back of his neck bristling with the stare that the armed guard aimed at him.

TEN.

"Hold on a minute," said Julian as they reached their hackney. "What have we *here*?"

Matthew turned to look. Another carriage was coming around the park, the horses' hooves making muffled thudding noises in the snow.

"You find who you're after?" Hermes' driver asked from his bench seat.

"Not yet," Julian answered, his eyes narrowed as he watched the new carriage approach, "but the night is still young."

"Gettin' toward midnight is what I'm thinkin'," the driver said. "If that's what you mean by *young*. And I'm too old to be out here shiverin' the rest of me life away!"

"Just a bit longer, if you please." Julian and Matthew saw the new carriage slowing down, and then its driver reined the horse to a stop in front of the gate. "A busy place tonight," said Julian. "I wonder what goes on in there."

Two men emerged from the hackney. They appeared at first to be dressed as clowns from a circus. One wore an enormous white polar bear of a coat, a white muffler around the lower part of his face, and had on a bright red tricorn with a half-dozen feathers of various dyed hues sticking

up from its golden band. The other man, taller and thinner than the first, wore a long coat of some kind of dark gray leather—sealskin? Matthew wondered—with a yellow cord as a sash around the waist, and perched atop his ridiculous pile of a curly white wig was a tricorn as purple as a new bruise. Matthew caught just a quick glimpse of his face, which seemed to be painted ghastly white with crimson arcs above the eyes to serve as brows.

"The carnival has come to town," Julian said with a smirk. "Let's see what these two do."

The two in question approached the guard. The man in the polar bear coat reached into a pocket, withdrew something and showed the guard, who nodded and opened the gate. The strange pair then proceeded to walk nearly in lockstep up the drive and up the steps to the door, where Sir Polar Bear used the knocker. After a moment the door opened and that same uniformed man looked out. Both of the new arrivals came to rigid attention and sharply clicked their bootheels together.

"Prussian," said Julian. "Have to be, with those military flagpoles up their tails."

Prussian, Matthew thought with a feeling in his gut like a twinge of rising bile. The one Prussian he had ever known—and one too many—was the deadly swordsman Count Anton Mannerheim Dahlgren, who at the moment should be bones in the belly of whatever Atlantic ocean shark had managed to digest the bastard.

At the door the uniformed man was speaking. Sir Polar Bear nodded, and then he and Clown Face came back down the stairs in their stately marching order as the mansion's door was shut and apparently the business finished. They came back through the gate, which was also closed behind them by the impassive guard. An instruction was given from Sir Polar Bear to the driver of their hackney, the two climbed back in, closed the cab's door, and the carriage started off, passing Matthew and Julian, their own shivering driver and the steam-snorting Hermes.

"More intrigue!" Julian called up. "Now follow *that* carriage!"

"Intrigue or not, my ass is an iceberg!" the driver complained, but he unlocked the carriage's brake as Matthew climbed up beside him again and Julian took his place within the hackney. With a whipstrike into the air Hermes started off, and this time the carriage ahead was easy to trail at least for a distance because they seemed to be the only two vehicles out and about in this vaunted area of London estates.

Back they travelled into the busier boulevards and thoroughfares of the city. It seemed to Matthew that the Christmas season had made London more of a beehive than ever, even at the midnight hour. Hackneys came out from all directions, veered off this way and that, but Matthew kept his focus squarely on the one carrying the two—Prussian?—clowns.

In another ten minutes they were stopping back where Benson had halted the coach to let the Turlentorts out: in front of the red-carpeted steps underneath a red awning that protected the entrance to the Mayfair Arms Inn, which was a huge elegant brownstone building that made New York town's finest Dock House Inn look like a near relation to The Octopus Garden. The edifice boasted four floors and had a castle-like turret up at each of its corners along with a forest of chimneys, all of which seemed to be spouting smoke into the snowfall. The two objects of current attention were disembarking from their carriage, the hackney's door being opened for them by a red-liveried footman wearing a ten-ton white wig and with white stockings up to his knobby knees.

As Hermes' driver pulled their carriage up behind the one ahead, Matthew saw Sir Polar Bear, who had in his grip a small brown satchel, gesturing for aid to unpack the bags laced up beneath canvas on the luggage platform at the rear of the hack. In turn the footman blew into a whistle that brought a pair of other similarly-clad attendants running. Sir Polar Bear paid the driver with glittering silver and then he and Clown Face marched up the steps and into the Mayfair Arms while the footman strode ahead to open all closed doors as if the strange guests had no arms of their own.

Julian was out of the carriage with his saddlebag over his shoulder and his sword's scabbard in its rightful place. He handed six shillings up to Matthew and Matthew passed them to the driver, who tipped his hat and said, "Thankee sir, and good luck with all yer intrigues."

Matthew climbed down and watched as Julian stood to one side observing the removal of the many pieces of luggage belonging to the two men they'd followed. As the canvas was unlaced, revealed beneath were a pair of large trunks, four smaller cases and four hatboxes. The attendants struggled to carry one of the trunks between them into the building. As noble Hermes pulled the trusty carriage away into the flurries, Julian said, "I think we should give them some help. *Here*." He tossed one of the smaller cases to Matthew and picked up another one.

"Hey! Hey!" called the hack's driver, who was on the ground feeding his horse pieces of a dried apple. "What're you doin' there?"

"We're part of the delegation," Julian answered with an upthrust of his chin. "And the last *servant* who spoke so rudely to me got a skewer in his kidneys." He put a hand on his sword.

The driver pulled his hat down lower over his eyes, so as not to see anything more. He shrugged and muttered, "I ain't speakin'."

"Come along, Manfred," Julian directed.

They went up the red-carpeted steps through the double oak doors into the Mayfair Arms. Matthew was struck with a myriad of impressions: first of all, blessed *warmth* and crackling logs in a huge fireplace with gold-hued marble tiles forming the mantle, colored lanterns and boughs of holly hanging from oak beams in a high-ceilinged lobby, a trio of musicians playing with dignified tones two violins and a flute, a number of seating areas containing overstuffed leather chairs and sofas here and there on the smooth and polished dark brown timbers of the floor, and above it all a massive chandelier that must contain at least sixty lighted candles. A distance away stood Sir Polar Bear and Clown Face at a desk where a slight young man in a dark blue suit and a restrained white wig was signing them in on a ledger book. A few other guests were seated

near the musicians for the late-night musicale, a grandfather clock ticked quietly in a corner, and all seemed right in this world of the wealthy.

The footman was coming toward Matthew and Julian on his way out again, with the two attendants at his heels. Over by a wide red-carpeted staircase with man-sized wooden statues of angels standing on either side of the bannisters the first trunk had been set down, the other baggage to follow in preparation of hauling all of it up to the new arrivals' chamber.

Julian reached out and caught the footman's arm, at the same time turning his back on the clerk's desk which stood perhaps twenty feet away.

"What kind of establishment are you running here?" Julian asked, his voice sharp enough to convey irritation but not so sharp as to prick the ears of anyone else. "Must your guests carry in their own bags from this frigid night and have no one to greet their carriage?"

"I...I'm sorry, sir. But due to the lateness of the hour and of course the weather, I have only these two attendants on—"

"No excuses! I am absolutely *mortified* that we have travelled so far to be treated as common...well, as *common*! What is your name?"

As this was going on, Matthew saw Julian sneak a glance at the clerk's desk and he realized this was a stalling game to get the two men up the stairs and out of the lobby. Sir Polar Bear and Clown Face were obviously in a hurry as well, because the key was already being offered and the clerk motioned with a sweeping gesture toward the staircase.

"Hold your place while I'm speaking to you," Julian went on, and the two hapless attendants—both young boys who looked terribly uncomfortable in their wigs and tightly buttoned uniforms—stood behind the footman as if seeking his protection, as much as frightened mice could seek the protection of a spindly scarecrow. "My associate and I have been guests in many inns across this country, and indeed across *Europe*, and I am simply *astonished* at the lack of—"

Matthew nudged him. The objects of interest were ascending the stairs with their quickstep military gait.

"Keep calm and carry on," Julian said to his audience, and just like that he released them from their state of siege. They rushed on out, Matthew followed Julian to the clerk's desk, and Julian set the case he was holding atop it. "Booking for Randolph Mowbrey," he said. "And associate, Mr. Spottle." While the clerk was checking the ledger for these names that were not there, Julian added, "That would be *Count* Randolph Mowbrey."

"Of course," said the clerk, whose brow was furrowing as his finger ticked down the list on his ledger. "Odd…I don't see those names."

"Our agent here made the booking some time ago. We're with the Prussian delegation who just arrived. The two gentlemen before us." To the clerk's blank stare, Julian said loftily, "We are the *interpreters*, and we would like the room next to theirs."

"Um…sir…I don't think I can—"

"This is quite the beautiful lobby," Julian interrupted with a smile, but his voice still carried a hint of disdain. "I'd say it's easily the equal to the lobby of the Imperiale in Konigsberg. Wouldn't you, Mr. Spottle?"

"Easily," said Matthew, wondering where that ridiculous moniker had come from.

"A room next to our patrons," Julian said. "We have just gotten off the ship, we are in need of shaves and baths—as I imagine you might realize—and the rest of our luggage has been delayed in being unloaded at the dock due to some error or another." He flipped a hand into the air to display further annoyance. "Therefore we are in no mood for further errors. A room, if you please."

"Well…Count Mowbrey…I can offer you a room on the same *floor*, but…it won't be a Grand Suite as Count Pellegar has been given."

"What room and how far from Count Pellegar's, then?" Julian spoke the name as if he heard it every minute of every day.

"Number twenty-six, on the second floor at the end of the hallway. Count Pellegar and Baron Brux are in twenty-one. The room is readied for a gentleman who has yet to arrive but I can place him elsewhere. Your window's view would unfortunately be of a brick wall."

Julian gave a frown of distaste. "Horrible! But…I suppose it'll have to do. You know, sometime in the future I hope inns are able to prevent these kinds of booking errors."

"Yes, my hope as well, your Excellency. If you would sign, here, please. And I might ask for the prepayment of the nightly rate of two guineas?"

"*Two* guineas? The night is almost done! And with such an unsightly view and disregard for our arrival?" Julian paused in his penmanship. "What say one guinea for tonight, and we shall pay for the remainder of our stay tomorrow once all is sorted out?"

The clerk was obviously taken aback by this suggestion, because he stuttered a bit before he said, "I do understand your meaning, your Excellency, but—"

"Agreed, then!" Julian was already drawing out his sword, which caused the clerk another few seconds of consternation, but his expression relaxed when he saw the golden guinea that Count Mowbrey removed from the belt and placed with great care exactly at the center of the man's open ledger. "Can't be too careful, with all the rascals about," Julian explained as he put the belt away and replaced the sword. "We'll carry our own bags. The key, if you please?"

"*Spottle*?" asked Matthew as they ascended the grand staircase.

"The name of a stray dog I took in when I was a small boy. I had to think fast. And I once killed a man named Randolph Mowbrey, so he won't mind."

The second-floor hallway was also richly carpeted in red. Matthew saw that there looked to be only six rooms per floor, three facing three. As Julian unlocked the door of number twenty-six at the corridor's far end, he said quietly, "We'll wait for their luggage to come up and everything to settle. We don't want any interruptions to spoil our party."

Matthew had dreaded this, but he'd known it was coming. They had to get into number twenty-one and find out whatever they could, and that meant Julian's penchant for violence might be at free rein.

Their room did have a window that faced a brick wall, but the space was perhaps three times as large as the dairyhouse that Matthew called home in

New York. The glow of a trio of oil lamps around the chamber cast merry light and spoke of the care the Mayfair Arms gave to its guests, making sure illumination was available to the gentleman who had booked the room but failed to arrive. Everything but the view was a study in good taste and expensive decoration, from the medieval tapestry that draped one wall to the black leather chairs situated around an oak table, a long black leather sofa and a canopied bed with an ornate carved headboard. The room smelled only faintly of the whale oil, but mostly of clean leather and fresh linens.

"A gold-plated bedpan is in here somewhere, I'm sure," said Julian as he put the purloined case down on the floor. Matthew put his own stolen case on one of the chairs and then walked to a washstand that held a small mirror on a pedestal, a washbasin, a cake of soap, a handtowel and a straight razor. "I presume the well is down in the lower cellar where the peasants are laboring night and day," Julian said. He took the saddlebag from his shoulder and tossed it on the bed, followed by his sword.

"Likely," Matthew answered. "We'll probably get a servant up here shortly with some water." He peered into the mirror and saw a weary-looking stranger with four days of beard on his face. Had he ever looked so old before, and so worried?

Julian took his tricorn off. His blonde hair stood up like hay that had been attacked with a pitchfork. He eased down into one of the chairs, removed the small spurs from his boots and put his feet up on the table. When he yawned and stretched a muscle popped in his shoulder. "I could go to sleep right now and remain unconscious until morning, but it's not to be. I'm interested in that satchel Pellegar was carrying so closely. Holding documents of value, do you think?"

"No idea." Matthew turned away from the mirror. "You're not going to have to kill anyone tonight, are you?"

"Absolutely not. Unless I have to."

"I'm not in this to murder anyone."

"Ah," said Julian with a faint smile that Matthew took as mockery, "the man on the high wire. Balanced between his values and his purpose.

If murder would save your Berry, would you refuse it? And by *not* committing murder, thus Berry would be doomed? What do you say?"

"I say that's a high wire I've yet to cross."

"Avoiding the issue," said Julian, his eyes hard again, "leads to a fall."

Matthew had no reply for this, nor did he wish to dwell too long on the matter. He sat down in one of the other chairs, took his tricorn, the woolen cap and his gloves off, leaned his head back and thought he too could close his eyes and sleep until morning, if not longer.

Sometime later there came a knock at the door. At once Julian was up and striding past Matthew's chair. "Yes?" he asked whoever was on the other side.

"Hot water, your Excellency."

It was a servant bearing the gift of a large ceramic bowl with a hinged metal lid on the top. Steam was rising through little holes in the lid and the bowl was so hot the youth was wearing soft leather gloves. He opened the lid, which revealed a spout, and poured water into the washbasin, after which he placed the bowl atop the washstand. "Anything more for you gentlemen?" he asked. "Another lantern or two? The Mayfair Tavern is closin' in half-an-hour, do you require any food or ale?"

"We're fine for tonight," said Julian, who gave the servant two shillings. "Oh," he said before the boy opened the door, "we're with the Prussian gentlemen in number twenty-one. Has their luggage been brought up yet?"

"Yes sir, it has. Well…except they say they're missin' two bags, and it looks like maybe they weren't taken off the hack, or…I don't know, sir, it happens sometimes."

"Indeed. And those gentlemen have been tended to just as you're tending to us?" Julian softened his tone when both he and Matthew realized the servant might wonder at this interest. "We're being paid to make sure they're comfortable," he explained. "They're a finicky lot."

"I see. Yes sir, I brought up their hot water before I brought yours."

"And they asked for nothing more? I mean…with the English they know to speak?"

"The bald-headed gentleman's hot about the missin' bags, but he asked only for peace and quiet," said the youth. "Nothin' more."

"Very good. It's comforting to know they're settled in for the night. Thank you, then, and goodnight to you."

The youth said goodnight and left with the shillings in his pocket.

When the door was closed again, Julian turned to face Matthew. "Someone's going to put two and two together here pretty soon, and that clerk or his manager will be asking us questions about missing bags. I don't think they'll do that tonight, though." He crossed the room and started to pick up his sword and scabbard but then thought better of it. He did reach down to rest his hand on the reassuring pistol, though, which would be out of view beneath the cloak. "So," he said, squaring his shoulders, "let's go meet the neighbors and take them their luggage, shall we? And don't fret, Matthew. Those two look like puffs of whiffle dust, so I seriously doubt murder will be necessary tonight."

"Says the man with a four-barrelled pistol," Matthew said as he stood up on aching legs.

"Accompanied by the man with a pistol *and* a dagger," Julian answered. He put his tricorn back on and tilted it at its usual rakish angle. "If anyone is dressed to kill, it's you. Come on, then, let us ease their worried Prussian minds."

ELEVEN.

Julian looked up and down the hallway. There was no one else in sight. He held the case he'd taken, and standing just behind him Matthew had hold of the second case. Julian gave a nod to Matthew, and then he walked to the door of number twenty-one and knocked.

A moment of silence passed. Then from behind the door came a voice: "*Was ist es*?"

"Pardon the intrusion," Julian said quietly, his mouth up close to the door, "but my friend and I have found your missing luggage."

"*Gepack*? That is...luggage?" The door came open wide enough to admit a face that was glistening with some kind of beauty cream. It was long, pale and angular with a thin nose that twisted slightly to the right on its steep descent from the high forehead and the totally bald pate. Matthew caught a glimpse of a dark purple robe under the man's pointed chin. The eyes in the pallid face were deepset and as black as inkwells under mere wisps of blonde brows. They found the two cases and the man's nearly-lipless mouth said, "Ah! Yes!"

"*Karlo! Sie haben unsere fehlenden Falle gefunden*?" the second man in the room called.

"*Ja! Diese beiden Manner haben sie genau hier*!" was the reply fired back.

"They were delivered to our room by mistake," Julian continued. He held the case up before the Prussian's face with his left hand. "You do speak a bit of English?"

"Yes, I do." The man opened the door wider and reached out to take the first case from Julian. "Marvelous! I had fear we would not—"

"Interesting you should use that word 'fear'," said Julian, who had dropped the case down to reveal the wicked pistol in his right hand that had been hidden behind it. Four barrels of hell were aimed directly at the Prussian's forehead. "It's my middle name. Put your hands behind your head and back into the room, please."

The man's eyes seemed to Matthew to have sunken down even further into his face and if possible had gotten even blacker. The thin mouth curled. "If this is a *robbery*, you should know—"

The Prussian ceased talking when his own case was slammed into his mouth. He staggered backward, making a choking sound, and fell full-length upon the floor's polished oak timbers.

At once Julian and Matthew were inside the room and Matthew had shut the door. "Latch it!" Julian said, but Matthew had already known to do so. *In for a penny, in for a pound*, Matthew thought, but he feared a pound of flesh might be in the offing.

The man sat up from the floor, his face contorted with rage and blood already staining his mouth from a split lower lip. Suddenly the second, taller and thinner Prussian came into the room from the suite's second chamber; he was also wearing a sleepgown, this one white with a black diamond design, a large lace-puffed collar and as near to a clown's costume as Matthew could imagine. This man had been removing his white makeup and had been interrupted with only half of the task finished, for the left side of his face was the ghastly color of a fish-belly and over the eye on that side remained the crimson arc of an eyebrow. He had a small brown skullcap of hair and ears that were best covered by his gigantic white wig, which currently burdened a wigstand upon the room's central table and had the selfsame bruise-colored tricorn perched atop it.

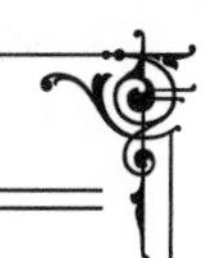

Clown Face took one look at the intruders and sprang for the corner of the room, where Matthew saw the red-and-gold embroidered bellpull ready to be used to summon a servant from below. As the man reached for the pull, Matthew had no choice but to throw the case he was holding. It was not a direct hit to the head but enough of a glancing blow to the shoulder to knock the man spinning, at which point when he righted himself he saw more clearly the pistol Julian was brandishing and he became a clown-dressed statue.

Julian stood over the man on the floor. "Count Pellegar, I'm guessing?" There was no reply. "I think so, since you seem to be the one in charge. Count, I just *hate* it when people don't do as they're instructed. It makes things turn messy very quickly."

"*Du kannst meinen Arsch kussen, du Schwein*," said the Count, who wiped his mouth with a sleeve but never took his ebony eyes off Julian.

"That doesn't sound very diplomatic. I know you speak English but I'm not so sure about Baron Brux. *English*?" he asked the second man.

"*Antworte ihm nicht, Jendrik*," Pellegar said.

"Dear me," said Julian. He glanced quickly at Matthew, who was more intent on watching Brux to make sure he didn't try for that bellpull again. "I think we have a failure to communicate. But I *do* have a solution for that." He placed the pistol downward on Pellegar's bald skull.

"Ha!" the man laughed with what was nearly a snort of derision. "You wouldn't *dare* to fire that thing in here! Half the inn would knock that door down, and for some reason—some very small but important reason, I am sure—you would not care for that, sir."

The man had spoken with no trace of a Prussian accent. "You're English," said Julian. "Why the Prussian masquerade?"

"No masquerade. Born English. Raised and educated in Prussia. Served honorably in the military, and so honored with a title and an estate. And you, I assume, are both common shits of thieves who've somehow profaned this establishment with your presence and…oh fuck it, I'm standing up."

He did, and Julian stepped back a pace but still kept the pistol levelled at him.

"*Bleib einfach*," Pellegar said to Brux in a quiet, almost casual tone. "*Diese Situation ist bereits unter Kontrolle*." Brux nodded, and then the baron sat down in a chair, crossed his thin legs and smiled at Julian and Matthew as if this were an occasion of great amusement.

As Julian considered his next move, Matthew took a quick look around the suite and saw immediately that to call it grand was a huge understatement. It was thrice as large as their own quarters, the bedroom separate from the sitting room. The black leather furnishings were the same but there were more of them, and more lanterns as well. Off to the left beneath a hanging tapestry of wolves and hunters stood a small but beautiful harpsichord on thin and graceful legs, painted gold with red trim and with pastoral scenes decorating the inside of the raised soundboard lid. A large blue bowl of apples, clementines and parsnips sat on the table beside Brux's chair, and behind him was a window that afforded a view of the snow-covered city to the south, even now the flakes continuing to blow up against the glass and whirl away.

"So," Pellegar said, as he dabbed at his mouth, "did you come in here to stare at us like *idioten*? What is it you want?"

"I presume your ship just arrived?"

The count shrugged.

"And you made a stop before you came here?" Julian said. "I presume also you stopped there to learn where you were staying for the night?" Julian didn't wait for an answer because he knew it wasn't going to come. "Whose house was that?"

"Whose house where?"

"No!" said Matthew suddenly, making Julian jump. Matthew drew his pistol from beneath his cloak, for he'd seen that Brux was reaching for an apple from the bowl and it wouldn't do to get one of those in the face. Brux looked at him blankly. Matthew recalled some of Dahlgren's language, but only the little bit: "*Nein*!" he said, and waved the pistol back and forth

until Brux smiled again and settled the hand back against his chest as innocently as a dove alighting on a church ledge.

"Whose house?" Julian repeated, his own gun steady.

"I'm going to sit down, as my tailbone is somewhat bruised." Pellegar backed away from Julian and took a seat on the room's sofa. He stretched his legs out and laced his fingers across his chest. "I have no idea who you two miscreants are and it appears this is not a robbery…or, not *exactly* a robbery. You have come here to steal information, yes?"

"I know it's the house of an admiral in the Royal Navy," said Julian. "I want the name."

"I want a large portion of weisslacker and a plate of wheat crackers to materialize before me, but one doesn't always get what one wants. Now what are you going to do? Shoot us for a name?"

Matthew's gaze found the brown satchel that Pellegar had been carrying sitting on a low table nearer the harpsichord. He said, "Let's take a look at *this*," and walked the few paces to fetch it. The item was much heavier than expected when he picked it up. There were two metal snaps, both with small keyholes. "It's locked," he told Julian when the snaps would not budge.

"Where's the key?" Julian asked Pellegar, who had not moved an inch on the sofa but was still smiling blandly, as was Baron Brux.

"I will tell you," said Pellegar, "that you are playing with fire, and if you do not leave this room immediately I will make sure both of you are burnt to crisps."

"Oh, will you?" Julian walked purposefully forward and placed the pistol's barrels against Pellegar's mouth. The man did not shrink back, but continued to smile up at his interrogator. "I won't shoot you," Julian said, "but if you don't produce that key your teeth will be lying all over this floor and—alas—your beauty cream will no longer be of assistance."

Pellegar pulled his head back a few inches. "*Er will den Schlussel zum Koffer*," he said to the baron. "*Ich werde gehorchen. Mach dich bereit.*" Brux gave a grunt and a nod.

Pellegar stood up and Julian retreated two paces. "Easy, sir," Pellegar said softly. "We wish no violence."

"That's up to you."

"Indeed." Somehow, Matthew didn't like the way that was said. He watched as the count reached behind his head with both hands and unhooked a clasp at the back of his neck. He offered to Julian a small gold chain draped around the fingers of his right hand, an equally small key dangling in the air. "My regards," he said, his bruised mouth twisting.

Julian reached out to take the key.

Count Pellegar dropped it before Julian's hand could get there.

In the instant that Julian's eyes left Pellegar's face to follow the key down, the count exploded into action.

His left hand clamped to Julian's gun hand to twist the pistol aside, while the right hand made half-a-cup and slammed with terrific force into Julian's chin. His tricorn went spinning off. At nearly the same time, Baron Brux picked up the bowl of fruit and flung it at Matthew, who suddenly found himself being assaulted by apples, clementines and parsnips to the head and shoulders; but right after them came Brux himself, who moved not like a drowsy joker but like a deadly juggernaut. Matthew realized his own gun was reduced to being a club, for he neither wished to murder anyone nor to fire a shot that would bring the management...but even as he prepared to bash Brux across the head with the implement the baron kicked up and out, the force of the violet-colored slipper knocked the pistol from Matthew's hand, and then the small table Brux had picked up in his rush across the room crashed across Matthew's right shoulder in a blast of breaking furniture. Stunned by this unexpected onslaught, Matthew fell to his knees.

Equally stunned was Julian, who in the few seconds after the half cup of a hand had made the stars shoot fire in his brain had taken a blow to the center of the chest that robbed him of breath and a following strike to the left side of the neck that paralyzed his arm on that side. His pistol was lost. It dawned on him through his pulse of pain, as it did at the same time to Matthew, that the bizarre costumes of these two had disguised the fact that they were highly trained military fighters and possibly assassins in their own right.

The whiffle dust had become a tornado of thorns. With brutal efficiency Count Pellegar drove a knee into Julian's midsection and slung him around in a circle before crashing him over the nearest sidetable. By this time Matthew had already taken another glancing kick to the side that he feared had broken ribs, but he got an arm up to ward off the kick that would've caught him in the face. He was trying to stand up when Brux grasped the back of his neck and under an arm and threw him with surprising strength into the harpsichord, which collapsed underneath him with a musical groan and caterwaul of splintering spruce and snapping wires.

Pellegar picked up Julian's pistol, quickly examined it with true interest, and then walked across the room toward his fallen opponent as calmly as if strolling in the park on a summer's morn. He kicked the shambles of the broken sidetable out of his path and leaned down to put the barrels against Julian's head as Julian struggled to his knees.

"I don't think," Pellegar said, "that anyone here will begrudge my killing of a common robber."

Baron Brux cried out in pain.

The baron had been coming in to deliver another more deadly kick when Matthew had twisted around in the ruins of the harpsichord and found his hand closing over a wire broken loose from the soundboard. The thickness of it indicated a use for lower notes, but Matthew thought it would now serve a higher purpose. He lunged forward, whipped out with it and drew a crimson line across Brux's pallid forehead.

With the baron's sharp cry, Pellegar's attention ticked toward the source and Julian chopped the gun hand away and hit him in the right knee with everything he had. Pellegar staggered sideways, his small teeth clenched and red whorls coming up on his cheeks, but he still had hold of the gun. At once Julian was up, mindful that if he let his pain slow him he was dead, and smashed Pellegar in the jaw with his fist, following that

with another blow to the temple. As Pellegar fell backward against the wall he swung out with the pistol to crack Julian's ribs but Julian was already upon him and trapping the pistol with his weight.

Brux was backing away from Matthew's makeshift whip. He retreated until he stepped on the huge wig that had fallen with its wigstand to the floor; he picked up the wig and held it like a shield before him, and Matthew realized that damned pelt could stop a rapier and it could also smother a face beneath it. Brux came in again and Matthew saw his eyes were judging distances in preparation to throwing the wig at him and rushing in. Now Matthew backed away, judging his own distances. When he got where he needed to be he stopped, and that was when the baron came at him like a whirlwind.

Matthew dropped the harpsichord wire, reached up with both hands to the full extension of his arms, grasped hold of the hanging tapestry and brought it down upon Brux's head. The baron flailed blindly, Matthew stepped aside to let the man pass and slam against the wall behind him, and then Matthew saw an implement that could be put to good use. He picked up a broken leg of the harpsichord and clubbed Brux on the head with it before the baron could get free of his entanglement with medieval hunters and wolves.

Julian and Pellegar were locked in combat with the pistol between them. They struggled in silence with deadly purpose. A hand with fingers outstretched to jab his eyes darted at Julian but he jerked his head to one side. Julian returned the compliment by twisting his body and slamming an elbow into Pellegar's face, but the man was a tough nut. With that in mind Julian's next move was to ram a knee upward as hard as he could into the count's groin, and a second time when the first reward was only a grunt of pain and a muffled Prussian curse. On the second knee to the nutcase Pellegar's knees began to sag. Julian wrenched the pistol free, swung it barrels-first into the side of the count's head and saw the man's inkwell eyes go blank, all the ferocity draining out. A second and third strike with the pistol to the brainpan sent Pellegar to his knees, but

incredibly the man held onto consciousness and began to try to crawl for some kind of cover.

Matthew had to hit Brux again with the harpsichord leg to put him down, and at last the baron lay still under the tapestry.

Pellegar was crawling across the floor, making gasping noises. Still dazed by all this violence and with a pain in his side as if his ribs had been staved in, Matthew watched as Julian walked over to pick up the fallen wig. Something about Julian's face had changed; it had gone gaunt, hollow-cheeked and severe, but there was no wildness in the eyes and that was what frightened Matthew the most. The bad man—one of Fell's killers—was in the room with him, and from this point on it was all cold-hearted business.

Julian kicked Pellegar in the side to throw the man over on his back. Then Julian straddled his chest, crushed the wig down upon the count's head, and holding the wig firmly with one hand he began to beat the mound of Pellegar's face with the butt of his pistol…once…twice… again…again…on and on as red bloomed up on the wig and Julian's face gleamed with sweat.

"Julian! Don't!" Matthew called, his own voice a croak, but the bad man was beyond hearing.

Pellegar's legs still twitched on, and methodically Julian beat him to death with the pistol butt though it was hard to say if the man perished by beating or being smothered. When the legs stopped moving, Julian lifted the wig to look at the misshapen face, his own expression utterly impassive. Then he covered it over and beat the dead man some more, as if now content to hammer a spirit until it fled from the room to the better climate of Hell.

At last Julian stood up, and as he approached Matthew the New York problem-solver shrank back from him because there was yet death on his face. Julian pulled the tapestry off the moaning Baron Brux and knelt down to give him the same treatment as the count had gotten, but he stopped and rubbed the tortured shoulder that did not want to lift any more heavy pistols.

Julian looked into Matthew's eyes and said, "Take out your dagger and kill him."

"I...can't...*murder* anyone..."

"*Worthless*," said Julian. He wiped sweat from his forehead. "Then give me the dagger and I'll kill him."

"Julian...no, I can't—"

"Oh, *shit*!" Julian answered in disgust. His eyes had found something he could handle. He reached into the rubble of the harpsichord and with a quick yank brought out a thinner wire suitable for a strangulation. Then he sat down behind the semi-conscious Brux, locked his legs around the man's midsection and in so doing trapped Brux's arms at his sides. He wrapped the wire around the white throat and began to pull the ends against the middle.

Matthew had to turn away. He had witnessed violent death before, of course, and had looked such in the face many times, but cold-blooded murder was something else. Even his execution of Count Dahlgren had not been exactly murder—or so he wished to believe—because his cutting of a rope during a storm at sea was not necessarily the man's death sentence, though it was hard to fathom that Dahlgren did not go down seven leagues to eternity. And Matthew would have even spared the life of Tyranthus Slaughter, if he'd had the choice...but *this*...this sickened him and sent a shudder up his bruised back as he heard the hideous noise of a windpipe being crushed and the heels of violet-colored slippers weakly beating the floorboards.

It seemed to go on a long time.

"This bastard," said Julian between gritted teeth, "will *not* die. Fuck if I'm—" He paused to give another fierce pull of the wire's ends. "Fuck if I'm not going to pass out myself," he finished.

At last, as Matthew stared down at the floor, there was a rattling sound, the slippers ceased their drumbeat of death and Julian said wearily, "That one nearly finished *me*." When he stood up, he staggered and steadied himself against the wall. He caught Matthew regarding him with a measure of repugnance, and his mouth smiled grimly below the red-rimmed eyes. “It had to be done,” he said. “You know that as well as I. But if it makes any difference to you in your opinion of me—which I care not—I’ll start anew and afresh tomorrow.”

But tomorrow might never come, for there came the pounding of a fist on the door and a voice calling, “Hello? Hello? What’s going on in there?”

TWELVE.

An index finger, somewhat red and swollen from its long acquaintance with the wire, flew to Julian's lips.

"This is the night manager!" called the man behind the door. "Open this *instant*, if you please!"

"Stand out of sight," Julian said to Matthew. He called, "Coming, sir!" and as he walked to answer the knock he blotted his face with his sleeve and smoothed his hair. He unlatched the door and cracked it open to a florid-faced, heavy-set man in a gray suit and a dark blue cravat beneath his three chins. Behind him, almost hidden by the night manager's bulk, was the young boy who'd brought the hot water to room twenty-six.

"What is going on in there?" the man asked. His furry eyebrows jumped up and down. "We have had a complaint from the next room and our lobby chandelier is swinging on its moorings!"

Julian stood so the night manager couldn't see the body on the floor under a bloodied wig; he had opened the door just as Count Pellegar had, only enough for a face to push through. "I am *terribly* sorry," Julian said. "I am Count Mowbrey, an interpreter for the Prussian delegation. I realize there's been a disturbance."

"I should say! Is someone destroying our furnishings in there? I feared the lobby's roof would collapse!"

"Baron Brux!" Julian suddenly called into the room. "Count Pellegar's condition has passed, has it not?"

It only took Matthew a couple of seconds to respond. "*Ja*!" he answered. What was the Prussia word for 'passed'? He knew not, so he said, "*Bitter*!"

"Sir, if I may explain." Julian slipped out of the room into the hallway and quietly closed the door behind him. He spoke as one reluctantly giving up a secret only because it was absolutely necessary. "Count Pellegar suffers from night fits. I'm sure you probably are aware of such, as many guests as have come through here."

The night manager blinked. "Your mouth is bleeding," he said.

"Oh. Yes." Julian dabbed at blood in the corner of his mouth and looked at the smear on his fingers. "Count Pellegar struck me. You see, right on the chin. I'm going to have a terrible bruise in the morning."

"*Who* did you say you were?"

"An interpreter for the delegation," Julian repeated. "The young man there knows, and also your lobby clerk. My companion and I came in after the count and the baron and took room twenty-six…oh, and incidentally their missing bags turned out not to be missing after all. Both were inadvertently packed by a servant in the baron's trunk."

"Ah!" The night manager nodded, liking this information. "I knew our staff hadn't misplaced anything! But…your Excellency…what is Count Pellegar's current condition, and what of the Grand Suite?"

"There has regrettably been some damage. A table has been broken and that beautiful tapestry has been pulled from the ceiling. As to Count Pellegar, he is resting comfortably now, but I'll tell you that it was a hard go. Sometimes—not very often, but occasionally—he awakens from sleep believing he is back on the battlefield leading a charge of grenadiers at the siege of Buda. Against the Turks, you know."

"Of course," said the night manager, whose overstuffed tone of voice told Julian the man did not know his world history.

"And therefore," Julian went on, "Count Pellegar comes out of sleep desiring to fight every Turk on the battlefield…and, unfortunately, everyone he sees through his burdened eyes is a Turk. Even me."

"Ghastly!" said the night manager.

"He has quite a punch. Baron Brux and my companion Mr. Spottle helped me subdue him, but not before he…well…did a bit of damage."

"I'd like to inspect it for myself, if you please."

"Certainly, but can't that wait until later in the day? I mean to say… Count Pellegar is quiet now, and I wouldn't wish to upset him from sleep again. It's a rather tenuous situation. You see? And," Julian continued before the other man could speak, "of course all damages—however slight—will be paid for in full, and for good measure I'm sure Count Pellegar will wish to pay double for his use of the Grand Suite, as His Excellency has already told me how much he prizes the quarters and that he wishes to be a regular guest here on his future visits." Julian smiled, in spite of the cut inside his mouth, the three loose teeth his tongue had found and the fact that he was standing on sheer willpower alone.

The moment hung.

Then the night manager breathed a huge sigh that must have been relief. "Pardon my rather rude knock at your door, sir. The couple next door rang for the boy here and said it sounded as if ten men were fighting in there." He lowered his voice. "Lord and Lady Turlentort are two of our favorites, but they *are* excitable."

"I understand completely," said Julian, his smile still firmly fixed in place.

Thus it was that after a few more apologies and pleasantries and wishes for the good health of Count Pellegar, the night manager and the servant boy withdrew, Julian returned to the room, closed the door and latched it again and stepped over the count's corpse in search of the chain and key. An exhausted Matthew had slid down against the wall near the destroyed harpsichord, but as far away as possible from the corpse of Baron Brux without crawling into the next room. He had done some self-examination

and determined that no ribs were broken but very soon he was going to become a blotch of bruises under his clothing.

"You all right?" Julian asked as he searched the floor. "You look like hell. Not about to be sick, are you?"

"I'm all right. And no, I'm not about to be sick."

Julian nodded toward dead Count Pellegar. "This little bastard here nearly caved my chest in. And that shot to my chin…I swear before Christ I've never had a harder knock. Came close to swallowing my own tongue. Ah! Here it is!" He held up the chain and key, which he'd found when he lifted up the corpse's left arm, as the item had slid across the floor during their battle and was hidden near the elbow. Julian winced as he stood up and it took him a few seconds to recover from a bout of dizziness. "My heart's still laboring," he said. "All right, let's find out what's in the satchel."

Matthew watched as Julian picked up the case from the floor. "Damned heavy. More than important papers, for sure." Julian inserted the key, unlocked and opened both snaps. Then he sat down on the floor across from Matthew, opened the satchel's pouch wide and with a violent—nay, *contemptuous*—thrust expelled its contents upon the boards.

Out clattered ten gold bars, each one about the length of an index finger and two fingers in width.

They glistened in the room's lantern light, as both Matthew and Julian stared at what had to be a very considerable fortune.

After a moment, Julian spoke. "How much do you suppose those are worth?"

"I have no idea," Matthew answered, "but I imagine they would buy at least a year's worth of Grand Suites. Maybe more than one Grand Suite."

Julian retrieved the satchel and peered inside. There was an arrangement of ten leather pockets sewn to the interior's dark gray leather lining. He pushed the satchel away. "Interesting that they brought gold *bars*, instead of coins," Julian mused. "Why do you think that might be?"

Matthew had a thought. "The polar bear coat," he said.

"*What*?"

Matthew was already struggling up. His first step almost sent him face-first to the floor again, but he maintained his balance and went into the bedroom where a marble fireplace burned logs. There on a gold-trimmed lounge chair next to the canopied bed with its ceiling-high headboard of a carved forest scene was the count's bulky white fur coat. "Whatever Pellegar showed to the guard at the gate…he put back in his coat," Matthew called to Julian. When he picked up the coat he marvelled that any man had the strength to wear such a beast. He went straight for the inner pockets. Only lint in the one on the right, but in the left his fingers found both the room's key and a square of parchment paper as stiff as a gentleman's greeting card. He withdrew the paper and took a look, aware that Julian had entered the room and was coming up beside him.

Written in a spiky penmanship were words in the Prussian language, which neither man could read, yet three items were clear to understand: the address, Number Fourteen Endsleigh Park Road, and a date and time, 20 December, 7:30 *Abends*.

"What's that word mean? *Abends*?" Julian asked.

"I don't know, but I'm going to assume this is an invitation to the house day after tomorrow at seven-thirty in the evening. I doubt these gentlemen were early risers."

"So Pellegar showed this to the guard to get past the gate?"

"Yes. As you said, Pellegar and Brux had likely just arrived by ship and they went to the house to learn where they were staying for the night. And obviously they're booked in here for the night of the 19th and likely the 20th and beyond."

"Interesting," said Julian. He took the parchment from Matthew's hand and studied it though Matthew had already deduced there was nothing more to be gleaned. "So…the Owl has been recruited to provide security for…what? A meeting at that house between the Prussians and our mysterious admiral?"

"It would appear so."

"But…why would *security* be needed? The Owl likely provided the guard at the gate and other guards we didn't see. Why go to all that complexity for a simple meeting?"

Matthew said the first thing that came to mind. "It might not be so simple." He walked back out into the sitting room and regarded the bars of gold upon the floor. "They brought a lot of gold for a simple meeting," he said quietly, his eyes narrowed in thought, as Julian joined him with the invitation still in hand. "I wonder…if the Prussians were not the only ones invited."

"Meaning?"

"Oh, I don't know, exactly. But the Prussians made a long and arduous journey bringing a satchel full of gold bars. With the Owl providing security, and that guard at the gate…showing his pistol to ward us off…it feels as if there's something larger going on."

"And what do you think it has to do with Cardinal Black and the book?"

Matthew nodded. "Now you're getting somewhere."

"Explain."

Matthew turned to face him. "I may be wrong and it may have absolutely nothing to do with Cardinal Black and the book, but…the book would be of great interest—and worth—to many people in the underworld, and not just in England. Criminals, terrorists, assassins…even some heads of state might like to get hold of it, and certainly Fell's name is known in those circles."

"Agreed," said Julian.

"I'm thinking that the Prussians have come here to *buy* it. The price is yet undetermined, which is why they brought all the gold bars. If that's true, this must have been planned for many months. I don't know how long it would've taken the Prussians to get here, but there had to be an exchange of messages that took a length of time, and arrangements to be made. This might have been Mother Deare's task for over a year, to get everything planned for the attack. Then…" Matthew shook his head. "But I still can't guess how our admiral got involved in this."

"So you believe the book is in that house?" Julian asked.

"If not there, then somewhere near."

"And the Prussians are expected at the house at seven-thirty two evenings hence to negotiate for the book?"

"If what I'm suggesting is a real connection, then yes."

Julian said nothing more. When Matthew looked at him, he saw Julian staring fixedly at first the body of Count Pellegar and then dead strangled Baron Brux.

The idea hit Matthew like a washbasin of freezing water in the face, because he could tell what was going through Julian's mind. "Are you *mad*? That would never work!"

"Why not? I'll wager neither Cardinal Black nor the admiral have ever laid eyes on these two. The only one who saw Pellegar was the man at the door. It was a quick exchange, and you saw that Pellegar had a muffler over most of his face. Brux likely didn't even get a glance. Pellegar is English-born, and if Brux only speaks the Prussian language, then you—"

"*You*?" Matthew interrupted. "How easily that's said!"

"I was going to say...if Brux only speaks the Prussian language, then all you have to be is silent. I'll do all the talking."

"If you happened to notice," Matthew said, "Pellegar had eyes as black as coals and he is completely bald. Now...the man at the door may or may not think he didn't register the correct eye-color, but your mop of blonde hair might—just saying *might*, you understand—tip the game."

"I'll buy a wig on the morrow."

"Fine. Then you'll look even less like Count Pellegar."

A cloud passed across Julian's face. "Damn," he said quietly. "You're right."

Matthew wandered over to another chair, where he could view both the bodies, and sank down into it. Was it *possible*? The size of clothing might be a problem. Definitely the boot size.

The style of clothing would have to be outlandish and so would the makeup, not just in keeping with the two original Prussians but as a way of preventing too close an inspection. No, it was impossible!

Or was it?

"You'd have to shave your head," Matthew said after another few moments of reflection. "I would have to wear a thick white face makeup. If Cardinal Black is present at this meeting, he would recognize me…and certainly by my scar."

Julian didn't reply, but he was listening.

"I would be the one to wear the mile-high wig," Matthew continued. "We could go through the luggage and see what might be used. I'm thinking we would both need to go buy new pairs of boots. And expensive ones. Ours are not fitting for titled Prussians. I would wear gloves to hide the Black-Eyed Broodie mark, which I'm sure Cardinal Black would also recognize. If anyone in that house speaks Prussian, we would both be dead. Any slip-up, however minor…we would both be dead. You understand that, don't you?"

Julian levelled his slate-colored eyes at Matthew. "Do you understand it? I mean…*really*?"

Matthew drew a long breath and let it slowly out. His ribs protested. "I do," he answered. "It seems to me there's no other choice. Two dead men on the floor with an invitation to the admiral's house, and we two alive to go in their places. And I have to say, after all the preparations we'll have to make, it had *better* be the admiral's house and not just someone who likes to play with ship's wheels!"

"Now *that* would be an evil trick of Fate, wouldn't it? Speaking of Fate, we'll have to be careful going in and out. Our next-door neighbors are the Turlentorts."

"Wonderful! Well, we can't risk them seeing us. Your charm may have worn off them by now and they would go directly to the manager," said Matthew. He spent a moment roaming in thought before he spoke again. "If there's any chance the book is in that house, we have to go. But even if we can somehow get the book and get out of there, we still have to find a chemist who can decipher the formulas."

"Correct," Julian said. "But first things first."

"Right."

"And the *very* first thing," Julian contended, "is to drag those bodies somewhere out of sight and out of mind. I don't want my Grand Suite marred by such trash on the floor. Then I plan to stretch out on that sofa and sleep for a few hours like a newborn, and you can either have the bed here or go back to twenty-six."

"I think I'd best stay out of the hallway." Even so, Matthew didn't care for the idea of sleeping in a majestic bed with two corpses rolled up in a tapestry and set in a corner like cordwood.

"Let's get to it, then," said Julian. "I'm very near passing out."

By the time they dragged the bodies into a small closet off the bedroom both men were spent to rags. Julian staggered off to the sofa and Matthew crawled into the bed without taking off a single item of clothing. Rummaging through the trunks and cases would have to wait, for Matthew had no strength to lift a lid. Knowing the dead men were curled up about ten feet from him had no effect on the willingness of his brain to go blank, and he knew not what dreams—or nightmares—might come ravening after him in the darkness of his own refuge, but blessedly so to sleep with the fireplace cackling like a crone's laugh.

THIRTEEN.

"*No*!"

Matthew heard the half-shout, half-sob echoing in his head as he came up from sleep. He lay on the bed staring up at the canopy and watching the low shadows of the fire dance. His body was one huge ache. Were the two corpses really in that closet over there? Yes, they were, and much work was to be done to get into that house on Endsleigh Park Road.

He heard footsteps on the floorboards in the other room. What time was it? The bedroom's lanterns gave off the same glow as before and it was difficult to tell how much of the whale oil had been burned. He felt as if he'd just thrown himself on the bed scant minutes before and he was still wrecked. But the footsteps meant Julian was moving about, and that cry meant...*what*?

Matthew mostly slid off the bed rather than sitting up. When he got to his feet the floor seemed to pitch like a ship in a wild storm, but that passed soon enough. With his balance under control he went out into the other room to find Julian standing before the window staring out at an overcast, snow-covered morning that might be anywhere from six o'clock to eight. The snowfall appeared to have stopped, but the city beyond the glass was a vast panorama of gray shapes crusted in shades of blue.

Julian glanced quickly at Matthew and then back out the window. He was fully dressed and had his cloak and his tricorn on.

"Did you cry out?" Matthew asked.

Julian didn't reply at once. Then: "I don't recall."

His voice was strained. Its timbre made Matthew think of Julian's reaction to the woman in Adderlane whose child had been sacrificed. "Do you have some kind of condition I should know about?"

"No, and no," said Julian. His gaze was aimed upon the city before him, and Matthew had the impression that Julian was looking—somewhat fearfully—at an old enemy.

"What time must it be? Is the sun even up?"

"I doubt we'll have much sun today. I think it's just after six. You should go back to bed."

"What's this about?" Matthew asked.

"It's about the fact that I am awake and I am going to take a walk."

"A walk? In this weather?"

"Good for the *soul*," Julian replied, with a slight grimace that might have passed for a smile. He turned away from the window. "I would think a servant will be bringing another supply of hot water sometime this morning. You might expect a knock at the door, I'd say in an hour or so."

"Excellent!" It was Matthew's turn to grimace, and it was far from being a smile. "Am I supposed to let him in to see all this mess?" Matthew had already noted that the washstand was in the bedroom, and it had occurred to him on the edge of sleep that the fine service given to guests in the Grand Suite meant hot water was going to be delivered after daybreak.

"Tell him the bedroom is full of sleeping beauties, we need no hot water until they awaken, and when that occurs we'll summon with the bellpull." Julian paused just short of the door. "I told the night manager that Count Pellegar will be paying double for the room. I doubt anyone will be coming up to check for damages, with that kind of promise. There's no reason for anyone to believe anything but what I said, that Count Pellegar suffers from night fits."

"The same as you?" Matthew asked, the question delivered as sharply as a dagger's strike.

"I'll return," said Julian, "when I return. Best latch the door behind me."

"Oh, I thought I'd leave it wide open for the Turlentorts to wander in for breakfast!"

Without another word Julian unlatched the door and left. Matthew immediately crossed the room and relatched it, thinking how if he turned around and the corpses of Pellegar and Brux were shambling toward him he was going right out the window.

He considered returning to bed. Though he knew his mind and body needed further rest, it was impossible to turn off the mental scenes of the count and the baron being murdered. Those...and that constant ticking...ticking...of time going past, and Berry still under the drug's power in Y Beautiful Bedd, and this shred of an idea that Pellegar and Brux's visit to London had something to do with the book of potions. They could be here for any number of other reasons, and for that matter it wasn't a sure thing that the house on Endsleigh Park Road was inhabited by the same man who'd partnered with Cardinal Black; the book could be on its way to another country by now, or being deciphered by some mad chemist in a cellar somewhere in preparation to poison the entire Parliament.

"Stop it," Matthew told himself, aloud, for he realized he was careening about in a dangerous circle that could only weaken his resolve. For the moment the impersonation of Pellegar and Brux—however insane that idea was—had to be done, and done *well*; it was all he and Julian had, and God help them in two ways: if they got into that house and discovered this had nothing to do with the book, and if they got into that house and discovered this had *everything* to do with the book.

To get his mind off these ramblings he set about returning the ten gold bars to their pockets in the satchel. The pockets seemed snug enough to secure them for the normal use of a gentleman, but not accounting for someone violently slinging them out. This of course would have to go with them to the house and the meeting.

When Matthew slid the fifth bar in, something made a strange rustling noise he could not readily identify.

He looked inside but there was nothing but the five bars in their pockets. Still…there had been a sound from within the satchel that signified something else was contained in there…somewhere.

He removed the five bars and put them aside. He sat on the floor with the satchel, his fingers searching within. In another moment he identified four small metal snaps at the corners of what he'd thought to be a leather lining but was instead a false front hidden behind the arrangement of pockets for the bars. He unsnapped those and was able to remove the entire back portion of the satchel, which he placed beside himself on the floor.

Revealed was a parchment document, larger than the invitation, about six inches wide by eight inches in length. As he drew it out, Matthew found that it was one sheet of five possibly cut from a roll of parchment due to the uneven edges. He put them out side by side on the floor, and then he got up and fetched the nearest lantern for better illumination than the dawn's murky light.

The first sheet showed a strange illustration that Matthew thought ought to be out of the pages of *The Lesser Key of Solomon*. It was the depiction of a dragon with four wings, the mouth open and breathing fire. The next sheet truly gave Matthew pause, for it was a painstaking study of the wings with measurements marked not in inches but in feet. The third sheet showed the same to the head of the dragon and the fourth to the body and the forked tail, all the measurements carefully marked. It appeared that a professional draftsman had produced these plans, because Matthew realized that's exactly what they were. And the fifth sheet: a clockwork mechanism operated by what appeared to be a large teakettle, with valves running the length of the dragon and into the wings as well.

He'd never seen anything like this and had no idea what it was for. The thing was a machine of some kind, certainly, but beyond that he was lost.

Plans for an Infernal Machine

Disturbingly, he calculated that the dragon's entire structure was somewhat over twenty feet in length, the span of the wings easily forty feet.

Matthew was still engrossed in studying the diagrams when a knock at the door almost gave him no use this morning for a chamberpot. He answered the knock by cracking the door open and found it was another servant with a bowl of water so hot that gloves were necessary for the handling. Matthew decided he would brave getting his fingers scorched for the opportunity to shave and clean up with the items on the washstand. The servant cautioned him not to do it, but Matthew explained about the "sleeping beauties" in the bedroom and took the bowl, instantly wishing he had not because the damned thing felt straight off the coals. The servant asked him for the return of last night's hot water bowl, which Matthew returned to him with numbed fingers and then closed and relatched the door once again.

He put the five sheets of parchment back into the satchel but left the arrangement of pockets out so as to show Julian what he'd found. Before he began the task of washing his face and shaving, he angled the hand-mirror so he could see the closet behind him where the dead men were stacked. It just made him feel better. He used the cake of soap and the razor that was offered by the inn, and lastly he soaked a handtowel in the wonderfully hot water and just let it rest on his face while he reclined on the sofa and listened to the whine of wind beyond the glass.

He was hungry and thirsty and yearned for at least a piece of toasted bread and a thimbleful of tea, but going down to the tavern was at the moment out of the question. He decided to take the opportunity to go through the belongings of the recently murdered, and so he began with the largest trunk.

Suits, blouses and stockings in colors that assaulted the eyeballs lay before him. He'd thought Prussians of the noble class would be more austere, given to blacks and grays, but the owner of this fashion festival knew no restraint. Matthew plucked out a robin's red breast of a jacket and tried it on, finding that it fit rather tightly around the shoulders but the length

was ample enough and the sleeves would allow the puffs of lace cuffs to explode forth. He held up a pair of yellow corduroy breeches against himself. The leg length looked all right but he wasn't sure about the waist; he declined to try them on, thinking that new breeches might need to be purchased before tomorrow night. The same with the two pairs of boots in the trunk, being too small for comfort. He found another huge wig and a teakwood makeup case full of jars of white cream, red and purple paints, sundry powders, black eyeliner and applicators for all of it and he knew he was rummaging around in Baron Brux's dandified atmosphere.

He had not checked the sealskin coat that Brux had been wearing last night. It was thrown over another chair in the bedroom. He picked it up and found it equally as heavy as the polar bear monstrosity. There was an object in one of the inside breast pockets. A powder-blue purse came to hand. Undoing the three brass buttons that secured it, Matthew cast his eyes upon a trove of coins both gold and silver. He angled the contents toward the light and made out a wealth of gold guineas and sovereigns, also a few shillings and some coins that appeared to be of Prussian mintage. Matthew had no idea how much all of it was worth, but it was clear that the count and the baron had come loaded for bear. Or, at least, a bear-like admiral of the Royal Navy.

He was still going through the luggage and sorting out the various articles of clothing when he heard a tapping at the door. He unlatched and opened it to Julian, whose newly shaven face was ruddy with the cold. There was another difference about him, as well; a few paces into the room, he removed his tricorn and displayed his perfectly bald head.

"Lock up again," he instructed before Matthew could speak. When it was done, Julian sent his tricorn spinning away upon the sofa. "How do you like the first step in the trans-formation from Devane to Pellegar?"

"Delightful," said Matthew. "Doubly cold up there, I'd think."

"I found a barber open early, he did the chore. Have you put the corpses in the fireplace and burned them up yet?"

"Uh...no, I was going to do that after I'd had a bite to eat."

"Well, say no more!" Julian reached into his cloak and brought out an object wrapped up in waxed paper. He offered it to Matthew. "A bakery was also open. A piece of raisin cake, specialty of the day."

"Much appreciated," Matthew said as he took what might be meager replenishment, but welcome all the same. "I presume you've already eaten breakfast?"

"A tavern around the corner serves very excellent beef hash and eggs. I deserved something substantial after having my head scraped."

"I might deserve a trip to that tavern for what I've found. Look here." While he ate the raisin cake, Matthew first showed Julian Brux's purse with all the money, and then he brought the diagrams out of the satchel. "What do you make of those?"

"Plans drawn up by a lunatic, it looks to me," Julian said after surveying all five of the sheets. "The measurements are...*twenty feet* in length? And the wing span *forty feet*? Of what purpose could this be?"

"I don't know, but evidently the count and the baron prized these diagrams highly enough to hide them in the satchel. And I believe the diagrams as well as the gold bars are destined for the admiral's house tomorrow night. Otherwise, what are they doing here?"

"Agreed. I see you've shaved. You let the servant in with the hot water?"

"I handled it," Matthew said. He motioned toward the bedroom. "I'm in the process of going through the luggage. I can wear Brux's jackets and blouses but not the breeches nor the boots. I found his makeup case too, which I detest to use but it's a necessity. You need to go through Pellegar's things and see what you can wear."

"Well," said Julian as he joined his tricorn on the sofa, "here is my suggestion. First I'll do as you say, and then we take some of their money, go out and get you an ample meal and after that we find whatever else is lacking. I'm sure we can locate a bootmaker with some ready-mades on hand. The same with a tailor and the breeches. I'll need to also use that makeup case. The bald head won't be enough, and at some point I'll have to lower the muffler from my face."

"All right, that sounds good."

"And further," Julian continued, "we dress up as the count and the baron *tonight*, and go have our supper."

"*Tonight*? Why?"

"Because we need to get used to the costumes. Starting tonight, when we have all the garments in order, we don't need to leave this room as anyone *but* those two. It will be *vital* that we play these parts as if we *are* the count and baron. Our lives may depend on it, and you know that very well."

"Yes," Matthew said, "I do." The idea made sense, however bizarre. But Matthew considered it as a dress rehearsal for a play…an extremely dangerous play, and one that had to be acted out with extreme vigilance.

Within the hour they left the Mayfair Arms, bundled up in their cloaks and walking into the bitter cold of the gray and snow-swept day. Julian had discovered that he could wear Pellegar's breeches and the tricorn adorned with the gaudy feathers, but the jackets were too small and the boots too narrow. The polar bear coat, being an extra-large monstrosity, did fit him and so that was a positive point. Matthew had shrugged into Brux's sealskin coat and found it tight around the shoulders but it would do as would the second outlandish wig and the purple tricorn. Pairs of calfskin, ostrich and what looked to be crocodile-hide gloves fit both men. Thus the conspirators had their tasks before them and set off first to get Matthew fed and watered, which occurred with a platter of baked chicken, green beans, yams and a mug of hot cider at the tavern a block away where Julian had secured his breakfast.

Though the day was inhospitable and the cold bone-cracking, the citizens of London were taking this in their stride. There was no shortage of people on the sidewalks, and on the streets a parade of wagons, carriages and coaches were carving paths through the snow. Matthew and Julian set off from the tavern in search of a bootmaker and had to visit several before they found ready-mades in their sizes and in the more exotic and expensive leathers suitable for Prussian noblemen.

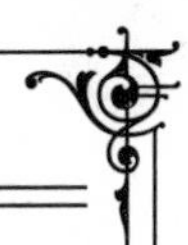

Then it was off to find a tailor, and in the area around the Mayfair Arms with its coffee shops, theaters and other refinements there were many to choose from. The second shop they entered supplied to Matthew a pair of brown-checked breeches that were the most flamboyant in the establishment, and to Julian a bright yellow jacket that the tailor explained was made for an eccentric nobleman who unfortunately—before claiming the item—died from heart failure after a night carousing with the wenches of Whitechapel, which to Matthew was many worlds away from the strange new land he currently explored. Matthew also purchased a purple cravat that was nearly the same color as Brux's bruise of a tricorn, and recalling a jacket in the baron's trunk the color of shiny brown mud with a bright red piping he considered his costume complete.

Upon the hour of seven o'clock in the evening, as the fireplace in the lobby of the Mayfair Arms burned its logs so quietly one might think it had been tamed by the management, and as various guests lounged about in the seating areas and the musical trio tuned their instruments for their nightly presentation, two men who might have hailed from another planet descended the staircase.

One wore a massive white polar bear of a coat, a red tricorn adorned with half a dozen feathers of various hues sticking up from its golden band, a pair of gray breeches with red stripes up the legs, gray stockings, an eye-stunning yellow jacket, a lavender-hued blouse and a white cravat wound around the throat. On his feet were greenish-black boots made from the hide of the South American python and his hands were protected by ostrich-skin gloves. It was apparent this gentleman was bald beneath his tricorn. His face was whitened by powder and the cheekbones heightened with red rouge.

The second man of the moment was taller and slimmer than the first. He was made much taller if one counted height by the elaborate white wig

that wobbled atop his head and was in turn topped by a purple tricorn. This curiosity of nature wore a long coat of gray sealskin, a pair of brown-checked breeches, pale yellow stockings, a maroon blouse, a jacket the color of brown street mud that yet had a strange and somewhat fascinating shine to its fabric, a pair of calfskin gloves and on his feet boots that few but the most seasoned world travellers would recognize as gray elephant hide. The gentleman's face was a white mask from chin to the hairline, with red arcs drawn above the eyebrows to give the face the illusion of further length.

As these aliens to the more sedate style of the London elegant came down the stairs, they gathered a few stares, shrugs and contemplative puffs of clay pipes from idlers in the lantern-lit lobby, but that was the limit of interest. The knowledge among the guests here was that if one could afford lodgings at the Mayfair Arms, one was entitled to show their colors to the world, no matter which world they represented.

"Ow," said Matthew very quietly, as his left ankle in its elephant-hide boot threatened to turn on him in anger for being pushed into such an unyielding enclosure. In truth, the boots would've needed a long breaking-in period before they were comfortable, and these bastards wanted to hobble their owner before the bottom of the stairs was reached.

Julian said from the corner of his mouth, "I can barely walk in this get-up, so keep your pain to yourself."

They reached the bottom. At his desk the clerk who had signed them in last night stood up from his chair to give a short bow, and to Matthew's amazement and horror Julian redirected his path toward the man. Matthew followed, thinking that all this weight on him was going to wear him out very soon and he felt like a true circus performer trying to balance a stack of plates on his head.

"Good evening, Count Pellegar," said the clerk, with a nod. And also, "Good evening to you, Baron Brux."

"Good evening," Matthew replied, which brought upon him a look from Julian that nearly fried his wig. *Oh my God*! Matthew thought. He

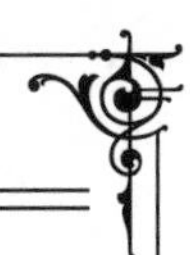

felt sweat spring out from his armpits. *I'm not supposed to know any English*! But after all it was a dress rehearsal, though it had to be treated as seriously as the real thing.

Speaking to the false Count Pellegar again, the clerk said, "How may I—"

"Your night manager. I wish to speak with him." Julian was making no effort to alter his speech, though the words were delivered with the haughty annoyance of a wealthy dandy who has little to do but belittle others. Matthew thought that was the wisest course since keeping up an affected voice would be most difficult.

"Oh...of course, your Excellency." The clerk picked up a small silver bell from his desk, rang it in what seemed all the cardinal directions of the compass, and here came three young attendants on the run. "Jackson!" the clerk said to the first youth who arrived. "Go fetch Mr. Brinewater. Tell him Count Pellegar wishes to speak with him."

"*Sir*!" The youth had nearly shouted it up to the gigantic chandelier. He took off at a run again and the other attendants went back to what they'd been doing.

"I am so pleased," said the clerk to Julian, "that your missing bags were located." Matthew noted that the clerk could not help but be a bit goggle-eyed standing so close to the furnace of all these flaming colors.

"I as well. Some fool of a servant packed them in the baron's trunk, as I suspect you heard."

"So pleased," the clerk repeated with a blank but polite smile, as it was not his place to repeat anything he might have heard that spoke against the efficiency of a Prussian servant.

Julian said haughtily, "I commend you and your establishment for finding a room for Count Mowbrey and Mr. Spottle. But I am not satisfied that acommodations were not made for them at the proper time."

Matthew grimaced for fear that Julian was going a room too far.

"Of course, of course! Ah! Here's our Mr. Brinewater!" It was said with relief that this international incident would go no further with him involved.

The heavy-set night manager who had come up after the disturbance was walking toward them. Julian gave him the shortest impression of a bow as he reached the desk. Brinewater's bow was deeper and more sincere, though his belly got in the way. "Firstly," Julian began in that same haughty tone, as Matthew hung onto a precipice of pins and needles, "I am in distress that our associates were not offered the glowing hospitality that Baron Brux and I received upon our arrival. Secondly, I wish to tell you that Count Mowbrey erred in not informing you that the damage to our suite is more severe than he revealed. That, unfortunately, is my doing though I have no recollection of such. Thirdly, I am paying now for both our suite and that little closet you've put our associates into." As he said this, he was drawing Brux's blue purse from within his coat. He snapped it open and gave the coins a jingle. "What is the price?"

"Uh…" Brinewater was taken aback by this performance and took a few seconds to regain his composure. "You're staying until *when*, sir?"

"At least the twenty-first." That irritated hand in the ostrich-skin glove came up and slapped the air again. "I don't tend to such things, my agent does."

Brinewater leaned over the clerk's desk where the clerk was already checking the ledger. "Ah! Staying through the twenty-third!"

"I thought as much," Julian said.

"And…pardon the reminder, but Count Mowbrey said you would—"

"I know exactly what Count Mowbrey said! Yes, I am paying double for the suite. At the end of our stay you may inspect the damages and inform me of that cost. Now please tally the price, we are on our way out."

A price was quoted that Matthew thought he could live on for two years. The golden coins came out of the purse and in truth made quite a dent in Baron Brux's finances.

When the money had changed hands, Brinewater said, "Your Excellency, I would be glad to give your associates a better room on the—"

"Nonsense!" Julian interrupted. "They're settled in now and in fact are tending to my business in another part of your city. Kensington, is it?

As for our own suite, have a servant bring up our hot water at ten o'clock. We intend to enjoy a leisurely supper."

"Our own tavern is but a few steps from—"

"Not a *tavern*," said the icy voice. "A *restaurant*."

On their way out with directions to what Brinewater said was an establishment that specialized in only the best, Matthew found his own voice where it had gone down to hide somewhere behind his knees. "I hope you're proud of nearly making me wet my new breeches."

Julian gave a twisted smile. "I'm damned good, aren't I?"

Matthew grunted. "For a bad man," he said.

During the course of the night Matthew understood the wisdom of the dress rehearsal. They had to become accustomed to these costumes and wear them as if they were born to the breed. Matthew also had to get used to wearing the gloves at all times, and even though they were relatively skin tight they still presented a challenge to handling small objects without fumbling, as he did with the knife and fork at their restaurant of choice. If Cardinal Black was present at the house and saw the Black-Eyed Broodies tattoo, it was the end of the masquerade and likely their lives.

Both Matthew and Julian took the opportunity to dine well on the Prussians' money, with a platter of beef ribs, bone marrow, corncakes and a selection of various stewed vegetables accompanied by the best two bottles of ale in the house. Neither man spoke about the forthcoming night, and toward the end of the dining experience Matthew was thinking that if this was a last meal it was a good one. But he shook that thought off so it wouldn't hobble him; he had to keep his focus on finding that book and somehow getting it out of the house—if indeed it was there—and anything else in his brain was mental debris.

Promptly at ten o'clock a servant brought the hot water to the Grand Suite, where Matthew and Julian were still in costume for his arrival but had removed their coats and tricorns. Matthew saw the young man cast a look of horror at the wreckage of the front room on his way to the washstand, and indeed he seemed to trip over his own feet when he spied the remains of the harpsichord. After the hot water was poured the servant offered to deposit their coats in the closet, to which Julian responded with a calm negative and Matthew breathed a sigh of relief that a third body was not going to be chucked atop the first two. Matthew thought the Mayfair Arms wasn't hurting for funds to buy a new harpsichord, they would hopefully be out of here before the corpses were discovered or began to be odious, so there was no need for any further concern regarding the state of the suite.

When the servant left, Matthew immediately threw off the hideous wig and got out of the elephant-skin boots and the shiny mud-hued jacket. He set about scrubbing Baron Brux's face from his own with the dreadful knowledge that the dress rehearsal was ended. Tomorrow night he was one of the principal actors in a deadly play, and he sent up a small prayer to God and a secret wish to Fate that they would both survive to the final curtain.

FOURTEEN.

"*No*!"

And there it had been again as last night, Matthew thought as he lay on the canopied bed: Julian's cry from the tortured depths of his sleep, which seemed to be a fearful place for him since it was a land beyond his control.

But this night, as the frigid wind whistled beyond the window in the front room, Matthew had also found sleep to be a horse that throws its master after a short spate of equine comradery.

He thought that since he'd prepared himself to rest he must've dozed, awakened, dozed and awakened eight or nine times. It was one of those nights when the pitiless hours moved past at a slow crawl, and one knew sleep was necessary for the rigors of tomorrow but...no, it wasn't going to be so simple.

He heard the sofa's frame creak softly as Julian shifted his weight upon it. Then there came a peculiar sound: Julian drew a long breath as if it were his last draught of air in the world, and when he let it out it ended in what was very much like a sob.

Matthew got quietly out of bed, put on the maroon blouse and the brown-checked breeches he'd worn the evening before and picked up a

lantern from the bedside table. He walked into the front room and found Julian standing before the window, his cloak bound tightly around himself, his face pressed nearly against the cold glass.

"Leave me," he said without a glance at Matthew. His voice… strained…terribly weak.

"What's wrong with you?" Matthew asked.

"I said…*leave me*."

"No," Matthew replied.

Julian's bald head swivelled around. The lantern's light fell upon a fierce, sweat-damp face in which the teeth were bared. "*Get away from me*," he breathed. The voice was all the more terrifying because it was a whisper instead of a shout. "*You don't know*."

"Don't know *what*?"

"What I have done. What I am capable of doing. No one knows… not really."

"I don't think you're as much the bad man as you pretend to be," Matthew said. "But you might think of giving up your present course of life so as to get a good night's rest."

"*Ha*," came the answer, delivered as if the solemn laugh of the dead from the city of graves.

There was a quiet in which the wind could be heard keening and crying beyond the glass. The early morning lamps of London burned out in the dark and once more everything out there was shapeless and ghostly white.

"Before I go out with you to that house," Matthew said, "I think I deserve—"

"*Deserve*," from the crimped mouth.

Matthew went on with hardly a pause. "I *deserve* to know what's wrong with you. At that house, if you have some kind of breakdown or something—"

"I do not *break down*," Julian said.

"Whatever's troubling you, you ought to let it go. It seems not to be worth keeping."

"Certainly. It's just as easy as you say. I shall begin anew and afresh tomorrow, and all will be right with the world." As Julian said this, Matthew got a glimpse of intense and harrowing fire in the other man's eyes, but it quickly flamed away. Left in its place was the smoke of sadness.

"Well," Matthew said, "I'm going back to bed. If you please, refrain from waking me again with your shouts."

"You weren't sleeping. Just like me…trying to grip on what we have to do tomorrow. I mean…*today*."

"All the same, I'm—"

"I was born not far from here," said Julian in a wan, distant voice. "On a street, not far from here."

"On a *street*? I thought you were—"

"Who I became. *What* I became," he corrected. "Born on a street not far from here."

Matthew didn't move nor say anything. After a moment he set his lantern down on a sidetable. There was more to come from the man who had confided Mother Deare's increasing insanity to Matthew, and who in the end had killed her.

"Aren't you going back to bed?" Julian asked, the acidity returned to his speech.

"No," Matthew answered. "I'm going to sit in that chair for a while." He eased into it and waited.

"What are you waiting for? A bedtime story?"

"I'm waiting for the truth," said Matthew. "Which can be as good for the soul as a solitary walk in the snow."

Again there was that small solemn laugh, but this time delivered not quite so harshly.

"Which street?" Matthew prompted, after another long silence.

Julian stood without response. Then he placed his forehead against the cold glass, beyond which the whirlwinds blew. "Not far from here." His voice was once more distant and haunted. "I could see it yesterday morning from this window. Oh…it's not near enough to this inn where

the guests would walk. It is a *low* street. But I could see it, all the same. I always see it."

"Something happened there?"

"Something," Julian replied. He once more drew a long breath and let it out. Before his face a ghost bloomed. "I committed my first murder on that street," he said. "I killed a little boy."

Adderlane, Matthew thought. The dead child in the tower, and the mother's reaction of horror.

"Does that shock you?" Julian asked, his face still against the glass. "Does that make you think I am among the most vile of men?"

"I don't know the story," Matthew said.

"The *story.* You say that as if it were something that made sense. Something that had a beginning and an end. It did not and does not. I killed a child on that street, and…he did not deserve such a death."

"Does any child?"

"Are you coming to my *defense*, Matthew? Now isn't that jocular…a member of the Herrald Agency…a law-abiding, stuff-shirted prick who thinks the world can be controlled by *order…*coming to my defense. It's all Fate, Matthew. And Fate knows only chaos and confusion. All right, if you wish a bedtime story, I'll give you one. A story to warm your heart on a cold winter's morn. Would you like that?" The face he turned toward Matthew was ghastly.

"I have time," Matthew replied.

"Time past," said Julian. "When I was *supposed* to be an officer in the Royal Navy. That was my father's plan. To make an upstanding officer out of the boy who had come upon the earth and killed his wife. He had no use for me, but I was supposed to follow my elder brother's course. Oh, what a *wonderful* time. He sent me to school here. The lessons he arranged for me, from the grand old men of the navy. Day in and day out…navigation and seamanship, and order and discipline and discipline and discipline and…" He stopped, because it sounded to Matthew as if he were starting to grind his teeth together.

"*Discipline*," Julian went on, when he could speak again. "I despised all that. It was supposed to be *good* for me. Poor Julian, that ill-starred boy who now and again stole small items from shops and thumbed his nose at the law. And thumbed his nose at the Lord…and the lords who swaggered on their decks and treated their crews like garbage in the streets. That's who I was supposed to be. One of *them*, and that would bring me into fine favor with society. *Society*," he repeated, with a caustic edge. "As if that ever mattered to me."

Julian was silent for a while, but Matthew did not speak or otherwise try to prompt anything more. If it was coming, it would come.

"On the day of my examinations," Julian said quietly, "I did not go. I had decided the life was not for me. But I knew what I was going to get from my father. More and more of the same. I went into a tavern and decided to drink. The whole day, I drank. Then I went out—stumbled out—and I got on the fine horse I had stolen the week before. Poor, poor Julian…that ill-starred boy." He shook his head back and forth like a wounded animal. "That fine horse got away from me. A second of inattention, an errant pull on the reins, too sharp a dig with a spur…whatever happened, it was fast, and suddenly the horse was running wild. I tried to control it, tried to get it off the street…and then there he was, right underneath me. And I ran him down. I ran him down as if he were a little bag of nothing."

On that street, Matthew thought. That street not far from here, and forever in Julian's nightmares.

"But the worst," Julian whispered. "The *worst*." His voice seemed to shatter like fragile glass. "I stood over the boy. He was a beggar child in rags. All broken, all done. But then…behind me…a woman screamed. *My boy*! she screamed. *My boy*! I turned…and there she was…a beggar woman, also in rags, her hair wild and dirty…screaming for her son. A woman my father would have called the dregs of the earth…*my boy*, she screamed…in anguish, I could *feel* her anguish…but her boy was dead… his skull was crushed…I said I'm sorry I'm sorry I didn't mean for this to—" He blinked, dazed by the impact of memories. It took him a moment

to go on. "She saw I was drunk, that I could barely stand. She fell upon him, cradled him…his head, all bloody. And she cried, as if the heart had been torn from her breast. That sound…her crying…I can't stop it. I hear it…always. And then she rose up…that beggar woman, suddenly as fierce as a queen who had lost the prince of her life…and she said into my face, *Murderer.* The tears were running down her cheeks…she was what my father would call a wretch but…in that moment…she had more dignity than I had ever seen in my life. *Murderer*, she said. Not loudly, but her voice carried."

Julian halted. He made a gasping sound, as if he were hearing that word flung into his face for the first time.

"Then…*then*," Julian continued, with an effort, "they came for me, summoned by her cry. They came from every nook and cranny on that street. They hobbled on their crutches and on their stumps. They crawled toward me like seething snakes, and they were *everywhere*. All the beggars and wretches of the world, it seemed, squeezing out from their holes and hideouts. Summoned by her cry. Yes. Murderer, she said. *Yes*. And they came at me with the filth of the street, flinging it in my face…my eyes…my hair. Someone threw a bottle. The first one hit me in the side. The second grazed my head. I ran, with that woman behind me trying to scream life into her dead son again. I ran…but the beggar army was on me…everywhere I turned, they were there. Pelting me with filth, and they took up the cry…*murderer, murderer.* It rang up and down the street like a firebell. There was no mercy for a drunken young fool in fine clothes who had let a fine horse run wild on the street…oh no…they were going to kill me, that much I knew. They were going to have their revenge…their *justice*…right then and there, and I was much too far from home."

Julian drew a ragged breath. "You see, Matthew? To them…I was Fate incarnate. I was the killing cough…the lost position…the crushed hope…the death that comes riding in on a golden summer's afternoon. I was everything that was ever wrong in the world, and they had had enough of wrongs. I understood that later, but not then. Just then, I was

only thinking of getting my stumbling legs moving, because I did not want to die. What I wanted to live for, I didn't know…but…there *had* to be something. And down an alley, with them closing in on me…I found it. A door in a wall opened and a man came out. He was holding an axe handle. He had seen it all from a window. *In there*, he said, and he motioned toward a dark room. He hit two or three of them as they got up closer. They retreated. I went into that dark room, to save my own life. It was the only choice Fate gave to me."

Julian offered nothing more for a while, which prompted Matthew to ask, "This man worked for Mother Deare?"

"Far from it." There was another long hesitation, while Julian obviously decided to go on with these revelations or not. Then: "He offered me protection and a job. Not much at first, just as a messenger. He was a rough, ugly man…but *smart*…and he saw that I could go places he could not. I could mingle with the wealthy. I could *talk*. I could hold a shilling in my palm and make someone see it as a sovereign. That was my gift, to blind people with their own greed. In time I met other people who were interested in me. They wanted me for other things. To talk my way into a room and steal something there…or use the knife or the pistol on someone's enemy, to settle old scores. I did those things. I was paid well. I had a purpose." He gave Matthew a tortured smile. "I'm a very fast learner," he said, "and I became better skilled in time."

"And one afternoon," he continued, "I had a visit from a man who introduced himself as an associate to a certain woman of business who had heard my name and wished to interview me for the possibility of future employment. That sounded like I would be taking a job at the permits office, sitting behind a desk marking in a ledger. It didn't sound like killing at Mother Deare's demand and *whim*, did it? But it was. More money, power over underlings, the excitement of the hunt…the deadly brew. Well, I'd been drinking it for a long time. It became my life's water. And what of it? Why shouldn't I take what I could, while I could? Nothing lasts forever, I know that. Why shouldn't I use my talents? Then Mother Deare began lending

me out to Professor Fell, and I got in with that crowd also. I *belonged.* I still belong. When I do a job, I do it to the best of my ability. I am relied upon and I have a reputation. I am *someone* in this world. You see?"

Matthew took his time in answering, weighing what he would say against the possibility of Julian Devane flying at him to take him apart. At last he said, "It sounds to me you decided that if being a good man was closed off to you—by what you consider to be Fate—you would be the best bad man you could be. Perhaps you're a walking contradiction, but there it is."

Julian did not respond. Matthew tensed, ready for anything.

Then Julian laughed, and it was genuine.

"Yes," he said. "I like that."

Matthew stood up, realizing the bedtime story had come to its end. Dawn was approaching, though again it looked as if the sun would be shrouded behind clouds for another day.

Julian yawned and stretched. "I think I can get some sleep," he said. "I didn't realize how tired I am."

Matthew nodded. He thought that Julian had likely never told this story in its entirety to anyone else in the world, and even if he'd related parts of it to his criminal friends he had certainly never revealed any of it to a law-abiding stuff-shirted prick such as had listened to it this morning. Maybe that made a difference, or maybe not, but already Julian was settling himself back on the sofa, his head on one of the pillows. He stretched out to full length and closed his eyes. Julian's hands were clasped across his chest in a way that Matthew thought was nearly an attitude of prayer, but he didn't dare voice that because he wanted to keep all the teeth he currently possessed. Matthew recalled that at the tower near Adderlane Julian had said he did not mourn the dead.

It seemed, though, that he did mourn at least one.

"We'll get in and out," Julian said with his eyes closed. "We'll find the book. Tonight. In and out. We'll take that book and then we'll find a chemist. Kidnap him, if we have to. We will.

Tonight…we will."

Julian was already drifting off. Matthew picked up the lantern and returned to the bedroom where he lay down on the beautiful bed with two dead men in the closet ten feet away and a tormented killer sleeping in the next room. He closed his eyes, but found that sometimes bedtime stories do not deliver peace.

Tonight. In and out. Find the book.

In and out.

Tonight.

FIFTEEN.

This was the plan agreed upon by the gentlemen in the first floor's Grand Suite: pack weapons, hire a hack in front of the inn, proceed to the destination, instruct the driver to go ahead just past the last estate on Endsleigh Park Road and wait for two hours, the payment supplied for his patience to be substantial. Then past the guard at the gate with the invitation, and in that house somehow find that book. If indeed it was there. If indeed this was the right house, which they were not absolutely sure of. Getting out of the house with the book was another kettle of fish, and they both agreed they might wind up fried before they could get to the hack.

Darkness had fallen, though the day had been so dark the disappearance of the meager sun hardly mattered. As Matthew readied himself in the white facial powder, wig and garb of Baron Brux—the same outlandish outfit he'd worn yesterday—he felt the immense pressure of the task ahead crushing down on him. It was truly a do or die situation; without that book, all was lost. So the plan might not be much, and certainly not to the standards that the Herrald Agency might have demanded, but it was all they had.

During the morning hours Matthew had considered trying to contact Gardner Lillehorne for help, perhaps getting a ring of constables around the house or even—in desperation—raiding the place, but he'd

dismissed the idea as unworkable. For one thing, time was of the essence and Lillehorne could not be counted on for speed in this matter. For the second thing, Matthew knew Lillehorne and certainly his superiors would wish to know why the book was so valuable, and he doubted that the legal arm of London would sit back and let it be returned to Danton Idris Fell, no matter whose sanity was at risk.

And contacting the London office of the Herrald Agency? Again, unworkable in the frame of time they had. Matthew would still be explaining the situation at seven-thirty tonight.

No, it had to be just himself and Julian, walking into that house dressed as Prussian clowns. He sorely wished Hudson Greathouse were here, if only for the benefit of advice…a better plan…anything to ease the tension that threatened to slow both his mind and his legs, and he had the feeling that tonight of all nights he would need them both to be quick.

"Remember," said Julian as he got into the polar bear coat. His face was powdered white up to the top of his skull and his cheeks were rouged. "You speak no English, correct?"

"*Ja*," the pallid-faced Matthew said, as he righted the wig on his head and secured the purple tricorn atop it. The last thing he did was pull on the calfskin gloves, and the Black-Eyed Broodies tattoo was out of sight. Beneath his sealskin coat, hidden away under the shiny mud-colored jacket, were his pistol and the ivory-handled dagger that had belonged to Albion. Under Julian's coat, the four-barrelled pistol hung on a belthook. They were as ready as they would ever be.

"Take along a vial of powder," Julian advised. "If you sweat, your scar may show and you don't want Black seeing it if he's there." As Matthew got the powder, Julian picked up the satchel containing the gold bars and the plans for the machine that resembled a winged dragon.

"Ready?" Julian asked.

Matthew nodded, because for the moment his throat had tightened to the degree that no English could pass even if he chose to speak it.

They left the room.

On the way down the stairs, Julian nudged Matthew with an elbow in the side, though Matthew hardly felt it through the heavy coat. But Matthew understood the meaning, for here came Lord and Lady Turlentort up the staircase, both of them wrapped in furs and silks and chattering to each other like happy shoppers, their faces ruddy with the cold. One glance at the pair descending toward them, and the Turlentorts shut up like clams feeling the steam from a cookpot. Matthew saw Lord Turlentort roll his eyes at his lady and she disguised a chuckle as a polite little cough. Then they were past, and Matthew realized that if anything, the duo of Scar and the dashingly charming but ominously wicked teller of exciting tales in a pitching coach were completely unrecognizable.

As they crossed the lobby, the grandfather clock began to chime the hour of seven o'clock. Outside, the night once more was bitterly cold. It seemed that the crust of snow would not melt a flake before May Day. "A hack, sir?" asked the attendant on the street, who having received a curt nod walked out waving his arms to guide a carriage to the curb.

When the carriage pulled up, the driver looked down at Julian from beneath his peaked cap. "Where to, sir?"

"Number Fourteen, Endsleigh Park Road," Julian replied, already reaching for the door. "And make haste, if you—"

"My destination, as well," a man said from behind them.

Matthew spun around, startled by the voice so close to his ear.

The man who had spoken wore a dove-gray greatcoat with a fleece collar and a gray tricorn adorned with a thin red band. He was tall and lean with a high forehead, dark hair, eyes so pale blue they were a shocking color against the deep brown shade of his face, a square chin and the kind of thin-bridged aristocratic nose with flared nostrils that seem to always be offended by odors from the lower classes, which contained everyone but his own ilk. Still, the man was smiling and there was no sense of either threat or snobbery. "Pardon the intrusion," he said, speaking with the trace of a foreign accent that Matthew found difficult to name. "But may I share your carriage, Count Pellegar?"

Matthew was both terrified and impressed; terrified by the man's use of the title and impressed by the coolness of Julian, who simply moved back and swept an arm toward the interior. The man placed a polished black boot upon the passenger's step. Matthew saw he was carrying a similarly polished black satchel. The man pulled himself up into the carriage, and Julian gave Matthew a look that even through the white face paint and the rouged cheekbones of a clown said *Be on your guard.*

Matthew and Julian sat across from the man as the hack started off. The interior's oil lamp rocked on its gimbal, throwing elongated shadows.

"It is a pleasure, sir," said the man, still smiling. "And this is Baron Brux, I believe?"

"The same. English is not his language. I have also the pleasure of addressing whom?"

"Um…you may call me Victor."

"But not your real name?"

"No." He shrugged. "What is a name but something applied to one that colors an impression?"

"And you know us how?"

Opening the sail in dangerous waters, Matthew thought, but he could say nothing.

"By your reputations, of course," said Victor. "And your clothing. Let me rephrase that: your *style.* Your handling of the situation with Prince Powalaski—was it three years ago?—was masterful. I dare say I can't think of anyone who could have gotten in there as you did, with all that security."

"Hm," said Julian.

"Well," Victor said with another slight shrug, "*I* might have been able to." His smile seemed now to Matthew to be more of the fixed grimace of a barely-contained animal, and the pale blue eyes burned with a frightening and powerful intensity. This, he thought, was a very dangerous man. A silence stretched, until Victor lifted his black-gloved hands in what might have been a suggestion of peace between nations edging toward the brink

of war. "But in any case," he said, still speaking with that accent Matthew could not define, "a job well done."

"My compliments for recognizing superior talent," said Julian, who Matthew thought must have decided that he could not only out-act any of Shakespeare's players but could also out-compose the plays themselves. He felt the pressing need for a chamberpot.

Victor continued to smile. Then he reached into his greatcoat and his hand emerged with a pistol. Matthew tensed, Julian shifted his position just a fraction, and Victor proceeded to inspect the pistol's barrel, cocking device and trigger as if he'd just bought the weapon. "Victor is not really my name, no," he said. "I feel it is appropriate in the situation, because I intend to *be* the victor of this particular event."

"Hm," said Julian, fast becoming the master of noncommittal utterances.

"We are all brothers, in a way. Do you agree?" Victor didn't wait for a response because it was obvious he didn't care if Count Pellegar agreed or not. "Here we are, though, on a field of battle of another sort. This does not involve our usual talents. This involves the power of the purse, and I can tell you that the power behind my purse is quite substantial."

"I see," said Julian. He smiled, which was grotesque on the painted face. "I am relieved to know this does not concern the size of one's gun." So saying, he pulled his own deadly weapon from its belthook and went about inspecting it as Victor had done his own. Matthew saw Victor's eyes narrow just a fraction, and with a satisfied and quiet grunt the man put his pistol away.

The rest of the trip was done in what Matthew felt was a tense silence. When the carriage stopped, Victor was the first one out. There stood the grand house beyond the gate with the guard at his post, the manse itself illuminated with lanterns in its windows as if for a party. Victor stood next to the carriage as Julian and Matthew disembarked, and at once Matthew realized there was no way to inform the driver to wait for two hours just past the last estate. The driver climbed down to be paid. Victor said,

"Allow me," and handed over the coins with an extra amount as incentive for his next statement. "We shall need a return to the Mayfair Arms. I expect the business should be done by midnight."

"Yes sir, as you say, and thank you kindly." The driver got back up on his seat, flicked the reins and started off, and Victor was already producing his invitation on parchment to show the guard.

"*Christ*," Matthew heard Julian mutter beside him. As the carriage went, so went the means of escape. They were caught here until midnight, for better or for worse.

Julian showed the invitation, which even though the same had admitted Victor still was subject to the guard's scrutiny. With a nod the guard released them. As Matthew and Julian walked a few paces behind Victor toward the manse's imposing front staircase they heard the solid metal clang of the gate behind being closed…and Matthew thought that now they were well and truly imprisoned, and this place might make the dangers of Newgate appear to be wraiths of fantasy.

Up the staircase, with its thick concrete bannisters on either side, and to the front door, where Victor was already using the knocker. Brass in the shape of a ship's cannon, Matthew noted. Almost at once the door opened and the man of the night before stood there, wearing a dark blue uniform with white epaulettes at the shoulders. His face was as grim as a closed tomb. He looked at the invitation Victor offered, then the one offered by Julian, they were admitted to the house and the door was shut behind them. Matthew's heart was pounding and his pulse raced and he was sorely glad he'd brought the vial of powder because he was going to need it.

Matthew had just time enough for fleeting impressions in the entrance foyer—rich dark wood flooring, sky-blue painted walls, the aroma of a bittersweet incense in the air—before he saw before them the white-suited Owl standing beside a sturdy oak table which supported a large wicker basket. Just beyond the Owl were two more men in dark suits, both of them looking as if they could bite the heads off poisonous snakes for supper.

"Weapons in the basket, please," the Owl said to Victor, who obliged by giving up not only the pistol he'd shown in the hackney, but a second smaller pistol and a curved dagger that Matthew thought might be of eastern European origin and some clue to his nationality. But Victor was not yet cleared to go through, for one of the two dark-suited men stepped forward, said, "Remove your coat and hat, hang them there and raise your arms." Hooks on the wall were indicated, which already held two tricorns, a bright red peaked hat of unknown origin, and three coats including one floor-length item made of a tawny animal skin. The second man grasped hold of Victor's satchel, took a key that was offered, unsnapped the satchel and peered inside.

Victor obeyed, revealing gray streaks at the sides of his ebony hair. The man commenced searching him from back of neck to back of boots before the satchel was returned. By this time Julian was depositing his pistol into the basket, and then came Matthew's turn. As Matthew gave up his pistol and dagger he noted that a number of other guns and knives were already in the basket, including a thing that looked like a knuckle-duster studded with small nails.

"One moment," said the Owl. He placed a pale hand upon Matthew's chest.

Matthew tried to stand very still, but his knees began to tremble. The Owl's protuberant golden eyes were unblinking, the eerie gaze moving here and there over Matthew's face. Matthew felt himself being examined down to the white-powdered pores.

"I know you," the Owl said. "Do I not?"

"Pardon," said Julian, "but Baron Brux speaks no English."

"Ask him then where I might have seen him before. His face...I know it from *somewhere*."

Julian hesitated only an instant. Then, in a clipped and harsh accent remembered from the real Count Pellegar: "*Hammer estad ugla kalein, ja*?"

"*Nein*," Matthew answered past the lump in his throat.

"He says *no*," Julian reported, speaking as sweetly as honey from the jar, "that you and he have not to this moment met. It would be impossible,

since the Baron and I have spent all our time at the Mayfair Arms. May I ask if you've ever travelled to Prussia?"

The Owl had given Julian only the briefest of glances; his attention was focused upon Matthew, who realized the man had looked into his unpowdered face before the fireplace at The Green Spot.

"Move along," said the Owl, but the way he spoke it held the underlying statement *I will be watching you.*

Matthew got his knees unlocked and lurched forward, and damned if that head didn't swivel on its neck to watch him continue to the next checkpoint, where Julian was already doffing polar bear coat, tricorn and giving up the satchel. "*Key,*" said the man who took the case, saw the keyholes and assumed correctly that all satchels coming through the front door tonight would be locked. Julian gave it up from an inner pocket of his jacket before being searched from backs of ears down to his heels. The satchel was looked into, returned to him and the way clear for him to follow Victor deeper into the house.

"Coat off, hat off, wig off," said the gent advancing upon Matthew, who had the sense to shrug and make motions in the air until the man removed the items for him.

As Matthew was being searched, he felt the Owl watching him. Damn the man! If he'd had his druthers he would poke those eyeballs out with a sharp stick. He felt woozy. If anyone in this foyer had known the Prussian language, he and Julian would already be on the path to reduction as dogfood.

But with a knock at the door another visitor's presence was announced, taking the Owl's attention. Matthew looked back to see what appeared to be a young boy entering the house and displaying his invitation. This person could not be over twelve years of age, was small-boned and slim, sharp-nosed and dark-eyed and completely out of the element here. He wore what was certainly an expensive black greatcoat, gray gloves and a gray tricorn with a single white feather sticking up from its band. He clasped a cowhide satchel under his arm. As Matthew watched, this new

arrival—a mere child, at that, and only in height perhaps three inches over five feet—stopped before the wicker basket and, smiling thinly at the Owl, produced from his coat first one pistol, then another smaller than the first, an even smaller pistol from his left boot, and lastly a short sword in a leather sheath from between his shoulderblades.

The man who had searched Matthew used the universal language of a thumb's jerk to order him to move along, and offered the return of the wig which now looked somewhat like a crushed dead animal.

He put it on, straightened it as best as possible, was grateful that he'd not had to take off his gloves, and again moved forward in a lurch to catch up with Julian. First no carriage, now no weapons…a fine plan, flying to pieces like an old grainsack in a hurricane.

What a house this was! Even with the present dangers Matthew could not help but be awed by the grand elegance of the place. Light woods were tastefully mixed with dark woods, everything was polished to perfection, a beautiful many-hued Oriental carpet graced the floor just past the foyer, and a runner of the same colored the wide staircase. From a large chandelier hung an array of illuminated ship's lanterns. Upon the sky-blue walls were mounted various paintings of seascapes, and a great white ensign of the Royal Navy was hanging from above. Its red cross served to remind Matthew of Cardinal Black's signature, and the fact that all this beauty was the smooth white powder on a killer's face.

"This way, sirs," said a gray-haired older man in that same dark blue uniform, motioning both Julian and Matthew in the direction Victor had gone. "Allow me," the man continued with a short bow, taking his place as an escort to the next destination. He opened a sliding door on the right and they were taken into a large parlor set down three steps. In that room the high ceiling was painted to resemble the vista of an evening sky, perhaps as seen from a ship at sea. The logs in a fireplace of sparkling white marble threw light and heat. The chamber was host to what appeared to be a party in progress, yet the mood struck Matthew as being more business than pleasure. He saw Victor across the room taking a glass of red wine from

a tray offered by a servant. The others gathered there—five more—were either seated on brown leather chairs or standing, seemingly all keeping to themselves and all with glasses of red wine. Everyone except Victor looked toward Julian and Matthew as they entered.

Matthew's attention went first to the sleek and quite beautiful black woman who stood at least six feet three inches tall, her long ebony hair adorned with combs of bleached bone. She was wearing a scarlet gown with a midriff section of that tawny animal skin, and Matthew reasoned the gown went with the similarly-skinned coat on its hook in the foyer.

A stocky, bald-headed man with the rough and pockmarked face of a brawler turned a cold eye upon the false Prussians, then sipped his wine and looked away. He wore an ill-fitting dun-colored suit and boots with metal tips, the boots currently propped up on an ottoman before his chair. Owner of the nail-studded knuckle-duster, Matthew assumed.

The next man was tall and thin, had a long almost cadaverous face, wore a dark blue suit with a white waistcoat and a white cravat, and possessed a full head of reddish-brown hair and a neatly trimmed beard more red than brown. He lifted his glass of wine toward Matthew and Julian.

The fourth man, standing with the black woman, was sporting a wig nearly as high and elaborate as Matthew's. He wore a gray suit with a blue-checked waistcoat and was of medium height and square of build, his chunky face ruddy-cheeked and the eyes reduced to small black holes. The cuffs of his gray blouse were explosions of lace. He regarded Matthew and Julian with a curled lip and an attitude of dislike that could be perceived across the room.

The fifth man wore the standard uniform and stood in the corner beside a table on which rested the satchels the others had brought in. Matthew and Julian's escort motioned toward that table. "You may trust that your offerings are safely watched," he said, and as soon as Julian placed the satchel down, the satchel-watcher set it flat and put upon it a card with the number five upon it. Matthew saw the others were numbered from one to four, and the case done up in the tawny skin bore a card with the

number two. The shiny black item Victor had brought in was number four. Matthew reasoned that the satchel the boy was carrying would be number six. So…who in the room had *not* brought an 'offering'?

A servant came up beside Julian with two glasses of wine on a silver tray. Julian took one, as did Matthew, who was still thinking about that word *offerings*.

Then the twelve-year-old boy sauntered in behind his own escort—the Owl himself, which made Matthew feel the sweat starting up at his hairline beneath the wig's weight. The boy's curly light brown hair was shiny with pomade and tied with black ribbons in a double queue down his back. He wore an amber-hued suit with a cream-colored blouse and a yellow cravat, bright yellow stockings and boots that appeared to be made of snakeskin. In one arm was cradled his cowhide satchel.

The boy's eyes flashed as he took in the gathering. He stopped in the doorway and grinned, showing front teeth that looked too large for a child's mouth.

"Is this a fucking funeral?" he asked, in the thin high voice that suited his age. "Who died?"

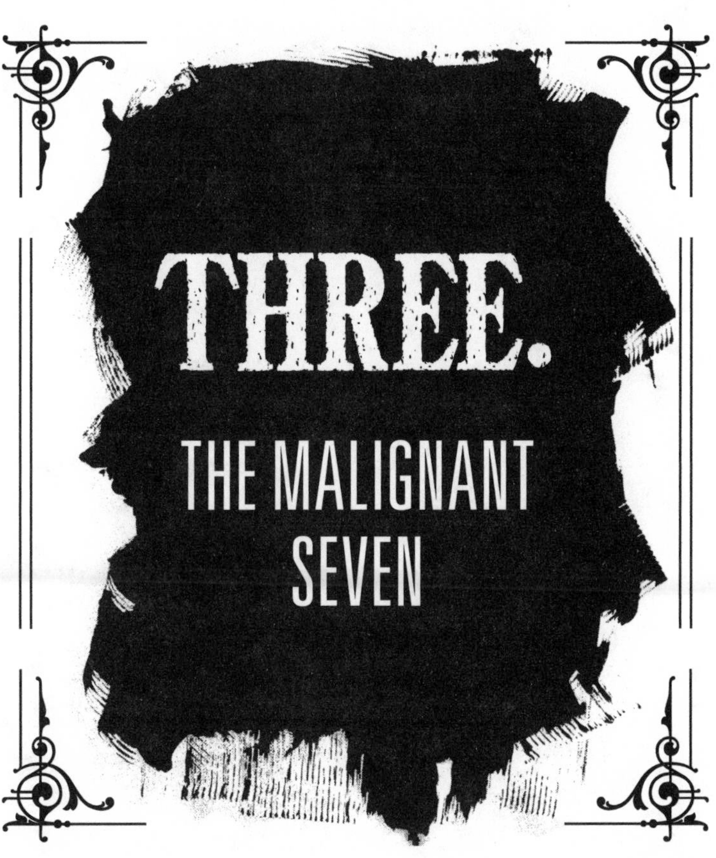

THREE.

THE MALIGNANT SEVEN

SIXTEEN.

The twelve-year-old boy with the mouth of a thirty-year-old sailor added his satchel to the table, took the glass of red wine from the silver tray that was offered to him and drank it down in one swallow. Then he put his hands on his tiny hips and again surveyed the other occupants of the room.

"*Everyone* here seems to have died," he remarked. "Why don't we liven this up?"

"Suggestions?" asked the man in the room's second outrageous wig. He also had an accent Matthew could not identify; he sounded mush-mouthed.

"Introductions. I'll go first. My name is Miles Merda. Merda with an 'e'. Representing French interests." He strolled over past the wig-man and the tall black woman to warm his small hands before the fire. "I am thirty-three years old and at birth was struck with a malady that at first would appear to doom my life yet has worked out perfectly for the occupation I have chosen. Or, let us say, has chosen me. I am an expert at appearing to be what I am not. I can't say the same for some of you." He cast a bemused gaze upon the pockmarked brawler. "All right, then. Next?"

No one spoke. The Owl took an empty chair and Matthew thought he was being watched, the Owl trying to place the face beneath the makeup.

"Come now, don't be shy!" Merda chided. "Tall lady! You don't look the shy type."

She smiled, but it was tight and held no humor. "Very well," she said, in a rather husky and well-educated, English-inflected voice with another deeper singsong accent behind it. Matthew had the impression that such a voice could be quite beguiling. "I am known as Lioness Sauvage," she went on. "Representing a consortium of African interests. I am a free woman and intend to remain so, and I will say that I have killed several men to gain that status."

"Bravo for you!" Merda grinned again. "My, you're a big one. You wouldn't fancy a small quick one, would you?"

"Too small for me," Lioness answered.

"You never know."

"Oh," she said, "I *know*."

"I turn from that crushing rejection to *you*, sir." Merda lifted a chin toward Victor. "Your name and affiliation?"

"Victor. As in 'the'," came the response. "Affiliated with parts unknown."

"A mysterious man," said Merda. He shrugged. "As you please. You two! Dressed in your best, I see. Pardon me if I take my eyeballs out to shield them against the glare. But I think I must know who you are! Count…what is your name?"

"Pellegar," Julian said.

"Oh, let's be friendly and do Christian names! Don't mean to offend, but you may call me Miles, if I may call you—?" He waited.

Matthew had a start. His mind raced. Back in the Grand Suite…had Pellegar's first name been mentioned by—

"Karlo," Julian said, and only Matthew could hear the small rush of relief in Julian's voice, that he'd remembered Brux saying *Karlo! Sie haben unsere fehlenden Falle gefunden*? whatever the rest of it meant. "But you may refer to me as Your Excellency," Julian added. "Baron Brux does not speak English, only the Prussian language."

"Well, what's *his* first name?"

"*Baron*," Julian replied, and having established his haughty bastardom to this room of like spirits he was dismissed by Miles Merda with a wave of the diminutive hand.

"You, sir?" Merda inquired of the red beard.

"Me? Oh…well…I am Lazarus Firebaugh." The man took another sip of his wine before he continued. He shifted his weight from one foot to the other as if he were standing on a bed of coals. "*Doctor* Lazarus Firebaugh," he said when he'd lowered the glass. "Chemist by trade and nature. I am simply…available to the winner."

Julian shot a quick glance at Matthew, who simply responded with a barely perceptible nod. Firebaugh was the one who'd not brought a satchel, because he was part of the prize.

"Splendid!" Merda next turned toward the brawler. "Sir?"

"Sandor Krakowski." This one's accent was thick. "Polish interests. I am a student of politics."

"Yes, I can tell you've carried out many studies. The school of politics is quite rough in Poland, I would venture. And *you*, lastly but surely not leastly?"

The bewigged gent had been addressed. He drank his wine and took his own good time in answering. "I am Bertrand Montague." His voice was like the first wheeze from a squeezebox before the notes issue forth. "Who I represent is my own business."

"All right, Berty, have it as you please. Now! Don't we all feel better, knowing who we're up against?"

Matthew didn't feel any better; in fact he felt as if the situation had tipped from the wildly difficult to the solidly impossible. Obviously this was to be a bidding for the book, with Lazarus Firebaugh to go along for whatever purpose was necessary. An auction, carried out by what must be an insane naval admiral and a child-killing demoniac, with members of assassins' guilds, criminal organizations, corrupt royal houses and whatever else in attendance on a scale far beyond the shores of England.

Matthew thought that if he could sit on the floor and weep for the loss of Berry Grigsby he would do so, for this was a hopeless case.

Yet…there was *something.*

The gold bars and the plans for the winged dragon in the satchel. Was it possible—just possible—that such items might constitute the *winning* bid?

His heart, which had tumbled into the cellar during this exchange of dark pleasantries, now lifted a little toward the lamp in the attic. Yes, he thought. Play this game out, present the bid and if all goes well walk out of here with both the book and a chemist supplied for its use.

And if all does not go well? Follow whoever wins and murder him—or her—before the night is done, seize the book from dead fingers and travel on? Because he was fairly sure the only way to get that book from the auction's winner was by bloodshed.

Oh my God, he thought. He was sounding in his own mind far too much like the bad man, but of what use at the moment was the *good* man?

He wondered when the admiral and Cardinal Black would make their appearances, and it struck him that the term 'cardinal' could be used to describe the primary colors from which all other colors are mixed. Black would be the darkest color, a shade without light or hue. He had the thought that if black could be termed a cardinal color, it ruled in this room among those assembled here. Black: the cardinal color of death.

Matthew was interrupted in these musings by someone else entering the room. Not the bearlike admiral with the flame-painted beard, nor the dark cardinal of evil, but a lithe sinewy young woman with short-cropped brown hair, a pretty heart-shaped face, expressive brown eyes and a warm smile. Matthew guessed she was in her mid-twenties. She wore a deep purple silk gown with a stitching of bright yellow flowers at the neckline. Her hands and forearms were adorned up to the elbows by silk gloves the same color as the dress, and it was difficult not to notice a striking musculature in her upper arms, not overly so but there all the same.

"Good evening to all," she said. "My name is Elizabeth Mulloy. Vice Admiral Lash wishes me to welcome you to his home."

Vice Admiral, Matthew thought. Lash? He glanced at Julian, whose painted face was as still as stone.

She went on. "Samson will be joining you in the dining room in due time. For the moment, I'd like to announce that dinner is served."

There was the name: Samson Lash. Again Matthew glanced at Julian to see if there was some recognition, but if there was Julian didn't show it. Then Matthew happened to look at the Owl and saw those damned weird golden eyes staring holes through him.

The Owl abruptly stood up. "Please, everyone, follow Miss Mulloy to the dining room." It was not so much a pleasantry as it was a command.

The dining room was festooned with greenery hanging from the exposed oak beams of the ceiling, along with a number of lanterns and naval signal flags. Logs burned in another marble fireplace. A long table was set with plates and silverware, but the food was not yet in evidence. Upon entering the room Merda stood next to Lioness, who was a true giantess in comparison. He pointed upward. "Mistletoe, I believe," he said, giving her a hopeful grin.

"In my country," she answered without a smile, "we kill under the mistletoe."

Which brought a shrug but did not diminish his cheerfulness, for he sat down next to her and puffed his chest out as if he were next in line for the kingship of the world.

"The places are not marked. Sit as you wish," Miss Mulloy said, though Victor had already seated himself across from Merda. Matthew and Julian sat down side-by-side, with Matthew facing Montague at one end of the table and Julian facing Lioness, while Krakowski chose the chair on the other side of Victor facing Doctor Firebaugh. The Owl had not entered the chamber, much to Matthew's relief. Where he'd gone, Matthew did not wish to know. Miss Mulloy waited until they were all settled at their places and then she said, "We'll begin in just a moment," after which she left the room by another door at the far side of the chamber.

Almost at once two servants appeared to pour more red wine into the glasses that were set beside each plate. Suddenly Julian lifted his glass. "A toast, if you will. To the great success of myself and Baron Brux."

"I'll toast that you fail miserably," said Merda, who lifted and drank. The others simply sat in silence.

But then Lioness Sauvage levelled her steady and transfixing gaze across the table at Julian. "How is it that a Prussian speaks the English so fluently?"

"Born English. Raised and educated in Prussia," Julian replied, parroting what the real Count Pellegar had revealed in the Grand Suite. "And I would say your grasp of the language is also exemplary. You had an excellent teacher, I think?"

"I killed the man who taught me English," she said. "That was all he was good for. He was a brute. Let me correct myself...I executed him for crimes against me I should not wish to relate at this table."

"Speaking of *crimes* against oneself," said Montague with that squeezebox wheeze, "you are sitting across from a—dare I use the word without being struck dead—a *gentleman* who is quite familiar with the conduct of a brute. An ignorant brute, at that. Isn't that true, Pellegar?"

Julian smiled silkily, while Matthew wanted to crawl under the table. "If you say so," Julian replied.

"You know full well what I'm referring to! The Hollenstein affair in 1698! Tell them all how you and Brux carried out that particularly charming solution!"

Julian retained his smile, but he did shift a fraction in his chair. "I find—as likely we all do—that any solution has its own charm. You tell them, Montague, since you're such the expert."

Bing bing bing! rang a fork against a wineglass.

"Sirs...please," said the obviously unnerved Doctor Firebaugh. "This is neither the time nor place for—"

"He and Brux murdered my *employer*," Montague wheezed on, aiming his eyes at Lioness as if she might rise up with him to strike down the

count. "Strangled him in his bedchamber! My golden goose! And for that I was behind the black balls for two years until I had atoned myself for *their* sin!"

"Unfortunate," said Julian, with a smirk that was right in character. "Ah, speaking of a golden goose!"

The food was arriving on three rolling carts, the first of which supported a green platter on which a very large cooked goose—its skin crisped to what really was a shade of gold—was being offered to the guests. Matthew's sigh of relief was a windstorm when Montague's attention shifted from the so-called crimes of Count Pellegar to the feast being rolled across the gray stone floor. He noted also that Julian's eyes closed for a few seconds, as if steeling himself for the next confrontation that he had to talk his way out of.

But any confrontations could wait. Soon on the table along with the cooked goose were platters of steamed carrots and turnips, fried potatoes, creamed corn, yams and asparagus as well as smaller plates of smoked salmon, fried cauliflower with mustard sauce, steamed mussels and a loaf of freshly baked dark bread covered with sesame seeds. The servants stood ready to pour more wine and attend to whatever was needed.

Weighty wig or not—and horrific circumstances or not—Matthew decided to eat as best as his stomach could manage in its current crimped state of tension. The others apparently the same, for the feast began to be whittled down by knives and forks and there was only the occasional comment from Miles Merda to interfere with the noises of gluttony, of which Matthew noted Montague and Krakowski were tied as most obnoxious.

Then came another noise…that of heavy boots striding from the passageway between the parlor and the dining room, and suddenly *he* was there.

To say that Vice Admiral Samson Lash was bearlike was to say that Lioness Sauvage was knee high to a cub. At six feet four inches tall and with a barrel-shaped frame, the man filled his space and more. He was as much an element of fire as Matthew had ever seen, even considering the

fiery Hudson Greathouse. This man's sharp blue eyes even seemed to be throwing fire as he stopped before the table and scanned the assembly. His nose was large and hooked, his forehead a battering-ram, the black beard that trailed down over the front of his medalled naval uniform was painted with orange and red flames, his mass of curly black hair hung shaggily about his monuments of shoulders, and his thickly veined hands bore knuckles that Matthew thought could knock a chunk of marble from the fireplace. The man was as scary as hell.

And there he stood, those huge hands on his hips, the fiery eyes peering at one and then the other. At last his broad mouth grinned and the teeth seemed to shoot flame also as they reflected the leaping firelight.

"Guests!" he boomed. "Honored guests! My hearty welcome to you all!"

"Hm," Matthew heard Julian mutter beside him, another noncommittal utterance but this time Matthew thought it was more an expression of awe...and the realization that *this* was the force of nature they had to bargain with.

"Please," said Lash in a more contained voice, "do continue your feasting." He drew from a pocket of his uniform a gold pocket watch, which he set upon the table between Matthew and Montague next to the bones of the cooked goose. "I will take this moment to say that I know you all have journeyed a distance to attend here tonight...some more distance than others...and I am gratified at the interest you and your affiliations have shown."

As Lash spoke, both the Owl and Elizabeth Mulloy quietly entered the dining room behind him, and again Matthew felt his stomach squeeze with tension around the grand meal he'd just consumed...and hoped to keep down.

"This is a momentous occasion," Lash said. "Great expense and precise planning had to be undertaken, but from the beginning I understood that I was not going to fail. I will admit to you that my associates and I—"

Yes, I know who those must be, Matthew thought: the fortunately dead Mother Deare and the unfortunately living Cardinal.

"—did fail twice in this attempt, as the plans went awry at the last moment. Therefore we had to wait until a more opportune time, which we of course seized…and the result is, I own a volume that has the power to change the world. You know it as a book of chemical and botanical potions once possessed by England's own Professor Fell, and I think all of you recognize the importance of that name." He paused. One wilderness of an eyebrow gave a slight twitch. "I mean to say…what *once* was the importance. Time does not stand still, gentlemen and madam. Neither does the control of power. This volume…whatever we had to do to get it, whatever risks had to be taken…well, the formulas in the book do speak for themselves."

Lash began to slowly pace from one end of the table to the other. "Let us understand the procedure." His boots made a clacking sound on the stones. "This has been a long time in the preparation—as you all well know—and I shall not rush it now. One by one, according to the number you were given that applies to your arrival here, I will see you privately in my study, and thereupon will hear the amount you have elected to offer in exchange for—"

"Just a moment, sir!"

The voice was startling, since everyone but the speaker had been so focused upon not only Samson Lash's speech, but his presence.

Victor had spoken. "I protest against that procedure! Why not have open bidding?"

Lash stopped pacing, stood very still, and stared at him.

The moment stretched.

Then Lash smiled, but there was something deadly playing at its edges.

"My house," Lash said quietly. "My rules."

Victor was silent.

"Let me reassure you—all of you—what your winning bid purchases." Lash walked toward Firebaugh and put both huge hands on the man's thin shoulders. Matthew thought those hands could break the shoulder bones

in two seconds of effort. "You are winning not only the book, but the services of Doctor Firebaugh for *one year* from tonight. The very talented doctor has given the contents of the book an intense study in the short period of time we have owned it, but let me assure you that he will thoroughly understand its directions before you reach your destination. Doctor Firebaugh has been trained in the knowledge of chemicals at the Royal College of Physicians by two of the most renowned names in London's medical profession, Doctors Lucian Crippen and Wilfred Jekyll, and you may not be aware of the intelligence of those individuals but I dare say you shall." Lash gave the shoulders a reassuring pat and strolled back down to the other end of the table, where he picked up the pocket watch, looked at the time and then set it back down.

"In addition," Lash said, "the winner of this auction shall have the benefit of two bodyguards chosen from this man's able team." He motioned toward the Owl, who briefly nodded. "These bodyguards will remain on duty until your ship leaves London, to prevent any of the saddened and disappointed losers from attempting to take what is not rightfully his—or hers—or *theirs*." He gave Matthew and Julian a pointed look. "These bodyguards will be armed and ready to kill, with my blessing. Doctor, are we nearing the time?"

"Yes, I would say so," Firebaugh responded.

"I foresaw," said the vice admiral, "that all of you might question the validity of the potions. Therefore I have taken the liberty of applying one of them—from the doctor's creation— to a glass of the wine that was partaken at dinner, and the effect should be imminent."

If Matthew's heart had been beating hard, now it began to gallop like a racehorse. His gloved hands grasped the arms of his chair. What if he or Julian had swallowed a truth serum? Christ! he thought. To have everything spill out here at the dinner table...disaster upon disaster!

"Soon now," said Lash, with another glance at the watch.

"I still protest this arrangement!" Victor argued. "It's unfair, not to hear what my competition is—"

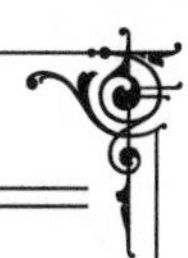

Sandor Krakowski began to laugh.

All eyes turned toward him.

Krakowski, still laughing, put a hand to his throat as if to clench the laugh off, but it would not cease. His pockmarked, battle-rough face had reddened. He laughed on, the sound of it getting louder and higher in pitch, and he looked back and forth at the others as if believing the wild laughter came from some other body than his own. He started to stand but suddenly he was laughing so hard he was unable to leave his chair, and on and on it went, until—

—very suddenly he burst into tears.

"Ah," said Lash. His eyes glinted with delight. "The next phase."

Krakowski not only was now crying forlornly but blubbering like a little boy who had just lost his last sugar candy. Then he began to wail like a child who had seen his mother beheaded before him, and in his seat Matthew cringed because it was a horrifying moment, to witness a man reduced to such a state of helpless pain.

Lash snapped his fingers. One of the servants came forward with a glass of white wine on a silver tray. Lash took it and said to the table at large, "Someone should hold him while I get this down his throat."

Matthew almost stood up, but Julian sensed it and grasped his arm to prevent a move that would betray Matthew's innocence of English.

Lioness rose from her seat, came around the table and clamped her arms around both Krakowski and his chair. With one hand Lash pushed Krakowski's head back, said, "Drink this, Sandor. Come on, like a good boy." He got the glass against the sobbing man's lips and started pouring, and somehow in his chemical grief Krakowski realized the antidote was at his mouth and his tongue emerged to allow as much as could be swallowed. After the glass was empty the man continued to cry for another moment while Lioness restrained him and Lash rubbed his bald head as an attempt at further ease. At last Krakowski shuddered, gave a last hideous sob and a croaking noise and laid his sweating face down upon the table.

"There," Lash said. "He'll be shipshape in a few minutes."

SEVENTEEN.

Matthew stood before the fire in Samson Lash's parlor. Everyone had returned from the dining room after the unsettling—at least, to him—demonstration, and first to be escorted by the Owl to Lash's office with his satchel in hand was Bertrand Montague.

All but Matthew sat silently in the chamber. Seated in his chair across the room, Sandor Krakowski was still recovering. Every so often he gave an involuntary shudder and put his hands to his face as if to blot out some horrific dream. As a reward for his participation, he'd been given a glass of what Lash announced to be twenty-year-old French Armagnac. Krakowski had taken it gratefully but was not exactly sure why it was being given to him, since he told Lash and the others that he recalled hearing someone laughing at the table and after that he couldn't remember anything until he'd found himself back in the parlor, being given a glass of Armagnac.

While Krakowski had been semi-conscious with his face against the table, Lash had said to the rest of the assembly, "And there you see the effects of just one of *many* potions in the book. Doctor Firebaugh informs me that this particular formula is simple to follow and has a result that can be effectively timed."

"All well and good, sir," said Victor with the hint of a sneer, "but of what use is such a formula? Laughing and weeping…it's not *lethal*, is it?"

Lash had stood where he could stare directly and quite forcefully into Victor's eyes. "No, not lethal. Does anyone have an answer to Victor's question?" His gaze roamed the table. Then: "Count Pellegar? Your reputation for creativity precedes you. Care to venture a guess?"

Julian tapped a finger against the table a few times, gathering his thoughts. Matthew waited for what was to come, thinking that it had better be convincing, "I believe," Julian said, "that the potion mimics insanity. There are times it might be useful not to *kill*, but to *destroy.* To ruin a reputation, to make a man fall from favor…particularly a man who might be valued as an advisor. On the battlefield, an officer under such a spell would be unable to lead or to write out orders. No, it's not lethal…but it is deadly in its own way, and could cause the actual deaths of—I would say—thousands."

"*Thousands*," Lash repeated. He smiled and nodded. "Precisely correct."

Now, in the parlor, Julian was sitting in a chair between Merda and Victor, his white-powdered brow furrowed in contemplation and his fingers steepled before him. Lioness had taken a seat as far away from the others as possible, and had been brave enough to ask for another glass of red wine from Elizabeth Mulloy, who seemed to be acting as their gracious hostess during this period of waiting. Firebaugh sat wearing a pair of oval wire-rimmed spectacles, reading what appeared to be a weighty medical tome he'd brought from another room, and Matthew figured he must be staying here at the house under Lash's watch.

Matthew couldn't help but from time to time steal a glance at Julian. That ready recognition of what the insanity potion could do bothered him; Julian knew his evil, that was for sure. But it had dawned on Matthew that Jonathan Gentry's book of potions would be worth an untold fortune in the underworld, which was exactly why these assassins and representatives of like-minded powers were gathered here. These people lived on the will to

destroy, either from their own motivations or the money being paid them from corrupted rulers or those who wished to seize the crowns. This book was akin to *The Lesser Key of Solomon*; one was a compendium of the demons of Hell, and one was a compendium of how to loose those demons upon the earth.

The demons of chemical poisons, all there for the taking, and Doctor Lazarus Firebaugh available for one year to coax the deadly imps from their bottles. Matthew figured Firebaugh would be free to negotiate his own terms after the year had ended, so he was pretty much set for life. He burned to ask questions of the man, to find out how Firebaugh had gotten involved with this…indeed, he burned to ask questions of all the assembly, but for once his curiosity could not be fulfilled and he felt like going to the wall and chewing the paint off it.

But…something had begun to work in Matthew's mind concerning Mister Julian Devane, and he did not like where it was leading.

Surely Julian had recognized the value of the book. Who wouldn't? With that thing in hand, Julian would owe allegiance to no one. Julian would be gone on his own path in a shot, Fell be damned and Berry forgotten. Indeed, that pistol of Julian's might have a ball with Matthew's name already on it, if they walked out of here as winners of the auction.

So, the questions Matthew realized he might face were terrible.

Might he have to kill Julian to save the sanity of the woman he loved…and intended to ask to marry him, when she was—by God's grace—recovered?

Might he have to kill Julian to save his own life?

Julian suddenly lifted his chin and looked across at Matthew as if reading his mind; then, without a change of expression, he averted his gaze and once more sank into contemplation.

The fire crackled and popped at his back, but suddenly Matthew felt very cold.

"Can't someone tell me? *Who* was laughing?" Krakowski asked, still befuddled. He had presented this question once before and gotten no reply.

Matthew wondered if he was going to be fit enough in the head to offer a coherent bid. "I am confused!" Krakowski said.

Firebaugh looked up from his book. "Breathe deeply a few times, Sandor. That should help."

"Help? Help *what*?"

"Just breathe and *relax*."

Krakowski muttered something that was in his own language and unintelligible, but he did as the doctor said and closed his eyes.

"You must have a big brain," Merda said to Firebaugh. "A fucking genius. Are you?"

"The creator of the book, Doctor Jonathan Gentry, was a true genius," Firebaugh replied, "I try."

"You'll have to do better than *try*, when I have you in *my* country," Victor said. "My employers will expect more than table tricks."

"I shall deliver," Firebaugh answered, with a measure of regal dignity. "And I can promise you, sir, that the book's 'table tricks', as you call them, have the power to turn the tables on any enemy your employers see fit to destroy."

Julian suddenly broke from his state of contemplation. "Fine words," he said. "But I'd like specifics that Vice Admiral Lash failed to supply. For instance, how many potions are inscribed in that book? Even…how many pages does the damned thing have?"

"You'll get to see that for yourself, Count Pellegar." Elizabeth Mulloy had entered the room, bringing Montague back to the group, and Matthew noted that she could move as quietly as a cat. "The book is in Vice Admiral Lash's study. Madam Sauvage, I believe you are next."

Lioness retrieved her satchel and went with Miss Mulloy, while Montague sat scowling in a chair as if things had not gone as well as planned. Merda aimed a little chuckle in Montague's direction but when he didn't get a bite on his line he reeled it in and sat twiddling his thumbs.

"Doctor Firebaugh," Julian persisted in a quiet, smooth voice, "how does a member of your profession—and your standing—come to be

involved in this matter? I would think with your qualifications you'd be quite happy with a profitable life in this city. Who knows where you might wind up?"

"Yes," Montague said, "he might wind up in that hellhole called Berlin."

"Or somewhere in Africa," Merda spoke up. "A good question, Your Excellency. Let's hear it, doc."

Matthew pretended to be intent on toasting himself before the fire, but he was listening intently.

Firebaugh put aside his book and removed his spectacles. He rubbed his forehead, gazed up at the blue-sky ceiling for a moment and then said, "It is true I graduated with high honors from the Royal College of Physicians. I have studied medicine and chemistry, it seems, for most of my life. I am forty-two years old and for the last six years have been practicing at the Highcliff hospital, which is not quite a half-mile from this house. In fact, that was where I met the vice admiral four years ago, when he came in to have a—" He paused, obviously not knowing whether to reveal this bit of information.

"Check of his ball sack?" Merda prompted.

"A boil lanced," Firebaugh continued. "A minor thing, but it can become complicated. In any event, we began talking about things. Life in general. The condition of the world. And I told him my secret, the thing that I knew to be true but that I believe for years I hid even from myself."

"Pray don't leave us hanging," Julian said when Firebaugh was silent.

"I *detest* people," Firebaugh replied, his eyes slightly narrowed. "I have never married, I have no children, my mother and father are deceased and my only relative—a sister—is married and lives in the colonies, in Boston. I was never meant to be a physician to human beings. One of my instructors told me as much, many years ago. That my so-called 'bedside manner' was, as he put it, somewhere between execrable and non-existent. Oh yes, the *people* element of medicine is what I have failed at. It's my nature, to want to work alone. To want to *be* alone. I find great comfort and pleasure in solitude…yet to continue to

rise in stature as a physician in this city, one must at least *pretend* to have care and empathy for his patients." He shrugged. "Not I. I am simply of a medical *mind*, and I do not wish to be bothered by the blatherings, woes and corruptions of the sick."

"Interesting," said Julian. "A doctor who despises the idea of having living patients!" Matthew thought he couldn't have phrased it better himself.

"Why didn't you simply become a researcher?" Victor asked, obviously finding some value in this conversation. "You needn't have dealt with patients in that regard."

"Money issues," Firebaugh replied. "Let us say, I have grown accustomed to a certain standard of living. Laboratory researchers find their income and their advancement quite limited. I choose not to accept limits. At one point I expressed these feelings to the vice admiral, and obviously I made an impression. Therefore when the vice admiral asked me to lunch at his club one day and broached the subject of a particular book he was proposing to seize—and the fact that a great deal of money would surely be in the offing—I listened with open ears. And so I am here, gentlemen, ready to turn my medical mind to research beyond my wildest dreams… researching items that, as the vice admiral has said, have the power to change the world."

Yes, but would it be a world worth living in? Matthew wanted to ask. The answer given to himself was: Definitely not.

Merda laughed. "That's a knee-slapper, doc. Damned if I ever met a doctor who wanted to *kill* people instead of heal them."

"All in the name of research," said Firebaugh. "I see myself in a solitary place—in some other country, yes—but surrounded by my papers and my books and my…my *peace*," he said. "Precious solitude, in which to exercise my mind. And who knows what might come from the potions in that book? In my estimation, the formulas are intriguing and at least on paper promise to be extremely effective, but also…I wish to use them as starting points toward greater experiments."

Matthew didn't like the sound of that. Greater experiments? What? Poisoning the water supply of entire cities? It seemed to him that Firebaugh might not be content in his pursuit of solitude until half the world had perished.

"That's my story." Firebaugh stood up. "Pardon me while I resume my reading in my bedchambers, as I prefer the privacy there." His reverie done, the good doctor left the room.

Miss Mulloy brought Lioness back within fifteen minutes, about the same amount of time as Montague had spent. Both of them had left their satchels with Lash. "Next will be Mr. Krakowski," the young woman announced. "Sir, are you ready?"

"Yes, ready!" He stood up, took one stumbling misstep but corrected himself. He got his satchel and followed Miss Mulloy from the room.

"That's one we can count off," Merda said. "He'll make a fucking hash out of his bid." Merda stood up from his chair, stretched to his not very impressive full height and strolled over beside Matthew at the fireplace. He rubbed his hands before the fire, and then his small dark eyes took Matthew's measure. "Doesn't the baron ever *speak*?" he asked Julian.

"When he has something to say," Julian answered. "And then only in our language."

"He looks like a painted dummy." Merda reached up and flicked Matthew under the chin. "No offense, but it's the fucking truth." Matthew simply stared back at him, then with a snort of disgust—both playing his part and expressing his own truth—he walked away and settled himself into the chair Merda had just vacated.

Krakowski was brought back into the parlor in around ten minutes. Miss Mulloy took Victor away and Krakowski took a chair, closed his eyes and seemed to go to sleep right then and there. In a few minutes Lioness got up from her seat and circled the room, examining some of the marine paintings and signal flags that adorned the walls…or at least pretending to. When she got close to where Julian was sprawled in his chair

she turned toward him as if she hadn't realized he was there. "I have heard quite a lot about you and the baron," she said.

"Positive things, I hope," Julian replied.

"*Ha*," Montague said bitterly.

"*Interesting* things," Lioness answered. "You and the baron recently had dealings in Portugal, is that correct?"

"Hm," said Julian. "You heard this in *Africa*?"

"In France, where I stopped on business. I understood your dealings had to do with Duke de Valasco." It was a statement, not a question.

"Madam," Julian said with a thin smile, "I never discuss business when I am at work. And this waiting game—this entire affair—is to me, *work*."

Lioness nodded, but Matthew saw the shine in her eyes and he thought her animal nature had been aroused. "I understood Duke de Valasco contracted you and the baron to murder his elder brother, and you were rewarded with an item of—shall we say—*importance*."

"Importance is in the eye of the beholder."

"You know what I mean," said Lioness.

"And *I* know what's going on here!" Merda crowed. "The tall lady desires some Prussian cream in her cookpot! Ha! I'd always heard the black skins were—"

He stopped speaking when Lioness came upon him like a whirlwind, grasped the lapels of his jacket and lifted him off the floor with one hand, pulling him up toward the teeth clenched in her otherwise impassive face.

Merda opened his mouth wide.

He reached up to grab hold of the teeth that appeared too large for their aperture. With a *pop* the entire set of upper dentures and the shiny red roof of his mouth was in his hand, and turning it toward Lioness there was another small *click* and two small but ugly hooked blades shot out from the device. He held the blades at the level of her eyes, and Matthew saw that the sharp tips were perfectly spaced for the task of turning light into permanent night.

"Temper, temper," he said, his voice a bit slurred and the real front teeth only tiny pegs beneath the hard wax dentures.

She didn't let him go at once. She smiled—a hideous grimace—while Montague laughed and clapped like a drunk monkey and Krakowski roused himself from sleep to wonder what the hell was going on.

Matthew found himself thinking that if these two killed each other right now it would be two less to worry about, and then he was horrified at himself because he was becoming too much of a bad man, pretend or otherwise.

Still, it would be beneficial.

"Truce, tall lady?" Merda asked. "It would be a shame." Whether he meant a shame to blind her or to be shaken like a dog's bone and thrown into the fireplace he didn't make clear.

At that moment Miss Mulloy walked into the room with Victor. In a flash Merda's bootsoles were back on the floor, Lioness had turned away as if nothing had happened and the blades were retracted into the dental device and inserted into Merda's mouth.

Miss Mulloy lifted her chin, as if actually smelling the aroma of impending violence. "Is there any trouble here?" she asked.

"Just a little show," Montague replied. "Quite entertaining."

"Nothing to remark upon," Lioness offered. "That is, nothing I can't handle in my own way."

"I see," said Miss Mulloy after a short pause, and Matthew suspected she really did. Her soft brown eyes turned upon Julian. "Count Pellegar? You and the baron, next."

EIGHTEEN.

With Pellegar's satchel in his grip, Julian walked alongside Miss Mulloy through a long hallway at the rear of the house, as Matthew followed a few paces behind. Matthew noted a peculiar thing about the hallway: its walls began as the light blue of the rest of the house, but as it continued on the paint became a darker and darker blue, as if they were descending into the depths of the sea. The candle sconces mounted here and there did little to lighten the atmosphere. It was as if the hallway in its emulation of the sea were depriving the lungs of oxygen. Matthew felt fresh sweat under his arms and he wished he'd had the chance to apply more white powder to further mask both his features and his scar, but he had not. There was some sweat at his hairline under the heavy wig, but unless rivulets ran down his forehead he thought—hoped—he'd be all right.

All right. Now that was a ridiculous thought, in this hallway that seemed to be twenty fathoms deep.

"What is your place here?" Julian asked as they approached a large oak door at the hallway's end where the walls were nearly black: the sea's bottom, which claimed the bones of so many drowning men.

"My *place*?"

"Yes. Your elegant gloves, the very beautiful gown...are you—let me put it as well as a poor Prussian can—Vice Admiral Lash's permanent hostess?"

She gave him just the hint of a smile, but it was guarded and careful. "My gloves are my style. I always wear them. Thank you for the compliment on my gown. I *am* the hostess at this particular event, yes, but I also serve as the vice admiral's business advisor."

"Oh?"

"I have a head for numbers," she said. "He trusts my judgement and in return offers me a very rich life. Here we are." She opened the door. "After you gentlemen, please."

Julian and Matthew entered the room. Its walls were painted as dark as the last few feet of the hallway, yet there were pools of light from strategically placed lanterns. A large oval window gave a view to a snow-covered courtyard. Across a dark blue carpet trimmed with scarlet, Samson Lash sat behind an imposing desk that had a ship carved upon its front. One of the pools of light spread across the desktop and reflected up into the flame-bearded face. And there before Lash—right there atop the desk—was the book bound in red leather that held the potions created by Jonathan Gentry. Right there...so near and yet so far. Even as Matthew's gaze fell upon it, Lash caressed it with his huge left hand.

On the floor to one side of the desk was a basket containing the satchels of those who had come before. To the other side of the desk was a chair in which sat the white-suited Owl, his golden gaze already fixing upon Matthew.

It took Matthew a few seconds to register that someone else occupied a corner of the room beyond the desk, where the light did not reach. His heart seemed to stutter in his chest.

Cardinal Black sat in a chair with his spidery legs outstretched, the boots crossed at the ankles. His thin, angular frame in a coal-black suit with an ebony cloak about his shoulders indeed made Matthew think of a spider that had spun its web and now waited for the prey to become entangled. On the pale long-fingered hands with their sharpened nails were the multitude of silver rings cast in the shapes of skulls and strange satanic faces. The mane of sleek black hair that settled around the shoulders simply made the cardinal's pallid, weirdly elongated face appear even more ghostly-pale, as if it were a thing of smoke that had somehow taken form and hung in the air, its puncture-wounds of eyes unblinking. The flesh was drawn so tightly over the cheekbones that Matthew felt pain looking at it, thinking that at any second the bones would burst through. But pain was not the central perception Matthew gathered; the centrality was that of a silent evil, watching and waiting...the spider for the flies.

Miss Mulloy closed the door at their backs. She came around to stand at Lash's right side. In the low light, even her cherubic countenance had taken on too many shadows for Matthew's liking. He felt a shiver up his spine. The Owl was still staring at him, and how long would it be before the man mentally unmasked him and recalled seeing his face at The Green Spot?

"Before we begin," said Julian, who sounded amazingly calm in this den of Hell, "a word to the wise." He was speaking to Lash, but directing it to the Owl. "The others out there are getting somewhat restless. Arguments have begun. I note that no one had the presence of mind to remove the set of fireplace tools from the room. With those, any of the creatures in that parlor could commit mass murder."

Lash nodded. "See to it," he said to the air, and immediately the Owl left the room and once more closed the door.

Matthew would've breathed a sigh of relief, but now Cardinal Black was watching him...and Black had seen him face-to-face in Y Beautiful Bedd, if only for a short time but time enough. *Mister Corbett*, Black had said that night in the village's hospital. *I've heard much about you.*

"Gentlemen," said Lash, "I have been looking forward to this meeting, most of all."

"The baron and I are honored."

"Show me what you have."

Julian took the key from his pocket and unlocked the satchel. Matthew thought Julian must have nerves of steel, to have fitted that key in the locks so smoothly; if it had been up to him he'd still be fumbling with a sweat-slick key from now past midnight.

Julian opened the satchel and shook it until all ten of the gold bars had left their pockets and lay on the desk just short of the book.

The gold gleamed up into Lash's face. He reached out to run his fingers over one of the bars, and then he said quietly, "Where is the other half of your offer?"

"Ah. Here." Julian unsnapped the inner compartment and brought out the five pieces of parchment, and Matthew thought that if these weren't what Lash meant, they were both dead. In dramatic fashion, Julian laid down one sheet at a time, and when he was done Matthew caught the briefest shine of sweat through the powder on Julian's forehead.

Lash said nothing as he studied the sheets. He took an arm and pushed the gold bars and the book aside so that he could further arrange them to his liking. Miss Mulloy peered at the drawings over one of his massive shoulders. In the corner, Cardinal Black shifted his position just a few inches, as if the spider were preparing to strike.

Lash spoke.

"Excellent," he said. Then, with a rush of emotion: "*Excellent*! I knew you wouldn't fail me. Even though after our last communication I heard nothing more." He lifted his gaze to Julian and presented him with a scowl that would've withered Matthew to his knees. "You should have written to tell me you had these. I was left hanging for much too long."

"My apologies. I...didn't feel a letter was secure."

Lash looked upon the drawings once again. His scowl evaporated. A smile kept pulling at the corners of his mouth. "I accept your apologies. And what you say makes sense. What do you think, Elizabeth?"

"They're magnificent," she said.

"More than magnificent. They are...*everything* to me."

"Your happiness, sir," said Julian, "is our happiness. Does this mean we win the bidding?"

"It means you are far ahead in the running," Miss Mulloy answered, rather crisply for her position as hostess. "Vice Admiral Lash will take his time in making a decision. Also, Miles Merda has not offered his—"

"Elizabeth, let us not be too opaque in our appreciation, lest Count Pellegar think we hold this collection in low regard," said Lash. "As far as I'm concerned, you *will* be the winners. And yet..." His hand again caressed the red book. "I do have the luxury of time in which to consider. In any case, I have an entertainment planned for later which I think you gentlemen will enjoy. So let us not rush to any statements of completion."

"As I say, your happiness is—"

Lash laughed. He grinned fiercely up into Julian's face. "Do you two even *know* what it is you've brought to me? Can you even guess why I went to all that trouble to contract your services to Duke de Valasco?"

Julian hesitated, perhaps a beat too long. Then: "Of course. For the plans you have before you."

What Lioness had said in the parlor, Matthew remembered: *I understand Duke de Valasco contracted you and the baron to murder his elder brother, and you were rewarded with an item of—shall we say—importance.* Matthew wondered if the gold bars were not from this Portuguese duke but from some Prussian criminal group that desired the book, and the parchment plans had come along because Lash had in some way arranged for them to be part of the bid. If that was true, Lash had reached a hand nearly fourteen hundred miles to secure the sheets of parchment that he now seemed to be viewing with such excitement, and Matthew reasoned that this plan must have been at least a year in the making.

"You don't *know*," said Lash, with a trace of pity for the uninformed and stupid Prussians in the room. "This is the *future* of warfare, gentlemen. You have brought me plans drawn up in 1664 by a Spanish inventor named Ferriz Maldonado. He unfortunately was also a drunkard, and he died of drink in 1670. His life's work was scattered to the winds, some of

it burned to ashes in a fire. Do you know what Maldonado's life's work *was*, Count Pellegar?"

"I fear I do not."

"The dream that all laughed at him for, and drove him further into decline. These are plans for an *airship*."

"A *what*, sir?"

"*Air*," Lash rumbled, "*ship*. In the shape of a dragon, with four wings, powered by a system of steampipes radiating from a central kettle. It was Maldonado's belief that a flame-throwing device could be rigged within the dragon's mouth—much like the mortar cannons currently used on a few of the ships in the Royal Navy—and in so doing make it into the world's most fearsome weapon: a machine to rain death down from the *skies*."

Matthew was nearly tempted to give a noncommittal utterance. He'd never heard of such a thing, and it sounded like madness. An *airship*? A flying dragon spitting flame down upon the battlefield? Well...yes, he saw how that could change the entire world of warfare, how the great ships of every navy would be in danger of the thing's fire, how no fortresses could stand before the thing—or God forbid a fleet of the things—and how the infantry would run for their lives at the dragon's mere shadow, but...it was *madness*! It had to be!

Wasn't it?

"I am going to build it," Lash said.

Did Cardinal Black give a quiet laugh from his dark corner? Or was it the laugh of Satan himself, awakened and listening to this most wonderful news of the night?

"Tell the baron," was Lash's next statement.

With hardly a pause Julian said to Matthew "*Airshippen, em builden*," and Matthew replied "*Jaaaaa*," as if this were the most interesting idea in the world.

Lash spent a moment surveying the plans once more, obviously enthralled by these five sheets of parchment. "When I was a small boy—a

boy," he corrected, for Matthew figured he was never considered small, "I was struck down with a fever. I lay in bed near death for many days. But in that fever I had visions of such things as this before me. Visions of great airships commanding the sky. Huge fleets of them sailing through the clouds and spitting fire on the enemy below. When I came out of that fever, I was consumed by another: the visions I had seen, and yet they seemed so *real*. I understood even then, as I played with my toy boats, what power airships might bring to whoever owned them. And as I grew older the resolve grew as well, that this was the future of warfare, and I would be the man to make it so."

"A worthy cause, indeed," said Julian, who shot a quick glance at Cardinal Black before returning his attention to Lash.

"Yes," Lash agreed. "Worthy. But expensive. My money comes from my family. Yarrow Huxley of the Huxley Shipyards was my grandfather, responsible for building many of the navy's greatest ships. My path to the vice-admiralty was greased by the oil of that labor. I long to make a name for myself, one that will stand for eternity. This before me…this is my destiny."

"Fate will smile upon you, I'm sure," said Julian.

Lash looked up into Julian's face. His mouth crimped and his eyes seemed to catch blue flame. "It will take more than the whim of *Fate*. It will take my working in secret, until the moment the airship is complete, the weapon is in place, and I will demonstrate it to—" He trailed off, and the flame of his eyes suddenly iced over.

"To whom, sir?" Julian prodded.

When Lash spoke again, his voice was hushed and it was as if he were talking to a league of ghosts in the room. "*They*," he said. "They…don't believe in my idea. Oh, I've presented it to them. The high officials of the navy. I have told them that someday the ship of the sea will be outdone by the ship of the air. I've presented all my reasons. I have described to them in detail the visions that came to me. But they don't want to hear it, and they cannot see the future. They look at me as if I have betrayed the

navy...or as if I have lost my mind. The ship of the sea, they say, will *never* be outdone, not in a thousand years." Lash lifted a thick index finger and tapped it against his shaggy skull. "I know better. I have been given these visions for a *reason*. I have been entrusted to build this airship. *Me*, out of all the people in this world who have ever lived. Do you understand the importance—the responsibility—that has been thrust upon me?"

Julian gave a nod. Matthew was thinking that if Samson Lash was not fully mad, he was only a few steps away from the tumble-chute to Bedlam. These visions of his had flamed his imagination yet at the same time begun burning his candle out at a young age. And how could he be certain this dragon of the air would fly, even if the plans were valid enough to build the thing? It seemed to Matthew that Lash desperately wanted to believe it was possible to create a working airship, if only to show the navy he was right—and not half insane—and to step out from the Huxley shadow.

But...the book. The book of potions, with its binding of red leather, was right there on the desktop before Matthew, only a few feet away.

No gun or dagger, Cardinal Black's eyes on him, Samson Lash big enough to strangle a horse and even Miss Mulloy now looking sinister in the low lantern light.

There was no way out but to play this game to the end.

"Thank you for your offer," said Miss Mulloy, as Lash had begun a closer examination of the plans. The gold bars remained untouched on the desktop. "I'll take you back to the parlor now."

"Very well," Julian answered. "But am I to—"

"Come along, please." Miss Mulloy was already at the door. Matthew's skin crawled as he turned his back on Cardinal Black, who remained sitting motionlessly in the corner.

With their return to the parlor, they found the Owl seated amid the group to prevent any further squabbling. They could only wait as Merda was escorted by Miss Mulloy back to Lash's study, and Matthew kept as far as possible from the Owl while the last bidder's offer was being contemplated.

Merda and Miss Mulloy returned after about ten minutes. When they walked into the parlor Victor stood up from his chair and asked, "All right, what happens now?"

"Now," said the lady, "you wait for the vice admiral's decision. In the meantime there is to be some entertainment I need to arrange, so if you'll pardon me. More wine is on the way."

"Dare we drink it?" Montague was on his feet as well. "It occurs to me that with all the treasure before him in that study, Lash could just poison us all and be done with it. Then he could put that damned book up for auction a second time."

"Ah," said Julian, who mirrored what Matthew was thinking to say, "a good point. What assurance do we have that we will leave this house alive? After all, as the vice admiral said…this is his house and his rules."

The Owl stood up. "Your caution is noted but unnecessary. As Miss Mulloy will verify, Vice Admiral Lash is an honorable man. He did not organize this event to offend or antagonize the various guilds and affiliations you represent. I daresay that if none of you returned to your bases of operation, those same guilds and affiliations might communicate with each other and take a dim view of the vice admiral's disposal of their finest resources. Thus this event is a legitimate auction, not a prelude to murder, and the winner will indeed leave here with the book and a pair of bodyguards."

"Good to hear," Lioness quietly said from her seat in the far corner. "It would displease me to be forced to end the vice admiral's life tonight."

No one spoke in the wake of that statement. Matthew thought that of all the killers gathered here this snowy eve, Lioness Sauvage and Miles Merda might be the most formidable, Victor next in terms of danger, then Montague and lastly Krakowski as an unknown due to the drug's effects. With the real Count Pellegar and Baron Brux in attendance, that would have made a malignant seven. As it was, it was still a malignant seven if one counted Lash and Cardinal Black. In any case…way too many killers in one room for his taste.

"The Owl is correct," said Miss Mulloy, who aimed her voice toward Lioness. "The vice admiral is an honorable man. Pardon me now, I'm needed elsewhere." She turned away and left the room.

Matthew settled himself back into a chair, as did Julian. The Owl walked over to warm his pale hands by the fireplace and Matthew suffered a start; if the Owl connected him with the memory of The Green Spot's fireplace…

But for the moment it did not happen. Matthew kept his face averted, staring at the floor. He wondered about Lash being such an 'honorable man'. How did an honorable man, even being so driven as he was to both seize the book of potions and get the airship plans, wind up in partnership with Cardinal Black? And this whole affair had the whiff of madness—or desperation—about it. Matthew wondered if the Owl was not the link that had connected Lash with Black, and Lash's money and warped purpose had found a ready hand from the cardinal and Black's gang of cutthroats—the same gang that had killed all the Broodies for their supply of the drug-laced gin called White Velvet. Again, the seizing of the book and this auction had to have been planned for nearly a year, and how Lash had gotten in contact with the various assassins' guilds and so forth was a mystery; perhaps that too was the Owl's doing. Matthew imagined that if Lash had not been successful in getting the book that night, these killers would've executed him on the spot for having come all the distances for nothing, so Lash had taken a dangerous risk indeed.

And also there was the second book that Black had been after but had failed to get: the copy of *The Lesser Key of Solomon* that had been in Fell's library. Surely Black realized that if Mother Deare had not met him at the tower near Adderlane, as planned, she had either been captured by the professor or had lost her life. So…though Lash's purpose for the raid had been carried out, the failure to get that second book must be a source of irritation—possibly anger—for the cardinal.

A servant with glasses of red wine on one of the ubiquitous silver trays appeared and roamed the room, but the wine was accepted only by Merda

and Krakowski, who evidently had not had enough of a bad thing. After a few moments, a second servant came in to say, "Gentlemen and madam? If you'll follow me, please."

"Be ready for anything," Julian whispered to Matthew as they followed at the end of the human caravan. The servant opened a door in another hallway and down they went along a set of lantern-illuminated stone steps. Further down and the walls themselves became formed of what looked to be ancient gray stone, and then the stairs led them through an arched passageway and by the light of several lamps Julian and Matthew saw a series of stone benches arranged above and around a circular dirt-floored pit.

Matthew noted chains hanging from the ceiling, ending in a set of manacles, and what appeared to be leg irons hammered into the earth directly beneath the chains. Whatever this was, it did not bode well.

Seated on one of the benches on the uppermost row of the circle were Lash and, a few feet away, Cardinal Black. Lash leaned forward to watch the procession file in, while Black simply sat staring down into the pit as if oblivious of everyone else.

Lash said, "Take your seats, wherever you wish. All the views are sufficient."

Matthew and Julian sat down behind and to the right of Lioness. Off to their left a distance was Victor. The others spaced themselves around the circle.

"What is this, a fucking dungeon?" Merda asked, his childlike voice echoing off the stones.

"My house is built over a Roman bear-baiting pit," Lash answered. "I didn't know it until the builder found it. Actually, there are Roman tunnels all through this area and leading under the park as well."

Matthew saw an oak door down in the pit's wall. As he was looking at it, there was the noise of a bolt being thrown and two of the guards came through dragging a naked man. A third guard followed behind. Rapidly the three men set about chaining the unfortunate's wrists to the manacles and then his ankles to the leg irons. The victim tried to struggle but

obviously he was in no shape to do so, for his pale and thin body already bore an ugly patchwork of bruises from earlier rough treatment. When they were done, the naked man was stretched to full length by the tautness of the chains, his arms up above his head and his body curved in what was nearly a half-moon crescent so that his chest jutted forward.

Matthew realized it was a position of complete helplessness. Whatever was to follow, the man might shake from side to side but he could not protect any portion of himself.

"I ain't done nothin'!" the man called out, his voice mangled by what must've been swollen lips and broken teeth. "Hear me?" He rattled his chains and his body swung a bit but no more; his arms appeared so strained they were about to be disjointed from the shoulders. He lifted his head and looked up at the gallery through terrified and bruise-slitted eyes. "Listen...please...I ain't done nothin'!"

"What kind of entertainment is this to be?" Montague asked, as the guards retreated to take up positions around the pit. "I fancy there is violence involved?"

Matthew was sure of it. He was braced for what was to come, and all he could do was sit and watch.

"Oh, indeed," Lash replied. "I have taken the liberty of plucking two constables off the streets. Two small men whose disappearance will hardly be noted." As Lash was speaking, Matthew saw the arrival of the Owl and a pair of servants; one of the servants held a drum and the other a penny whistle. The Owl took a seat between Lash and Cardinal Black but the servants remained standing nearly side-by-side at the top of the gallery.

"I have come to despise dumb authority," Lash was saying. "Over the course of years, I have seen how small men destroy large—and great—ideas. If I had my way, all the small men would be trussed up in that pit. It would be better for London, and for the world, to be rid of the stumbling-blocks to true progress. I realize also that you gentlemen and madam have had your own misfortunes with such men, whether they represent a tainted law or a tainted house of royalty. And also...I have a companion

who needs…shall we say…proper expression every so often, therefore I have used this pit several times in the last few years. It is a release for her, and I believe you will all enjoy the spectacle." He waved toward the two servants. The one with the drum started a steady beat with the palm of his hand while the other began a weird, lilting melody on the whistle.

"I give you the hidden animal within Elizabeth Mulloy," said Lash. "In this arena, known as RakeHell Lizzie."

One of the guards, on cue, opened the door down in the pit.

A few seconds passed. The drumbeat and the weird melody kept going. Then suddenly a completely nude Elizabeth Mulloy came through. Her lithe body glistened with oil under the lantern light. Her eyes were sunken in pools of dark purple makeup, and black lines had been drawn on the angles of her face as if to resemble a painted doll. As she took appraisal of the hanging man it seemed to a dazed Matthew that he could see in her eyes the leap of a red spark, like a tinderbox just about to birth its flame.

She had removed the elegant gloves that she'd remarked were her style of fashion, yet had replaced them with elbow-length gloves of another nature.

These were made of black leather and bore long curved talons of blue-edged steel.

RakeHell Lizzie advanced upon the helpless constable, and Matthew realized he was about to witness murder on a scale beyond the horrific.

NINETEEN.

The creature that had been the demure hostess was gone. In its place was another killer to add to the list, and RakeHell Lizzie wasted little time in displaying her talents.

As the drumbeat and the penny whistle played their strange carnivale, the woman slinked in a circle around the chained constable, her rhythms that of the drum. Then upon completion of the circle—as if she had been an animal looking for the right place to strike—she leaped upon her victim with a bound of her gleaming body, her small breasts pressed against his gray-haired chest, and she began to lick his face with her legs wrapped around his hips and the deadly claws at his shoulders. The chains rattled and the man cried out for mercy. Someone in the gallery laughed. Matthew chose not to lay eyes upon whoever it was, for he felt that all of them held sadistic glee in their dark hearts, and none more so than Samson Lash and Cardinal Black.

RakeHell Lizzie climbed up the man and then up the chain, her blades striking sparks against the iron. She stood on his manacled hands and swung his body from one side to the other, again in keeping with the drumbeat. Sliding back down again, she peered into the constable's face for several seconds, what Matthew thought was a terrible stare of triumph

for whatever demons ruled Elizabeth Mulloy. The man moaned "No… please…no," and then with a dramatic flourish of her boyish arms her blades bit into his shoulders.

Matthew could not close his ears to the cry of pain, but RakeHell Lizzie was only playing with the man for the cuts hardly drew blood. The blades caressed his face, roamed across his forehead and combed through the sparse gray hair of his scalp. Matthew shot a quick glance at Julian and saw that he was completely without expression, but Matthew had to wonder if the bad man was not at least a little intrigued by this danse macabre.

The woman writhed upon the constable in a parody of sexual intimacy. The claws touched here and there, but lightly, drawing not blood but cries from the helpless man. Matthew thought it could be upon him to save the constable's life…but how? It was impossible! No, he had no recourse but to sit and watch, and squirm on the stone bench as the others seemed to be leaning forward for better views into the pit.

And as he was thinking this, suddenly RakeHell Lizzie lived up to her name by sinking her claws into the man's sides. While he screamed and thrashed to no avail, she drew the deadly gloves up along the bleeding sides to his armpits…and then she did it again, slowly and methodically. The claws left his sides and went to his face. In a matter of two seconds they had torn away chunks of flesh and the crimson blood streamed down in rivulets. She pressed herself against the bleeding body, her legs locked around his hips, and to the beat of the drum and the whistle's eerie tune she began to shred the flesh from his back with long, slow strokes. Through his pain the constable tried to bite at her face but she was too quick for him; her head jerked from side to side, and Matthew saw the terrible smile on her twisted mouth.

Now the claws really went to work. RakeHell Lizzie was so fast her movements were nearly a blur. Matthew realized how she had gained the musculature of her upper arms; it was hard work to butcher a human being, but she made it look easy. Before Matthew's eyes the constable

In the Pit with RakeHell Lizzie

was being shredded to pieces, and though the man's tortured body violently shook the chains he could not shake her off. His ragged screams filled the chamber but there was no mercy for him. He was doomed. Blood had pooled on the dirt below him and he was only a few minutes from being a ghost.

A few minutes? No, not that long.

The claws crisscrossed his chest, piercing deep. A mist of blood swirled in the air. The smell of it made Matthew's temples pound and his stomach writhe. He must've shuddered as if he were fighting off sickness, because suddenly Julian's hand was gripping his shoulder like a clasp of iron, and when he looked into the bad man's painted face Julian mouthed a single word: *No.*

RakeHell Lizzie dropped off the dying man. She stepped back a few paces to admire her work. Her head cocked to one side, deliberating.

And then, like an artist completing her work, she darted back in. With a flurry of strikes that threw bits of flesh and streamers of blood into the air she opened up his stomach. All the blue-tinged, ruddy and pink-edged insides that the body concealed slid out from the gaping wounds, and at this someone—Montague?—gave a shout of appreciation for the kind of art he obviously admired. The constable's hollowed-out body continued to thrash and writhe, but the mouth was open and the eyes stared blankly in the fish-belly-white face, and Matthew knew it was just the muscles contracting at the last moment of life. He looked down at his boots, his own face flaming red with shame behind the white powder of his masquerade.

"Bravo!" said Merda, who accompanied his statement with hand-clapping. He was addressing Lash. "I admire your definition of *small* men, sir!"

That brought a laugh even from Lioness. The music had stopped. Matthew didn't wish to watch, but he could hear the chains rattle as the body was being taken down by the three men who had trussed the constable up.

"Your Excellency!" It was Lash speaking. "Is the baron not one to enjoy such entertainment?"

Matthew looked toward the vice admiral and saw that the Owl had leaned over to whisper in the man's ear; he made a presumption that 'the baron' had been noticed averting his eyes from the bloodshed.

"Not at all!" Julian replied, with the nudge of an elbow into Matthew's ribs. "He, like I, am in amazement at the lady's prowess. It seems to both of us that she should be a member of the profession. As long as she stays out of Prussia, I might add."

Lash shouted a laugh at what was to Matthew an odious witticism, but neither the Owl nor Cardinal Black allowed a smile to cross their faces. Both of them were staring daggers at Matthew, who gave them a nod of the head and then forced himself to gaze upon the result of the carnage below.

The dead constable had been dragged aside and left lying. The men who had taken him down were gone, the pit's door still open. RakeHell Lizzie was stretched out on her back in the dirt, her eyes closed in whatever state of repose she could find...which meant to Matthew that this spectacle was not yet ended.

Suddenly another naked man was dragged in through the doorway, struggling against his three escorts but obviously weakened from having been beaten about the face.

It took Matthew a few seconds to recognize who it was. When he did he gave a gasp, his body involuntarily shuddered and his first impulse was to leap to his feet, but again Julian's iron hand gripped Matthew's arm to hold him in his place.

"Steady," Julian whispered. And then: "You know this man?"

"*Ja*," Matthew answered, dazed. He cast off the pretend language. "*Yes*."

Down in the blood-stained pit, the men were chaining up Dippen Nack.

"God save me, I never did a thing again' ya," Nack was blubbering through a mouth swollen by the impact of hard knuckles. The ruddy-faced little bully's right eye was completely closed and a goose-egg of a knot adorned his forehead. "Never a thing, I swear to Christ!" he said, and when he broke into a sob the mucus ran from his nostrils down onto his white and hairless chest.

"Make him beg!" Victor called out. "That first one went too easily!"

With a pitiful cry Nack broke loose from his captors, but one leg had already been trapped by a manacle and so all he did was fall into the blood and guts left by the previous victim. He was hauled up, stretched out and his wrists cuffed to the chains above him, then the other leg was locked in the second iron and he was shackled and ready for the kiss of Lizzie's blades. The guards once more took up positions of watch within the pit.

Matthew again gave a shudder. He had never been able to stand Dippen Nack—who could, but his mate in stupidity Gardner Lillehorne?—and yet…God, this was a terrible way for any man to leave the earth, sobbing and trussed up for the slaughter, soon to have his insides sliding down his legs like so much wet garbage. Matthew put a hand to his forehead, both to think and to determine what he should do, for it seemed to him that sitting watching these murders along with the others made him too much of a bad man for his comfort.

"Listen to me," whispered Julian, leaning close to Matthew's ear. "I know you by now and I know what you're thinking. Firstly, drop your hand before you rub the powder off that scar. Secondly, you can do *nothing*. Hear me? *Nothing*. Nod your head that you understand."

Matthew dropped his hand, but he did not nod. He had already scarred himself with a deeper mark by sitting still while that first innocent man was murdered…now, to sit still a second time *knowing* what was to happen? Dippen Nack or not…it was a mark of cardinal black against his soul.

The drumbeat started up again, slow and methodical. The penny whistle began a different tune, but still eerie. Matthew saw RakeHell Lizzie turn over on her belly and begin to crawl toward Dippen Nack, and Nack shook his chains and screamed like a little child, his pudgy nude body ripe for the slashing.

"Mark this," Julian whispered, but now with grit in his voice. "You say *anything*, and we are dead. Your ladyfriend is lost forever. So whatever you're thinking in that primrose garden of your mind, come back to reality. Hear me?"

RakeHell Lizzie was up on one knee. She held her deadly gloves out toward Nack and clacked the blades together…*clack clack…clack clack…*

"Swing on him!" Merda called. "Go to it, dearie!"

She stood up from the bloodied dirt. She circled him, as she had the first man, as Nack whimpered and fought weakly against chains that would not be broken.

Then she leapt upon him.

Once more she climbed up his body and then shimmied back down to peer into his swollen face. Her legs locked around his hips. The claws caressed his cheeks, and this time she kissed his forehead as a prelude to murder.

Matthew felt near passing out. The chamber swung about him. Merda clapped his hands in time with the drumbeat and Krakowski followed suit. Matthew looked toward Lash, Cardinal Black and the Owl, who were all leaning slightly forward in anticipation.

Nack let out a scream, because one of Lizzie's claws was travelling down his chest—slowly, slowly—drawing lines of blood in their wake.

"Sit *still*," Julian hissed.

Sweat was on Matthew's face. Bad man or good man? To speak out… what good would it do? It was a hopeless situation…to speak out…hopeless…Nack was doomed…to speak out…he and Julian would also be doomed…and Berry lost in the grip of her insanity…hopeless…

"Please…please…I ain't done nothin'!" Nack begged, and once more he screamed as RakeHell Lizzie's other glove travelled down his chest and more lines of blood bloomed.

Hopeless.

But when had that ever stopped him from doing what he knew to be right?

The claws made circles over Nack's belly. In a matter of seconds Nack—for all his boasts and bullying and prideful strutting—would be on his way to becoming a sack of dead meat.

No, Matthew thought.

He stood up, and as he did Julian grabbed at him but he shook the hand off.

"Stop this!" Matthew said.

The drumbeat and the whistling abruptly halted. All eyes—even those of RakeHell Lizzie—turned upon him.

"Oh dear God," Julian muttered, and lowered his head.

"My name is Matthew Corbett," was the next thing from Matthew's mouth, and it seemed extraordinarily loud in the chamber, echoing around the walls. Matthew had an instant of thinking himself to be utterly insane, but he steeled himself and plowed onward. "I am a member of the Herrald Agency," he decided to say. "Right now this house is surrounded by armed men. It is useless to continue this…if I and the man before you are not allowed to leave—with the book of potions in hand—they will storm this house and—"

Cardinal Black was on his feet. He came toward Matthew like a walking storm.

Julian stood up. "This man killed Baron Brux and took his place! He forced me into this!" Even as practised an actor as he was, the desperation in his voice was evident. "But what he says is true! The house is surrounded!"

As Cardinal Black reached Matthew, Lash and the Owl were on their feet. Lash struck the Owl with an open palm on the shoulder and the white-suited security man hurriedly left the chamber through its archway to presumably check outside. Black stood before Matthew, yanked off the high wig, spat into his hand and rubbed the spittle across Matthew's forehead, wiping off the powder and revealing the scar he had seen in their encounter at Y Beautiful Bedd.

Cardinal Black smiled. On that weirdly elongated face it was more of a grotesque leer.

"Indeed it is Mister Corbett," Black said. His eyes went to Julian. "And here we must have…Julian Devane, I presume, with a shaved head? Making inquiries of Geoffrey Britt…we knew you were in London, nosing around. And here you are, the both of you."

Trapped in the spider's web, he might have said.

Matthew saw that the others were all now on their feet, some watching in bemusement and others more concerned according to their temperaments. Lash settled himself back down upon the stone bench. "I'll be damned!" he said, with a whoosh of breath that could've filled a mainsail. "You two have got some cannonballs in your breeches! Look at them, friends! Come here to join our auction under false pretenses! What happened to the real Prussians?"

Julian lifted his chin. He gave a smile that said he was not dead yet, and far from it. "We carved them up and threw them in the gutter with the other pieces of shit. By the way, they had execrable taste in clothing."

"*Matthew*?" A weak voice called. "Matthew...where are you?"

It was Nack, calling from the lip of the grave with RakeHell Lizzie still entwined about his body.

"Here," Matthew answered, though he still stared into the merciless eyes of Cardinal Black. "We're going to get out of this house, lest it be attacked by the thirty men out—"

"*Only* thirty men?" Lash interrupted. He gave a short, harsh laugh. "Why not *fifty*? Hellfire, why not *one hundred*?"

"He's lying, isn't he?" Montague asked, with a measure of fear. "I didn't bargain for this!"

Lioness reached out a long arm, roughly took hold of Matthew's chin and turned his face toward hers. Her nostrils flared as she sniffed the air. "He's lying," she said. "I can smell it."

"Really?" Matthew had a fire in his belly now, and his painted eyebrows went up. "Why would we be so *stupid* as to come here alone?"

Beside him, Julian gave a cough and sounded for a moment as if he were choking.

"They have come—alone—to steal the book back for Professor Fell," said Black, speaking to all the group but to Lash in particular. "Tell me this, Devane: what happened to Mother Deare?"

"Dearly departed," was the reply.

"I thought as much when she didn't meet me as planned. So Fell still has the book *I* wanted...which is a great shame and angers myself and my master." A thin finger traced a Devil's Cross on Julian's forehead. "Soon to be departed, yourself."

"Well," said Julian with a shrug, "every dog needs a master...and I had a looksee in that tower at your work on a small boy. I'd like to have five minutes in a room with you to show you how a big boy fights."

Lash laughed again, the booming voice circling the chamber. "Listen to him go on! But you won't get your five minutes, sir. In fact, your clock is fast ticking down."

"Matthew!" Nack called. "Please...I'm beggin'...get me out of this."

"Kill 'em all and be done with it!" said Merda. "I'm wanting some desert to go with my dinner."

"Yes," Victor added, as he sat back down on his bench. "Finish them all."

"Patience," Lash said. "We will wait for the Owl to return. Hold your place, Lizzie, I doubt your dance is done for the night."

Julian sat down and stretched his legs out over the bench below him. "You do understand, Lash, that Matthew and I brought you what you wanted. Doesn't that mean we win the auction?"

"You were not *invited*," said the vice admiral. "You brought what the Prussians offered. I'll take it, with my thanks. Otherwise, I will continue to consider who wins the book and the services of Doctor Firebaugh. *The end*," he added.

"Of both of you," said Black.

In the space of a few minutes, as Nack continued to struggle weakly and Lizzie clutched to him like a leech, the Owl returned. "I sent some men out into the park," he told Lash, while his head slowly turned nearly over his shoulder to take in Matthew and Julian. "The first report is that there are no footprints in the snow. If there's a raiding party out there, they are hiding up in the trees."

"An invisible raiding party, I presume," said Lash. He stroked his flame-streaked beard. "So much for a delay to our entertainment. Musicians, begin. Lizzie, continue."

As the drum and the whistle started up once more, RakeHell Lizzie's claws went to work again on Nack's chest. Nack screamed out Matthew's name…once more…and a third time, his voice rising to heights of utter terror…until the blades slashed his throat and the blood filled his mouth and spilled over in a torrent.

Matthew looked down. Cardinal Black seized his jaw and twisted his head toward the unholy spectacle of Dippen Nack's body being opened by the gore-clotted blades.

At last, as Nack's insides tumbled down from the steaming cavity to the dirt, the bloodied RakeHell Lizzie fell off him and sat on her knees a distance away, her head bent forward and sweat shining on her back. Nack was already dead, but his body trembled on in spasms of muscle making the chains rattle their own weird tune. To add to the horror, Matthew realized the final sound from Nack's mouth was the cry of his name, begging for help that would not be given.

"Well done," said Lash. He motioned for the musicians to stop and at the final note he led the applause. RakeHell Lizzie remained on her knees, obviously winded by her efforts. "Dear?" he asked. "Are you able to dance with two more?"

She breathed in and out a few times, and then she answered, "One."

"Good enough," Lash agreed. Again he stroked his beard as he regarded the false Prussians. "All right," he said, coming to a decision. "Let us prepare Mr. Corbett."

TWENTY.

Matthew regained consciousness as his arms were being stretched above him and secured by the wrist manacles. The pit spun about him, his eyes were unfocused and his brain dazed by the blow that had been given to him on the back of the head, but even so he realized the three men—whether the Owl's security men or Lash's attendants, what did it matter?—had not yet trapped his ankles in the irons, and so he fought.

It was a losing proposition. One of the men hit him in the ribcage with the same short wooden club that had previously clouted his head, the pain blew the air from Matthew's lungs and the next blow from a fist to the side of his jaw rocked his head and sent him once more into a haze. He felt the irons clamp around his ankles. His spine was stretched by the tension of the chains above, and so his naked body was bowed slightly forward as had been the other two men who were torn apart this night.

"Wait a moment until he recovers." It was Lash's voice, seemingly speaking from a great distance. "We want him fresh." That brought a spate of sadistic laughter from the assembled killers, and in his state of disrepair Matthew thought he had reached the position of being a low-hanging apple on a tree, ready to be turned into pulp.

He had been taken from the gallery by the three men—Owl's or Lash's, whomever—and marched down a set of stone steps, then across the bloody pit where RakeHell Lizzie sat on her haunches watching him, her taut nude body gleaming with gore and the sweat of her exertions.

He was pushed through the doorway along a stone-floored passageway, the ceiling barely above his head, and then into another small lantern-lit room where obviously the first constable and Nack had been kept, judging from the scatter of clothes on the floor. In this room he received an initial blow from the wooden club across the shoulderblades and a punch to the belly that made his knees sag, at which point the trio of toughs went about tearing the gloves, jacket, blouse, breeches, stockings and boots off him. He tried to fight once more, and then the club got him on the back of the head and that was all he knew until he felt his arms being pulled up nearly to the edge of having his shoulders dislocated from their joints.

Now, hanging from the chains with his ankles locked into the irons, Matthew Corbett looked up toward the gallery and saw Julian sitting with Lioness on one side of him, Victor on the other and Cardinal Black behind him. The cardinal had a length of rope looped around Julian's throat and had situated himself so that he might increase the pressure should Julian's chin drop a fraction of an inch.

"He's come around!" Merda said. "Go to it, darling!"

"I give the commands here, sir," said Lash. The vice admiral leaned forward, his palms on his knees. "Well, Mr. Corbett! You shall be the last act of our entertainment for the evening. I'm sure the pleasure is all yours."

What use was there to struggle? The sweat was running down his face and burning his eyes. His backbone felt stretched into fiery pain. It occurred to him, oddly, that upon his death he would probably have gained two inches in height.

Did he have a reply to this? Some sort of witticism that would delay the onslaught of those deadly blades? Something? *Anything*?

No. He did not.

Lash motioned to the musicians. The drumbeat began. The whistle started up, a different weird tune to escort Matthew to the grave.

RakeHell Lizzie stood up, leaned over to touch the blades upon the earth so as to stretch her own muscles, and then she straightened up and advanced upon Matthew like a slinky cat.

"Take him!" Montague called. "Carve his guts out!"

But Lizzie was in no hurry. It was her performance—her last dance of the evening, as it were—and she was going to take her time. Which Matthew realized was to heighten his suffering, because the end would be prolonged. As the girl circled him, Matthew cast another look at Julian, who appeared nearly strangled by Black's rope. The bad man could do nothing but sit and watch with the others.

Hopeless, Matthew thought, and this time he knew it was true. But could he fight her off when she jumped at him? Could he get his teeth on her—

She jumped.

And she was fast. She wrapped herself around him, and though she was lithe and small-boned her weight further bowed his back and almost brought a cry of renewed pain from him. Before it escaped he caught it in his throat. She stared into his eyes and lifted her eyebrows as if expecting—or asking—him to beg for mercy. Matthew was determined not to do so, for what would it accomplish? He was not afraid of death—not very much, at least—but his impulse at the moment was to weep…not for himself, but for the waste of the beautiful Berry Grigsby who was now doomed to a further and irreversible descent.

Lizzie's claws were at his sides. They picked and probed at his ribs, but they did not yet draw blood. Matthew closed his eyes. He could shake his body from side to side, but this would simply increase his pain and it certainly would not shake her off. He felt her breath on his face…and then her tongue as she licked his cheeks.

Up she climbed upon him, licking at his arms and then at his hands trapped in the manacles. It was just a matter of time now before the claws

truly went to work, and what good had it been to try to save the life of Dippen Nack? The good man had made a blunder and the bad man had been right. It was just a matter of time, as the drum beat on and the whistle shrilled.

She came back down. Her claws clamped to his sides, but again not yet drawing blood.

He braced for the hideous pain.

But suddenly he felt the pressure of the blades ease.

He opened his eyes.

RakeHell Lizzie was still staring into his face, but something about her had changed. He didn't know what it was, or why, but something… her face…a softening…a departure of the desire to murder, just like that in an instant.

Abruptly, the nude girl climbed off him and left him swinging in his chains.

"Samson," she said up to the gallery, "pardon me, but I believe you're making a business mistake." The music ceased, on a note of bewilderment.

"Oh? What mistake would that be?"

Lizzie walked away from Matthew, through the blood and insides of two butchered men, and looked up at Lash with her gloved claws crossed in front of her chest. "They came here to get the book back for Professor Fell. The professor must want it very badly. Why not give him a chance to make a bid?"

"*What*?" Victor had nearly screamed it. "That's outrageous!"

"I protest against this delay!" Krakowski said, standing up. "Kill the man and let us continue our own business!"

"Damn right!" Merda chimed in. He was on his feet as well, but it hardly made a difference. "Lash, you've got all the bids you're getting!"

Lash was a moment in replying, but his reply was to Lizzie. "Go on," he said.

"You have what you've wanted," she answered, referring obviously to the airship plans. "But…there's a second book *he* wants." She pointed with

the blade of an index finger toward Cardinal Black. The way she'd spoken the word 'he' was with a hint of a foul taste in her mouth. "Why not keep one of them here and send the other back to the professor? Let Fell offer a bid, and make him include that second book in the offering."

"This is not *acceptable*!" growled Lioness, who also stood up. "I came here and presented my bid in good faith! You cannot change the rules now!"

"I agree!" Montague's sallow face was pinched with a scowl. "The rules for this auction were set up long ago!"

"One moment." Cardinal Black released the rope from Julian's throat. He wore a ghastly smile. "This proposal has merit."

"No no *no*!" Victor shrieked. "I'll not stand for it! Rules are rules!"

Lash regarded the others, then stroked his beard as he gazed upon RakeHell Lizzie, who seemed to be at least halfway returned to her less violent identity of Elizabeth Mulloy. "My house," he said. "My rules."

"Well spoken, sir!" said Julian as he rubbed his throat.

"*Shut*," Lash told him. He returned his attention to Elizabeth again as Merda muttered curses and Victor let out an unintelligible holler. "And which one do you propose to send, dear? I would think it would be Corbett, as from what I know about Devane, we would never see him again."

"Yes. It would be Corbett."

"*Insanity*!" Montague raged. "You've lost your senses, Lash!"

"It's an outrage!" Lioness seethed. "I protest this act of betrayal!"

"Everyone *shut*." Lash stood up. He put his hands on his hips and took a stance as if he were captain of the ship and the rest were unruly crewmen at the point of mutiny, which Matthew even through the pain of his bowed back thought was probably an accurate assessment. "Listen to me and hear me well!" Lash's voice was not a bellow, but it had strength enough to drown out the mutterings, ragings, seethings and curses. "I say it will take Corbett one week to go to Fell, secure a bid and return. At least, that's what I'll give him. I'll also supply one of my private coaches, two drivers and a bodyguard. He can start out before dawn. The rest of

you can make your decisions now: if you want your offerings returned and to be sent on your way, you are welcome. As Elizabeth said, I have what I wanted from the Prussians. Therefore the *next* highest bid will be the winner. I am still contemplating such. If Fell makes a bid I feel to be—"

"This is damned treachery!" Victor shouted. "If you're intent on creating enemies, you've made a hell of a start! I'll make sure my guild exacts full payment!"

"—feel to be inadequate," Lash went on, "it shall be rejected. Even with the object of the cardinal's desire." He walked toward Victor amid the stone benches. When he reached the man he produced a small pistol from within his medalled naval jacket and cocked it.

He levelled it at Victor's head. Victor's eyes widened, but he had no time for any further reaction.

The shot blew a sizeable chunk from Victor's skull. Blood spattered into Julian's face. In an instant the body had slithered down as if the bones were turned to jelly.

"One less enemy, it appears," said Samson Lash after the echoes of the gun's roar had faded. He waved the pistol's barrel beneath his nose to smell the pungent perfume of its blue smoke. "I dislike threats. Now it also appears our friend Victor is no longer a valid participant in this auction. Any further questions or comments?"

"I need a napkin," said Julian, his voice unusually shaky.

"Are you planning to murder us all?" Lioness's gaze was fixed on the pistol. "If you are, I will say—no threat implied, sir—that our affiliations might wish to remedy their losses."

"Murder you all? Of course not! I see that the rest of you are hard-nosed people of business who understand my position. And…that you understand your own positions…no threat implied, madam. Besides, Victor offered a terrible bid. I nearly dispatched him right there in my study."

The childlike voice of Miles Merda piped up. "I don't give a fuck. My bid'll stand up against anybody's."

"Let me understand this," said Krakowski, whose head might have still been befuddled. "You are asking us to wait in London for one *week* until this boy comes back? And not until then will you have decided who has won the book? But…sir…what if the boy does *not* come back? What if when you let him go, he is just simply *gone*?"

Lash spent a moment holstering his pistol underneath his jacket. "Simple answers," he replied. "If Corbett does not return, the book goes to the winner here. Mr. Devane becomes another dance partner in this arena, I will give you all a feast by which to remember this event, I will see you off at your various sailings and all will be well with the world."

"I do not like it," said Lioness. She lifted a hand that was almost as large as Lash's and showed her palm in order to prevent the reappearance of a pistol. "But I do not fail to appreciate the fact that you wish as much gain as possible for your possession. Therefore I protest only in spirit."

"My spirit thanks yours," Lash said, with a slight bow. He gazed around at the others. "Any more objections?"

"I have a comment," came Matthew's tight voice. He felt as if either his shoulders were about to pop free or his back about to break and possibly both at the same time. The smell of the blood and intestines around his leg irons was a sickening miasma. "If I'm to take a trip," he went on, painfully, "my first step should be getting down from here."

"Oh!" Lash pretended to give a startle as if he'd completely forgotten. "Pardon me, young man! Where are my manners? Get him down!" he instructed the guards. "Corbett, we'll bring you a washbucket and a glass of the fine Armagnac to calm your nerves. You may rest and dress at your leisure. That suit you?"

"Of course," said one gentleman to another, though the naked former was near passing out and could not bear to set eyes upon the hollowed-out corpses that lay in the dirt on either side of him. The guards unlocked the leg irons and the manacles, at which moment Matthew found he was hardly capable of walking and sank down into the bloody mess, where he gave a bone-wrenching shudder and from his stomach boiled up most of the night's dinner, in particular the steamed mussels and the fried cauliflower. He was hauled up by the men and guided toward the pit's door, whereupon in his state of delirium he stepped on the face of Dippen Nack and again fell, was again sick, and heard Lash laughing up in the gallery as if watching a comedy of Shakespearean proportions.

Thus, then, went Matthew through the door and again into the bare room where the clothing of a Prussian baron and two dead men lay scattered on the stones. A moment after the door was closed and he heard a key turn in its lock, he sank down to the floor. Under the lantern that hung from a hook at the ceiling, Matthew brought his knees up to his chin and wept in the grief of his own personal tragedy.

TWENTY-ONE.

Had it been an hour before Matthew heard the key unlocking the little room's door for a second time? The first had been when one of the guards had brought a bucket of water and a cloth for him to wash the gore of dead men off himself. But time had lost its bearings. He recalled that Victor had requested a coach return at midnight to pick him up, but was it now past that haunted hour? It seemed to Matthew that every hour would now be haunted, for Berry was surely doomed. Professor Fell was not going to give up even one copy of *The Lesser Key of Solomon*, and certainly not to Samson Lash nor to Cardinal Black. Matthew's bargain with Fell had been to locate Brazio Valeriani in exchange for the chance to get the book back and find a chemist to save Berry. Just the *chance*, not the certainty. So Fell's part of the bargain was done, and when Matthew returned to Y Beautiful Bedd the coach's driver and the bodyguard would likely be pulled apart by red-hot pincers and the whole episode of the potions book put aside in favor of the impending voyage to Italy, with Berry's sanity an unfortunate liability in this game of thugs.

The door was opening.

Matthew had no further reason to fear whoever was coming in. He had washed himself as best he could, leaving the bucket's water stained

red, and then dressed again in the atrocious garments of a clownish baron. At least now he had no need to wear white facepaint and balance a weighty wig on his noggin. He stood back from the door as Elizabeth Mulloy entered, bearing a silver tray on which rested a glass of amber liquid: the French Armagnac that had been promised to him.

She had returned to her civilized persona. She was freshly scrubbed, fragrant of a cinnamon-based perfume, and wore a sea-green gown decorated with pink curlicues around the neckline. Her arms were adorned by sea-green gloves up to the elbows.

In spite of himself, Matthew found himself continuing to retreat from her. There was not a stick of furniture in the chamber, so nothing to use as defense if the tiger jumped out of the cat once again.

"Your Armagnac." She held the tray out until he took the glass. "How are you?" she asked.

"A good question. I'm not quite sure." Matthew lifted the glass up toward the lantern light to look for anything suspicious that might be floating in it.

"It's not drugged," Elizabeth said. "He doesn't want you sluggish."

"What time is it?"

"Just past two o'clock. And snowing heavily outside again. The others are in the parlor. Samson has said he'll feed them a good breakfast at dawn for their troubles. Anyway, some of them are playing at cards."

"A delightful picture," said Matthew with a sour smile. "What about Julian?"

"He was taken upstairs. I believe they've given him the room next to the doctor. Locked him in, of course."

"Of course," Matthew said. He frowned. "So...why are *you* here? Why didn't one of the guards bring that?"

"I wished to speak with you." She held the tray down at her side. Matthew tensed, thinking she could probably cut his throat with its narrow edge if she liked.

"Well, I do like speaking better than killing." He took a sip of the Armagnac, found it good and strong and just what he needed for a shot of

extra courage. Still, he kept retreating until his back was nearly wedged into a corner. "Speak," he said. "I seem to be at your disposal." Instantly he thought that was a very poor choice of words.

She nodded, and for a silent moment she just stared at him with the soft brown eyes that had so recently appeared intoxicated with murder.

"You," she said, "are a total fool."

"I bow before your appraisal."

"I'm serious. Do you know how many men I have killed—slaughtered—in that pit?"

"I don't wish to know, thank you."

"You would have been number eight."

"Must be my lucky number," Matthew said. His next drink almost sapped the glass. He realized that if he pushed himself into the corner any further he would be stuck until the New Year.

"It comes upon me," she continued. "I have to have it, as other woman must have…well, whatever they must have. I live in a different world, Matthew. My world…few would understand it."

"Fine. As you say." He wondered about the use of his name. She seemed awfully familiar to have been gutting two men and then climbing up his own body not too long ago.

"I was jarred out of my state tonight," Elizabeth said. "My *state*, being my condition. I was jarred out of it, and I had to think of something to save your life…from myself…and from Samson and that thing who calls himself a cardinal."

Matthew was taken aback. All he could think to say was, "*Huh*?"

She came toward him. Did he cringe? Probably so, but she came on anyway. And when she was almost in his face she peeled off the glove from her right hand and showed him the tattoo of a stylized eye within a black circle embossed between the thumb and the forefinger.

"When I climbed up on you," Elizabeth said, "I saw the tattoo on your hand. You're a Black-Eyed Broodie, the same as me."

If God had not fixed Matthew's teeth to the gums they might have fallen from his mouth at that instant, or his mouth opened in amazement so wide an army of flies might have gotten in, set up camp, and buzzed happily for the space of time it took Matthew to recover from this shock.

He remembered the oath he'd taken, given by Rory Keen and verified by being spit in the face from twenty-six members of the Broodie clan: *I solemnly swear to be faithful and true to the Black-Eyed Broodies and hold my brothers and sisters in the highest regard and respect, show no mercy to their enemies, and do no harm to nobody who is or ever was a Broodie.*

And here before him stood a contradiction to his belief that after the murder of Rory Keen by Mother Deare he himself was the last of the Black-Eyed Broodies. But no, no…this was his 'sister' standing before him, the young woman who had slaughtered Dippen Nack in front of his eyes and very nearly had emptied his own innards out upon the ground.

His 'sister' Elizabeth Mulloy, otherwise known as RakeHell Lizzie.

She put her glove back on. "Your eyes almost popped out," she said.

He nodded, dumbly, and finished off the Armagnac.

"Now you've got to get out of here," she told him.

"Pardon me?" Was his hearing failing, to add to this wonderful evening?

"*Out* of here," she repeated. She held up the large brass key she'd used to open the door. "This will unlock a door further along the passage. There are tunnels that go under the park. Samson says they're what remains of the old Roman streets. You'll come to a chamber where they throw the bodies, but don't go in. Keep going straight. I've never been very far in there, but the tunnels *must* come out somewhere close, because they bring the men through there." She jerked a gloved thumb up toward the lantern. "Give me a boost and I can pluck that off the hook for you. You'll need the light."

Matthew was again struck dumb.

"You can't waste time!" she urged. "They'll be coming for you soon. Listen, you'll have to hit me with something. Have to make it look real, like you took me by surprise." She looked about the room, bent down and

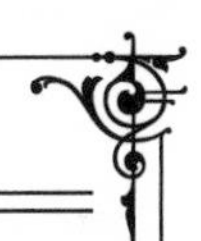

picked up a dead man's boot. "Hit me with this. Back of the head. Hit me hard, I can take it. Have to put a lump there. Go on, do it."

"I…I…" What was he trying to say? Had he lost his senses? He felt as if his tongue were mired in mush and his brain no better. "I…" He forced it out: "I can't leave here."

"*What*?"

"I can't leave here," he repeated, "without the book of potions and Doctor Firebaugh to go with it." He realized he was omitting something. "Oh…and Julian. I can't leave here without all three."

It was Elizabeth's turn to be open-mouthed and struck dumb for a few seconds. Then: "Are you *insane*? I'm offering you a way out!"

"Through tunnels that may only get me lost in a maze without an exit? I can't risk that. Thank you, but no."

She shook her head and let go a long breath of frustration. "They're talking about you up there. Samson and that so-called cardinal. Black told Samson you really do work with the Herrald Agency in the New York colony. He said he learned that from the woman who calls herself Mother Deare. *Called*," she corrected. "I understand she's dead."

"As the proverbial doornail," Matthew said.

"No matter. I do know about the Herrald Agency. I have no idea how you've gotten mixed up in this, but I doubt you're completely and willingly affiliated with Professor Fell. Don't you want a chance to get out with your skin?"

Matthew decided he had to trust this young woman, even in spite of her deadly instincts. "I am here to retrieve the book and to take Firebaugh with it, because Fell's previous chemist used a formula on the woman I love, to turn her into…well, into the shell of what she once was. If I don't return the book and a new chemist to decipher the potions, she will continue to mentally decline into an infantile state. Fell agreed to let Julian and me at least try to get the book back. But I don't think he cares much about the book itself anymore. He has bigger fish on his plate." He paused, watching her expression as she took all this in; it was perhaps of sisterly

concern, but still not enough to fully understand. He decided also to open another tin of worms. "Do you know that Cardinal Black and his gang murdered every Broodie but Rory Keen and myself? And then Mother Deare shot Rory in the head. I was there to see it happen, but I couldn't stop it."

"Wait…*wait*," she said. "Murdered all the Broodies? *When*?"

"Not a month ago. I was present when Black—with Lash's help—raided Fell's village in Wales and took the book of potions. By that time, Berry—the woman I love and plan to marry, if I can bring her back—was already under the drug's influence. Obviously Lash was the one who wanted the book, but Black wanted a second book that concerns his interest—obsession, I would say—with demonology. So that's the story. I do appreciate your saving me from yourself, but I doubt Fell is going to offer any further bid to get the book of potions back. He's not going to want Black to get his hands on the second book."

Elizabeth appeared still shaken by the news that the Broodies had been murdered. "I…can't…why did Black kill all of them?"

"He was after the supply of White Velvet the Broodies were keeping for Mother Deare's gang, which was part of Fell's organization."

"White Velvet?"

"A drugged gin that Fell created by using one of the book's formulas. Mother Deare was losing her mind and had been working with Black for some time. How those two got together, I don't know. But I suspect Black knew he had to kill the Broodies to get the cases of Velvet out of their warehouse. Mother Deare likely knew that as well. I don't know if Lash was in on this or not, or where the cases of Velvet wound up, but I do know for certain: I cannot leave here without the book, Firebaugh and—" Could he leave Julian to the wrath of Black and Lash, if it came to that? "And Julian," he finished.

"Murdered all the Broodies?" she said quietly. "Every one?"

"Every one," Matthew answered. "And I won't go into great detail, but they did not die easily."

She was silent for a while, as she digested this foul information.

"The Broodies took me in off the street when I needed refuge," Matthew continued. "In their own way, they were kind to me. I believe I came to look on Rory as a true brother, of a sort. I would venture to say that Samson Lash is driven by his need to build this airship and prove a point to the Royal Navy—a point they will likely always refuse to grant him—but that Black's influence is corrosively evil, and under it Lash will be drawn into deeper and darker depths." He refrained from stating his belief that Lash was probably already at dark depths even without Black's demonic hand pushing him deeper; it seemed to him that the airship idea had unhinged the vice admiral and made him believe that any wretched crime and murder was done for the advantage of England in her future wars.

Elizabeth stared for a moment at the discarded clothing on the floor, but Matthew saw that she wore a blank expression as if she were regarding items for paper dolls that had been torn in two and tossed into a fire. "I didn't want Samson to become involved with Black," she said. "I advised against it when the Owl came to speak to him about the collaboration. Yes, the Owl put all this together. It was quite a pretty penny for him, and another feather in his—" She paused, deliberating, and then said, "*Tail*."

When she didn't go on, Matthew decided to push her for the sake of his own curiosity, and possibly there was some information he might grasp upon and use. "How did all this begin?"

"It started several years ago," she said. "I had only been living here a year before it began. Samson had heard about the airship plans from the captain of a Portuguese vessel that was wrecked off the Canary Islands. It was what he'd been envisioning all his life. He made inquiries from some people he thought might help, and one day the Owl came to visit. For a fee, the Owl learned that Duke de Valasco owned the plans and would give them up in exchange for the assassination of his elder brother. So—again with the Owl's help—connections were made with the Prussians, who had a reputation for excellence. The duke didn't wish the assassins to be anyone in Portugal who might be traced back to him and Samson didn't wish to use

anyone with an English affiliation, so the Owl—or someone the Owl considered a loyal confederate—served as the go-between. Then there was the matter of paying the Prussians for the work. Something had to be found that would be of extraordinary value to those who could make use of it. That's where Black came in. The Owl introduced them to each other. Black told Samson about the book and about what *he* wanted from Fell. The scheme took over a year to put in place and had some fits and starts. But I told Samson from the beginning not to put too much trust in Black. That was one time he disregarded my advice, and I believe he's yet to pay for it."

"A scheme that must've run on many wheels," Matthew said. "Tell me this: if Lash really only wanted the airship plans, why did he include the others in this auction?"

"He wasn't certain the Prussians could get the plans. They might have failed in the attempt, or been caught, or whatever. He—and I—thought it best to bring others into the fold. Once again, the Owl took care of this through his contacts. You can be sure he's nearly as powerful—or as ambitious—as Professor Fell *once* was, but his true talent is in diplomatic communication. And another reason: when Samson builds the airship he wants to be sure there are other markets for the vessel if the Royal Navy refuses to buy it. In that regard, he's announcing his name to the guilds that the ones upstairs represent."

"I don't think Victor's guild is going to be too pleased," Matthew said.

She shrugged. "Everyone here understands that it's business. Yet Samson draws the line at personal threats, and it was a wise thing to show them what crossing that line will do."

Matthew nodded vacantly; he decided another line should be crossed. "What are you to Lash? Besides his business advisor and a source of rather cruel entertainment?"

Elizabeth lifted her chin. "I am his figurehead," she replied. "I live in great wealth and luxury, to be—"

"A wooden effigy?" Matthew interrupted. "Is that all?"

"He enjoys my company and my advice."

"That's all he enjoys?"

"It is," she said. Her eyes narrowed. Matthew felt a heightening of danger in the room. "I cannot be touched by any man. I refuse to touch any man, except for what you've witnessed. Samson has never seen my tattoo, for I always wear the silk gloves…unless I'm wearing the others. If you wish to know more, I would warn you that travelling in that direction has the effect of awakening my condition."

"Well, let's park the wagon," Matthew said quickly.

"I agree." She reached out and took the empty glass from him. "Now… if you are so stupid as to remain here when I'm offering you an escape, that's all I have for you."

"Not quite," Matthew said before she could turn for the door. "As you say, Lash has the object of his desire. He doesn't need the book, and Black doesn't need that other book, either. God can only dare guess what use Black would put it to. So I am asking you as a sister to *help* me."

"You've already rejected my help."

"No. Help me to get the book, to get Firebaugh, to get Julian, and escape from this place with a good chance of finding my way back to Fell's village."

She allowed herself an incredulous smile. "Impossible. As much as I might like to sever the relationship between Samson and Cardinal Black, Samson's planning for you to leave in the coach before dawn."

Matthew grunted. His mind was working furiously and it seemed he could smell the friction of his brainwheels burning themselves. The tunnels…she said they brought the men through there for her to kill in the pit, but where might be the nearest entrance and exit?

He had a thought to bend down and examine the discarded clothes. He searched the pockets, not knowing what he was looking for…the spark of an idea…a shred…anything that might—

He felt something grainy on his fingers. A further inspection and he discovered that the substance grimed both sets of clothing. He stood up and held his hand where the light would benefit his vision.

"Coal dust," he said. "On the clothes. Your victims aren't delivered through a coal chute?"

"Samson uses wood in the fireplaces, not coal. As I say, they come through the tunnels. And my 'victims', as you call them, have been up to this point drunkards and the dregs of London gathered up from the low streets. Small men, as Samson would say. They only come in at night, and I'm sure Samson takes great precautions not to be seen."

"I'm sure he's a fine provider," Matthew replied. He rubbed the grainy coal dust between his fingers. "Coal dust on both sets of clothing."

"That tells you something?" Elizabeth prodded.

"Possibly that the constables were brought here on a coal wagon, and I doubt they didn't have to be knocked senseless and covered over. But it would be a risk for Lash. A little screaming and commotion if one of the men happened to break free, and this quiet, privileged neighborhood would be looking askance at the vice admiral. If indeed they came in a coal wagon they were taken off somewhere not too near the house just in case of such mishap, but not too far away either." Matthew realized he was basically thinking aloud, for he had no surety of any of this. "I doubt that Lash would like his neighbors to know what goes on in here," he said. "He might be booted off the park."

"Samson would be the one doing the booting," she replied, with a haughty air. "He owns the park. Now, I don't believe I can help you any further. What you're asking is out of the question."

"Two things you *can* help me with," Matthew said. Again his mind was racing, trying to solve the problems that lay before him. It seemed that Julian was right, and everything was left up to the whims of Fate. "Number one, tell no one what we've been talking about, and number two—" and here was the real risk at hand, "—make sure that when I'm taken away in the coach, the door to which that key is suited is unlocked."

That gave her pause. She frowned and her mouth twisted. Whatever she was about to say, it would have to be left unsaid because the chamber's door suddenly opened and two of the Owl's toughs were there.

"Come along," one said to Matthew. "He wants you."

"Am I presentable enough for a chat with the vice admiral?" Matthew asked Elizabeth as, smiling tightly, he brushed the last of the coal dust from his fingers.

"Not Lash," said the guard. "Cardinal Black. Come on, he's waiting."

TWENTY-TWO.

"You interest me," said Cardinal Black, fully three minutes after Matthew had been escorted into what had to be the library at the rear of the house, for all the books on the oak shelves and two large wooden models of naval frigates mounted on stands. Wood crackled in a fireplace of rough gray stones. On the floor was a dark blue rug with a golden pattern at its edges. To the right, an oval window showed curtains of snow flying in the wind.

Black was seated on a red leather lounge chair with his long legs stretched out and his boots up on an ottoman, a low table at his side bearing a glass of red wine. Overhead, six candles burned in a brass chandelier of intricate design. Black had told the two guards to leave and close the door behind them, and then Matthew waited for Black to take his time in filling a clay pipe with tobacco, fire up a tinderbox, touch flame to the bowl and start puffing out blue clouds that slowly changed shape as they drifted toward Matthew's face. Matthew thought it was quite ironic that Cardinal Black's pipe of choice was called a churchwarden for its long curved stem, but he decided against pointing it out.

Matthew had not made a move to sit in any of the other two chairs, nor had Black suggested it. After Black had made the single statement, eyes

that seemed to hold centers of scarlet in the long-jawed, pallid face fixed upon Matthew as if regarding another feast. He smoked in silence.

"It interests *me*," said Matthew at last, "that you chose to have this presumed discussion in the library. A certain book on your mind, is it?"

"Of course."

"And what would you do with that book if you had it? It's not one for bedtime reading."

"Speak for yourself," said Black, with a thin little smile.

"I've looked through a copy. Several copies, in fact. One in New York, one on Fell's island and the one you wanted in the village."

"You must know that Fell has bought up every copy in existence. At least, I've been unable to secure one...and you can be sure I have shaken the trees."

"Unfortunate that one didn't tumble down and knock your brains out," said Matthew. He walked past Black to the hearth to warm himself. Any fireplace implements here, poker or tongs? No...likely recently removed just for this meeting. He held his hands out before the fire. His bravado toward Black was both a shield and a valve to relieve pressure, for standing here he could put himself back in an instant among the dead Broodies, their faces eyeless, their eyeballs having been plucked out and put into an empty White Velvet bottle down in the warehouse's cellar, their throats slashed and upon their foreheads the bloody Devil's Cross courtesy of the monster who sat across the room from him, smoking a churchwarden pipe and puffing small exclamations of smoke like the scrawls of a secret language.

"The *reason* you interest me," Black went on after a short pause in which Matthew heard the wind shrilling and whining beyond the glass, "is that you are *here*. I can understand Devane being sent by Fell to get the book...but sending *you*? Whatever was he thinking?"

"That I could get the book back, I suppose."

"Ohhhhh no." Black puffed another blue cloud of smoke and wagged a slim finger back and forth. "There's more to it than that. Isn't there?

You know, Mother Deare confided something to me that you might care to hear: the professor *likes* you, in spite of your misdeeds toward him. It seems…now how did she put it?…oh…it seems you remind him of his deceased son. Or…of what he might have been, had he not been beaten to death at a young age. But, Matthew…let us be honest…he doesn't like you enough to set you loose from that village of his, not even with Devane riding on your back. What's the truth?"

Matthew continued to warm his hands. He thought it was Black's presence that was making the room so terribly cold.

"We can get it out of Devane," Black said. "I'd like to cut him up a little."

Matthew looked over at the demoniac and saw that Black had set his pipe aside on the low table, had drawn a curved dagger with strange markings on the blade from his jacket, and was commencing to use it to clean his long sharp fingernails. "Come now," Black urged softly. "Confess it."

Still Matthew remained silent.

"Let me play at being a problem-solver," Black suggested, as his blade continued to probe. "That's what you are, correct? Mother Deare told me about that episode on Fell's island. That he *hired* you to act a part? And now here you are again, acting a part, but I suspect it wasn't planned this time." He paused in his nail-cleaning to draw on his pipe once more. "Your agency excels in such work. I mean to say, the work of solving problems for your clients. Such as…oh…finding objects that have been lost. Or…people who have for some reason been lost. I put my mind to this, Matthew. I shunted it back and forth, trying to make sense of *why* Fell would send you after the book. I came to the conclusion that…and I hardly could believe this myself…you *volunteered* for the task. Likely Devane didn't, but he was made to come along. Now…with that in mind, why would you volunteer for this? Well, is it to win freedom for those two friends of yours, the man and the girl Mother Deare told me she took to the village? But no…I don't think that's all of it. I think you bartered with Fell for something else, if he would allow you to come after the book and

win the freedom for your friends. Fell is not that easily bargained with. He would want more than the book. He would want…shall I tell you, or do you already know?"

"Is it your voice or the whine of the wind that's making my skin crawl?" Matthew asked.

"You already know," Black said. He blew a ring of smoke. "He wants you to find Brazio Valeriani. That's the other part of the bargain. He must have great confidence in you, believing you would come back from this house *alive*." Black held up the dagger, its tip toward Matthew. "Don't waste time trying to deny it. Your agency is well-known for such exploits as finding missing persons. I have to say, if you weren't looking for Valeriani on Fell's behalf, I would be glad to pay you your asking price to find Valeriani for myself. What would that price be, Matthew?

"Your head on a stick," was the answer.

"Rage clouds the mind, Matthew. It doesn't suit you." Black returned to cleaning his nails. "Do you even have any idea why the professor wants so badly to find Valeriani?"

Matthew realized that remaining silent and sullen at this point was not beneficial to his interests. Was Black offering to tell him? Matthew said, "I know it involves the book of demonology and Valeriani's father, Ciro."

"Ah, the book of demonology." Black gave another thin smile. "What if I told you one might regard *The Lesser Key of Solomon* as a *catalogue*?"

"A catalogue of what?"

"Demons, of course. There they all are, with their names, titles and powers spelled out on the pages. A catalogue, Matthew, of what demon can be chosen for what kind of *work* on the earthly plane."

It took Matthew a moment to formulate an answer. "You don't really believe that, do you?" Instantly he thought *yes of course Cardinal Black believes it…and so too must Professor Fell.*

Black laughed. It began as a chuckle of glee and ended up sounded as if he were grinding his teeth on a bone.

"That was a stupid remark, wasn't it?" Matthew asked.

The cardinal's pipe smoke drifted through the air, curving toward the fireplace's flue. As the whorls approached him, Matthew imagined they took the shape of grotesque faces and creatures with claws and horns. One skimmed his cheek like a rude phantasmic kiss as it went past and was caught by the updraft.

"The tale I have been told," said Cardinal Black, "is that Brazio's father—a scientist of some note—suffered a mental breakdown at the death of his wife. In that condition, Ciro Valeriani actually had an enlightenment. All the false beliefs were extinguished. He came to know the true ruler of this world, and to both respect and yearn for that kind of power."

"Satanic, I'm assuming you mean."

"He became quite interested in *The Lesser Key of Solomon*, and in other tomes even more far-reaching but difficult to obtain. My understanding is that Ciro made contact with a man in Rome who could not only furnish him with some of these—for a hefty price—but who could also introduce him to Senna Salastre."

"A new flavor of tea?" Matthew asked.

"Senna Salastre, who was ninety-four when he passed into the master's hands last August, *wrote* some of the books Valeriani was seeking. Matthew, you are *so* uneducated. You have no idea how Maestro Salastre has worked to benefit the true believers, what he has done in this world to overturn the fictions that you and others of your ilk labor under. You don't see that the master's way is *freedom*. Total, unadulterated freedom the like of which you have never known."

"Freedom to cut the hearts out of children, is what you mean?" said Matthew. "And gouge out as many eyeballs as will fill a White Velvet bottle?" He felt the heat rising in his face. He brushed away a floating specter that seemed to be formed of scrabbling claws and a blue tongue a foot long. "And, oh yes, the freedom to cut as many throats as possible and carve that ridiculous symbol on their foreheads, as if it really means you have any power at all? Your freedom, sir, will end when the rope drops you, and I will be there to—"

"From one of Maestro Salastre's books," Black went on, as if Matthew had not spoken a word, "Ciro Valeriani created in his workshop a free-standing, full-length mirror. Valeriani as a scientist had been interested in mirrors for years, so this project intrigued him. Maestro Salastre helped him with the construction and added the mirror's reflective element from his own workshop. I understand that very soon the glass turned dark, as expected."

"A dark mirror? To what point?"

"With Maestro Salastre's guidance," said Black, "Valeriani created a mirror that is not *simply* a mirror. It is a passageway. Can you imagine in your earthbound mind what planes of existence are connected by that passage?"

"I don't wish to imagine," Matthew quickly replied, though he knew fully well what Black must be getting at.

"A demonic being can be called to come through." Black put the pipe's bit between his sharpened teeth. "A chosen one, of the caller's choosing. I understand that there is a time limit and a risk of injury, but—"

"Good Christ, you *are* mad, aren't you?" Matthew felt ready to explode. "Demons coming out of dark mirrors! That's sheer insanity!"

"Ah," said Black, with a slight nod. "Would you say the same thing to Professor Fell?"

Matthew was struck into silence. Behind him the fire burned brightly and before him the wind of a pre-dawn storm blew currents of snow past the oval glass.

"Fell wants to call forth a demonic presence as much as I do," Black said. "Why, I don't know. For me, it would be the ultimate power…to have such a presence in my grasp…for that creature to know I have been faithful and true to the master we both serve…and then…what my command would be…I haven't yet decided, but mark this…that it would shake the world, Matthew. This I can vow."

It took Matthew a moment to regain his reeling senses. "*Insanity*," he breathed, but he feared it was much more than that. "You do realize that

Ciro Valeriani came to his senses and tried to destroy the thing?"

"He was unable to do so. My understanding is that at the last moment, when the presence he called forth was in the passageway, he must have lost his nerve—known he was unworthy—and shattered the glass. Some time later he was compelled to repair it."

Compelled might be the right word, Matthew thought. What Valeriani created would not let him destroy it, Fell had said. "And then he hanged himself soon after?" Matthew asked.

"Very soon after. With his death, the mirror disappeared. His son must know what happened to it, and—if it still exists—where it is hidden. That is why Danton Idris Fell wants you to find Brazio. Find the son, find the mirror. Simple enough?"

"Italy's a big country."

"Oh, not so big for a grand problem-solver like yourself." Cardinal Black stood up from his lounge chair and came across the carpet toward Matthew with a smooth, gliding gait. The man was fearsomely tall and in this firelight his weirdly angular face itself had the appearance of demonic virtues. Matthew wondered if this was the sight the little boy in the tower at Adderlane had seen: Black coming at him like a long-legged spider with a dagger in hand. When Black stopped before him, Matthew was treated to the cardinal's blade being drawn back and forth across his chin.

"You'll soon be leaving for Fell's village," Black said. "They're harnessing the horses right now. I will tell you that if you do not return with the book *I* want, I will personally cut Devane's heart out. The master demands that it's done while the offerings are still alive. You may not care that Devane dies and you may get to that village and think you can hide from me, but you are wrong."

"What, are you going to get Lash to sail the *Volcano* back and bomb the place again?"

The dagger stopped moving. Black angled it so the point was just beneath Matthew's lower lip. "You know too much, little man. Lash

anchored the *Volcano* off Newquay just as it's supposed to be, so when I come for you it won't be with bombshells, it will be with…" He paused, conjuring up an appropriate term. "Deathknells in the night," he said. His mouth of sharpened teeth grinned. "Bring the book back to me, Matthew. That's what my master demands of *you*." The dagger's tip was just about to draw a droplet of blood, but Matthew steeled himself and didn't move.

There was a knock at the door.

"Yes?" Black called.

"The coach is ready for him." It was the Owl speaking. "Bring him to the dining room."

Black motioned with a flourish of the blade. "After you."

On the way from the library to the dining room, Matthew was taking in every detail he could gather about the house…where the central staircase was, how far it was from the staircase to the entrance foyer, how far the door down to the murder pit was from the dining room, the distance from the dining room to the parlor, and everything else he could slip into his brain. He was going to need the details for what he was planning. Of course it was a desperate plan and might go wrong in the first few minutes. He was unsure he would be up to the beginning of it, but he had no choice. It was either try this or be taken on the road back to Y Beautiful Bedd and there was no time to even pretend Fell was going to give up the book. Fell might have a dozen copies hidden away somewhere in the village—if indeed there were a dozen copies of that thing in existence—but to make a gift of one to Cardinal Black? No, it would never happen.

"Here's our morning traveller!" boomed Samson Lash as Matthew entered the dining room. The others seated at the table for the breakfast feast Lash had promised regarded Matthew with less enthusiasm and more pure disdain. At the far end of the table Elizabeth Mulloy did not look up from her platter of scrambled eggs, ham and corncakes. Matthew noted that Lazarus Firebaugh was absent, likely either sleeping or having breakfast in his quarters. "Ready for the journey, I hope!" Lash said.

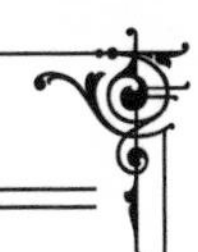

"Here's some breakfast for him," said Merda, who followed it with a thrown biscuit that hit Matthew squarely in the middle of his forehead. "Want another?" He reached for the tray on which the other biscuits rested.

"Come now!" Lash chided. "Let's don't be antagonistic! You have a week of being perfectly ordinary citizens and enjoying all the charms of London!"

"I am far from being a perfectly ordinary citizen, thank you," said Lioness. She bit a sausage in half and turned her dark, sullen eyes from Lash upon the object of the moment's contempt.

"I miss the charms of my own country already," Krakowski said, with a sour expression. "I didn't think I was to be held hostage here!"

Before Montague could voice his own bitter sentiments, Matthew took charge. "I regret you all feel so...would the word be *betrayed*? I wish I could alter the situation, but unfortunately it's not within my power." He tensed momentarily as Cardinal Black came up beside him and patted him on the cheek with those hideous and murderous fingers before the cardinal took a seat across from Elizabeth. "That said, I *am* hungry," Matthew continued. "Where should I sit?"

"In the coach that is waiting for you outside," said Lash. "You'll find a basket of edibles there for your breakfast, which you'll need to share with the able bodyguard the Owl has provided. His name is Bogen. He'll be here directly to help you along."

"Travelling in this snowfall?" Matthew asked. "We won't make much time."

"You'll be leaving as soon as possible because my experience at sea tells me the weather is only going to worsen. There's no use in dawdling. The directions I've given my driver are to stop at inns only to freshen the horses and feed yourselves. He knows the way, you may count on it."

"Here's butter for your biscuit, you sorry shit," said Merda. This was followed by a thumb-sized bit of butter hitting Matthew on the side of the face.

Lash took a drink from an ale mug before he went on. "Make sure you take that nice warm coat of Count Pellegar's. It does look to be a frigid

morning. You also may count on the fact that Bogen will be well-armed. The Owl tells me he is capable of extreme violence, if it comes to that. Also, he is instructed to shoot you in the head if anything even appears to his careful eye to be going wrong up there in Fell's little corner of Wales."

"Tell him he should save a ball for himself, because after he shoots me they'll start by sawing his feet off and go up from there by inches."

"I am sure there will be tensions." Lash wiped his wet mouth with a white napkin, dabbing gently at the corners. "It will be to your benefit to ease them, keep both death and dismemberment at bay, and lead all events to a happy conclusion."

"Happy for *whom*?" Montague threw his own napkin down onto his plate. "I dislike this arrangement to the marrow of my bones, sir! You know I must make a full report to my guild!"

"As you please," Lash replied easily. "It was my error in not inviting Professor Fell to join the bidding, and so I take full responsibility. But let us not be hasty in our judgments, as we must take the long view on this matter."

"A long *dim* view, sir!" Montague snapped, unwilling to empty his cup of anger.

"He lost at cards last night," said Lash to Matthew in a tone of confidentiality. "That does tend to annoy someone who thinks he's a better bluffer than he is. Ah, here's your escort now!"

The Owl had entered the room. He was accompanied by a square-shouldered man of medium height, stocky with a thick bull neck. Bogen wore a dark blue cloak over a gray suit. Beneath a gray tricorn was a face hewn from a slab of granite and then squeezed under pressure. Matthew thought Bogen's formidable nose could be mistaken as a third elbow and his chunk of chin an extra six-knuckled fist. A pair of pig-like eyes stared from the holes in the work of stone and fixed upon Matthew, whose heart rose into his throat at the same time his knees sagged as if struck from behind. This man was a beast.

"All is ready," said the Owl.

"Get him that coat Devane wore," Lash said. "Find him a hat, we don't want him catching his death. Then search him again before you put him in the coach. Good journey to you, Matthew. Now run along." He waved an indifferent hand and returned to the consumption of the breakfast feast.

Matthew cast another glance at Elizabeth. She kept her gaze averted. Now he felt his heart sink. If his plan was to work at all—and to call it a plan was to call Cardinal Black the most handsome of angels—he needed her help. Of course it all might go to hell in the first minute, so there was that possibility, and then what?

He dreaded to think.

Bogen took hold of Matthew's upper arm. "*Move*," he said, in a voice like the sound of the chisel that had shaped his face.

Shit, Matthew thought.

"Hurry back!" piped Merda's childlike voice as Matthew was marched out of the dining room with Bogen on one side and the Owl on the other. They passed the central staircase and entered the foyer where the coats and hats were still hanging and, as Matthew noted while the Owl gave the polar bear coat a good going-over, the weapons were still piled up in the basket atop the table. Then the Owl frisked Matthew again, he was made to shrug into the coat, the bruise-colored tricorn of Baron Brux was smashed down upon his head, the front door was opened and the pre-dawn cold hit him in the face like a freezing sledgehammer, and once more he was marched along between the two men to where his coach awaited at the gate.

Never mind the airship, Matthew thought. The coach was a leviathan, a landship twice as large as an ordinary vehicle of its purpose. It suited the outsized swagger of Samson Lash. The thing was shaped like a ship, with a sharp prow and a flatter stern. Its main body was painted a cream color with doors of navy blue and scarlet, two on each side, and at the back the baggage compartment was not a regular canvas tarpaulin but another pair of doors. The four horses that were destined to pull the thing were also of the larger and shaggier variety. Matthew didn't know their breed but figured the Vikings had brought their forebears over from the frozen north.

Two men bundled in heavy coats and hats sat up on the leather-padded driver's bench, one to relieve the other when necessary. By the light of the lanterns that hung from ornamental pedestals on either side of the bench, Matthew saw through the falling snow that the relief driver had easy access to a musket secured in a cowhide holder just beside his right leg.

So far, his feeble plan was going to the domain of Cardinal Black's master.

"In you go," said the Owl, as he pulled a release lever that lowered a small set of collapsible wooden steps below the doors on the coach's side. Matthew saw the guard opening the gate. He was in for it now, no matter what happened. He went up the steps, turned a brass handle and was instantly pushed from behind by Bogen into the coach.

"Good trip!" Matthew heard the Owl call. There came a whipcrack and the driver's voice shouting "Hiiiiiyupppp!" The coach gave a shudder and began moving, but slowly through the gate and onto Endsleigh Park Road.

"Settle back," said Bogen, who sat down across from Matthew. He moved his cloak aside just enough for Matthew to get a glimpse of the pistol's handle at his belt. For emphasis to this implied threat, Bogen reached into his jacket and brought out a powder horn on a leather strap, which he placed around his bulk of a shoulder.

Matthew took quick stock of his surroundings. The dark blue interior was built to carry six passengers facing each other on bench seats of red leather, with an uncommonly generous space for leg room between. A pair of lamps built onto the sides gave off enough light for a small chapel, but even Lash's money and influence couldn't reduce the fishy odor of the whale oil. White linen curtains covered small round windows—portholes—on either side. Matthew saw on the floor near his feet a wicker basket. The promised breakfast, of which he might make a use.

The coach was still not moving very fast, due to the horses plodding their way through what must've been five inches of snow. But Matthew realized that his time to act was fast running out. Still, if he was to make a

move at all, he had to wait until the coach had gotten some distance away from Lash's house and that guard at the gate.

He had decided he had only one option, in this wonderful plan of his formulated when he'd found the coal dust on the clothing of the dead constables.

He had to break back *into* the house.

But first…there was this beast of a bodyguard to take care of.

Matthew picked up the basket and opened it. Bogen watched him with his piggish eyes. Inside the basket were some slices of ham and sausages wrapped up in waxed paper, another packet of biscuits, a few slices of apples, and a wooden flask that Matthew presumed held water. "Biscuits?" he asked Bogen, offering him the packet.

Bogen took one and instantly pushed almost the whole thing into his mouth.

Matthew uncorked the flask and took a drink. Yes, it was water. He drank again. His pulse was pounding. The horses were moving steadily though not yet fast and there was no need for the whip. How far were they from the house? It was hard to tell, but—

"Water," said Bogen, holding out his hand. The biscuit crumbs were still falling from his mouth.

Matthew gave him the flask.

It was now or never.

When Bogen put the flask to his lips and tilted his head slightly back, Matthew drew a deep breath. He grasped the edge of his seat for traction and swung both legs up to kick the flask squarely into the man's teeth.

TWENTY-THREE.

Maybe it was the toughness of the elephant-hide boots.

Maybe it was pure animal desperation. Or maybe just pure fear.

Whatever it was, the power of Matthew's double kick to the flask as Bogen held it to his mouth broke the front man's teeth out and down into his throat. Bogen's head rocked back and cracked against the coach's wall behind him. Matthew had an instant to think that surely the drivers had heard it…but then with a dazed blink of his eyes and a smear of blood at his mouth Bogen righted himself and reached for his pistol.

Matthew seized the gun hand before it got there and held on for dear life. Bogen was making a strangling noise but nothing else was coming out through the crimson foam at his lips.

A hard fist with plenty of strength behind it struck Matthew's left shoulder and nearly broke his grip, but the heavy polar bear coat took most of the impact. The second blow that grazed his jaw sent stars flying through his head. He hung on as the pistol came up out of Bogen's cloak like a cobra and also like that deadly reptile swayed back and forth, Bogen trying to get a bead on Matthew and at the same time to secure his finger on the trigger.

They grappled at close quarters in the coach. Bogen got his hand under Matthew's jaw and shoved his head back with a force that sent spears of

pain through his skull, and then Matthew twisted around and slammed an elbow into Bogen's face. The pistol came loose and fell to the floor. When Matthew went for it Bogen got an arm around his throat from behind and starting choking him, all the time making an unintelligible wheezing noise as if his lungs were laboring for air. Matthew shot an elbow into Bogen's ribs, which did absolutely no good. He kicked out again, this time against the seat before him, and drove both himself and the bodyguard crashing backward.

"What's goin' on in there?" Matthew heard one of the drivers shout, the voice muffled by the wind. Bogen reached up to open the sliding viewslit between the drivers and the coach's interior but his arm was stopped when Matthew hit him in the face once, twice and again in rapid succession.

The bloodied Bogen bore down on Matthew with ferocious strength and crushed him to the floor. The man's hands clamped to his throat and began to squeeze. Matthew hammered at Bogen's sides but it was like beating on solid stone.

He heard the noise of the viewslit sliding back from the other side. "Christ, they're fightin'!" one of the men cried out. "Pull the horses up!"

Bogen was strangling Matthew, who felt the blood pounding in his face and his lifeforce ebbing by the second. Matthew got a hand up and tried to push at Bogen's chest but again it was a shove against heavy stone.

Then Bogen's wheezing turned into a gurgling noise, he suddenly let go of Matthew's throat to grasp at his own, his small piggish eyes were bloodshot and his mouth dripped ruddy foam. He began to thrash like a man gone mad, kicking at the air and clawing at his throat, and through his own considerable distress Matthew realized that Bogen was strangling on the teeth that must've gone down into his windpipe.

The coach had stopped. In a few seconds one or both of the drivers would be upon him, and one might have that musket in hand.

Matthew found the pistol as Bogen rolled this way and that between the seats, gasping like a dying fish. As he cocked the hammer, the doors to his right opened.

He put the pistol in the faces of the two men who stood there, one indeed with the musket in hand but not yet levelled to take aim.

"Drop that," Matthew said.

Either the ferocity of his command or the blood coming out of both his nostrils spoke for quick obedience, because the musket fell into the snow.

"Don't shoot, sir," the other driver said, lifting his hands. He cast a quick glance at the strangling and thrashing Bogen, and then he said, "I'm a hired man, sir, I don't have no dog in this fight."

"Move back. Both of you put your hands behind your heads." As they did so, Matthew climbed down from the coach on the little wooden steps one of the men had lowered. He kept the pistol aimed somewhere between them. If they knew how wrecked he felt they might have rushed him; he only had a shot for one man, but it appeared that neither one wished to take a ball for the vice admiral and certainly not for Bogen.

Where were they? Matthew quickly took his bearings. A faint purple blush had begun to paint the darkness of the clouds. Through the falling snow he saw they were still on Endsleigh Park Road but the illuminated windows of the Lash mansion looked to be at least a hundred yards away. Was the guard still at the gate? Had he seen the coach stop? Possibly he'd gone into the house for warmth after the coach had pulled away? Matthew couldn't worry about that at the moment; he had to move and move fast while that party of killers still sat at their feast.

"Both of you start running," Matthew said. He kept the pistol as steady as a man suffering with the shakes could. He pointed with his free hand in the direction opposite Lash's house. "That way. If I see either one of you coming back, I swear to God I'll shoot to kill."

The two drivers might fear the wrath of Samson Lash but since Lash was not present, they feared the wrath of Matthew Corbett much more, particularly as he was wild-eyed and spraying spittle, hoarse-voiced and most importantly with that gun in his grip looked like a very bad man.

"Go *now*," Matthew croaked. "Be glad you didn't wind up as shark food."

They went, without realizing Matthew had likely saved them from a horrible death at the hands of Professor Fell. Within seconds they were taken from sight by the currents of snow.

But he doubted they'd go very far without trying to get back to the house. They would hunker down somewhere, probably in the park, and wait until their courage had—

Bogen fell on him from the coach.

He went down under the man's weight, but desperately he held onto the gun as he clawed himself out from underneath the body.

When he recovered his wits he realized it was indeed a *body*, for Bogen's face had taken on a blue tinge, his hands were still clutched to his throat, his eyes and mouth were open and the snowflakes made little hissing noises as they melted upon flesh soon to be as cold as the wind, for Bogen the bodyguard was dead.

Matthew didn't know if this made him a murderer or not, but he doubted very many people had been killed by a water flask.

He made the quick decision to shrug off the polar bear coat, for its weight would be an impediment. He tossed it into the coach. A rapid search of Bogen's jacket under the cloak turned up a small fringed leather pouch that Matthew's fingers could feel contained ammunition balls and extra flints. He put that into his own jacket. The powderhorn had come off Bogen's shoulder and lay up on the coach's floor next to the flask, so Matthew retrieved that and bound its strap over his head and across one shoulder. He scanned the darkness and saw no return as yet of the drivers, but he pushed the musket deeper into the snow with his foot so it would be too wet to fire. His own pistol was probably too wet as well, in this weather, but he knew from experience that flintlocks were finicky things. After he had crushed the musket down, he turned his attention toward the park itself.

Through the snowclad trees he could see the gazebo at the park's central point. The multicolored lanterns had gone out. Matthew figured that as owner of the park, Lash probably had his servants attend those festive lamps as Lash desired to appear a herald of the Christmas season to

the residents of this exclusive neighborhood; he thought that Lash might disdain the small man, but the vice admiral wished to curry favor with those of equal wealth. In any case, Matthew had decided that if a coal wagon pulled up alongside the park and delivered warm bodies to the house for RakeHell Lizzie to slaughter, the entrance to a tunnel might be thereabouts—near enough to the manse but far enough away that no disturbance would draw unwanted attention. The gazebo, being a solid structure, might be concealing a trapdoor to a tunnel.

He climbed to the driver's bench, unhooked a lantern from one of the pedestals and made his way through the snow to the gazebo, which had a peaked roof and stood up from the ground a few feet by a set of four wooden steps. He ascended and by his light searched the gazebo's floor. The place looked fairly new, maybe built in the last few years; the floorboards had received a dusting of snow, but the roof had kept any real accumulation away. He was looking for pieces of coal that might have been caught in the clothing of the constables, but he found none. Dropping to his knees for a closer search, he could find no hatch nor other obvious opening in the gazebo's floor.

A feeling of panic gnawed at him. If he was wrong about this, all was for naught. He didn't have much time to spend scrabbling about trying to find a tunnel entrance, if indeed one existed here. But where else would it be? This seemed the most logical place. His light uncovered nothing, no bits of coal…nothing.

An image came to him of the lever that operated the coach's collapsible steps. A nice invention. Might Samson Lash, being of a mechanical mind, have put that idea to use elsewhere?

Matthew went back down the steps and searched around them. Again, the lantern's light revealed nothing. He felt along the edges of the steps. Nothing but weather-roughened wood. His sense of panic—and impending doom—flared higher. At the bottom of the steps he got on his knees once more, brushed away as much snow as he could, and felt along the ground level.

At the center, just beneath the lowest step and certainly impossible for anyone who didn't know it was there to find, was a bolt. He threw it from its latch. Nothing happened. What now?

He put the lantern aside, lodged the pistol in his waistband and used both hands to push the last step upward, thinking that maybe the whole thing collapsed in some way.

There came the rasping of a hidden hinge. The entire set of four steps, hollow within, lifted up. Revealed beneath was a dark cavity from which bloomed the dank odor of old stones. Matthew continued to push the set of steps up until they rested against the gazebo's floor. He shone the lantern down upon another set of steps, these also of wood—certainly of modern construction instead of Roman—that descended into darkness beyond the light.

He went down.

The staircase descended about twenty feet and had been built with a railing. At the bottom the floor was composed of what appeared to be old flagstones, worn smooth possibly by the ancient traffic of the Roman city. The passage was at least ten feet wide and the walls were formed of rough and broken stones though some of it had fallen to piles of rubble, exposing the dark earth behind. Matthew judged the direction from the gazebo to Lash's mansion to be to the northwest, and he began following the lantern's light.

He came across three small pieces of coal on the floor that must've been caught in the constables' clothes. So far, so good, but not far enough nor good enough.

It was soon apparent that he might not be striding along Roman roads, but instead following passageways in what could have been an ancient fortress. His light showed cavernous chambers on both sides. Here and there stood columns of stones that rose up to the ceiling. He was aware of the shrill squeaking of rats scampering away from beneath his boots, and he mused that the rodents had no respect for the glory of Rome.

He reached a fork in the passageways and took the one leading off to the left, thinking that was a more northwesterly heading. Within half a minute he came to a solid stone wall. He retraced his path, took the other passage and sped his pace, for if the drivers regained their courage and got back to the coach or the house before he did, all was lost. He was wondering also if Lash wouldn't use his second private coach to soon take Lioness, Merda, Krakowski and Montague back to their inns or wherever they were lodged, and in so doing the halted coach and Bogen's body would be found.

It all added up to the fact that he had to hurry.

The passageway narrowed and its ceiling dropped lower, nearly brushing the top of Matthew's head. The rats were bolder here and made hissing noises of anger beneath his boots. He passed a chamber where the rats were nearly climbing over themselves to get down into what looked to be an old well or something of the sort, and Matthew reasoned the bodies of the first constable, the loud-mouthed Victor and Dippen Nack—God rest a hopeless bully—had been thrown in there and served to feed the rodents as had RakeHell Lizzie's other victims.

He came to a door.

Now before him was the real test. He put the lantern down and took hold of the door's handle.

He turned it.

Or tried to turn it.

Because it would not turn.

The door was locked.

All the breath came out of him. His brain burned with the idea of defeat. So much for the brotherhood and sisterhood of the Black-Eyed Broodies! What now? was the question that rang like an alarm bell in his ears.

There was a quiet *click*.

The door opened, and before Matthew stood Elizabeth Mulloy.

Her mouth was a grim line. Her eyes took in the damage done by Bogen. "I was waiting for you," she said. Behind her about thirty feet was

the light of the open door that led out to the pit. "They're finishing up their breakfast. Samson will be taking them to their inns in about half an hour. What did you do with the coach?"

"It's up the road, not far."

"You had to kill the bodyguard," she said, with a glance at the pistol.

"Not directly, but he's taken care of." He left the lantern where it was and passed her, walking cautiously toward the pit. "The drivers are out there somewhere." He stopped just short of the pit and turned to face her. "Where are they keeping Julian?"

"The second floor, the third door on the right. There's no guard but the door will be locked. I can't help you with that."

"And Firebaugh?"

"The first door on the left."

"All right. Thank you. Will you do me one more thing?" Before she could reply, he said, "Bring me the book of potions. *Please*."

She shook her head. "No. I'm sorry, I can't do any more for you. I've got to make it appear that the door was left unlocked by mistake, so I have to return this key to the study. Then I wash my hands of it."

Matthew doubted that any amount of washing could remove the bloodstains. "Very well. Just stay out of my way."

She grasped his arm. "I ask you not to harm Samson." Her eyes were imploring. "He's all I have."

Whatever the depth of their strange relationship was, Matthew had no time to ponder. He said, "I hope there'll be no further violence. Go back to the others."

She turned away and left him without another word. Matthew used the powderhorn to ready the pistol with a dry primer. Then he crossed the pit, climbed up the stone steps past the gallery and continued upward until he reached the closed door that led to the hallway. To the right would be the stairs and the entrance foyer, to the left would be the dining room with the parlor in the middle on the other side of the corridor. Where would the Owl's men be? Still guarding the gate and the door? Scattered throughout

the lower floor? In the parlor warming themselves? And how many were there? All questions he could not answer, but risks that must be taken.

Matthew eased the door open. The hallway was clear. He quickly came out, hearing Lash's voice talking from the dining room behind him as they were likely finishing up their breakfasts. He passed the parlor and had a start as he saw two men standing with their backs to him before the fire, one listening to the other speak. The foyer and the front door were unguarded, and there before him was the table on which stood the basket of weapons. He reached in and retrieved his ivory-handled dagger, which he slid into his waistband. Then he took hold of Julian's four-barrelled wonder, and the wonder of it was that anyone could manage as heavy a thing as that. He put both guns down on the table and opened the front door. At the gate the guard was still there but was smoking a pipe, looking out toward the park, and evidently had not seen the coach stop through the snow.

Matthew returned to the table, picked up the basket of weapons—a heavy weight indeed that made his shoulder muscles crack—and moving quickly he went out the door and dumped the whole load into the snowy shrubbery off to one side of the entrance staircase.

At that moment the guard turned, saw him, and spouted a huge cough of smoke.

Matthew threw the basket aside, went back in, closed the door and threw its latch.

"Hey there! What're you doing?" someone called out.

Matthew spun around. The man who had just come down the stairs was one of those who had taken him to the room behind the pit and clouted him before stripping him naked. The man at first didn't recognize Matthew. He came striding closer, as Matthew reached the table and picked up Bogen's gun. The man abruptly stopped with a cry of alarm. He whipped open his jacket and began to pull out a pistol.

Matthew had no choice but to lift the gun and fire.

The sound of the gunshot was a small explosion. Through the bloom of acrid blue smoke Matthew saw the man clutch at his chest and fall, his

own pistol going off and firing a ball into the ceiling. The racket was loud enough to raise Dippen Nack from the dead. Matthew grasped Julian's gun and raced past the wounded man up the stairs.

The third door on the right. No need to try the lock. Matthew kicked at the door and felt as if his kneecap would burst. But he had no choice. As he was about to deliver another kick, the first door on the left opened and Lazarus Firebaugh emerged, wearing a gray silk nightgown and his eyes groggy with sleep. "Stay where you are!" Matthew shouted, levelling Julian's pistol at him, and instantly his mouth dropped open and he froze.

"Matthew?" came Julian's voice from behind the door. "What the *hell…?*"

"Stand back!" Matthew told him, and again gave the door a kick. The thing splintered but would not yet yield. He heard upraised voices below and the sound of someone coming fast up the stairs.

"Help me!" Firebaugh shouted, regaining his senses if not his courage to flee. "A man with a gun is up here!"

The moment swayed on the edge of disaster. Matthew kicked at the door again as hard as he could, his kneecap be damned. The door burst open on one hinge. At the same time, Firebaugh tried to run. Matthew scrambled after him, grabbed him by the back of his nightgown and put the gun to his head.

The man climbing the stairs—one of the Owl's crew who had escorted Matthew in to see Cardinal Black—had reached the second floor and also gripped a pistol. His steely gaze registered the gun at Firebaugh's head and said, "Let him—" but *go* would never be spoken, for a heavy blue flower vase went flying past Matthew's left shoulder and made a direct hit to the man's face, toppling him back down the way he'd come.

"I've got this," said Julian, who put one hand on the four-barrelled bastard of destruction and the other on the back of the red-bearded bastard's neck. Matthew stepped aside. A glance at Julian showed the guards had enjoyed some exercise at the bad man's expense, for Julian's left eye was bruised dark and dried blood crusted his swollen lower lip. Though

the garish yellow jacket had been taken off him, he was still wearing his Count Pellegar clown costume of gray breeches with red stripes up the legs, gray stockings, a lavender-hued blouse—now speckled with blood-stains—and the python-skin boots. He held the pistol against the back of Firebaugh's head so hard it made the doctor's eyes bulge.

"Hear me!" he called around the corner to those downstairs. "If we're not allowed free passage out of here, we'll find out if the good doctor is well-named or not!"

Lazarus, Matthew thought. Able to rise from the dead, is what Julian meant.

"He won't be of use to any of you with his brains blown out!" Julian continued. "Are you listening?"

"Listening." It was Lash's voice. "'*We*'? Who is—oh my Lord! Is *Corbett* up there with you? I thought you'd broken out on your own, but… Corbett, are you there?"

"Present," Matthew answered.

"Well, I *am* impressed! Come down and let's talk. You can tell me how you got back into my house, and perhaps we—"

"Perhaps my *ass*," Julian interrupted. "We're going out. One move I don't like and Firebaugh is a useless bag of bones." To Matthew, in a quieter voice, "Stand behind me."

"Kill him and you both are dead," said Lash. His voice was easy and betrayed no sign of distress. "Haven't you considered your situation that far?"

"You may not care, but ask the others if they want a dead chemist to go along with the winning bid!"

There was a long silence. Not quite a silence: both Matthew and Julian could hear urgent whisperings from below.

"We need to go *now*," Matthew told Julian, before Lash could think clearly enough to send men out to find the coach or to take up firing positions in the park.

"Start walking," Julian told the doctor.

"Please…let me at least get my cloak."

"*No*." Julian gave him a hard shove with the gun's barrel to the head, and Firebaugh began walking toward the staircase.

As Firebaugh, Julian and Matthew came around the corner, two pistols were levelled at them by a pair of men standing on either side of the Owl. The front door was wide open, someone having unlatched it to let in the gate's guard. Everyone had taken positions below the stairs, including Cardinal Black who stood toward the rear next to Montague. Matthew saw Elizabeth Mulloy at the very back, and when their eyes met she shook her head as an entreaty not to harm Lash. But not harming Lash was far from Matthew's mind at the moment; getting the book and getting out of the house with their skins were the foremost problems.

"Back up, all of you," Julian said. The man who'd been hit with the vase was at the bottom of the stairs next to the one who'd been shot, the former sitting up and rubbing his bloodied face, the latter stretched out moaning and clutching at his wound with both hands. Matthew saw on the steps a few risers down the pistol that had been dropped when the vase crashed home. "Keep moving," Julian told the doctor. As they went down, Matthew picked up the fallen pistol and cocked it.

"Everyone be easy," said Lash. He wore a bemused expression. "Surely you gentlemen don't think you're going to get very far, do you?"

"Shoot 'em now!" Merda urged the gunmen. "Go on, take 'em!"

"Keep your teeth in your head, shorty," Julian said. "As Lash says, everyone be easy and just keep backing up."

"You won't get out of here alive," Lioness promised, standing between Lash and Merda, with Krakowski just behind her. In her eyes burned the flames of impending violence.

"Then neither will the doctor. And we'll be able to send at least one of you to the grave. *You*! Come here!"

Matthew had no idea who Julian was addressing. Then Julian said, "*You*! RakeHell Lizzie or whatever you're calling yourself! Get over here!"

"Stay where you are, Elizabeth," Lash directed, with perhaps in his voice the faintest of quavers.

"Matthew," said Julian, "shoot her in the head if she doesn't come here in three seconds."

Matthew realized he had no reason not to obey, at least by Julian's understanding and the understanding of the others. How could he refuse? Because he was not the bad man? No, if he didn't, someone—like the Owl or Cardinal Black—might get the slightest sense that he had gotten into the house with her help, and she might be Lash's dear companion and advisor but her skin would be in jeopardy after he, Julian and the doctor had gotten out.

He aimed his gun at her head. "*One*," he said.

"Let me through," she told the others, because she too had recognized the inherent danger…not because Matthew would shoot her, but because a brother Black-Eyed Broodie could *not*. "It's all right," she said to Lash when he took hold of her arm. "No one should be hurt on account of these two. Especially not for that doctor…or for *him*." She lifted her chin with disdain toward the cardinal.

"*Two*," Matthew said.

Lash let her go, but he glowered pure hatred at Matthew and Julian.

When Elizabeth reached Julian, he grasped the neckline of her gown and turned her so his pistol barrel was between her head and Firebaugh's. "Everyone into the parlor," Julian said. "Go in and slide the door shut. Matthew is going to stand here with his gun on Firebaugh, and Lizzie is going to take me back to get the book. After that, we'll be on our way."

Brave words, Matthew thought, because Julian had no idea the coach was up the road about a hundred yards.

"You won't get far," Lash said. His eyes were cold and dead. "You have two guns but not very many shots, it appears."

"We have enough, and I hope you'll keep your own gun in its place. Firebaugh is going to be standing up against the door if anyone has the idea of shooting through it."

"So what good is that bastard if you've stolen the book?" Montague said at the parlor's threshold. "That's not much of a—"

"The book is more easily recovered than the doctor replaced," said Lash, still with a withering glare aimed at Matthew and Julian. "I know where they're taking it and the route they'll be using to get there. Unless they want to kill me right now, and use up one of their shots, I can get that book back within a day."

"Are you tempting me?" Julian asked, with a curl of his injured mouth.

"Go ahead," Lash replied. "Use that shot and see what happens."

"*Please*," said Elizabeth. "Samson, just do as he says."

Matthew realized Elizabeth was trying to protect both Lash and her brother Broodie. Also that since Lash had the airship plans he didn't give much of a damn about the book any longer, but he could not reveal that to the assembled group. He had the plans and a fortune in the Prussians' gold, and that had been the point of the entire endeavor.

"We shall," he replied. "Let us retire to the parlor, everyone. Owl, you and your men go ahead."

Cardinal Black strode forward so quickly Matthew hardly had time to swing the pistol in his direction. Black stopped a few feet from Matthew, cocked his elongated face to one side, and with a grim smile said, "You and your friend are declaring war not only on me, but on all gathered here. Devane is a killer. *You* are not. And here he is leading you to your destruction. Be certain that I will follow you to the ends of the earth to—"

With an explosion of anger, Matthew hit him across the face with the barrel of his gun. Black's nose crunched and the blood burst out. He staggered back into Lioness Sauvage, who thrust him away from her as if he carried leprosy. Krakowski made a move to lunge at Matthew in the confusion of bodies, but the black-eyed brooding hole of Matthew's gun in his face drained his enthusiasm for attack.

"Calm, everyone," said Lash. "We have time to correct this situation." To Elizabeth he said, "Don't fret, dear. We'll all survive this minor setback. I trust Mr. Devane has a light hand with a lady."

"Into the parlor," Julian said.

They all obeyed, including Black with his bloody, broken nose. The last in was Lash, who slid the door shut. True to his word, Julian pushed Firebaugh up against the door. "Stand behind him," he told Matthew. "They won't shoot through the door…I don't think. If they do, the ball won't reach you." To Matthew's dismay, Julian's light hand with a lady included twisting one of her arms behind her back. "To the study," he said, and he marched her off along the hallway.

In Lash's study, Julian released Elizabeth to pick up the red leather-bound book where Lash had left it on the desk. He paged quickly through it by the light of the desk's lantern to make sure it was the real thing, and though he couldn't make heads or tails of it he did see that it was composed of chemical formulas. He slid it down in his blouse.

"Satisfied now?" Elizabeth asked. "Just take it and get out."

"Not satisfied yet," Julian answered. He had seen an edge of the airship plans protruding from beneath the desktop's blotter where Lash must've put them before Merda's visit to the study. He drew out all five sheets of the parchment. Then he pulled the lantern closer and removed its glass chimney to reveal the naked flame.

"What're you *doing*?" The young woman's voice carried a note of alarm.

"I don't care to be held down and beaten. This is my payment." So saying, he held the first sheet to the flame.

She attacked him, not with the supple grace of RakeHell Lizzie but with the wild desperation of Elizabeth Mulloy. She got an arm around his throat and squeezed but in her current state she was no match for Julian; he threw an elbow into her jaw that knocked her nearly senseless and then he tossed her like a bag of rags against the wall.

Methodically and with great joy, Julian burned all but one sheet to brown crisps that he scattered across the top of Lash's desk. When Elizabeth started up off the floor, he kicked her down again. The bad man was in his full glory. He set fire to the fifth sheet and when it had burned nearly to his fingers he blew it out so only a charred remnant remained.

"Get up," he told her.

"You don't know what you've done!" she said as she staggered up, her eyes wet with both rage and pain.

"I know." He shoved her out of the study. "*Move*."

Instantly Matthew saw that violence had been done to Elizabeth. "Julian! What have—"

"He burned the plans!" she said, nearly sobbing. "This insane *idiot*! He burned them!"

"Not all of them." Julian moved Firebaugh back from the door with an elbow to the ribs and dropped the remaining fragment on the floor. "Now," he said triumphantly, "we have the book, we have the chemist, and I presume the coach you obviously escaped from is somewhere near."

"A hundred yards up the road," Matthew said.

"Good. Our hostage won't have to walk too far in the snow, will she?"

"Our…*hostage*?"

"We're taking Miss Mulloy," Julian said. "No resistance from you, please." He put the gun to her head. She looked at Matthew for help, but he was unable to give it. Julian was already pushing both Firebaugh and Elizabeth toward the foyer and the open door.

Matthew started after them, but stopped to look down upon the remnant of the airship plans on the floor.

All that was left was about the length of a man's thumb. Matthew had the bad feeling that Julian had just declared war upon Samson Lash, and combined with Cardinal Black and the other killers who would want both the book and their revenge…

…it was going to be a very long way back to Y Beautiful Bedd.

Someone had begun to slide the parlor door open, an inch at a time.

"Elizabeth?" Lash called. And again, more urgently: "*Elizabeth*?"

Matthew turned and ran.

FOUR.

SQUIRRELS AND CATS

TWENTY-FOUR.

"What are we to *do*?"

Samson Lash did not answer. He sat at his desk in the study. Before him was a white clay cup bearing the brown ashes he had gathered from the desktop. The remnant of parchment paper he'd found on the floor lay under the fingers of his right hand. Every so often his fingers trembled.

"What are we to *do*?" Cardinal Black asked again, through the bloody cloth pressed to his battered nose. Both his eyes had turned a shiny shade of purple.

"Do," said Lash after another moment of silence. His voice was distant, his eyes unfocused. "Yes. We must do *something*."

"The others want to know! We must get *after* them! Every minute we dawdle, they—"

"*Hush*," Lash whispered, and though it was only a whisper it was enough to make Cardinal Black shut his mouth in obedience, for beneath the soft voice was a sound like a blade being sharpened on a grinder. Lash turned the cup of ashes between his hands. "Bring the Owl to me," he said.

Black left the study, and the vice admiral sat alone turning between his hands the cup of his burned dreams.

Not quite one hour ago, Lash and his guests had emerged from the parlor. "Elizabeth!" Lash had cried out, and when no answer was given he knew the worst. Then, upon the realization Elizabeth had been taken by Devane and Corbett, he had seen on the floor at his feet the most horrible thing…the thing that stole his voice and made his heart hammer and killed something in his soul…for immediately he knew what it was, and running at breakneck speed to his study there was the rest of it scattered atop his desk, and at that moment an icy cold and frozen grip seized upon him that was like falling from the world he had held under firm control onto the threshold of another where chaos and insanity ruled. Thus he was made small and shivering as he stared down upon what had been mockingly left for him to find.

In the space of time since Devane and Matthew had departed, the Owl had sent the remaining four of his men who could walk—minus Perry with a bullet wound in his upper chest—out into the park, where Bogen's body had been found and one of the coach's drivers had emerged from his hiding-place to relate the story. Bogen was brought in and deposited in the foyer, and Samson Lash had sent a man down into the pit to find that the door to the passages had been unlocked. How Corbett had discovered the entrance beneath the gazebo's steps and who had left the door unlocked—or who had unlocked it on purpose—were questions that Lash was not yet prepared to consider.

After a few minutes in which Lash continued to turn the cup between his hands and contemplate the bitter twistings of fate, Cardinal Black returned with the Owl.

"Close the door," Lash told the cardinal, still speaking in a wan and quiet voice. Then, to the Owl: "Your men are gone?"

"Just now. I instructed that Perry be taken to the Highcliff hospital."

Lash nodded, staring at the cup. The Owl had previously arranged for two coaches to arrive at six o'clock to transport his team of six security guards back to their homes. By their agreement, payment for the Owl's services was now due and then he was to be ferried to his own townhouse in Southwark by one of Lash's coaches.

"Sit down," said Lash.

The Owl pulled a chair up before the vice admiral's desk while Black stood in a shadowed corner probing at his blood-crusted nostrils and occasionally making a noise that was between a growl and a spit.

The Owl said, "Sir, I regret—"

"Don't speak," Lash interrupted. He kept turning the cup of ashes around and around, and then at last he released a long quiet sigh and put it aside. "Well," he said. "Here we are."

"May I say something?" the Owl ventured, and when Lash did not reply he dared to go further. "They can't be travelling very fast in this weather. I'm sure you know the route they must be taking, and—"

"The northwest pike," said Lash. "Yes, I know."

"—and also I doubt that either Devane or Corbett have much experience in handling a coach of that size or a four-horse team. They will be hobbled by their circumstances. You, on the other hand, do not have to concern yourself with guarding two hostages and I presume you have another driver at hand."

Lash gave a brief nod, though he was staring through the Owl.

"They might get as far as the first coach inn," the Owl went on, "though I doubt that as well. In any case, the horses must be stopped to rest, and sooner than later in this snowfall. My opinion is that—as you yourself have stated—you can catch them within the day."

"Thank you," the vice admiral said, "for your opinion."

A silence stretched.

The Owl shifted nervously in his chair. "Samson...we have worked together...been compatriots...for these last three years. I have served you to the best of my ability, and certainly I have proven my worth in supplying the...um...raw material for Miss Mulloy's episodes. I will continue to serve you in any way I can...and as a matter of respect and trust, I shall adjust my payment for this past night to half of what we have agreed upon." He blinked, as this news had not caused an iota of reaction from Lash. "Is that not a fair accounting?"

Lash leaned back in his chair. "I want to know," he said, "who left that door unlocked. When your men took the bodies in they were given the key, which was returned and is now in the first drawer of this desk. Whoever failed to lock the door allowed Corbett to get in here. Who was it?"

"I would have to make an inquiry. And believe me, I shall!"

"No inquiry is needed," said Lash. "I hold *you* accountable, and that I consider fair."

"Yes, of course, but…those men are my regulars. My *best.* They've done this before, they surely haven't forgotten their instructions!" The Owl's head swivelled around, more quickly than usual, to take note of Cardinal Black standing in the corner, and then came back around to face the vice admiral once again. "Something I noticed…something *strange*…about Corbett and Miss Mulloy." He hurried on before Lash could respond. "It happened so fast…just an impression I had…that when Devane told Corbett to shoot her after the count of three…he *hesitated.* And what passed across his face was an expression of…I don't know…reluctance or repugnance, whatever it might have been. It was *there.* I see those things, Samson. I *sense* them. You know I do, and that's part of what you pay me for."

"Corbett didn't wish to kill a woman," said Black. "He's funny that way."

"*More* than that," the Owl rushed on. "The whole thing about Miss Mulloy climbing down off him in the pit, and wanting you to send him back to Professor Fell. It seemed to me at the moment to be…well…an *excuse* not to kill him. I didn't say anything, because I know you trust her as your advisor, and rightly so. But…even there when Corbett had his gun on her…something passed between them. I saw it in their faces. He was not going to shoot her, Samson…and she *knew* he was not going to. Right after that, *she* was the one who said no one should be hurt on account of those two!" His mouth twisted below the protuberant golden eyes. "Her! As many as she's put to death!"

Lash's solemn face was immobile.

"And...*and*," the Owl said, "consider this! She excused herself from the breakfast table. It wasn't ten minutes after she returned that we heard the first gunshot!"

"He's blathering, Lash," said Cardinal Black. "About to start weeping, I think."

"No, listen to me! Is it possible...at all possible...that she went down and unlocked the door for him? That she told him how to get in through the gazebo? That she has some kind of connection with him that we don't know?"

It was a moment before Lash replied, during which he reached out for the cup again and stirred the ashes gently with his index finger. "One of your men made the error," he said. "You shame yourself by trying to muddy my Elizabeth. She has never known about the gazebo. I built that some months after I brought her home, and there was never any need for her to know."

"And I know why!" said the Owl, whose face had begun to display a sheen of sweat. "You didn't want her running off into the city and murdering someone the law might take notice of! Because you could barely control her yourself, when she goes mad!"

"Control your tongue," Lash said softly. He stood up, which made the Owl also start to stand up but Lash said, "Stay seated. I have a complaint against your service that you may wish to weigh against your future value." He walked around behind the Owl and placed his huge hands on the man's frail shoulders. The Owl's head turned to an impossible angle to look up—fearfully—toward the hulking giant at his back.

Lash leaned down and spoke quietly into the Owl's right ear. "For all your vaunted service and *sense*, you allowed two imposters to enter my house on the most important night of my life. You allowed them to take my Elizabeth and the book. You caused my airship to be lost... *forever* lost..."

"I did my duty I swear it how was I to know—"

"*Shhhhhh*," Lash whispered. "You are paid to know. And here you are, adjusting your payment downward to account for the negligent act of—"

His hands clasped the sides of the Owl's head.

"—destroying *everything*," said Lash, and suddenly his face flamed red, his eyes widened and in an instant were shot through with blood, his teeth clenched together with a ferocity that nearly shattered them from his mouth, and the muscles in his arms beneath the medalled jacket jumped and twisted into knots as his hands began to squeeze.

The Owl cried out and tried to stand, but already the power of Lash's hands was crushing his skull inward. Four seconds after the pressure had begun the Owl's body began to writhe and jerk, the golden eyes rolled up to show the whites, his own teeth chattered like a symphony of bones and his hands flailed as if trying to find a grip in the air.

Lash gave a bestial shout that made the wall shake behind Cardinal Black and trembled the glass window that looked upon the courtyard. His face was bloated with blood. As he continued to crush the Owl's skull, his next shout to the god of vengeance made scarlet burst in a spray from his nostrils. Cardinal Black, for all his callous bloodlettings to the dark entity he called 'master', pressed himself deeper into his far corner and tried to become as thin a presence as possible, for it was apparent that Samson Lash's rage had been released and with it the raw power of madness.

Blue veins stood out in Lash's hands and pulsed at his throat. There was a sudden loud broomstick *crack* of breaking bone followed by the lesser cracklings of sinews and muscles giving way like the timbers of a house in a hurricane. The Owl's face collapsed inward. The left eye exploded from its socket and hung down the concave cheek by its oyster-colored string. Still Lash's hands clutched the sides of the Owl's misshapen head, and still the head became more misshapen as Lash's strength put paid to the bill.

The Owl's open mouth released a shuddered moan. The body writhed in its chair, a bizarre sight as the arms and legs were set in one direction and the broken skull in the other. Blood gouted from the mouth, the nostrils and the ears at the same time. Lash hauled the Owl up, swung his body

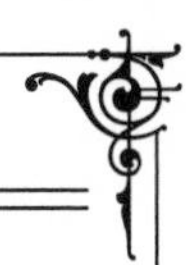

around and sent it smashing into the wall five feet away from Cardinal Black. As the Owl's limp form sagged to the floor, Lash again picked the body up and hurled it into the wall, which cracked at the same time as did most of the Owl's remaining intact bones. For a third time Lash heaved the body up and crashed it against the wall, his face a swollen rictus of rage. Then Lash began to stomp his heavy boots upon the crushed head, and at that time the study's door flew open and Lioness Sauvage stood in the opening with Meacham, the uniformed doorman, behind her. Both of them recoiled from the sight before them. Lash shouted, "*Get out*!" as he continued to stomp down upon the ruined mass at his feet.

They retreated. Lash gave the body a few final kicks and then, his face shining with sweat and the breath rasping in his lungs, he leaned over his desk and placed his hands upon the edges for support. With a grinding of his teeth he picked up the cup of brown ashes and threw them into what had been the Owl's face, now become a scarlet crater with its lower jaw hanging off and its remaining eyesocket somewhere up where the forehead used to be.

Lash stood breathing heavily and looking down upon his work.

"*If*," Black said quietly, still pressed into his corner, "I may speak?"

"Speak."

"For all his negligence, he presented some valid points. Devane and Corbett must be followed and taken. They cannot be allowed this insult to your honor. You have a second coach and you have a driver. You have—*we* have—an auction to conclude."

"Go on," said Lash, continuing to breathe hard.

"In this house," Black said, as he slid forward, "is one of the greatest assortment of killers you might ever hope to find. Tell them that the auction will conclude when the book is recovered, and when that is done you will announce the winner. I'm sure they would much rather join a manhunt than spend fruitless time twiddling their thumbs in their rooms. Yes?"

Lash spent a silent moment pondering the suggestion. Then: "That will set them against each other, will it not?"

"We will all be travelling in the same coach, with you as the arbiter of this contest. And with your dispatch of Victor you have demonstrated your willingness to command order from chaos. I, of course, will be there as well to…as the saying goes…watch your back." Black approached nearer to the vice admiral, minding his footing on the mess below. "Use what is at hand," he said. "Four killers of international renown—and you and myself—against Devane and Corbett. They don't stand a chance, but we must hasten our path."

Lash stared down at the last of the ashen crisps being dissolved into the bloody swamp that had been a human face.

He straightened up.

"Go tell Meacham to wake Hodder, if he's sleeping." Hodder was the alternate driver, who kept a room in the coach house next to the stable. "Give word to Hodder to harness the second team and ready the coach. I'll expect to be off within the hour. Then tell Meacham to gather up the empty wine bottles, fill them with gunpowder and…no, I don't want Elizabeth or Firebaugh blown to bits. Fill them with lamp fuel, cork them and stand them upright in a box. Gather also some cotton wadding. And," he added before Black could leave the room, "tell the others I will address them as soon as I clean myself of this mess the Owl has made."

"At once," said Black, and he departed.

Lash's rage was not yet subdued. As soon as Black had left the study, the vice admiral overturned his desk and threw it aside like so much straw stuffing. He took the basket of satchels and flung them against the blood-smeared wall, for in his fury he had no interest in gold.

Standing in the shambles of his study with the corpse at his feet, Lash put his hands to his head, squeezed his eyes shut and cried out a curse to the gods. Taking Elizabeth was one thing, but destroying the airship plans…that was a death sentence for Devane and Corbett, and the book of potions be damned. All Lash desired now, to stem these currents of rage that were sweeping him toward the deeper and darker waters of madness, was to get his hands upon those two, tear them to pieces and dance upon their broken bones. He had to go out and address the others. They would go, all right. Such a hunt would be a pleasure for them, and with the book in the balance…yes, they would go. But there was one small item that Lash thought neither Devane nor Corbett had considered, and because of it their coach might not get very far. In fact, their journey might end before they even got to the northwest pike.

If Elizabeth had one of her spells and could get hold of a blade, she would kill them both. Unfortunately, in that unfettered condition she might also dispatch Firebaugh.

Lash wanted to wash his hands of the Owl's fluids and change his clothes before he spoke to the others, and with revenge and murder foremost in his fevered mind he left the study and strode along the corridor, leaving bloody bootprints in his wake.

TWENTY-FIVE.

"By way of introduction," said Matthew over the pistol he held on Lazarus Firebaugh, "my name is Matthew Corbett, the man driving this coach is Julian Devane, and we're taking you to Professor Fell's village in Wales, where you will search the book I'm sitting on to prepare a potion. After that, you can jump off a cliff as far as I'm concerned."

Firebaugh, ashiver in his nightgown for the cold was a steely presence within the coach, gave a slight, crooked smile. "Prepare a potion? Why?"

"Never mind that now. Just settle back and enjoy the—" The coach felt for an instant as if the wheels had lost traction and the whole thing was sliding to the right, but before Matthew could register the fear of an impending wreck the wheels caught the road once more. "Ride," Matthew finished.

Elizabeth was staring burning holes through him. She had the polar bear coat draped over her as a blanket, only her head showing over its bulky folds. She said, "He was a fool to destroy the plans. You should've told him...take the book, take the doctor, take me along if you please...but don't touch those plans."

"I didn't know what he was going to do. I couldn't have stopped him anyway."

"You'll wish you had," she answered.

"You'll wish you'd never been born after the vice admiral finishes with you," said Firebaugh, crossing one thin bare leg over the other. "He'll be on the road by now. You won't make it to Uxbridge before he nabs you."

"We'll see," Matthew said. Julian was driving the horses as hard as he could, but in this weather it was an iffy proposition. The team could not gallop full out and they were constrained to a canter through the snow. Even so, it was a hard go for them and Matthew realized—as Julian must—that they were not going to last more than several hours. Certainly not a full day. Could Julian get the best out of them? It was difficult to say, because before climbing up to the driver's seat he'd told Matthew he had limited experience driving a four-horse team and none with a coach of this size and weight. So indeed the future seemed, like the breaking dawn, dark and stormy.

"This is a farce," said Firebaugh. His eyes glinted with what Matthew considered to be the cunning of a trapped animal, though from time to time the animal shivered from the chill. "If you need me to concoct a potion, then surely you're not going to use that pistol. I don't think you'd shoot Miss Mulloy, either. You're not the type. So what is there to stop either one of us from jumping out of this coach at the very minute? We might have a rough landing, but I think we'd survive."

"Damage would be done, snow or not," Matthew replied. "You wouldn't get far with a broken leg, and I can tell you that you'd receive rougher treatment from Julian than you would care to experience. So again I advise you to settle back and don't consider anything stupid."

"What is *stupid* is this entire enterprise." Firebaugh's upper lip curled in a sneer of disgust. "Thinking you could get away with this?" He leaned forward slightly. "You have begun a game of squirrels and cats, you and your accomplice being the squirrels. You can run all you please, but the cats are on the prowl and when they get their claws into you it will seal your graves. But then again, the vice admiral might save you and your driver for his pit." He shrugged and settled back against his seat once more. "Didn't you witness the entertainment provided by the lovely RakeHell Lizzie?"

"Please, Doctor," said Elizabeth. Her countenance had darkened. "Don't."

"Oh, but I *must*," Firebaugh answered. "It is my duty, to explain to this young fool that sitting before him in these close quarters is a far superior killer to the ones who now are likely coming after him with blood in their eyes. Mr. Corbett, haven't you heard of the Spitalfields Murderess?"

"*Please*," Elizabeth repeated.

"The Spitalfields Murderess," said Firebaugh, who spoke with an expression of sadistic delight. "Otherwise known as RakeHell Lizzie or her Christian name, Elizabeth Mulloy. Yes, here she is, right before you." He frowned at Matthew's blank stare. "Don't you read *Lord Puffery's Pin*? It was a featured story for almost four months!"

"I'm not a regular reader of that publication."

"Well, you missed it then! All the gory details of how a young woman who has been victimized for years by unscrupulous and conniving—and brutal, I would say—men finally toppled over the edge from disturbance into madness. And forming her leather gloves with the extended razors—as she is actually and has been a very talented seamstress—she began to go out at night into the heart of Spitalfields to lure men into alleyways from which they did not return. Am I giving you fair enough credit, dear Elizabeth?"

"I want you," she said evenly, "to stop talking."

"But Mr. Corbett should know one more important thing, should he not? That you and I have a long history, before Samson Lash took you away from me. Oh, yes. Truth be told." Firebaugh offered a chilling smile to Matthew. "You see, I told a little lie when I explained how Samson Lash and I connected with each other. He came to Highcliff hospital not to have a boil lanced, but to have a conference concerning placing his insane wife in the asylum I directed there. And lo and behold...in those halls of bedlam he met an *angel*."

"I think that should be enough," Elizabeth said, but her voice was weak because she knew it would not be enough.

"Met her that day when he came to my office," Firebaugh went on. "After the treatment she had become good with figures and I let her do some accounting. The work seemed to calm her, and by all means I intended to keep her calm…because, as you no doubt know, she can be a trifle *active*." Firebaugh paused for a moment, as the fine landship of a coach sailed along the snowy road on the western side of London and the sound of the horses' hooves were like muffled drumbeats against the frozen earth. His eyes narrowed. "Just a moment. *Matthew Corbett.* I am familiar with that name, from somewhere. I can't quite place it. Oh…a favor, please. Would you remove your finger from the trigger of that pistol? If we happened to hit a bump, my usefulness to you might come to a sudden end."

Matthew did as Firebaugh asked. He lowered the gun but kept it in his lap. Of course the doctor was right; the gun was simply a hollow threat. Matthew drew the ivory-handled dagger that had belonged to Albion out of his jacket, pretended to inspect the blade so Firebaugh could get a good look at it, and then set it at his side. Such a dagger was a better threat, for a cut could be delivered whereas a bullet could not be.

"Oh look, Lizzie," said Firebaugh in a silken voice, "he's brought a nice sharp toy for you to play with."

"I know what you're trying to do," she said. "You're trying to awaken it."

Matthew definitely did not like this avenue of conversation. He thought he probably should put the blade back into his jacket, but before he could do so he felt the coach begin to slow…slower…slower yet…and the coach stopped.

"Stay still," he told both of them. He drew aside the white linen curtain at the porthole on his left and was greeted by the sight of snow falling upon a stark gray tableau of shops on some street it appeared the dawn had not yet awakened.

The doors on the right opened. Julian peered in, his gun in hand. His face had taken on a blue cast and he was shivering. Snow frosted the cloak and the tricorn he had taken from Bogen's body. Found in a buttoned pocket

within the cloak were four crowns, sixteen shillings and a few pence, a goodly amount but quite a comedown from a satchel full of gold bars.

"I'm freezing out here," he managed to say to Matthew, though his tongue was thickened by the cold. "Need a heavier coat and a woolen cap. Gloves, too. We're stopped alongside a goods shop. I'm breaking in. Need anything?"

"I could use a coat, sir," said the doctor. "Winter stockings for my legs as well, and while you're at it find me a jug of some nice hot cider."

"I wasn't talking to you, shithead."

"Oh, but you *should* be. Corbett tells me I'm needed to prepare a potion of some kind at the end of this delightful journey. How can I do so, if I have frozen to death on the trip?"

Julian's blue-lipped mouth set into a grim line, which told Matthew that he was thinking exactly what Matthew had considered: the doctor had them over a barrel of sorts, and he must be protected—if not downright coddled—to get him to Fell's village in working order.

Julian gave not a glance to Elizabeth. He closed the doors. Matthew watched through the porthole as Julian approached one of the shopfronts, swung with the butt of his pistol and broke the glass. Another swing, and more shattering of the display window followed. Then all was silent but the soft shrilling of the wind around the coach, as obviously Julian had gotten into the shop.

Suddenly Firebaugh moved.

It was so fast and unexpected that he had burst the doors open and was halfway out of the coach before Matthew could react. Matthew reached out to grab the nightgown but the man in it had already leaped from the coach and was running through the snow. Matthew let out a "Hey!" as if that would stop the doctor's flight. He had an instant of quandry: leave Elizabeth and the book? Leave the dagger lying on the seat?

"Julian!" he shouted, but Julian was inside the shop looting the goods which was exactly what Firebaugh had been waiting for. Matthew had to make a split-second decision. With the pistol in one hand he caught up the

dagger and jumped out in pursuit. His boots sank into the crust, but that same crust was hobbling Firebaugh. Still, the man was running as if his ass were aflame. The nightgown flew around his thin body like a distress flag. Matthew had a quick sense of the street being deserted, the morning's light hardly the glow of a few candles against the clouds. Firebaugh was running for an alley up the way. Suddenly he slipped and fell, got up and ran on and then Matthew's feet slipped out from under him and he also went down. Firebaugh was about ten yards from the alley. If he got into it and into the maze of streets beyond, he—

—*might* have escaped, but for Julian coming in at an angle across Matthew and hitting Firebaugh with his body like a four-horse team.

Firebaugh gave a squalling sound as he fell. As Matthew reached them Julian was standing over the doctor with his free hand gripping the front of Firebaugh's nightgown and the pistol at his forehead.

"Go ahead," said Firebaugh. Snow whitened his red beard and his eyebrows. He grinned. "You wouldn't *dare*."

Julian shot a glance at Matthew. He let go of Firebaugh and said to Matthew, "Hold this." He offered the pistol, and at the same time he took the dagger from Matthew's hand.

Then without hesitation he grasped hold of Firebaugh's left ear and drove the dagger through it.

Firebaugh's scream echoed up and down the street. Dogs started barking from somewhere near.

Julian tore upward with the blade. Though the dagger was not so useful in cutting as it was in sticking, it still took away a large part of the upper half of Firebaugh's ear. The man screamed and thrashed and threw blood upon the snow. Then Julian grabbed the front of the doctor's nightgown again, pulled the man's horror-stricken face up close to his and said in a voice matter-of-fact and without emotion, "You will not try to run again. You have another ear and a nose. Understand?"

Firebaugh nodded. But Julian wasn't finished. He sliced a thin groove with the dagger across the doctor's forehead and through his right eyebrow.

"*That,*" said the bad man to Firebaugh's sobbing, "is so you really *do* understand."

"*Yes yes I do I swear it!*"

Julian caught Matthew giving him a look that said he'd gone a slice too far. "I'll start anew and afresh tomorrow," Julian said. "So shut up."

And with that, fresh terror leaped into Matthew's heart and as he turned to run back to the coach, Julian shouted "The woman!" It was not so much losing Elizabeth as a dubious hostage that sped his legs, but the idea that she might have taken the book. Still, the doors on the righthand side of the coach remained open and neither he nor Julian had seen her emerge; and yet of course she might have slipped out the other side, and gone.

When he peered into the coach he found that the Spitalfields Murderess had pushed aside the heavy coat and opened the breakfast basket where it lay on the floor between the seats. She was eating a biscuit and a slice of ham.

Her eyebrows went up. "Caught him, I'm guessing."

Matthew nodded. The red leatherbound book remained exactly where it had been when he'd sprang out after Firebaugh. In another moment Julian arrived with the doctor in tow. He shoved the whimpering and bloody man into the coach. Firebaugh curled up on a seat and clasped one hand to the wreckage of his ear and the other to his sliced face.

"Here." Julian gave Matthew back the blade and retrieved his own gun. "There are two people watching us from a window and three others have come out to stand across the street. I'm going back in and grab what I can." He registered Elizabeth sitting quietly and eating her ham and biscuit. "Better not try anything," he warned her, but Matthew thought it was just to hear himself say it. Then he closed the coach's doors and went about his looting in earnest.

"The smell of blood," said Elizabeth. "Thick in here."

The way she said that made his stomach give a twinge. She kept unhurriedly eating her food. When she was done, she brushed the crumbs from her sea-green gloves and said, "You should put that dagger away."

Did any man on earth obey a suggestion as quickly? The dagger, which Julian had been thoughful enough to wipe clean in the snow, went into Matthew's jacket and out of sight.

"Monsters!" Firebaugh groaned. "You both are—*oh my Jesus*!" He tried to sit up and nearly tumbled down between the seats. In his blood-smeared face his widened eyes were fixed upon Matthew. "You!" he wheezed. "Matthew Corbett! Oh my Jesus…the Monster of Plymouth! In the *Pin*! I knew I recognized your—" He gave a groan and clutched at the remnant of his ear, after which he huddled himself up on the seat and seemed to go into a delirious daze of muttering and shivering.

"He's gone 'round the bend," said Matthew, unwilling to answer any questions concerning the murderous and quite false reputation bestowed upon him by *Lord Puffery's Pin*.

"Interesting you should say that, since he made a living off those who had—as you put it—gone 'round the bend. I should hope he recovers enough not to wet himself, or otherwise."

"Ho there!" a man called. "You in the coach! Is someone hurt?"

People would be gathering in the aftermath of Firebaugh's scream. Matthew peered out the porthole on the right side and saw four men standing on the other side of the street. If they had seen Julian robbing the goods store, they had not yet taken action…but then again, unless one of them owned the shop it was unlikely they would.

"Anyone hurt in there?" the man called again.

Then Julian's voice replied, "Hold where you are, gentlemen." It was spoken with a measure of threat.

"No trouble, sir! We want no trouble!"

"Be mindful of that." The doors opened and Julian, who had made sure the gathering Samaritans had seen the weapon of a Philistine, threw into the coach two horse blankets, a quilted red-and-yellow plaid banyan robe and a blue woolen cap. He himself had found a pair of deerskin gloves and a brown woolen cap to wear on his bald head under his tricorn. "I'll take that coat, madam," he told Elizabeth. "You can warm yourself under a blanket." He glanced at Matthew's disapproving expression. "They only had *children's* coats in there. Must've sold out the others before this snow. Your *coat*, please." He gave the men across the street another view of the four-barrelled widow-maker. "A wagon's coming," he said, taking the polar bear coat that Elizabeth offered. "It's time to go." He closed the doors once again and in another moment he was heard to flick the reins and call out, "Giddap!" He had to do this twice more to get the team moving, for evidently they were used to the regular driver's voice and hand on the reins.

The coach, frosty at its joints, creaked forward. Elizabeth pulled one of the blankets up to her neck. Matthew put on the blue cap and got under the second blanket. When Firebaugh recovered, he could put the banyan on over his nightshirt and his bare legs would have to do without winter stockings.

Matthew set the book beside him and placed the pistol on top of it. It seemed that the Spitalfields Murderess and his Broodie sister was in no hurry to leave the company. He took a biscuit and a slice of ham from the basket and chewed on them. By this time Julian had urged the team to a canter again, and they were obviously strong horses but they weren't going to last too many hours in these conditions. At any rate, Lash's second coach would be facing the same difficulties though that team likely had a driver with more skill than Julian.

He finished off the food before he asked Elizabeth the question he'd been holding. "Why didn't you run?"

"I don't like the cold," she said.

"A flimsy reason. Any one of those men gathered out there would've helped you."

"Help from *men* is what I do not wish. Anyway, I didn't care to be mauled by your associate. And there's another reason that you probably should take into consideration."

"What might that be?"

"I am staying with you," she said, "in order to uphold my vow of loyalty to another Broodie. But when Samson catches you, I won't be able to

save your life. I am staying with you—and I will not attempt an escape—so that I might plead to Samson that you deserve a quick death."

"Oh, well I'm relieved to hear that," Matthew said with a twist of his mouth.

"I'm absolutely serious." Her calm, level gaze said she was. "He will kill you. He *has* to, not just for taking me and the book but for destroying the plans. Your associate—Julian—will likely wind up back in the pit with RakeHell Lizzie. You, on the other hand, will receive a bullet to the head if I'm successful."

"If I had a cup of ale," said Matthew, "I would offer a toast for your success."

"Make humor if you please, but this is the best I can do for you. I would say I'm sorry, if there were any other way."

"Don't be sorry on my account. I plan on getting to Fell's village alive, with the doctor and the book...and you as well, because you're right about Julian doing you harm if you tried to run. That would put me in a very difficult spot."

She nodded, watching him thoughtfully. "If you were in my place, would you have done for me what I've done for you?"

It was a good question, and one that Matthew could not honestly answer in the affirmative. Opening the door in the passageway was a real act of Broodie sisterhood that might have cost her her life, and might yet if Lash figured out the connection. "I appreciate all that you've done," he said. "And especially that you didn't kill me."

"Kill me...monsters...both of them...monsters," Firebaugh muttered in his stupor. His eyes opened and he sat up as if not realizing where he was. Then fresh pain hit him, he made a sobbing noise and curled himself up once more. Matthew tossed the banyan robe over him, and moving in slow increments the pitiful doctor drew it around his body like a shroud, even though its plaid was so gaudy it wouldn't be suited for a Scottish funeral.

"What's all this about the Monster of Plymouth?" Elizabeth asked, as she took another biscuit from the breakfast offerings.

"No idea. I think he has the wrong Matthew Corbett in mind. I'm sure there are several in London."

"True," she answered, eating her biscuit with small little bites. "For a man who seems so...shall I say...unimposing, you made quick work of that bodyguard. And you sure don't seem the type who would run with the Broodies. When I saw that tattoo on your hand it was nearly the shock of my life."

"It was nearly the *end* of mine," said Matthew.

Elizabeth was quiet for a while. She finished her biscuit and ate a few slices of apple. She looked out the porthole at the passing snowscape, for by this time they had left the confines of London and were moving through the small villages that stood just to the west of the great city.

"Are you afraid of me?" she suddenly asked.

"Yes," Matthew said. No use to mince words on that question.

"I can feel it. I could always feel fear. I thought I felt it in the parlor, but I reasoned it was the tension of the group. I presume it was coming from you and your associate."

"From me, most certainly." He gave her a wan smile which she did not return.

"You're fearful in the presence of the Spitalfields Murderess?"

"I'm most concerned that RakeHell Lizzie not make a return appearance."

"Ah," she said, with a nod. "That one. I hate her and I love her. She is my worst enemy and my greatest friend. She is—"

"A different part of you?" Matthew asked.

"A part hidden in most people. In me, she comes to the surface now and again and takes control." She motioned with a lift of her chin toward the sleeping Firebaugh. "He gave me the treatment."

"The treatment? Of what kind?"

"In the asylum. Where he brought me when he took me out of prison. He gave me the drug treatment to keep Lizzie quiet, but it didn't work the way he wished. Or perhaps it did, because I believe he enjoyed the fact

that once Samson took me out I would have to keep taking the drug or she would come out when she was least expected. And Samson paid quite a bit for that drug."

"I see." Matthew also saw how Lash must've decided on Firebaugh to be involved in this affair. "But…the drug. How often do you take it?"

"I drink it twice a day," she said. "I took it early this morning, just before I let you through the door. My next sip would be due around six o'clock in the evening. It remains to be seen if I'll get it or not."

"It helps you keep *her* at bay?"

She smiled, showing her teeth. "She is *never* at bay. She only chooses sometimes to be quiet, and to wait. With the drug, she is put back into her bottle after a killing or two, which she needs as others need air to breathe. *Without* the drug…well, I don't dare think, because it's been so long since she's been…" She paused, finding the word. "*Unchained*," she said.

"Hm," said Matthew, who felt rather uneasy along the spine with this young woman so near to him, Black-Eyed Broodie or not. He shifted uneasily in his seat, and Elizabeth Mulloy gave a soft laugh.

"Fear," she said. "It tingles the back of my neck." She leaned forward. Matthew saw that her brown eyes seemed to have gotten darker and there were cinders of red in them, just like Cardinal Black's. "We have time, dear brother," she told him. "Dear brother Broodie. Though I think you have lived a life so different from mine that this brother can never fathom his sister. Yet we shall attempt it. Would you care to hear my story?"

Matthew's first response would be *No*, prefaced by the word *Hell*. But he thought better of it, for it appeared his sister wished to tell the tale, and as they were travelling in the same direction for any number of hours it might be wise to listen, and heed the warning that was sure to be in it.

Thus Matthew settled back in his seat, as the coach's wheels crunched along the snowcast road and the wind made little whines and shrieks past the portholes. She gave him a smile that was not really a smile but more of a grimace, like she was about to open a door that led to a chamber where grotesque figures of the damned danced and capered at a party far beyond Matthew's understanding of good and evil.

Her smile faded. Her face became a blank, and though she was still a lovely young woman Matthew thought there was something horrific in that empty stare, and he wished to look away but he could not, for he had an inkling that this was part of how she lured men into alleys and tore them to pieces: she looked so lost, so innocent, so needful of a guiding hand.

"I will begin," she told him, and the Spitalfields Murderess opened that dreadful door to the party.

TWENTY-SIX.

The first one I killed, *she said*, bore a remarkable resemblance to the man who murdered the only mother I ever knew and raped me at the age of ten.

But…I'm getting ahead of myself. Let me go back a distance.

What are you before you're born? I ask myself that question, and there is no answer. But is there something in you, even as a seed before birth, that might someday catch fire depending on the circumstances? Something that might, once begun, become a driving need in a person as much as the need for food and water? I suppose, Matthew, that I am touching on facets of good and evil that no one can fully understand.

Am I evil?

I'll let you decide.

I was given up as a baby to an orphanage in Spitalfields, so perhaps it was only natural that I return there. I did not know my mother or father. I received my name of Elizabeth from the first woman who found me wrapped in a blanket in their barn. I simply recall growing up in the orphanage, surrounded by the others and with kindly people there to assist us. The games of children. I remember them well, and I think that was a happy time.

At the age of eight I was adopted by an older woman—she was in her late forties—and taken with her to the boarding house she ran in

Walham Green, southwest of the city. Her name was Nora Mulloy, a widow of a few years, whose daughter by blood had married a tobacco merchant and moved with him to the colonies. I was to call her 'Mum', and I was pleased to do so.

Yes, Matthew, I did know love at one time in my life. And that was a wonderful time. The boarding house was kept spotlessly clean, my mum was a grand cook famous in the area for her soups and chowders, and we had quite a good business due to those qualities and the fact that our house stood near Sand's End and the harbor there, so we had many travellers passing through.

In her youth Mum had been a street dancer with a group of other girls. She had never lost her flair. She always dressed well and wore an assortment of gloves such as those I have on now, and those I always wear. She taught me how to dance, how to express myself with the movements of legs, arms, head and hands. It was quite a gift she had. How flawlessly she could move, how effortlessly...but I can tell you that learning it takes a great deal of effort. She said I was born to the dance. In time I put on little shows for some of the boarders, with her playing the flute and sometimes the drum. The next year she proclaimed me ready for the public, as she called it, and she sent me out to dance at the harbor and give out broadsheets advertising our house. Oh, it was a harmless thing, Matthew...she always accompanied me and it was all good business...but how were she and I to know what it would soon attract?

Yes, what you're thinking is correct. One morning a man came off a ship with a bag of his belongings and stood watching me dance. I remember his face very well, though at that moment it meant only that we might have a new boarder. It was later, during the thing that was to come, that his face was burned into my memory: A nose long and a shade crooked, as if broken more than once, a high forehead with many furrows, a thick chin adorned with a short brown beard, brown hair also cropped short and pale green eyes. It was only later, during the moment, that I thought they were the eyes of the cats that roamed the harbor creeping up on birds and

mice and tearing them to shreds. And sometimes—ofttimes—those cats never ate what they killed. It was for the pleasure of the hunt. It was for the killing, and that was all.

This man's name—or at least the name he put down on the ledger—was Broderick Robson. A false name? Yes. The constable who investigated the incident later learned the man had arrived from Newcastle on the ship the *Broderick Robson.* It was a fitting name, for he robbed both my mum and myself...she of her life, and me of everything but that...and I suppose, that too.

I will take a moment to think on some things. I do not like the cold, but I like the sound the wind makes. It's almost like music, is it not?

So. This man Robson. He was in London for a week, he said. Here to see an attorney and settle a score. That was all he said and we knew better than to ask, for it seemed to be a private trouble. During that week we had three more boarders, but they stayed only a few nights and then they were off again. Robson kept to himself, took his meals in his room, went out walking at night and slept long past the breakfast hour. Then one afternoon he asked my mother if I might dance for him after his evening meal, in his room, for his entertainment. He said that was why he had come to our house, because of my dancing. Such a perfect little girl, he said. I brightened the world, he said, and the world needed brightening because it was such a dark place. He called me a little candle. I recall very sharply that he said that. Well, my mother agreed that I should dance for not only him but for Mister Patrick and Mister and Misses Carnahan who were staying there, and I should perform in the parlor that evening.

When the appointed time came, all gathered but Robson. Mum went up to knock at his door, and she returned with an ashen face. I danced for the group, and later Mum said Robson did not answer the knock, but that she could hear him as if he were two persons, talking to each other. One was cursing in a brutal voice, and the other was sobbing. From that moment, Mum wanted me to stay far away from the man and she wished him to leave but he'd already paid for the week and he had two more nights.

In the room I had, which was just off my Mum's chambers, I could hear Robson walking at night in his room. Back and forth and back and forth… the thudding of heavy boots upon the boards. Then stopping. Silence for several minutes. Then again…back and forth, as if he were walking the distance to London. Mum took him his meals on that last day and was told to leave them at the door. They went untouched.

What is it, Matthew, that makes a man an animal? What is it that makes the hidden beast rear up and strike out at the world?

Who can answer such questions? Certainly not my Mum or myself. Little did we know.

On the last night.

He was to leave the next morning. The Carnahans had departed that evening. We were alone in the house with Robson. It was raining. Late October. Raining steadily. In my room I heard him walking again. The sound of it had wakened me.

Then I heard him cry out. It was a cry unlike any noise I had ever heard, and it terrified me to my very soul. It was the noise of the beast emerging. Or rather the cry, possibly, of a man trying to keep the beast from coming out, and commanding it back to its cage.

But on this night…the last night…it would not obey, and it had become the master.

My Mum came into my room in her nightclothes, carrying a lantern. She said for me not to be afraid. She had heard the cry as well—how could she not have?—and she was going to have to go upstairs to knock at his door. She told me to stay in my room, and she told me to latch my door after she had gone.

I was ten years old, Matthew. Can you imagine the moment? Mum left with the lantern, I latched the door, I stood in the corner where I felt safe, and I prayed to God as I heard Mum climbing the stairs.

I heard her knock at his door.

'Mister Robson!' I heard her call. 'Mister Robson, would you come to the door?'

Rain was beating at the window next to me. I heard voices. My Mum's and…a voice I did not recognize. A low, harsh voice…I could not hear the words, but it was almost as if I could feel the entire house tremble.

Then…let me take a breath, if you please.

Then I heard a sound that could only have been a body falling to the floor. There was no scream, no cry for help. She was not given time. It came upon her so fast, she had no moment to defend herself. And who can defend against a razor, Matthew, when it comes at you without warning, and you are standing close enough to feel the other person's breath on your face?

After the body fell, I heard the noise of…I can only describe it as pounding…a pounding…pounding. His boots upon her, as she lay in the hall. Pounding. It went on until it stopped.

'Mum!' I cried out. 'Mum!' And I crossed the room and reached for the door's latch, and then I heard him coming down the stairs. My hand froze on the latch. He came down no longer as a guest, but as master of the house. He came down slowly, whistling a tune. An eerie sound, dissonant, discordant, disordered. A tune from the mind of the monster.

At last came the hand upon the door's knob, turning it and turning it. And then followed the knock at the door.

'Elizabeth?' he whispered. And it was not fully the voice of Mister Robson. It was partly his, and partly some other voice that I can only say sounded harsh and bestial and…yes, I would say demonic. 'Little candle,' he said, 'open the door and shine for me.'

You don't have to go on, Matthew said.

Oh yes. Yes. Only partway out will not do…it has to be told all the way, as it happened. But thank you for your consideration.

I was not going to open that door. I was going to get out the window and run for help, because I knew my Mum…if she was not dead…she was not able to save me. And as I backed toward the window he kicked the door open and he came in with Mum's lantern lifted high and blood on the razor and all over his shirt and his teeth bared. And his eyes…the cat

eyes, the predator eyes…they glinted with pleasure in the light, for they had found a mouse to play with.

He put the lantern down very softly upon a table. Very softly. It hardly made a noise.

He put his hand in my hair. It was long then. Down over my shoulders. He put his hand in my hair, and I felt it tighten.

'Please,' I said. I do remember I said that. My sight was blurred. There were tears in my eyes, because I knew something terrible had happened, and something terrible was yet to happen.

He leaned down and he kissed my forehead. And then he drew the razor up and down each side of my face, as if sharpening it on a strop… but carefully, so no cutting was made. He whispered in my ear. 'Dance for me,' he said. 'And smile, little candle. Smile!'

I could not move. My feet were rooted to the boards. He closed the razor and slid it into a pocket of his breeches. Then he began to clap his hands in a rhythm, while his grin showed his teeth and those pale green eyes glittered in the light.

I don't remember starting to dance. I just recall moving…swaying… beginning to sob…and he said 'No, no, don't cry! Here, my love,' he said, 'let me dance with you.'

And there I was in that room with him, a room where I had always felt so safe and secure, and before me he was clapping his hands and moving forward to rub his body against mine…and when I moved back he moved forward again…and the next time I moved away from him he let out the kind of half-scream, half-bellow that I had heard from his room. His face…contorted in some kind of unknown agony, horrible to behold. He grabbed my hair with both hands and he flung me onto the bed, and then…well…then he was upon me.

Don't, said Matthew.

Do you say that because you wish me not to recall this thing? Or because you wish not to hear it? But it is central to my story, Matthew, and it must be told.

He was upon me. Worse than the pain was a crushing sensation. All the breath smashed out of me. I thought I was about to die, because I couldn't breathe. The pain…I was being torn. Torn apart, it seemed. And yes, perhaps I was and I would never again be whole. His hands… rough flesh, sharp nails. His mouth on me…his green cat eyes, staring down into my face with what later I realized was the perverted joy of the hunt.

Rain beating against the window. Late October. Did I say that already? Raining steadily. That last night my Mum was alive. That last night.

When he finished with me, he pulled his breeches up, took the lantern and left the room without a word or another glance. After he was finished, I was no longer there. I got out of bed and curled myself on the floor. I heard him walking in his room. Then silence. He had gone up to pack his bag, for his stay at the boarding house of Nora Mulloy and her adopted daughter Elizabeth was at an end. Later I heard him come down the stairs. I heard the front door open and shut. Then there was just the sound of the rain and the breath hissing between my teeth.

And do you know what I thought then? After all that…what I thought in my dazed ten-year-old brain was: that man must be crazy, to go out walking in this heavy rain.

It is a fact that people in their most dire situations think of the most inane things to shield their minds from shattering. Doctor Firebaugh told me that.

When I was sure that Robson was gone, I lit a candle and went upstairs.

What I saw in the hallway was the worst of it, Matthew.

The very worst.

I do think my mind shattered. I believe I felt it come apart like a house that had suffered too much shock in a storm…too much for the joints and the foundation to withstand. I felt my brain bleeding as it was torn asunder. My head and face became burning hot. I ran down the stairs and out into the rain screaming for help.

It seemed a very long time before anyone answered.

Well. Poor little girl is without a home now, and without a mum. Poor little girl witnessed a murder and was raped by a madman. But you know...poor little girl likely is not all blameless, they said. A cute little thing, dancing and prancing like that at the harbor to draw business in for the widow Mulloy. And no matter that the widow Mulloy was always there with her at the harbor...that pretty little poor little girl...her dancing drew the murderer in, and there you have it.

Spoken in the most fashionable of low and dirty dives, I later heard.

But the little girl must now return to an orphanage. And there I learned that a child who had been raped and overheard the most vile of murders was not quite suited for the stamp of quality, and certainly not the pretense of innocence. Especially since I carried a darkness within me from that time on. The others—the children and the ladies at the home—could sense it. I could no more play children's games than fly to the moon on a hog's back. If my mind had been shattered, it healed itself with crooked scars. I became as Robson was: alone in my flesh, carrying private torments I would show to no one. And the result was that on the days when people came from outside to view the orphans with intent to adopt, I was the one they could not bear to look at and rushed past. I was the dark blot on the white sheet of paper. I was the ugly scowl in the picture of smiles. I was thirty years old at the age of twelve.

I remember that I was chosen as a challenge by a well-meaning reverend and his wife. They returned me after almost two weeks. When he told me that God loved me and had a plan for my life I laughed in his face. And I called his wife a fat old cow, which she was, and threw a soup bowl through the window.

But let me move ahead two years. In that span of time I was released from the orphanage in the custody of a man who—honestly speaking—craved young girls. The ladies at the orphanage were glad to be rid of me, so what was the difference? And not only did this man crave young girls, but he craved using the whip on them. As he did to me. And then he revealed his nice little plan: for me to go out posing as a young innocent

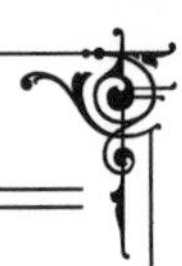

in the city's parks and playgrounds, and to draw other young girls to him with the promise of sweets. I ran away from that house the very night, and then I was on the street.

What could I do to survive? I was fourteen years old. What could I do, except for what to me was the unthinkable. Well, I realized I could do what my mum had trained me to do: I might become a street dancer and earn some coin from the passersby. And I did that through the spring and summer, living in an abandoned warehouse in Whitechapel with a number of other castaways like myself. You knew them as the Black-Eyed Broodies, though I imagine my group was not the same as yours. My relationship with them began as a threat of violence. Since I was dancing on the streets of their territory, I was made to give up half my earnings to their treasury. In time we worked out an arrangement. I would *only* dance on their territory, and only if I was made a Broodie and came under their protection. And so that was how I got the tattoo and went through the same initiation ceremony you likely did.

And now, Matthew, we come to the part of my life when RakeHell Lizzie began to awaken. Or perhaps she was already awake, and just waiting.

We were four and we were attacked by six of the Mohock gang. You might have had some encounter with them yourself. It was late night, we were coming back from the tavern that fed us—in our territory—and they jumped us from a passing wagon. They were painted up like the savages from the colonies. As I say, six of them—all male—and four of us, two male, myself and my friend Audrey. The Mohocks had daggers and sabers. They cut down the two boys before one of them could blow his warning whistle. Then they were on us. We fought, but they had very hard and capable fists. They threw us in the wagon and were off, and the whole thing probably didn't take over a minute.

They blindfolded us and took us somewhere that smelled of old damp. A cellar, of course. I was prepared to be raped again and killed, but it wasn't to be. Oh, they kicked me around a bit but they laid off the other. I found out later that they'd hit Audrey too hard in the first attack and she died early the next morning. So they were in trouble because they'd been paid to deliver two girls of a young age to a house that I learned was in Shoreditch, close to the prison.

I learned that because that's where they took me the next night. That's where I met Missus Spanner, who ran the house, and the other seven girls who ranged in age from twelve to fifteen. I was the oldest, at sixteen, but I'd always looked younger and they figured I could pass for fourteen. Of course I tried to get away, several times. Missus Spanner had a couple of Arab men who worked as guards. They couldn't touch the girls…that was for the dandies who paid high coin for the privilege. So I was there to stay, and it was made clear to me that if I didn't work I didn't eat. Well, I didn't eat for a while…but you know, sooner or later you get so hungry nothing else matters. And so I did the unthinkable, to survive.

Missus Spanner wasn't all bad. She was a business woman and she had to eat too. She'd been a seamstress by trade, many years before, but her hands gave out and her eyes weren't what they'd used to be either. I wasn't there very long before Missus Spanner asked me to help darn the girls' clothes and to add little puffs of lace and flower decorations and such on them. She said if I did that she'd go easy on me and wouldn't make me work when I was tired out. And she was true to her word.

Then one day I met the man who owned the house. Not only that house, but several others around the city. He was involved in many things, Missus Spanner told me. Better not to know too much, she said, because that was the way to get your throat cut.

His name was Maccabeus DeKay. He arrived in a coach that made this one look like it belongs to a mule train. I would say that if the Devil decided to come to this earth in human form, he would choose to resemble the extraordinarily handsome man who strode into the house that afternoon, accompanied by his two bodyguards. This was a man to whom nothing would be forbidden nor denied. And he knew it. He was there to inspect his merchandise. We had all been made to wear our nicest dresses and told to curtsey before him as if he were royalty. He himself was dressed in the

finest suit I had ever seen. We lined up and he went along the line checking our teeth and such. When he reached me he ran his hand along my cheek and I shivered because his touch was icy cold.

Right there I realized that evil existed to corrupt innocence. To take innocence and turn it into an ugly thing that could be bought and sold like any commodity. At that moment I wished with all my heart to kill him, to rend him to pieces and to rend to pieces all the evil men who preyed on those who could not fight back. RakeHell Lizzie awakened and began to think on murder as a remedy…if not a remedy for the whole world's evil, at least a remedy for evil in the small world I knew.

I bided my time. I was at the house for nearly a year, Missus Spanner began to trust me to accompany her out to buy fabrics, but always one of the Arab men went with us. I acted as docile as I could, until the moment was right. Then I bolted into the crowd of people on the street, and I ran and ran until I had to collapse in an alley.

I hope Missus Spanner was all right. DeKay might have had her killed for losing one of his properties, but I knew I had to get out. But where to go next? We had been in the Spitalfields district where most of the textile work in the city was done. I could sew and weave. Many of the workers in the mills were children. I had no trouble finding a job for a few pence a day, and at that time I had just turned seventeen—much older than most of the other workers—and I also had no trouble finding a little hovel near the mill.

On my walk from work one evening I saw a man take up a little girl by the neck and drag her into an alley. I realized—RakeHell Lizzie realized—that here in Spitalfields was a paradise for evil. The predators came from miles around to get at the children, most of whom were orphans and lived in groups in small rooms like myself. I began to roam around at night and recognize the signs of the predator who was looking to further corrupt innocence that the world had already touched. So I—she—bought a knife. It became her obsession…a driving need, to strike back at the Robsons and the DeKays. It was on her all the time, and she realized it was the only way for either of us to not lose our minds to madness.

She dressed as a younger girl and made herself look like a child. The first man who came at her got away because she swung with the blade and missed. The second one she only cut on the arm. She realized she needed something better, something more efficient. Thus I bought for her ten blades and I stole some leather, and I sewed the gloves for her.

She had some trouble. The gloves were hard to handle. She cut herself the first few times, getting them on in haste from the bag she carried. She had to learn the art of killing and not injure herself. That took practice. So while Elizabeth Mulloy worked in the day among the children at the mill, by night RakeHell Lizzie—the name I gave her, as the public only knew the title of the Spitalfields Murderess—walked the streets of Spitalfields, and so it began with that man who she thought looked so much like Broderick Robson. She made a fine mess of him. She learned to cut their throats first before they could cry out, and she learned also where the most blood would jump from so as to diminish the spatter on her clothes. That was a difficult thing for her and meant a lot of clothing stolen from clotheslines, but again…she learned.

She took down six of them. With the seventh, she was too confident and a shade slow. She took off the side of his face, but he was able to run screaming for help. He was the one who gave the law our description. After three months, they trapped her in a blind alley. Four constables who had come to track her. They took her to jail, to the court, and to prison. After two years behind bars we were removed by Doctor Firebaugh to the asylum at Highcliff where he was doing his experimental treatments on what was termed criminal minds. They even sold him the original gloves, to put in a museum he was planning to build there on the grounds.

I was not the only one at Highcliff, but a few of the others died from the drugs. I survived, and so did Lizzie. And even though she was contained, she was not dead.

Samson Lash brought his wife in. She had lost all knowledge of who she was and who he was. She could not dress herself, feed herself or anything else. She babbled and cried and made no sense. The doctor

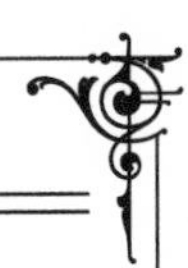

announced her as a hopeless case, but Samson returned to see her nearly every day. Eventually he and I began to talk, as I had been allowed to do some clerical work in the doctor's office. I was as amazed as anyone might be when, after a period of some weeks, he paid the doctor to take me to his house, and also paid for a regular application of the drug.

Lizzie slept most of the time. But when she awakened, Samson arranged for there to be an outlet for her violence. Without victims she would perish, and I told him that I feared part of me would die with her. I think he feared I would diminish in mind and spirit as his wife had, and he enjoyed my companionship. He has always been kind and gracious to me and considers me a fine lady, but of course untouchable. His figurehead on his grand ship, he calls me.

Well, the victims need not be child molesters at this point. Lizzie was beyond that, as someone used to dining on roast beef will eat beef hash if necessary. It was an urgency in the blood. He could tell the signs of agitation that began well in advance. But with the drug's continued application, I found that Lizzie could be released when the time was appropriate and then—with a bit of effort—confined again. She doesn't like it but she has to live with it. As I say though, I don't know what the effect will be without the drug. Samson thought that particular gathering would be entertained by the show of the constables, as such a display would impress upon them the fact that he disdains the law of small men and that his ambition is on a greater scale. It was good business, and Lizzie needed the exercise.

My story. I consider that Lizzie put to death six men who might have preyed upon the mill children in Spitalfields, and they would've been back for further victims. She could not save all the innocence of those children, which was likely already lost, but she could keep the corruption from spreading and destroying more of them, body and soul, as it had very nearly destroyed me.

My story.

TWENTY-SEVEN.

At Elizabeth's final two words, Matthew felt the coach slowing.

Firebaugh made a muttering groan from his huddled bundle of tormented flesh.

"We're stopping," said Elizabeth. "Why?"

Matthew peered out the porthole to his left. He felt a twinge as he turned his attention away from the woman and he figured the back of her neck was tingling aplenty. Through the falling snow he saw only dim gray light and the further blue darkness of a forest.

The coach stopped with a crunch of wheels.

"I think we're in the middle of nowhere," Matthew said. "Do you see anything out there?"

She looked out the porthole on her side. "Woods," she answered. "Nothing else."

The doors on the right side opened and Julian stood there shivering. "Spell me on the reins, Matthew. I'm freezing and my back's a wreck. God knows how these drivers do it."

"*Me*? Spell you? I've never driven a coach this size or handled a four-horse team!"

"Understood. It's time for you to learn." He motioned with a thumb for Matthew to get out.

"What is it? *What*? Where are we?" Firebaugh had been roused at the sound of the earcutter's voice. The eyes were wild with fear in his swollen face, and it appeared he was trying to desperately squeeze himself into a seam in the coach's wall at his back.

"Settle yourself," Julian told him, as one might tell a dog to behave. "Here, take the coat and the gloves," he said to Matthew, but before he removed the items he waved his pistol in Elizabeth's face. "No tricks from you, miss murder."

"I'm content to watch," she answered coolly, and Matthew had the creepy feeling that she might be speaking on behalf of her other half.

He got into the polar bear coat and put the gloves on. The air was bitterly cold and the wind blew the snow at a slant, whistling past his ears. He pulled his woolen cap lower. Before he climbed up to the driver's seat and before Julian could get into the coach, Matthew said, "Don't injure Elizabeth. Hear me?"

"I won't if she doesn't try anything." He frowned. "What's your concern for her?"

"She and I are both Black-Eyed Broodies. I made a vow not to—"

"What's *that*?" Firebaugh had leaned forward to hear through his good side.

Everyone ignored him. "I made a vow not to injure a brother—*sister*—Broodie," Matthew went on. "She made the same vow. That's why she didn't—"

"Well, I'll be damned!" said Julian. He tapped his chin with the pistol's barrels. "But she's not *my* sister, Matthew, so if she makes a move I don't like…I told you before, I'm the bad man. What else do you expect of me?"

"A bit of honor."

Julian grunted. "What you haven't yet seemed to realize, Matthew, is that very often it takes a bad man to do the things that have to be done. Would we have gotten this far if our main concern was *honor*?"

"I made a vow. I stand by it, no matter what."

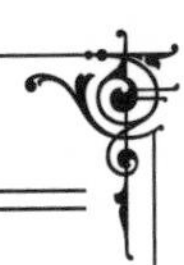

"Let him come inside," said Elizabeth, with a silky smile. "She won't bite him. Yet. And please close the doors before I turn to ice."

Julian wore an expression that told Matthew he might be weighing the cold and his aching back against the wisdom of being in close quarters with RakeHell Lizzie, but then he climbed into the coach. "Just keep us on the road," he said grimly before he shut the doors, leaving the problem-solver on his own.

Matthew put his gun into the waistband of his breeches and used a handgrip and a bootstep to haul himself up to the driver's seat. From here the landship looked truly immense, as did the south ends of the horse team. Julian had left the reins tied around a railing beside the seat. With the snow flying into his face he took the reins and looked ahead at the road that curved to the right between stands of forest. How far they were out of London he had no idea, but there was no use dawdling; the further they got away from that city, the better.

He flicked the reins. "Giddap!" he shouted.

The horses didn't move.

He tried it again. "Giddap!"

Two of them snorted gouts of steam in derision. One shook its mane as if saying *no*, and the fourth just stood there like a huge chestnut-colored statue.

Matthew remembered the driver's command. He gave the reins a harder flick and shouted, "Hiiiiiyupppp!"

They started off with an irritated rumble and a force that jerked the coach. The power of the horses against the reins gave Matthew the first inkling of what his back and arms would feel like after a few hours of playing at being a driver. Still, they were moving...not very fast, but moving all the same, and Matthew tried to settle back against the cold-hardened cushion but found that the heavy pull of the horses was not going to let him relax one iota. It seemed they were in full command of this coach, and they knew it.

As he sat in obedience to the team, Matthew reflected not only on

Elizabeth Mulloy's tale but upon everything that had brought him and Julian to this point. He thought of Elizabeth saying *had very nearly destroyed me* and considered that she was likely more insane than she knew, for if anyone had been destroyed in the story of her life it had certainly been she.

And Julian's comment: *Very often it takes a bad man to do the things that have to be done.* True, Matthew thought. If Julian's nature weren't what it was, they would neither have the book of potions nor Lazarus Firebaugh. Of course cutting the doctor as Julian had done was not a thing to be praised, but still…there would be no more attempts to escape, so the bad man had done his deed to its ultimate success.

And of ultimate success: on the road to Fell's village was no promise that they'd get there, as Matthew was sure Lash was following in the other coach. How fast that coach was being driven was another question mark that seemed to hang in the snowy air before Matthew's face.

And would Firebaugh be able to reverse Berry's condition? Even at the point of a dagger threatening his other ear?

And of the mirror purportedly created by Ciro Valeriani with the aid of an Italian sorcerer…a mirror that could summon a demon up from the depths of Hell? If Matthew had vowed to help find Valeriani's son in the search for that mirror, what kind of accomplice to the act of demon-raising would that make him? Such a thing if true would mark a soul forever.

Of course it wasn't true. It couldn't be. Could it?

Well, by Matthew's reckoning they had quite a way to go yet. It had taken thirty-eight hours from Bristol, but that had been in much better weather and the horses able to be driven harder and faster. Matthew recalled that the condition of the roads—the cart tracks, would be a better description—was not ideal for fast travel up into Wales, and particularly around Y Beautiful Bedd. So say forty-eight hours plus another twelve? That, he thought, would likely be a conservative estimate, particularly as the wind was picking up and shrilling past himself and the coach. Seventy-two hours from London to Fell's village, say? And that was with hardly stopping at any of the coaching inns along the way except for resting the

horses and the necessities, just as they'd done on the trip from Bristol.

There was nothing to do but to flick the reins every so often, to try to convince the team that a driver was in charge, to count off the miles and keep this polar bear coat wrapped around him, and God bless the taste in clothing of dead Count Pellegar, whose corpse and that of Baron Brux had surely by now been found at the Mayfair and would cause a profitable spike in the business of *Lord Puffery's Pin* when Lady Puffery got hold of the story.

The miles rolled on. The snow fell. The coach passed through several small villages in the early dark. There was little activity, here and there horses standing in pastures watching their brethren pass and a few villagers out doing whatever labor was essential, which didn't seem to amount to much. Then the forest closed in on both sides of the road once more. They had come this way from Bristol, it being the central pike northwest and southeast as far as Matthew knew, and this was also the route he'd been taken by Mother Deare to Fell's village in the first place. But it was far from being familiar, and the covering of white made everything even less so.

How long was it before Matthew felt as if his face had frozen solid and the exertions of the drive began to ache in his bones? He figured he'd been up top close to three hours. Steam curled from the horses' nostrils. Even with snow on the road, the coach juddered to its joints and swung back and forth with alarming abandon. He had just about reached his limit. Therefore when in the next twenty minutes he saw off to the right a stone cottage with smoke rising from its chimney, a barn and a corral and a neatly-painted sign out front that read *Travellers Welcome*, he made a decision for resting the horses and getting some hot food, and he began the rather strenuous task of slowing the team and guiding them off the road toward the chosen destination.

The viewslit came open. "What're you doing?" Julian asked from within; more of a demand for an answer than a question.

"I'm stopping at this inn ahead. I need to get warm, I need food, and I

need to do everything that I've been holding back for a solid hour. I expect our guests would wish the same."

Julian paused for only a few seconds. "All right. Agreed. We might be stopping too soon, but I'd care to get a warm cup of ale at least. But we're not staying here very long." He slid the viewslit shut, and Matthew said, "Whoa, whoa," to no avail and felt as if he needed the strength of three Hudson Greathouses to get the damned team to stop in front of the inn.

At last he fought them to a compromise, halting about fifty feet from a snow-laden green awning that hung above the front door. As Matthew performed his last pull on the reins, the door came open and a stout figure bundled up in a gray woolen cap and a brown coat with a fleece-lined collar hurried out to meet them.

"Hi hidy!" called the man in a voice as rough as the weather but sunny with good cheer. "Welcome, all! How many there be?"

"Four," Julian said as he came out of the coach. He had put his gun out of sight for the sake of not scaring the innkeeper to death. "All cold, hungry and in need of some rest. The horses too. Can you handle them?"

"Cack a bull, what a team!" The man stepped back, hands on his wide hips, to regard the coach as Matthew climbed painfully down from his perch. "I have *never* seen the like of such a wagon! Too handsome for *this* road, by a cannon shot! Well, I reckon I can handle them giants and my teeth hope so. Get 'em unhitched and into the barn, feed 'em and let 'em warm up a bit. That suit?"

"Suit," Matthew said.

"Afternoon, lady," the man said to Elizabeth, with a polite little bow. "Dark like the stroke a' midnight, but there you have it." And then Firebaugh got out, barelegged and wearing the plaid banyan robe. The innkeeper gave a whistle. "Zonders! You're toggin' a nightgown in this foulness? And...what got at your *face*, sir? Highwaymen?"

"He had an accident with a knife," said Julian.

"Bloody tinshears, that was some accident then! Go on inside, my Greta'll put the balm to it. I'm Oliver Autrey, by the by."

"Pleased," Julian said, but offered no name in return. "We can't spend more than an hour here, understand?"

"In such a hurry? An hour'll hardly do for the team!"

"It'll have to do." And the way Julian said it, there was no room for disagreement.

"'Gainst my nature as an innkeeper and stablemaster," said Autrey, "but I'll do my best with the time. Horses won't like it, though, goin' from cold to warm to cold again so—"

Julian had already turned his back on Autrey and was shoving Firebaugh toward the cottage. Matthew followed behind Elizabeth, and he heard Autrey speaking quietly and reassuringly to the horses as they were approached to be unhitched.

They had not stopped at this particular coach inn on the way from Bristol with the Turlentorts, as they had paused for a couple of brief hours at one that Matthew figured was about fifteen miles further to the northwest. For their purpose, the inns were havens to the weary traveller, offering food, drink, and a place to sleep—bed, cot or barn, depending on the size of the establishment. Matthew was glad to be getting in out of the weather, as the wind had picked up strength and the trees in the forest on three sides of the cottage were losing their coats of snow in long white streamers. He had a sudden thought that locked his knees. "The book!" he said, and he was relieved when Julian turned at the door and touched the breast area of Bogen's cloak, indicating a second buttoned pocket—or pouch in this case—large enough to push the book into.

A green curtain at one of the cottage's two front windows moved aside, a face peered out, and the door was opened before Julian could reach it. "Come in, come in, and *willkommen bei dir*!" said the short, rotund woman who stood smiling on the threshold. Matthew thought her language sounded like it must be Prussian, of all things. Well, he wouldn't begrudge her being Prussian and miss the warmth of a hearth and a hot meal, so long live Prussia. He tramped on in across the stone floor with the others and in the cheerful yellow lamplight the fireplace with its bounty

of burning logs was a thing of true beauty, and beautiful too was the fact that the cottage was warm enough so one wouldn't need to climb into the flames to thaw out.

The fireplace drew an immediate crowd, including Firebaugh who shivered and shook as the warmth chased the chill from his bones.

Greta Autrey closed the door against the wind and had a look at her guests. "*Oh mein Sterne*!" she gasped, as she saw the doctor's injuries. "What happened to you, *mein herr*?"

"An accident," said Julian. "He'll recover."

"Such an accident I never saw before! I have some balm that could ease you, but I'm thinking you need to see a doctor! And in your night-clothes you're travelling?" Matthew saw the expression on the woman's seamed and ruddy-cheeked face change in an instant from concern to suspicion. "*Was ist das*? No one travels in this weather in such clothing!" She backed toward the far wall where a musket sat on a shelf within reach.

"Ma'am," Matthew said before anything could get out of hand, "this man is our prisoner and we're taking him to a special prison in Wales."

Firebaugh gave a half-laugh, half-choke.

"My name is Matthew. My associate Julian and I are constables."

Now it was Julian who nearly choked.

"We had to take him from a place where he had no chance to change into warmer clothes. Unfortunately he was a bit roughed up in the doing. We intended to find something for him on the way. Perhaps you have something? At least a pair of winter stockings you might sell us?"

"This man is a damnable liar," Firebaugh suddenly spoke up. "I'm a respected London doctor and these two criminals have kidapped me! Look what they did to my face and my ear! Would constables of the law commit such violence on a person?" He motioned toward the musket. "If that's loaded and primed, I'd thank you very much if you would—"

"Matthew is telling you the truth," Elizabeth interrupted. "The man before you is indeed a doctor, but he is also a criminal of the lowest kind

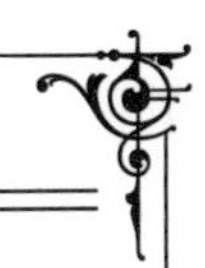

and quite cunning. Greta is your name? Well, Greta, I can vouch for these two constables because this doctor committed several murders in the Spitalfields district of London several years ago. One of the victims was my sister, and I am accompanying these men to see that justice is done when the doors slam shut on him in prison."

It did not help his case that Firebaugh at that moment gave a crazed laugh.

Greta Autrey stood open-mouthed. She blinked twice but otherwise did not move.

When he was done with his strangled chortling, Firebaugh might have continued to plead his case if he hadn't felt Julian's hand clenched to the back of his banyan robe and tugging him very slightly down toward the red-hot center of the flames.

"*Tar und Feder mich*," said Greta. She shrugged. "I'm thinking my Oliver better figure this one out, because I am *verdutzt*!"

"And I am *hungry*," Matthew said, glad to get past this little mountain in the road. "We all are, I'm sure. May we impose upon you for at least some soup and a bit of bread?"

"But it'll have to be fast," Julian added. "We can only stay an hour at most and the sooner we're out the better."

Greta Autrey might be a simple woman who helped run a small coaching inn, and she might be in the twilight of her fifth decade with a cloud of gray hair and a ruddy-cheeked, gap-toothed countenance, but Matthew could tell she was not stupid. This comment from Julian put the mortar to her construction that likely no one of the four was telling the truth. Her eyelids might have drooped to a suspicious half-mast, but what was she to do?

"I have a pot of chicken soup with barley and enough bread for you all to have a slice," she said. "The pot's in the kitchen. You can eat at the table in there if you please."

"Excellent!" said Matthew. "Speaking of pots, if I'm not too indelicate might I ask also if there's a room with a chamberpot available?"

"Back there." She motioned toward a hallway. "One chamberpot will have to suit all. And I ask that you use it, take it outside, dump it and clean it with snow. *Ja*?"

"Yes, absolutely."

"What is *this*?" Elizabeth suddenly asked.

Matthew and the others turned to see what had caught her interest. She had walked a few steps to the other side of the room, where a small fir tree was planted in a dark green pot of earth. The tree was decorated with small paper roses in the branches and strands of multi-colored beads were wound around and around, giving quite a beautiful effect.

"Oh," said Greta. "That's the *tannebaum*. It's a custom in the country of my birth to bring a fir tree in and decorate it this time of year. Here you would call it a Christmas tree."

"A tree in the *house*?" Elizabeth went on. "How unusual! It's very pretty, though."

"I like the good cheer it brings," said Greta. "Now, if you'd care for some soup? And those who wish to visit the chamberpot may do so as well." She motioned for them to follow.

Julian drew aside a window curtain to check outside and saw Oliver approaching through the swirl of snow. Matthew observed Firebaugh's lip curl as the doctor stood beside Elizabeth and regarded the fir tree. "Most *ridiculous* thing I have ever seen," he said. "A tree in a house! That'll never catch on! As equally ridiculous as you taking sides against me with those two. Have you completely lost your senses?"

"You're simply asking for more injury," Elizabeth answered quietly, as the kitchen Greta had retired to was not so far distant. "Where could you go, even if you did manage to get away…which you *cannot*? Bide your time, doctor. That's all I can say."

"And this betrayal is because you and Corbett were in the same *gang*? I'm sure when Samson catches up to us he'll like to hear that explanation."

"Not betrayal. Common sense, which you seem to have left with your ear in the snow."

The door opened and Oliver Autrey entered. "Whew!" he said, stalking past the others to the hearth to warm himself. "A cold night ahead, mark it! Well, the horses are taken care of, so that's not to worry." He shrugged off his coat and removed his cap. Matthew thought he was probably a few years older than his wife, and he also was as gap-toothed as the missus. But he had a friendly, heavily-jowled face and from the very front of his liver-spotted scalp there curled a single tuft of white hair like a tiny angel's wing. He took the measure of Firebaugh's wounds again. "Trimmin' your eyebrows and cleanin' your ears with a blade," he said with narrowed and serious eyes, "is not the smartest thing to do."

Greta returned to the room, her face expressionless. "Ollie, they have given me the *pferdefedern* story. It is best not to ask questions of these people, and whatever they are up to we are not wishing to know. Come along now, the soup's ready." She turned away, a stately presence in the little homey cottage.

"What did that word mean?" Matthew asked, and with a lift of his furrowed forehead that made the angel's wing dance Autrey said, "Horsefeathers."

Matthew made a trip to the chamberpot room and in obedience to the lady of the manor went out through the cottage's back door, passed the woodpile and a little toolshed and ventured a distance into the forest before cleaning the thing out with snow. Elizabeth was the next to go out, and Julian waited for her at the back door in spite of her assurance that trying to run away was not on her agenda. Firebaugh was next, and he refused to clean his pot out so Julian took care of both his own and the doctor's but not without the grim lip that said Firebaugh would pay for the indignity. Coats and hats went up on hooks and it was time to fill bellies.

In the small but well-kept and clean kitchen where another hearth blazed, everyone gathered around a sturdy oak table to partake of the chicken soup and the thick black bread that Matthew reckoned came from a Prussian recipe. Before any eating could commence there was a short period of haggling between Julian and Oliver over the price of their stay, Autrey saying they had never had anyone stop over for a single hour in their whole eight years of working the inn and he didn't know how to set the charges. Four shillings was agreed upon. As the soup and the bread were going down into hungry gullets and followed by strong hot tea, Greta pulled up a chair beside Firebaugh. From a little green jar she applied a white ointment that smelled of ginger to his wounds. He cried out with renewed anguish but she assured him the ginger root paste would do wonders at healing him up…unless, she added with a quick wink at her husband, he suffered any further accidents on the way to Wales.

"It is up to the prisoner to behave," said Julian as he got down to the last of his soup and dipped a hunk of bread into it to chew on. "Matthew and I thank you for your hospitality, but it's past time for us to go."

"The team won't be ready," Oliver said. "Those steeds are strong, but you can drive 'em 'til they're ruined."

"They can take it. They'll have to. Out of pity for this *gentleman* before you," and here Julian motioned with his bit of bread down the table at Firebaugh, "do you have a pair of woolen stockings we can buy? It seems he says his legs are cold."

"I have two pair but none I can sell," came the reply. "My woolens are hard to come by and expensive to boot."

Matthew had a thought and realized he should've come up with it sooner. "The baggage compartment in the coach," he said to Julian. "My… um…escort must've been carrying a bag or two for the trip. There might be some woolen leggings in there."

"Your *escort*? No questions from me!" said Greta, who began to clear away the dishes.

"Please do check the coach!" Firebaugh was nearly begging. "If you want me alive to reach that damn village, for God's sake show some mercy!"

"No questions from me, either," said Oliver, who finished the last of his tea with a single slug and left the table. "Bringin' more wood in," he told Greta on his way out the back.

"Go take a look," Julian decided. "Then we've got to get back on the road, whether those horses are ready or not."

Matthew paused to put on the polar bear coat and his gloves, then went out into the cold. The snowy wind hit him in the face so hard he was staggered. At what must've been three o'clock in the afternoon the light was a dim gray dusk. Across the road the forest was a mass of dark seen through a fogged lens. Matthew put his head down against the elements, trudged to the coach and opened the baggage doors. He was gratified to find that inside was indeed a brown canvas bag.

He took the bag, closed the doors and started back, and that was when he heard the horse whinny.

He stopped in his tracks.

Had he heard it, or not? The wind was playing tricks, but he thought that the sound had not come from the barn about thirty yards away and behind him; he thought it had come from off to his left where the road curved into the forest.

But no…no, of course it was one of the team in the barn.

The wind was playing tricks, and how could one tell exactly where a sound had come from in this weather?

He was on edge, that was all.

But then from the corner of his left eye…was there a quick movement from tree to tree, just a dark shape moving among dark shapes? He couldn't tell for sure, and the movement was not repeated. Snow and wind…blowing across his field of vision.

Better to get inside, he thought. Better to go through this bag as fast as possible, and get moving again.

Within the cottage, Matthew opened the bag on a table as the others watched—Firebaugh in particular with expectant hope—and found a number of blouses, two pairs of breeches, a pair of scuffed black boots… and a pair of woolen stockings.

"Thank God!" said Firebaugh, snatching up the stockings, a blouse, a pair of the breeches and the boots. "I'll try these on right here!" And

without further decorum or regard to his hosts he stood before the hearth, threw off his banyan robe to expose his thin nakedness, sat on the floor and pulled on the stockings, which fit well enough. The breeches were problematic in being too large around the waist, and Firebaugh grimaced as he fought his feet into the boots. The blouse went on and fit reasonably well though it flagged around the shoulders, but when Firebaugh stood up the breeches fell to his knees.

"Hmmm," said Autrey as he and his wife watched this display with amusement. "I've got a length of cord might do to hold those breeches up. Extra shillin' buys it."

Julian offered the coin with no comment, and Autrey handed it to Greta with the flourish of a triumphant businessman and went to the back to fetch the cord. Firebaugh was left securing his baggy breeches with both hands, causing Elizabeth to laugh at the sorry spectacle.

Matthew wandered over to one of the windows and moved the curtain aside.

"What is it?" Julian asked sharply, coming over beside him.

"Nothing. But you're right, we ought to be going." The tension in his voice surprised him and also worried him; had he seen something—or *someone*—out there, or not?

"We should've gotten out of here already. Autrey!" Julian called. "Hurry up, will you?" He too peered out the window, but the dark and the snow obscured vision beyond a very few yards.

Autrey returned with a length of cord and a small knife. As Julian stood guard to watch Firebaugh in case the knife intrigued him as much as had the musket, Autrey cut several holes in the waist of the offending breeches and threaded the cord through them to create a makeshift belt. "Cinch that in and give it a knot," he directed, and when the doctor did as ordered and the breeches stayed up Autrey nodded with the satisfaction of a job well done. "There you go," he said. "Handsome as a stag's skin on a beaver's butt."

As Firebaugh was getting into the banyan robe again for extra warmth, Autrey suddenly stopped still in the middle of the room. “Hear that?” he asked.

Matthew only heard the whine of the wind and the noise of wood crackling in the hearth.

“There! Again! A horse screamin’!” Autrey strode past Matthew and Julian to a window, as obviously his hearing on such matters was acute from eight years of minding the coach teams.

He drew aside the curtain, and as he did an orange flicker of light licked his face.

“Oh my Christ!” he said, his eyes wide and his voice strained with true horror. “The barn’s on fire!”

TWENTY-EIGHT.

Both Matthew and Julian were instantly at Autrey's side to peer through the glass, while Greta rushed to the second window. Matthew could see firelight leaping between chinks in the barn's boards, and now he thought he did catch the high terrified scream of a horse carried by the moaning wind.

"Ha," Firebaugh said tonelessly. "The cats have caught the squirrels."

Without a word, Julian turned from the window, took two paces toward Firebaugh and laid the doctor out upon the floor with a right fist to the jaw.

"I have to go out!" Autrey was going for the door.

"Don't!" Julian said, and the urgency of his voice stopped the other man. "They're waiting for whoever comes out!"

"I…I *have* to," said Autrey, all the blood seemingly drained from his face and his lips a waxy gray. "The *horses*! They'll burn alive!"

The moment hung.

Matthew swallowed the gritty taste of his own fear. It had to be done. "I'll go with you," he said, reaching into the polar bear coat and his jacket to pull out the pistol.

Autrey's eyes widened further. Elizabeth said, "Let me go out to him, Matthew. I can—"

"Yes, let her go out!" Firebaugh taunted from the floor. "Once I tell him what a traitor she is, he'll—"

Julian put a boot upon his throat, which turned the doctor's voice into a strangled gurgle.

"I never heard a chamberpot talking before, and I don't like it," he said.

"I'm going!" Autrey opened the door, and Matthew cocked his pistol and followed him. Julian shouted for Matthew to stop and there was real fear in the shout, but then Matthew and Autrey were out in the snow and both were running toward the barn, where the firelight glowed orange between the boards and tendrils of smoke were being whipped back and forth by the wind.

They had gotten about twenty feet from the cottage when Matthew saw the white flash of a gunshot from the woods across the road and a heartbeat later heard the *crack* of the blast. At his side, Autrey gave a shout of pain, clutched at his right thigh and then he staggered and went down. Matthew instantly fell to his knees beside the man, who grasped at Matthew's coat with a bloodied hand and cried out, "The horses! Don't let 'em burn!"

There was no time for weighing life and death. There was no time to decide if the next bullet would be better aimed than the first.

There was no time.

Matthew leaped up and, crouching low, ran for the barn. He expected another shot but it did not come. Whoever had fired it was getting into a better position, or crossing the road, or whatever. Odds are Lash had brought others with him, and maybe the entire gathering. If so, the odds against himself and Julian were very bad indeed.

When he reached the barn and threw the heavy locking board off its latch, the second shot sizzled past his right ear and thunked into the wood. Whoever was firing could indeed hit a barn, though this was not its broader side. He didn't wish to pause for a third attempt; he pulled the door open and the heat and noise of the flames growled out at him and he realized he was silhouetted by the light and made to be a better target, so into the fire he ran.

The place was not yet an inferno, but a large pile of hay was burning fiercely and the flames were beginning to lick up the wall on that side. Matthew caught the smell of whale oil over the odors of burning hay and wood. One of the big horses had already pulled free of its tether and it nearly trampled Matthew as he jumped aside in its swift passage out the door. Another smaller horse that must've belonged to the Autreys also ran wildly past Matthew and out. Not only were the remaining three horses of their coach pulling at their tethers and screaming in distress, but one other smaller steed was trapped by a second pile of burning hay toward the rear of the barn and it was screaming, spinning around and kicking at the walls.

Matthew had to untie the horses but he was in triple danger: from the unknown gunner, the fire, and the hooves of those Viking monsters. Again, there was no time. He saw a shovel leaning against the wall near the door. He pushed his gun into his waistband, got the shovel and ran to free the Autreys' horse at the far side of the barn, using the shovel to push aside enough of the mass of burning hay so that the animal could recognize a way out. And indeed it did, rushing past him and gone. Then Matthew turned his attention toward freeing the other three, and that was when the figure came walking toward him through the swirling smoke.

"Ah," said Bertrand Montague. "The Baron Brux imposter, come here to die." He lifted his pistol, which Matthew no doubt knew had been reloaded and ready for murder.

Before Montague's finger could pull the trigger, another shot rang out and the man lurched forward and spun around as if dancing a strange minuet. The pistol in his hand went off with a loud report and the bullet went into the burning hay.

Montague fell to his knees and then onto his face, and Matthew could see the blood rising on his coat from the wound at the center of his spine.

"Any man who shoots my husband and tries to burn horses," said Greta Autrey as she held the smoking musket at her side, "is not fit to live." She blinked, perhaps stunned at what she had just done. Then she added, "No questions asked."

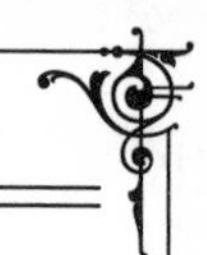

"Help me," Matthew said.

Together they braved the terrified animals and the flashing hooves. They got two out but the third huge horse was thrashing and jumping so hard neither Matthew nor Greta could get in close enough to release the tether. The fire was getting hotter as more hay caught, and smoke was filling the place. Matthew kept looking toward the open barn door, expecting at any second for another shot to come at him. He and Greta were about to try the task again when the third beast pulled not the tether free but the wooden bar that the lines were tied around, and off the horse galloped, dragging the bar behind it and missing trampling its would-be saviors by mere inches.

The fire would either have to burn itself out or take the barn down in flames. They had to get back thirty yards to the cottage. Matthew figured any gunner out there was in a good firing position and aiming at the opening. Where might a gunner be? Across the road in the woods? No, probably closer by now. Where, then? In cover behind the coach?

He heard a voice outside call for Montague. He recognized Sandor Krakowski's accent. Had Lash brought the whole group with him? Cardinal Black and the Owl as well? He remembered how many weapons were in that basket he'd dumped into the hedges; if they'd brought all those, this was going to be like battling a small army. He realized he'd left Bogen's powderhorn in the coach though he still had the fringed pouch of flints and ammunition in his jacket. Was it worth trying to get the powder? He would have to, because Julian didn't have any.

All these things spun through his mind in a matter of seconds. He was going to have to go for the coach. He had one shot in his pistol, which he drew from beneath his jacket and cocked. Greta was peering out, the musket at her side and smoke whirling past her. "Greta!" he said, coming up behind her. "Any more bullets for the musket?"

"A box," she said, still warily looking toward the sinister line of forest across the road.

"Gunpowder?"

"A pouch about half full."

"Good." Matthew was relieved he wouldn't have to run for the coach after all, as that was surely tempting a mortal wound. He looked past Greta's shoulder and saw that Oliver was crawling toward the cottage. "I'm going to step out in front of you and fire," he told her. "I want you to run when I pull the trigger. Are you ready?"

She nodded.

Matthew took a breath, almost choking on the billowing smoke that was blowing past him, and stepped outside. He chose to fire his single shot in the direction of the coach—an ear-shattering blast—and Greta ran. Almost at once Matthew realized a figure was on its stomach *under* the coach, and as he turned to follow Greta the next gunshot flashed and boomed. Matthew felt a heavy tug at the left sleeve of his coat just above the elbow. Someone else fired from the woods: a sputter of sparks and a hiss, a misfire from wet powder. Then Greta had reached her husband and helped him up, and together they made for the cottage door, which Julian opened for both them and the shivering young man who threw himself into the cottage at their heels, knowing how close he'd come to being the recipient of two pistol balls.

Julian slammed the door shut. Elizabeth was standing back against the far wall and Firebaugh had not moved from his position on the floor. Even with his newly-split lower lip, he was grinning like a fool and daring another visit of violence from Julian.

Greta eased Oliver down to the floor. "Damn!" the man said, breathing hard and obviously in severe pain, as the ball had likely cracked his thigh-bone. "Took a good gooser that one, lady! Busted somethin', I can tell!"

She looked up at Julian, who had produced his own pistol and had drawn the curtains aside from a window. "Who are they?" she asked.

"Bad men," said the bad man.

"Horses are gone," Matthew said, examining the two burn-edged holes in the left sleeve of the polar bear coat where the ball had torn through.

"I saw."

"Montague came in," said Matthew. "Greta shot him, and thank God for that."

"Montague," Julian repeated. His eyes were narrowed as he scanned the snowy dark. "Lash has brought the others, then."

"Let me go talk to him!" Elizabeth insisted. "*Please*, Matthew!"

"And say what?" Julian asked; in this moment of extreme stress his voice was calm and even, as if conversing quietly over social affairs in the lobby of the Mayfair Arms. "Bargain with him? To what end? We need the book and we need the doctor and by God we're not giving either of them—"

A pistol shot flashed out, again from beneath the coach. The window beside Julian's face suddenly grew a hole and a spiderwebbing of cracks and there was a whine as the ball hit the stones of the hearth and ricocheted off.

"—up," Julian finished, speaking calmly again. "Lash intends to kill us anyway, even if we were to give him the book, the doctor and yourself, so what might be the point of that conversation?"

"I would ask him to deliver quick deaths instead of slow," Elizabeth answered. "You know you're outnumbered, and by now he's got this place surrounded."

"What have you people brought upon us?" Greta asked as tears reddened her eyes. "*Mein Gott*, are we to *die* here?"

"Everyone dies, madam," Julian replied without looking at her. "It is unfortunately a fact of life that most times we cannot choose our fate in that regard. I will say that if my last meal was your very fine chicken soup, I will not go wishing for better food." At last he gazed down upon her and perhaps only Matthew saw the fleeting expression of sorrow that passed across his face. "My regrets," he said. "But we're not dead yet. Please reload that musket and afford me some gunpowder and bullets if you have a supply. Things may get hot here very soon."

"I have bullets and extra flints." Matthew took from his jacket the fringed pouch that had belonged to Bogen.

"I saw you fire your shot. You reload first and go man the back door. Madam, the musket and the powder?"

Greta hesitated, the shade of doom still upon her face, until Oliver urged her to go on and to hurry. She left the room. Matthew reloaded his pistol using a ball and a bit of cotton wadding from the pouch, then when Greta returned with the powder he applied the necessary amount for ignition and tamped everything down with the small ramrod that fit in a groove under the barrel.

He started for the back of the house when a voice came, eerily whipped up and down in volume by the whirlwind beyond the broken window.

"Your position," Lash called, standing in the shelter of the coach, "is untenable! Shall we call an end to this nonsense?"

Firebaugh scrambled up from the floor and shouted, "Lash! Get me out of here!"

"Go to the back, Matthew," Julian said quietly. "Be ready to reload."

"Lash!" Firebaugh pushed his face toward the second window. "Help me!"

"Patience, Doctor!" the vice admiral answered. "All in good time."

"They're sending Corbett to the—"

Before Firebaugh could get that out, Julian was upon him. As Matthew was heading to the back, he saw Julian catch hold of the doctor's banyan robe and swing him around with such violence that Firebaugh almost went into the flames of the hearth.

Matthew felt the chill of the wind blowing through the hallway, and he realized he was two steps and a moment too late.

Sandor Krakowski, wearing a brown corduroy coat and a woolen cap on his bald head, had just crept in through the back door. They saw each other at the same time, and at the same time swung their guns up and fired at a distance of twelve feet while they both twisted their bodies to avoid the bullets.

In the roar of gunfire and the explosion of blue smoke, Matthew felt a hot sting across his right cheek and the force of the shot staggered

him back along the hallway. He had stars and pinwheels in his eyes, and for an instant everything turned blood red and the hallway itself seemed to pulse like a labored heart. He knew he'd been hit, but had he hit Krakowski?

The answer came at him like a maddened bull.

Krakowski struck out with the empty pistol, caught Matthew on the left shoulder and drove him down. Matthew lost his own gun in the impact but had the sense to roll away from a steel-tipped boot that kicked at his skull. He was not dazed enough to miss the fact that he was fighting for his life, and Julian could not help because as soon as Firebaugh got out the door the rest of Lash's group would charge in. Matthew felt the blood running down the side of his face from the bullet that had creased him, and in desperation he pulled the ivory-handled dagger of Albion out from his waistband and stabbed at the smoke-stained air where Krakowski had been a second before but now was not.

A pistol swung, a knee came up, a fist chopped down and Matthew was flattened. The dagger went spinning from his nerveless fingers. He tried to scramble away but a hand caught the back of his coat and then an arm went around his throat and the immediate pressure caused his eyes to bulge from their sockets.

He was facing the front of the house as he was being choked to death. And through the smoke that blew past him he saw her pick up the dagger.

And he saw her look at the blade, and he saw her change.

She was bringing up RakeHell Lizzie from the depths. She was doing it to save a brother Broodie, and even so close to passing out Matthew thought that Sandor Krakowski did not realize who had just entered the hallway. If so, he might have let Matthew go and run for his life.

But it was too late.

Elizabeth's face had become a waxy mask. It was as if the creature underneath it had in an instant manufactured its own disguise. Her eyes, so warm and brown, took on a cold, hard black shine. Her mouth crimped, as if thirsty for murder. Her entire body tensed like a spring about to

uncoil, and with it a need beyond anything Matthew could ever begin to fathom that would only be sated by blood.

She came at Krakowski like a silent spirit drifting through the gunsmoke, her eyes ashine, her mouth twisted slightly to one side, the dagger upraised.

She struck, fast as a blur.

Matthew couldn't see where she cut him, but he howled and suddenly Matthew was gasping on the floor. Krakowski stumbled over Matthew and fell, and then Matthew saw that RakeHell Lizzie had slashed him across the right side of his face and turned that eye into a white, oozing ruin. Krakowski made an animalish noise that was a combination of fear and rage and then he came up off the floor with nearly superhuman strength. As he did, Matthew saw he had scrabbled into his coat and upon his right hand was the ugly nail-studded knuckle-duster Matthew had seen in the weapons basket at Lash's mansion.

If RakeHell Lizzie saw it, it made no difference to her. Or perhaps it made all the difference, and that was why she flung herself at Krakowski with a warped sense of joyful abandon and Albion's blade went up and down like a piston in the meat of his face, neck and chest.

Matthew grabbed hold of Krakowski's legs. The man staggered but stayed upright, dragging Matthew with him. Matthew could feel him swinging back and forth with the deadly duster. RakeHell Lizzie clung to him like a deadly vine, and Krakowski was bellowing like a dumb injured brute who was staying on his feet by sheer willpower, and there was nothing Matthew could do to bring the man down.

Then suddenly Krakowski fell like a huge thick tree that had at last received its final axeblow. His body lay quivering as Matthew sat up and saw that Elizabeth too had slid down against the wall, and she was staring blankly at the dagger in her hand as the life streamed from the wounds that had torn her throat open.

Someone else was in the hallway. Greta Autrey, holding the musket. Matthew got up as if in a slow-motion dream, and he saw through his own

haze of pain Greta's eyes tick toward the back door and her face tighten, and when he turned from her he saw Lioness Sauvage in her lion-skin coat coming through the open door with a pistol in each hand.

At that instant he gave himself up to Fate.

With death and blood all around him, with his ears half-deafened by the pistol blasts and the red haze pulsing in his eyes, everything seemed to him to have become eerily calm, even his own breathing and the labor of his heart…calm, as if chaos itself had reached its limit and collapsed, and what was behind that tattered veil was the glimpse of another world where life and death had become a strange and stately dance.

Matthew took the musket from Greta.

He walked—or rather, drifted in his dream—toward Lioness Sauvage, who also in slow-motion lifted one of the pistols into his face and pulled the trigger.

Fizzzzzzz… The snow-damp gun shot out from its flint three sparks and a ghost of smoke, but no bullet.

Matthew saw her face contort. Saw her teeth clench. Saw the other pistol coming up.

He pulled the musket's trigger, though he had no memory of aiming it. His thought was that if Greta had not yet reloaded the weapon, the hammer was falling on his grave.

Greta's powder was dry.

The musket was loaded.

In the burst of blue smoke that followed, Lioness Sauvage simply fell away out the door and was gone as if she had never been there at all. When Matthew pulled his reluctant legs after himself and peered out, he couldn't see her anywhere but there were dark streaks on the snow. He closed the door softly, as if not wishing to disturb the dead, and he lamented the fact that there was no latch on this door, as the country thereabouts was a trustful land.

He found himself standing over Elizabeth. He looked into Greta's blood-blanched face. He handed her back the musket. "Thank you," he

said. And then: "I'd like a cup of tea," but why he said this he had no idea because he didn't really want any tea, he wanted to find a place on earth where human beings did not murder each other for profit or for entertainment, and as Greta backed away from him obviously realizing he was on the brink of madness he sank down beside Elizabeth with a weary sigh and put a brotherly hand on his sister's arm.

She had been cut badly in other places and those wounds might have healed, but she would not recover from the throat wound. Matthew saw it was a matter of time, and time was short. He just sat with her, in the mess of the hallway, and he put his arm around her shoulders as she leaned her head against him and bled out.

She angled her face up toward his ear and whispered something. A garbled sound. He couldn't make it out.

She tried again, and this time he caught the first word.

"*Save*," she said.

He nodded dumbly. Yes. Save.

"*Save her*," she said.

He knew what she meant.

She was speaking about Berry. *The woman I love and plan to marry, if I can bring her back*, he'd said to Elizabeth in the room near the pit. *I am here to retrieve the book and to take Firebaugh with it.*

Perhaps at the last Elizabeth respected that effort, more than she respected Lash's auction of the book; perhaps even RakeHell Lizzie thought it was a noble thing, because what man had ever held her in such high esteem? What man, indeed, would have died to save her?

Lash's figurehead, deciding which way to steer her own ship.

And perhaps also, Matthew thought as Elizabeth took her final breaths, she was weary—so very weary—of being two people, and being burdened by all she'd told him in the coach.

Matthew realized she was setting him free of her own affection for Samson Lash—who had likely rescued Elizabeth Mulloy from the madhouse because he purely and simply desired a companion—for while she

was living she could not have allowed violence to be done to Lash by Matthew or Julian, and thus she was not only torn into two people but torn by two purposes.

Her ship was sailing.

"Rest," he told her, but she was already gone.

He tried to take from her hand the dagger but he found he was unable to open her fingers. He decided to leave it with her, because in her own way she had been an Albion of sorts, fighting a battle she could never win, but doing enough to make a difference for someone, somewhere, and they would probably never know it.

When Matthew staggered back into the front room with the pistol he had retrieved in his hand, Julian looked at his bloodied form—the polar bear coat soaked on the front with it—and the bullet gash across his cheek and brief expressions of both sickness and relief passed across his face.

"I couldn't leave here to help you," he said, "but she said she would."

Matthew just nodded. He saw the Autreys huddled on the floor together, and he wondered how they could ever see the world again in the same light as before.

Julian peered out the window and quickly drew his head back. He asked, "Is she—"

"Dead," Matthew said.

At once Firebaugh rushed toward the broken glass and screamed, "Lash! They've killed Elizabeth! Do you hear? They've—"

Julian put him down again with a kick to the groin, after which the doctor crawled off to a corner sobbing in pain.

"Who was it?" Julian asked.

"Krakowski. And Lioness. I shot her. She's out in the back somewhere."

Julian grunted. He brought up a wry smile that his eyes did not share. "Well, that just leaves us with—"

Something on fire came flying through the spiderwebbed window and shattered the rest of it to pieces. A wine bottle with a flaming cotton wick broke on the stones of the floor; there was no explosion, but the whale oil spilled in a small brown wave rippling with blue fire. Almost immediately following that one came another bottle through the other window, breaking on the floor and throwing the burning oil in all directions.

Julian had seen a figure darting in through the barn's heavy smoke to throw the second bottle—a large figure, Lash it looked to be—but there was no time to aim and no use in wasting a shot. When the third bottle came in through the window it broke on the sill and the flaming oil splattered a curtain, burning shilling-sized holes into it.

Smoke began blowing in from the barn. A fourth bottle came out of the murk and passed Julian's face by a few inches. As it came in, shattered on the floor and spilled its sizzling oil a shot rang out and fragments of stone from the sill whined about the room.

Matthew found a place to sit away from the oil and went about reloading his pistol. His fingers fumbled. He couldn't get his thinking straight. Another shot was fired and the bullet thunked into the wall above his head.

"You do know you've loaded that gun with three charges, don't you?" Julian asked him.

Even in his dazed condition and with a dozen places of pain in his body, Matthew realized it was pointless to stay here. He stood up in a crouch.

"We've got to go," he said, his eyes watering from the smoke. "We've got to circle through the woods and get that second coach."

"Agreed," Julian said with hardly a pause. "Pull your balls in and stand up," he told Firebaugh.

"Come out!" It was Cardinal Black's voice from the whirling curtains of smoke. "Devane, you and Corbett have *no* chance! Make it easier on yourselves!"

"Easier, he says. Fuck him. Stand up, I said, or I'll haul you up by the nuts." Julian looked down upon the Autreys. "You two need to get out of here."

"And go *where*?" Oliver asked, his face still pinched with pain and his eyes now gray-rimmed with the same shock that affected his wife and Matthew.

"Anywhere but here," Julian answered.

"Wouldn't get very far with a broken leg, would I?"

"You might hobble as if your life depends on it, which it does." Julian advanced upon the doctor, who shrank back in fear. "One word from you, and by God your teeth will be down your gullet. Matthew, don't put another charge in that damned gun. Get yourself under control."

"Yes," Matthew said. Had he said that? "Yes," he said, loudly to make sure.

"If you decide to stay here," Julian said to the Autreys, "reload that musket and shoot the first man who rushes through that door…which will happen anytime now." He sighed heavily. It turned into a series of coughs for smoke was filling the room through the broken windows.

"Get out while you can," he told Oliver and Greta, and then he motioned with his gun at Firebaugh. "You first. Out the back door. Matthew, you're behind me. Be watchful. Ready?"

"Yes."

"Thank you for the hospitality," Julian said to the innkeeper and his wife. There was nothing else to say, and with a solemn glance to see that several of the paper roses on the Christmas tree had begun to crisp and burn from the splatters of whale oil he put the four barrels of his gun against Firebaugh's back and shoved the doctor toward the blood-soaked hallway.

TWENTY-NINE.

"Gone," said Cardinal Black.

Lash did not answer. Black gave the old man and woman who clung together on the floor a look of disdain. He wiped his watering eyes with the back of a long-fingered hand, coughed a few times to clear his lungs and then picked up the musket he had his boot on. He walked into the hallway the vice admiral had just entered, and there he saw the picture.

Lash had knelt down beside her body. He had one hand in her hair, supporting her head, and the other against her cheek.

"This is a damnable mess," said Black.

Lash was silent. His huge body gave what might have been a shiver of either anguish or rage.

"They're going for the other coach," said Black. "Whatever happened here cannot be changed." When Lash still did not respond, Black prodded a bit harder. "Lioness and Merda may be able to stop them in the woods but if they slip past, Hodder will be no match for Devane."

Lash gently laid her head to the floor. He picked up the gun he'd set aside, stood up and stared at the open back door. Smoke was whirling through the hallway, drawn from both the burning barn and one of the window curtains that had caught fire. When he turned his gaze upon

Cardinal Black again his face was a blank mask but Black recognized in the vice admiral's piercing blue eyes the writhing flames of Hell.

He strode into the front room. The Autreys clung to each other on the floor, surrounded by little blue oil fires that shimmered on the stones. When Lash had thrown the last oil bottle in and followed it by breaking the door off its hinges with a tremendous kick, he'd found a musket pointed at him. He'd stopped dead still and bellowed *I am a vice admiral in the Royal Navy, madam*! The statement had so unnerved Greta that before she could compose herself Cardinal Black was in the room, and had driven the musket to the floor with his boot.

The flame-bearded Lash, a towering and terrifying presence, stood over the couple with his pistol at the ready.

"Please, sir," said Oliver, "we want none of this." His voice broke. "*Please, sir.*"

"Allow me," Cardinal Black requested.

Lash's voice was like a doom bell. "Make haste."

Black drew from his raven's-wing coat his ceremonial knife, its hooked blade marked with the symbols and lettering that to him spoke of absolute freedom in the name of Satan, which to the mind of the normal person would mean all forms of the darkest, most brutal evil without regard for consequence or conscience.

Black was on Oliver Autrey even as the man put his arms up in an effort to protect his wife. The blade slashed across Autrey's throat, a target upon which Black had had much practise.

When the bloody knife was turned in the woman's direction, Greta Autrey got up on her knees and spat at him with the tears running down her cheeks, and she said fiercely, "*Rot in der Holle, du Schwein.*"

After the work was done—quickly and efficiently, as was Black's method—the cardinal cut the sign of the Devil's Cross on the forehead of both bodies and said, "I commend your souls to the Master." Then, to Lash, "I'm ready now, sir. The Master will speed our cause."

"Fine," Lash rumbled, with a grim glance toward the horror that lay in the hall. "Just keep your damn master out of my way."

They struggled on through the woods and eight inches of snow. The wind was still blowing hard, sweeping snow from the tree branches, but the snowfall itself had ceased. Behind them the low clouded sky was smeared with orange from the burning barn, and before them was the dark of the unknown.

When they had come out of the cottage, they'd found Lioness Sauvage lying next to the woodpile. Blood had seeped through her lion's-skin coat on the left side of her body up near the collarbone. When she made out who was there, she made a gasping noise and tried to lift one of the pistols she held—the one that Matthew realized had not misfired—but she was unable to do so. In any case, snow had already blighted that weapon as well, and also lay in an icy gleaming upon her face and the mane of her hair.

Matthew paused to look down upon her and was struck with a feeling of pity, his senses still stunned. As he was doing so the axe that Julian had picked up beside the woodpile came down into her head with a definitive finality, and Julian said, "Don't waste our time. *Move.*" He pushed the doctor ahead of him, and Matthew followed as they trudged away from the cottage.

After another moment Matthew asked, "Do you think the Autreys will be all right?"

There was no reply from Julian.

"The Autreys," said Matthew. "Do you think they'll be all right?"

"They're already dead," Julian said. "Now be silent."

Of course they were. Matthew knew it. Lash and Black would not let them live to tell any tales. Of course they were dead, their throats likely cut and that Devil's Cross sliced into their—

Matthew nearly fell. The night and the woods and the world spun around him. He had to grab hold around a slim pine tree to keep from

being flung off into infinity, and he realized he deserved to be flung off. He should be, because he had killed Oliver and Greta Autrey. He had killed Elizabeth too, and for what? Because he'd thought Dippen Nack should be saved? And even when he'd done the foolish thing and spoken out, it hadn't spared Nack's life. He realized that if he'd remained silent in his role as Baron Brux, he and the false Count Pellegar might very well have gotten out of that house with the book of potions and the doctor and not a drop of blood had to be shed for it. Lash would have his bars of gold and the plans for the airship he was obsessed to build, and that would've been the end of it until Julian and Matthew had told Firebaugh where he was going.

No one had had to die, least of all the Autreys. Matthew thought that good and bad were mixed up in his mind; he no longer could tell one from the other. Had it been a good thing to try to save Nack? But that deed had led to bad consequences. Had it been a bad thing to kill Brux and Pellegar in their inn suite? But that deed had led to getting into the house, which would be a good deed in favor of saving Berry.

And just now…the axe to the head of a defenseless woman lying in the snow. Good or bad? A cruel murder? Or a defense against her regaining her feet and her senses and—

A hand gripped the front of the bloodied polar bear coat.

"Listen to me," said Julian, his face up close to Matthew's. "I don't know *exactly* what's in your mind but I don't think I like it. You're no stranger to bloodshed. Oh, I see…the Autreys, and you can't stomach that, can you? Well, neither can I but it's not going to get me killed. Our task was to get the book and the doctor…however we could. We have done that. Now the trick is to get both of them back to where they'll do some good for your lady. You go to pieces now and everything—*everything*—was for nothing. Say you understand." Matthew was slow in responding and Julian shook him. "*Say it.*"

"I understand," Matthew answered, and whether he truly did fathom this deadly chess game of good and bad played by the hand of Fate, it did not matter. Julian was right. All the deaths, all the violence…it would be

for nothing if they didn't get the book and Firebaugh back to save Berry, and that was the very most important thing.

"Keep moving," Julian said. Matthew let go of the tree that was holding him onto the earth. He did not spin away. He followed Julian and Firebaugh through the snowy woods, remembering that in his state of delirium in the house he had loaded his pistol with three charges, one ball and one pour of gunpowder on top of the other, and he thought that without a bullet extractor tool the gun was now useless except as a bomb to blow his hand off, so Julian's four-barrelled pistol would have to see them through the next encounter. Lash, Black and Miles Merda were still out there, and they were not going to let that coach go without a fight.

Julian pushed Firebaugh to the right, in a direction that would curve them through the forest back to the road. As Matthew's head cleared—and the bitter cold had a great deal to do with that—he reasoned that the second coach had come upon the Autreys' cottage and its driver had seen the first coach situated in front, thus had pulled the horses to a halt and backed them up around the road's bend so as to be out of sight. Montague had likely started the fire either to drive the team away or burn them, if they weren't set loose. The others had probably either elected their own plan of attack or been directed by the vice admiral. In any case, now there was the unholy three to deal with, and maybe the worst of the lot though Krakowski had come within a gasp of finishing Matthew off.

"*Stop*," Julian said quietly.

Through the trees could be seen the yellow glow of the coach's lanterns, one on either side of the driver's seat. The driver himself was not perched up top. "Driver's inside keeping warm, if he's got any sense," Julian told Matthew. He withdrew from his cloak his gun, which he'd been trying to keep dry during their trek from the cottage. "If you have any thoughts of shouting out," he said to Firebaugh, who appeared utterly exhausted and in no shape to protest, "I can still pour you a cup of suffering."

"No, please," the doctor murmured listlessly. "Please…I won't shout out."

"Go." Julian shoved Firebaugh forward.

They crossed from the woods onto the road, which itself was thick with snow. The orange glow of the barn's fire lit the clouds. Matthew looked back to see the spectacle of thousands of sparks blowing with the wind. The coach's team grumbled nervously and shifted in their traces, smelling the smoke. Then they were upon the coach, and Julian threw open the doors on the side facing them.

The man inside was bundled up in a heavy brown coat and a brown woolen cap with a white tassel atop it. He gave a start and instantly lifted his hands at the sight of the four barrels looking him in his sharp-nosed face.

"Take off your coat and cap, get out the other side and run," Julian said.

It was done at once and without protest. As soon as the driver was gone, Julian put on the coat and the cap and said to Matthew, "Both of you get in. I'll get us the hell out of here." When they were inside, Matthew put the useless gun on the seat beside him and Firebaugh collapsed into a heap on the other side. Julian closed the doors and climbed up to the driver's seat. A movement to his right caught his attention: a small figure, crouched down and running as fast as possible across the road behind the coach. Julian had no time to dwell on Miles Merda; he flicked the reins and shouted "Giddap!" but the horses would not move.

Julian saw the whip upright in its stand. He put his gun aside to pull it out and crack it across the reluctant rumps. "Giddap, damn you!" he shouted, and with this added incentive the team lurched forward, the traces jingled, and the coach's wheels began to roll.

A shot rang out and the lantern to Julian's right exploded. He saw Samson Lash coming like a destructive force of nature across the road in front of the team, followed at a short distance by Cardinal Black. Before the team could pick up any kind of speed, Lash had thrown himself at the horses and grabbed hold of any leather strap he could find to stop their progress. Julian reached for his gun but Lash was too close to the team and shooting a horse was not productive; as the coach rattled to a stop, Julian struck out with the whip at Samson Lash, who took two strikes

The Demise of Admiral Lash

until he grasped hold of the whip's bitter end. Before Julian could let go of the whip's handle he was yanked off the driver's seat, cast into space, and down upon the crust of the road.

The breath bellowed from Julian's lungs. Lash gave him a kick to the side that Julian instantly knew through the searing pain had staved his ribs in. Julian desperately gripped the gun; he rolled away from the next kick, which grazed across his shoulder, and heard Lash shout, "Finish him, Black!" as the vice admiral tore away toward the coach. With two more strides Lash reached up, grasped one of the door handles and ripped the entire door from its hinges, exposing within Firebaugh and a terrified Matthew whose first impulse was to kick out at Lash's face.

Black's gun was drawn. As he reached Julian and took aim, Julian twisted his body and pulled one of the pistol's triggers. Sparks flew, a small flame gouted, there was an instant of a sizzling sound during which Julian feared the first chamber had misfired…and then the pistol went off with a blinding flash, ear-cracking blast and a whirling dervish of blue smoke.

Lash gripped one of Matthew's legs and started pulling him out. "Get him! Get him!" Firebaugh screamed, his voice as shrill as a woman's. Matthew kicked out with his other boot and caught Lash on the side of the head, but it was as a slap against the brow of an enraged bull.

Matthew reached to the seat beside him for his pistol to use as a club, but before he could get it the huge man had nearly climbed into the coach and the vice admiral's hand closed on the weapon.

"*Now*!" Lash shouted, a shout of triumph to go with the fierce red gleam of near madness in his eyes, and he lifted the gun and pulled the trigger.

When the blast came, Matthew Corbett had known what was coming. He had thrown both his gloved hands up to protect his face and tried in the instant of recognition to twist his body to one side, but even so the flash was like a sun exploding and his ears rang with the shriek of a thousand of Cardinal Black's demons. When he dropped his hands and uncoiled, through the roiling smoke he first saw that Samson Lash's gun hand had

been reduced to a red mass of two twitching fingers around a twisted thing that had once been a pistol.

Lash stared at his own misshapen hand. His right eye was a red, sunken hole. Around it the bones of the skull had caved in from the concussion. In his right cheek and forehead above the ruin of the eye had been driven pieces of metal from the gun that had exploded with its three packed charges of lead balls and gunpowder. Blue flames rippled in his beard. Some of the metal bits of the gun had blown out sideways and were imbedded in the walls of the coach, and they too glowed as if on a blacksmith's forge. Sparks flared and flickered in the air, which smelled not of a winter's snow but of summer's hot lightning.

It also smelled of blood, scorched flesh and burning hair.

In another instant the vice admiral's face had become a distorted bloodmask. He fell back out of the coach, but he did not go down nor did he make any sound. He began to stagger back and forth beside the landship, shaking his destroyed hand to which the mangled bomb of a pistol had melded. Matthew watched him as he took one arm with the other and seemed to want to tear it off, so fiercely did he wrench at it. Then he did fall to his knees, and his gory face turned to behold the man who was coming toward him, the specter of approaching death.

Julian Devane stood over him.

Lash's mouth worked but no sound emerged. The remaining eye still held its red fire of both hatred and a refusal to plead for life. He puffed his chest out, and Julian caught the shine of his medals in the leaping firelight.

He brought up his pistol, cocked it, and put it against Lash's head.

Lash pushed the gun away with his good hand. The vice admiral grinned, as blood ran from his nose and down into his beard, and his eyelid in the gruesome face began to fall to half-mast.

Julian put the gun against Lash's head once more.

Lash spat blood at Julian and made a noise that might have been a laugh.

Matthew saw Julian hesitate…still hesitate…and then the bad man stepped back. Clutching his left side as if to hold his entrails in place, he hobbled to the coach. Julian croaked, "You're driving. Get us out of here."

"What happened to Black?"

"Gone. I think I hit him. But when the smoke cleared…gone. Get up there, Matthew. Firebaugh, I can still hurt you. Hear me?" Julian kept his grip on the fearsome pistol, and though his face was dead white and sweating even in the cold and his voice was a harsh whisper, he was yet enough threat to keep the doctor at bay.

As Matthew shook off his own pains and weariness in the cold and got the team moving, he looked back to see Samson Lash still on his knees in the snow. Did the vice admiral fall at last, as Matthew took the coach around the curve to pass the burning barn and the house where the Autreys lay dead?

He wasn't sure, but he did not look back again.

THIRTY.

Night and the wind. The horses, exhausted, had slowed to a walk and would not be urged to go any faster. The driver too was exhausted, and he clung to the reins as if fearful of falling asleep and toppling from his perch, which was true.

Two hours had passed since Matthew had guided the team past the Autreys' cottage. He could see stars between the clouds as they moved like gray wraiths across the heavens. His body seemed to be one pulsing pain. Any broken bones? He didn't think so. The pain of his shoulder where Krakowski had clouted him with the pistol was bad, but the worst pain was in his heart.

He fought against sleep. How many hours had it been since he'd slept? Many. The wind in his face was a double-edged sword; it was helping him win the fight, but his eyes were so narrowed against the blow that they kept wanting to close altogether.

He heard the sound of the viewslit sliding open.

"Stop the coach," Julian said, his voice now even more ragged and pain-wracked than before.

"What is it?"

"Just stop. Right here, right now."

Matthew pulled back on the reins. "Whoa, whoa," he said. The team needed no coaxing. When the wheels had stopped rolling Matthew saw that they were on what appeared to be a desolate road with flat, snow-covered moors on either side. There were no lights but the single remaining lantern to his left, the lanterns within the coach, and the stars.

"Come down here," Julian said, and then he slid the viewslit closed.

Matthew climbed down. His back protested. He dreaded what a mirror would tell him; the only demon in it would be himself, because in his sorry state he was sure he resembled the very Devil, if that creature were covered in black and blue bruises. Before he went to the place where there had been two doors, reduced now to one door and an opening that allowed the passengers to freeze to death, he stopped to scoop up a handful of snow and press it against the bullet crease on his cheek because that too was stinging like Satan's most favored scorpion.

Julian was already climbing out, but with the pained slowness of an elderly man. Again he clutched at his left side. "Here." He gave Matthew his pistol. "Hold this beast for me, and watch *that* bastard." He motioned toward Firebaugh, who sat shivering in his banyan robe. "I'm going to see if there are any blankets in the back. Hoping a horse blanket, at least. A rope to tie *him* up with would be good, too, because I'm about to pass out. Watch him," Julian repeated, and then he went to the landship's stern where the two doors were closed over the baggage compartment.

When Julian got around to the back, he noted that one of the doors had been jarred a crack open, likely from the motion of the coach. He grasped both handles and pulled, and as the doors came fully open starlight glinted on the snout of a pistol that was thrust into his face.

"Jack in the box!" said Miles Merda with a toothy, lopsided grin. The man who resembled a twelve-year-old boy was wrapped up in a heavy coat with a blanket draped around him. His grin widened. "It appears to me I have won the—"

Three things happened almost at once.

Julian slammed the doors upon Merda's wrist and the gun went off, but Julian had already jerked his head aside and the ball hissed past his left ear. With a move that sent excruciating pain through his injured side he reached into the baggage compartment where the small killer had lodged himself during the fight with Samson Lash and waited patiently for the moment when the guns were silent and the defenses down.

Merda was already reaching for a second prepared pistol, but Julian got hold of Merda's coat and threw him out of the compartment into the snow before small hand could latch onto large gun. The little man nimbly scrambled up. A knife that a butcher would envy glinted in the wash of the coach's lantern light. Merda rushed in jabbing the blade at Julian, who dodged one strike and then another but felt the third tear through his cloak. The blade snagged in the cloth. Julian chopped Merda's hand away from it. He hit Merda full in the mouth but Merda delivered a fist that got Julian in his damaged ribs, and as Julian fell with the breath knocked out of him and pain sawing at his side he saw Merda reach into his mouth and pop out the false front teeth that turned into a pair of deadly blades.

At once Merda was sitting astride Julian's chest, one hand up against his chin and the other pressing the blades into his throat, about to pierce the flesh.

"*No*," said Matthew. He cocked the second chamber of Julian's gun, which had seemed of its own accord to have taken aim at Merda's forehead under the mass of curly, oiled hair.

Merda looked up at him. At that moment the doors on the other side of the coach banged open. Firebaugh was out and running.

The blades remained pressed against Julian's throat. The slashing of arteries was an ounce of pressure away.

The grin was fixed on Merda's mouth but his eyes were dark and dead: the remorseless, conscienceless eyes of a painted doll. It was clear he meant to kill Julian and take his chances with the Herrald Agency's problem-solver, whose sympathetic nature—weakness would be the correct word—could be easily used against him.

"Corbett," Merda said quietly and soothingly, as if the child were speaking to another over the matter of sharing sugar candies. "You and I both know you're not a killer. You're a man of the law." He spoke it like a curse. "Of *justice*. You wouldn't *stain* yourself by—"

Matthew pulled the trigger.

The blast of the double shot took most of Merda's skull away. The small man seemed to fold up as if made of flimsy paper and blow before the wind, the staring eyes beneath the cratered skull now truly dark and dead.

Julian sat up. He coughed up blood.

Matthew offered him the smoking pistol. "Here," he said tonelessly, and when Julian took the weapon he began walking away.

Julian wiped his mouth with the back of his hand and regarded the result. "Where are you going?" he asked, his own senses stunned and sluggish.

"To fetch a doctor," Matthew answered.

Firebaugh didn't get far, maybe only a hundred yards before his borrowed boots cracked through the crust into boggy earth that stopped his progress as surely as a pair of leg-irons.

"On your feet," Matthew commanded when he reached the man by easily following his tracks. He could hear in his voice—as the doctor could—that something had changed about him. Something was different, and this difference had perhaps become complete in just the last few minutes. Was this change for good or for bad? At the moment, it was difficult to say.

"Oh yes," Matthew added, as he stood over the doctor and found himself wishing Firebaugh to try to run a bit more so he could take the man down like a sack of dirty laundry. "They don't call me the Monster of Plymouth for no reason."

The rope that wound up tying Firebaugh's arms behind his back in the most uncomfortable position possible was the cord that had previously held up his breeches. With Firebaugh trussed and the yellow cravat of

the formerly living Miles Merda stuffed into his mouth, the doctor was secured enough so that Julian could sleep under the blanket that Merda had used to stay warm in the baggage compartment, and thus Matthew got his balls under himself—as either Julian or Hudson Greathouse might say—and continued on as driver.

When two more hours had passed and the road seemed to go on forever across the moors, Matthew knew he was near passing out. So it was with great relief that within the following half hour he steered the team toward the lamps of a coaching inn made of white stone and at least twice the size of the Autreys' cottage, which would hopefully mean featherbeds and a chance to bathe. They had stopped here briefly with the Turlentorts on the way in to London, but the stop had hardly seen them out of their coach.

How to explain the situation to the innkeeper Edmond Varney and his wife Ann, when they as loyal helpers to the riders of the roads came out wearing coats over their nightclothing and shone their lanterns upon the battered faces of their newest visitors?

How indeed?

The first item of business before Matthew stopped the coach before the inn was to shrug off the polar bear coat that was freighted by so much blood. It would not do to scare the wits out of the Varneys before a word could be spoken. He threw the coat over the side of the coach into the snow on the right, still perhaps thirty yards from the inn, and hoped it was far enough not to be discovered, at least for tonight.

When he reined the team in, he climbed down and rang the small bell that hung beside the front door. Above the door was a sign he'd noted before, but now seemed more poignant: the name of the inn, The Flying Dragon.

"We are constables escorting this violent criminal to stand trial in Bristol," Matthew decided to say when the pair emerged as predicted, with coats over nightclothes and lanterns ashine. "Yes, we did pass this way just lately, and we were coming from Bristol, as you know. Well, this one gave my associate and me quite a run and we've suffered some injuries but at last we brought him to ground. He's tied up now, and it's best he remain

tied up and stoppered up because I can tell you, sir and madam, he is one cunning sonofabitch. Might we have a room for the night and some food? Also, the horses are very much in need of attention."

"Of course!" said Varney, who stated that they had three rooms vacant and food aplenty, since it being so near Christmas all were at home with their families, and no one was travelling the roads except the express post coach.

Varney's quick and hospitable acceptance of the guests changed noticeably when a gray-faced and wheezing Julian brought Firebaugh out of the coach like a bound-up beast. Both the innkeeper and his portly wife retreated from the doctor as if from a carrier of plague, and at the inn's door Varney caught Matthew's sleeve and asked nervously, "Sir? My wife and I are not to be in danger, are we?"

Matthew said, "Absolutely not," and unless Samson Lash still lived and could stride the many miles with his face nearly torn off its skull and Cardinal Black could fly through the night in his raven's-wing coat, he believed his statement to be true. "And for your help in this matter," Matthew said, as he felt the weariness closing in around him and trying to drag him under, "you will be paid handsomely, I assure it." And thank God for the fact that Julian still possessed Bogen's four crowns and most of the shillings, which would never be put to a greater or more welcome purchase.

Within the Flying Dragon, Julian swigged down one mug of hot apple cider and then he and Matthew tied Firebaugh to the wooden bedframe of the room the criminal was consigned to. The cravat was left in his mouth and any needs he had for food, drink or evacuation delayed until after Varney had finished tending to the team. Julian warned him forcibly that any mess upon the featherbed would earn him dire regret. Then Julian staggered to his own room, collapsed on the bed, got himself into as much a comfortable position as possible, and immediately fell asleep, leaving Matthew to explain to Ann Varney that they were travelling with no baggage because their cases had been left behind in their haste to escape the criminal's accomplices.

It was the best story he could concoct, but he knew at once that Ann Varney was not so rural a spirit as to fail to have some sophistication in the aromatic tales of travellers, and this one did not pass her smell test. But there was naught she could do except demand that her husband throw the trio out upon the road at this wee hour, which she evidently decided against. However, as she prepared a pot of turnip soup while her husband attended to the horses she gave Matthew a show of producing a small pistol from a drawer and keeping it close at hand in her kitchen.

Matthew didn't blame her. Who would? The story's rope had to be fashioned with some stronger fiber, otherwise the nearest sheriff might be summoned, and in any event he had important business with the doctor.

As the woman worked in the kitchen, Matthew entered Firebaugh's room with a cup of the hot cider and took a chair beside the bed. Firebaugh's eyes were closed. Matthew turned the lamp's wick up and prodded the doctor in the side. Firebaugh jerked awake and pulled his knees up to his chin in an effort to make himself a smaller target for violence.

"I just want you to listen to me for a minute," said Matthew. He took a drink of the cider, which had to rank among the most delicious liquids he had ever put down his gullet, or maybe it was just part of the joy of still being among the living. "You're a man without a country right now. You know that, don't you?"

From the doctor there was no response, just the sullen glaring of a caged animal.

"Where you're being taken," Matthew went on, "may well be your finest dream. Professor Fell needs a chemist. I have no doubt he is willing to pay you anything you ask. The village isn't the worst place on earth, and I believe—hear me now, don't try to blank me out—that if you perform your duties to his expectation, you will have the solitude you require, all the research materials you could ever wish for, and—" He paused, but he had to say the next part. "And all the test subjects you might want. The whole place is an experiment in chemistry. What would be better for you? A long sea voyage to some foreign country where the intrigues might get

you killed before you even settled in? Well, there would be nothing to keep you from journeying to London or wherever you'd like, once you proved your worth to the professor. You would *not* be a prisoner there, if that's what you're thinking."

There was still no response from the doctor, but had a fraction of the angry glare in his eyes softened?

"All I want from you is the application of an antidote to the drug that is killing the senses of the woman I love," Matthew said. "That's what this has all been about. The formula for that antidote is somewhere in the book. I have as much faith in you as Lash did. Do you understand that? I have faith that you can concoct and apply that antidote, and that will finish the business between you and me. But it will only *begin* the business between you and the professor, if that is what you wish." As he spoke these words he couldn't believe he was hearing himself. Matthew Corbett...speaking on behalf of Professor Fell...building up that damned village...offering its trapped inhabitants up as chemical experiments, which of course they already were. And Matthew had made a promise to the kidnapped Italian opera star Madam Alicia Candoleri that he would somehow free everyone from Y Beautiful Bedd.

He imagined how Julian might grin from ear-to-ear if he could hear all this.

Welcome to the club, Julian might say. *We are always in need of another bad man.*

In essence, Matthew realized, he was sitting here talking to Lazarus Firebaugh as a member of Professor Fell's organization.

He took a deeper drink of the cider, because the taste in his mouth was terribly bitter.

"Just consider these things," Matthew continued. "Money...freedom...solitude...research...and *respect* from the professor. He needs you, Doctor. *I* need you. But all I ask at the moment is that when our innkeeper comes through that door and I remove the gag from your mouth, you go along with the story we have invented for our passage."

Did Firebaugh's eyes glaze over? Did a muscle twitch behind his red beard? It was difficult to tell.

In a few minutes, as Matthew finished off his drink, the door opened and Varney peered in. "Ann said you might be here. Is…um…everything in order?"

"Yes." It was apparent Ann had been telling her husband that these men were not to be trusted. Well, some men had to be trusted whether you wished it or not. Matthew stood up and pulled the cravat out of Firebaugh's mouth. "Tell Mr. Varney exactly what you have done, Sir Cunning," he said, "and why you are on your way to stand before the docket in Bristol."

Firebaugh didn't reply.

The moment stretched.

Firebaugh gave a short, harsh laugh.

"Spill it, sir," Matthew said. "Then we can get you a bowl of soup, a cup of cider, a chamberpot and a night's rest. I'll even sleep on the floor in here on guard, so that your bindings might be loosened. But only a bit, I will assure our gracious innkeeper, because our culprit here has three murders in his history. Isn't that right?"

Firebaugh laughed again; the laugh turned into a grunt, and then became a heavy sign of resignation.

"Three you *know* about," the doctor said, with a curl of his lip.

THIRTY-ONE.

On the early afternoon of Christmas Eve, Matthew chose a slim volume from the shelf of books in the parlor of the Flying Dragon. The title did not matter, nor did the subject of the book itself. He paused for a moment to watch flurries of snow sweep past the window that looked out upon the road, and then he walked into the kitchen where Edmond Varney and Ann were at work preparing the evening's holiday feast, which included the pheasant Varney had shot that morning on the moors.

"Some help, please," said Matthew to his hosts. He held up the book. "Firebaugh wishes to do a little reading and he's without his spectacles. Do you have anything that might suit?"

"Say no more." Varney reached up into a cabinet and brought down a small canvas bag. He unlaced it and opened it wide to show Matthew its contents: an assortment of keys, two pocketwatches, three small knives, a compass, a little black book, and four pair of spectacles.

"People leave things here all the time," he explained. "Wonder we don't find a head or two in a closet someday." Ann jabbed him in the side with a hefty elbow; it was an unwise remark, with a killer of three Bristol men in the house. "Take your pick," Varney said, regaining his composure as well as his balance.

"I'll let him decide." Matthew took all the spectacles. "Thank you very much."

"Supper at six o'clock," said the woman of the house. Her face darkened. "Do you think he'll be up to eating anything? Some beef broth, perhaps?"

"I'll ask. Again, thank you." Matthew left the kitchen with the book and the spectacles in hand. He walked past the room where Julian had been in bed for the two days since they'd arrived. He went into Firebaugh's room. The doctor was sitting in a chair with his banyan robe on, his feet up on an ottoman and the red leatherbound book of potions in his lap. In case the innkeeper or his wife happened to look in—which they certainly were not going to—Firebaugh kept the ropes loosely about his wrists and the other end tied to the bedpost. Matthew closed the door behind him. "Four pair for you to try."

"Ah." The first pair brought a wince and a comment of, "This person was born of a bat." The second: "Not too bad." The third and fourth did not suit, so the second pair went on the doctor's face and he opened the book of potions. Matthew put the book he'd selected as a decoy aside on a table.

"Quite a chemist, was this Jonathan Gentry," said Firebaugh as he turned through the forty or so pages of the book. "Some of these are devilishly intricate. What became of him?"

Matthew had known this question was coming sooner or later. "He passed away. Thus his place was taken by a chemist named Gustav Ribbenhoff. He was unfortunately dispatched on orders from Cardinal Black."

Firebaugh gazed at him over the rims of his spectacles. "I hope I don't see a pattern developing. That of a short life for the professor's chemists."

Matthew offered a faint smile but could go no further in his assurances.

The first full day of their arrival all three of them had slept like the dead, Matthew keeping his vow to sleep on a pad at the foot of the murderer's bed, and with Julian's pistol at the ready to further comfort their hosts though the gun was not loaded. On the second day, yesterday,

Firebaugh had told Matthew he wanted to start re-reading the book of potions so he might be as best informed as possible when they reached Fell's village, but his mind was still somewhat fogged and it needed to wait for another day.

The reason they had not left the Flying Dragon was that on the previous morning Julian had begun throwing up blood. Varney had taken a horse to Whistler Green, the nearest village six miles to the west, and returned with a thin but wiry and white-bearded doctor named Adam Clark following him in a buggy. Clark had gone in to see Julian, with Matthew standing at the bedside, and at once the assembly—including Varney and his wife—could see that the pallid and sweating man in the bed was not only in extreme pain but had sustained life-threatening injuries.

"Four broken ribs on the left side," said Clark once the examination was done and they were in the parlor. "Internal injuries as well. It's possible the sharp edges of the breaks have caused further wounds. Terrible bruises. What hit the poor man? And you also...that's the mark of a bullet crease on your cheek, is it not? And you too are not wanting for bruises."

"They are constables on official business," Varney explained before Matthew could speak. "They have captured the murderer of three men and are transporting him to Bristol for trial. Obviously it was a violent encounter."

"Oh?" The doctor's white eyebrows went up. "Well, then...it seems your man nearly has committed a fourth murder. And I have to say..." His voice quietened. "There may yet be another charge."

That statement sent a shrill of alarm through Matthew. "*What*? No! Julian needs rest, that's all."

"I can bind the ribs tightly so the pain is lessened, but it will not magically disappear and that process in itself will be painful...to say the least. I have some laudanum in my bag that will soothe him and help him sleep, though I am not particularly a great advocate of that drug. Still, it *does* work. As for the internals, that is a different story altogether. It may be

that excreting the corrupted blood will help, but then again…to speed the process I may need to apply cupping and the lancet."

"What?" Again Matthew felt a shiver. "Oh my God! I know what bleeding does to a patient, doctor, and I'm not at all sure it's for the positive."

"Young man, I have no other suggestions. His fever is running high and his heartbeat is labored. Ordinarily broken ribs will heal themselves in a matter of perhaps two months, but here we have further complications. Your associate could very well die in that bed, and it could be quickly if infection takes hold."

"No bleeding," said Matthew. He put a hand to his forehead, recalling the death of his mentor and great friend Magistrate Isaac Woodward some years ago. The—to Matthew's mind—hideous process of cupping and cutting had in his opinion worsened the magistrate's illness and likely killed him. "Please," Matthew said to the doctor. "No bleeding. Not yet, at least."

"Very well, I'll wait on that. But by your opinion, which is *not* mine. Understood?"

"Yes."

Laudanum was given, the binding was done, and thankfully Julian slept. Matthew left him alone, because there was nothing else to be done. Clark had left a small bottle of the drug with precise instructions on how much to use if Julian should awaken wracked with pain, and then the doctor had spent a few moments cleaning Matthew's cheek wound with a stinging red solution, had covered it with a plaster bandage, asked for five shillings in payment, and when the coins were paid wished the house a merry Christmas and went on his way.

"Devilishly clever, some of these," said Firebaugh as he continued through the book, stopping at certain formulas that he found intriguing. "Some of them simple enough, though. Just depending on the strength of the botanicals."

Matthew had to ask the question: "Do you think you can help Berry?"

"Honestly, I can't say until I've seen her. There are three formulas in here that might have been the one Ribbenhoff used. I'll have to examine the subject, and that's all I can say."

*Subjec*t instead of patient, Matthew thought. That was Firebaugh, all right, the doctor with the bedside manner suiting an automaton. But it was the best he could do, and that was that.

Matthew left Firebaugh with his reading and quietly slipped into Julian's room.

The figure in the bed was gray-faced. His eyes were closed and Matthew could hear the soft wheeze of his breathing. Matthew was about to retreat when Julian's eyes opened and he asked in his quietly tortured voice, "What day is it?"

"The twenty-fourth."

"Time?"

"About two o'clock."

"Has that doctor gone?"

"He was here yesterday," Matthew said.

"Laced me up," said Julian. "Tighter than a tick's asshole. Damn, I can hardly breathe."

"Are you in any pain?"

Julian looked at him as one would peer cockeyed at a madman. "Ha," he said.

"Do you want some laudanum? The doctor left a—"

"No. Hell, no." He moved slightly under his blanket and winced. Then he managed a harsh little laugh. "I'm not good for very much right now, am I?"

"Neither am I. Last night I slept maybe two hours. I had a dream that Lash and Black were chasing me in a landship that actually *was* a ship. It was pulled by giant seahorses and bristled with cannons."

"Did they catch you?"

"No. They were about to, and I was on the ground watching them float nearer and nearer…and then they melted away."

"Maybe you need the laudanum to clear your brain," Julian said.

Matthew pulled a chair up beside the bed and sat down. Julian's face was damp with sweat and dark circles ringed his eyes. Matthew imagined he could feel the heat of Julian's fever.

"I was asked," he said, "by the missus if you'd care for some beef broth."

"I would care for a *side* of beef, but I'd just throw it up like I did the breakfast. Damn that Lash! He got me good, Matthew. That giant-sized boot…I can still feel it knock my ribs in, damn him." Julian blinked and brought a hand up out of the covers to wipe his forehead. "What day is it?" he asked. "Feels like it should be August by now."

"Christmas Day tomorrow," Matthew said. "You've got to get well enough for us to finish our task. We don't have very far to go now."

"Two days travel, at least. I won't be up to that for a while."

"But you will be."

"Remains to be seen. Is Firebaugh behaving himself?"

"We've come to an understanding," Matthew said.

"Good for you. Smack him in the head if he gives you any trouble. Then kick him in the nuts for me."

"I'll keep that in mind."

Julian was silent for a few moments. He shifted again and once more winced with the pain. "You may…may have to go on without me. Have you considered that?"

"No."

"Then you're a damned fool. Time's wasting."

"There's time. We have the book and the chemist, and we have a coach. There's time."

Matthew heard the bell ring at the front door. A visitor? Clark making another call, perhaps?

Julian suddenly tried to sit up, but he made a noise of pain and settled back against his pillow. "Can't even sit up in bed!" he said. "Pitiful!"

"I wouldn't be moving those ribs around like that, if I were you."

"Pah!" was the answer. Then Julian was silent again, staring up at the ceiling, until finally he asked, "Am I going to die, Matthew?"

"I'll tell you what I think," Matthew replied. "I think you're too bad to die in bed laced up tighter than a tick's asshole. I think you have a long life ahead of you and when you die—many years from now—it will be because you've raced the moon one too many times, or glared too often into the sun, or walked too close to some or another cliff of destruction. But for you to die in *bed*? No, that's not your fate, Julian. You won't go quietly into the night. It's not your style. You have too many more razor edges to climb upon. So yes…in the long run, as you told Greta Autrey… everyone dies, and it's the truth. But for the here and now…no, you will not die."

"A nice speech," said Julian. "You just…you just don't want to have to handle that team by yourself."

"That's also true," Matthew said.

There came a knock at the door. Varney looked in. "Matthew, there's someone here to speak with you."

"To speak with *me*? Who?"

"Sheriff Lancer. From Whistler Green. He's waiting in the parlor."

Matthew stood up. His heart was beating harder. A sheriff, here to probably ask questions? Who had told him? Doctor Clark, of course. Two constables escorting a triple murderer to trial in Bristol. *Oh shit!* Matthew thought.

"Matthew?" Julian said as he started to follow Varney. "Thank you."

"Just make up your mind that a bed in a coach inn is not a suitable place for a man of your talents to die," Matthew told him. "Now be still and rest." He left the room, quietly closed the door and went out with Varney to the parlor, where a broad-shouldered man in a dove's-gray cloak and a black tricorn with a crimson band was standing before the hearth smoking a pipe that had a black bowl the size of Samson Lash's fist.

"Matthew Corbett, Sheriff Gideon Lancer," said Varney.

The sheriff shook Matthew's offered hand with a grip that Matthew thought he would feel until the new year. "Smells good, whatever Ann's cooking," Lancer told Varney.

"You're welcome to stay with us and have a plate."

"That wouldn't suit Becca. She's already hung the pot over the fire and she's furious I came out here to see this young...constable," he answered, deliberately laying in the pause. He smiled, showing teeth that looked to Matthew like the jaws of a bear trap. "So I'll pass this time, but some other?"

"Of course."

"Fine. Now...might I have a moment with this Mr. Corbett?"

Varney retreated, leaving Matthew in the clutches of a man whom the New York problem-solver instantly thought could see through the entire charade before a word was spoken. Gideon Lancer removed his tricorn and cloak and hung them up beside the door. He wore a gray jacket with black patches at the elbows, black breeches, white stockings and a plain white blouse. There was nothing about him that might be called ostentatious, except that the pipe's bowl was awfully big. Matthew judged him to be in his mid-forties. He was of medium height with a stocky build, had a scalp covered with gray sand and owned a pair of deep-set brown eyes that Matthew thought could go from warm to accusing at the hint of a lie. His nose was the rugged, crooked sort seen on street brawlers, and a small scar curved upward across his rock of a chin.

All in all, the man scared Matthew to the marrow of his bones.

"Sit," said Lancer, motioning toward one of the two brown leather chairs on either side of a small table before the hearth. Matthew did, and Lancer took the other chair. The sheriff spent a moment firing up his plain pewter tinderbox to relight his pipe, and then he blew out a curlicue of blue smoke and said, "What's the story?"

"Pardon?"

"Story," Lancer repeated. "Doctor Clark came to my office yesterday afternoon. Said there were two constables from Bristol out here, both of

them damaged and one most severely. Said one of them had broken ribs and the other had a bullet crease across his right cheek. I see that's you. Doctor Clark said these two constables were escorting to Bristol from London a man who had committed three murders. So…what's the story?"

"Well…sir…that *is* the story."

"That is *a* story," Lancer corrected. He put the pipe's bit in his mouth and chewed on it. His brown eyes had taken on a chill. "The coach you constables came in on…that's quite a vehicle. I'm sure there's a story behind that, too."

"We had to steal the coach. We had to spirit our man away from the house his…" Think, think! Matthew told himself. "His gang was holed up in. We didn't have much choice."

"Where was this house?"

"In London. Of course."

"The area. Where?"

"Um…Endsleigh Park Road."

"Hm." Puff, puff. The smoke, smelling of spicy Virginia tobacco, wafted past Matthew's face. "I know that area. I lived in London for many years. My two sons live there now. That area is a fine neighborhood. Not a place where one usually finds gangs of killers."

"Nevertheless," said Matthew, "that's where it was."

"And you and your other…*constable*…were charged by the court in Bristol to attack this house on Endsleigh Park Road and arrest this murderer? What about the rest of his…" He puffed smoke again. "*Gang*," he said.

"They came to bad ends," was Matthew's reply.

"Pardon my saying, but you don't look the type to be attacking a murderous gang."

"Well," said Matthew with a tight smile, "I suppose that makes me all the more valuable." Before Sheriff Lancer could respond, Matthew plowed on: "As a matter of fact, sir, I am more than a constable. And as a matter of fact, I am an associate of the Herrald Agency. Have you ever heard of that organization?"

Lancer smoked his pipe in silence. He watched the smoke slide into the fireplace and slip up the chimney.

"Certainly," said the sheriff, his expression blank. He took two more pulls on his pipe before he spoke again. "When I lived in London, I was an associate of the Herrald Agency for…oh…was it five years? No. *Six* years. And four months. Yes, almost exactly four."

Matthew sat still, but his mouth had dropped open.

"I suppose, as an associate of the Herrald Agency," said Lancer, "you know the first name of its founder."

Matthew found his missing tongue. "Richard. Unfortunately passed away."

"And you must know his charming widow, Caroline."

"His charming and gracious widow, *Katherine*," said Matthew.

"Oh yes." Lancer nodded. "So she is."

Matthew didn't know what else to say, so he just sat there like a frog on a log and waited.

"Those were the days," said the sheriff of Whistler Green. "*Dangerous* days, to be sure. I was not married then. I wouldn't have put a wife through that. When I married, I settled down. I started out as a lawyer in London, actually. But I wanted *action*, and lawyering…well, not so much action. Intrigue, yes, but not what I desired. An interesting thing though, Matthew—if I may call you Matthew?—is that as sheriff of a small town, I find both intrigue *and* action. Oh you wouldn't believe what goes on in a small town."

"I think I would," said Matthew. "I live in New York. That's in the colonies."

"Yes," Lancer replied, and his gaze for the moment was colder than the December night. "I do know where New York is, son."

"I meant no offense."

"None taken." He shrugged and went back to smoking. "Very interesting work, being a sheriff. A cry in the night from an empty house…a runaway horse with a dead man roped to it…a scarecrow in a field that

turns out to be a bit more gruesome than straw…a man dressed as a jester who has lost his memory but cannot cease laughing…a woman who continually dreams a warlock has commanded her to kill the sheriff of Whistler Green, or her own family will die…very interesting work. Now, as for *your* work…and your being here with the other man who has suffered the broken ribs, and you with the bullet wound and all bruised up, and the biggest and most ornate coach I have ever seen, and one door torn off it, and a loaded pistol lying in the baggage compartment, and dried blood and what I believe to be brain matter stuck up on the back of the coach, and this story about a Bristol murderer that I think is complete… how shall I put it politely?…bull figs, and I thought that immediately upon hearing it from Doctor Clark…well…you understand my position."

Matthew swallowed hard. Merda's second pistol, forgotten in the baggage compartment? And Merda's brain matter, splattered there by Matthew's shot?

"Anything to say?" the sheriff asked, behind a cloud of smoke.

Matthew was at a loss, but something came out. "Hudson Greathouse is my friend."

Smoke spun slowly around Lancer's head.

"If I—we—don't get to where we're going, Hudson will be in danger. He is in danger *now.* I can't…and I won't…tell you anything more."

The words were spoken quietly: "Hudson's in Bristol?"

"No, not Bristol. That's not our destination."

A long pause followed. Then: "Do you need help?"

Matthew thought about it. He said, "I would like a letter of passage, signed by you stating that my friend and I are constables en route with a murderer to Bristol. We will likely have to stop at least twice more at inns. It would help if we didn't draw the attention of any more sheriffs."

"A letter like that would need more than my signature. It would need an official wax stamp." He lowered the pipe. "Otherwise, easily forged."

Matthew waited for more, but it seemed that Lancer was also waiting. Matthew asked, "Will you help me in that way?"

The sheriff folded his hands together and regarded the knuckles, which Matthew noted were as scarred as Hudson's. It was a time before he spoke. "I do recall my days with the agency. I was fortunate to get out alive from some of those escapades. Many I wouldn't dream of telling Becca about." He gave a wry smile. "*Most* I wouldn't tell her about. But…I do also remember that sometimes I was called upon to do things that…well…the law might frown on, and might serve to put me behind bars. Hudson the same. It was all for the good in the long run, and I suppose that's what you're looking at now."

"Correct, sir," said Matthew.

"Yes," Lancer replied, but whether he was simply affirming Matthew's comment or saying he would supply the document, Matthew could not ascertain. Suddenly Lancer stood up. "Edmond!" he called. "I'm shoving off!"

Varney and Ann came out from the kitchen. There was a bit of small talk about the season and Becca Lancer's own holiday feast preparations, some conversation about a missing blacksmith and a bag of money, and then Lancer took his coat and tricorn from their hooks and put them on. "Pleased to meet you, Mr. Corbett," the sheriff said, and once more there was a handshake that Matthew thought could crack bones with just a fraction more pressure. "Enjoy the company of these fine people. Here's hoping the other constable regains his health very soon, for you both to move on with your…*catch*," he said. "Good day to you all." With that and a last puff of pipe smoke, the sheriff of Whistler Green left the house and walked out through the flurries to where his fine-looking dappled buckskin horse was tethered to a hitching post. Matthew watched from a window as the man mounted up and rode away toward the west.

"A productive meeting?" Varney inquired.

"We'll see," said Matthew.

THIRTY-TWO.

Christmas Day dawned with sun across the snow. The clouds had cleared, the morning was bright and the sky a dazzling blue. Edmond and Ann Varney sat before the fire, with Matthew seated nearby, and over cups of hot tea spiced with cinnamon the innkeeper read the story of Christ's birth from the Bible, which Matthew figured was a tradition in the house.

Matthew took a bowl of oatmeal in to Firebaugh, who had also enjoyed a plate of the pheasant, yams and fried corncakes from the evening before, and found the doctor still engrossed in the book of potions. The better for all that, Matthew thought as he left Firebaugh to his reading. Then Matthew went in to see Julian and noted that there was no change in the sleeping man's condition, at least not any he could detect. A touch to his forehead showed the fever was still there. Julian stirred and moaned but didn't awaken. He had not eaten yesterday but had gotten down a half-cup of tea, and one good thing—Matthew supposed, though Doctor Clark might disagree—was that Julian was no longer expelling blood.

Matthew left him, put on a woolen cap and one of Varney's coats with a warm fleece lining and took a walk across the snowy field outside. He wandered over to where he'd thrown the bloody polar bear coat and found

it vanished beneath the new snow of the previous days. It was a wonder, he thought, that Sheriff Lancer hadn't discovered it. Or...perhaps he had.

With his hands in his pockets, Matthew walked on.

His sleep lately had not only been haunted by Lash and Black, but by the others as well: Merda, Lioness Sauvage, Krakowski, Montague, and even Victor and Bogen. Making their presences known in his nightmares were also Brux and Pellegar, who kept knocking and knocking at the door of their closet, and though they never physically appeared in all their gruesome glory Matthew was struck with terror that they would come lurching from the closet and want their wigs back.

He had dreamed of sitting in the coach with Elizabeth Mulloy, and her relating her life's story. And while she was speaking Matthew had sensed another presence in the coach, and looking to his right had seen RakeHell Lizzie sitting there wearing her bladed claws, her face waxy and blank and her dark eyes shining. Suddenly then, as Elizabeth spoke, RakeHell Lizzie began to claw at herself, to cut away her flesh in red ribbons that whirled off as if by a demonic wind, and as she whittled herself down to her core there sat at her center a little girl with terrified eyes, who whimpered and drew herself into a tight knot of self-protection that could never again be unravelled.

And he dreamed of Berry.

She was as he had known her before the drug: beautiful, vibrant...a bit headstrong...no, *much* headstrong...but that was her. They were walking together in a park of some kind, and oddly enough it seemed very clearly to be autumn, for the passing breeze blew red and yellow leaves from the trees. She put her hand in his and her shoulder against his own, and then she said—again, very clearly and right up into his ear—*Help me.*

Yes, he'd answered in the dream. *I will, I promise it.*

And there in his dream before them was a small pond of shining silver, calm and unrippled even as the breeze blew past. As they stood together at the pond's edge, the pond itself began to rise up from the earth, to elongate and change shape, until it was standing upright and reflecting both their

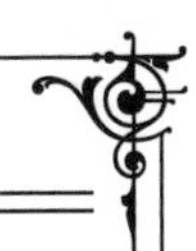

figures. It had become a mirror, and as both Matthew and Berry looked upon it something dark and terribly dangerous—something hideous and vile—began to stir in the glass, began to loom larger and larger, to spread wings and grow the wart of a head, and amid streaks of lightning that shot through the glass and wound about the reflections of Matthew and the woman he loved like the tentacles of Professor Fell's man-eating octopus, Matthew saw that the grotesque figure wore a raven's-wing coat and had the face of Cardinal Black.

He wasn't sleeping much.

He walked through the snow, the sun upon his face and yet the cold bracing and in its own fashion exhilarating. How lucky he was to be alive, after all that. How Fate had smiled upon him—or, at least, had offered him a chance for success that he had to risk taking. Returning to Fell's village with the book and the chemist…looking back, it had seemed impossible. And Julian? Without Julian it would have truly been impossible. Without a bad man guiding the way…impossible.

In the middle of a snowy field where the footprints were his alone, Matthew sent up a prayer for Julian Devane. He did not linger on it, because if someone were listening his heart had already been heard. It seemed to him that maybe a bad man needed a prayer more than the good. So there it was, and after standing for a while with the sun as warm as summer on his face and his shadow still in winter he turned about and retraced his steps.

As the afternoon progressed, a rider dismounted his horse in front of the Flying Dragon and tied his steed to the hitching post. He was a young man, bundled up in a new woolen coat and an equally new woolen cap, both Christmas gifts from his mother and father in Whistler Green. He took from a saddle bag a leather cylinder, approached the front door and rang the bell.

"Hello, Billy!" said Varney when he opened the door. "Come in and have a cup!"

"No, sir, but thankee," said the young man. "Got to get back. I've been sent from Sheriff Lancer. He said to give this to Mr. Corbett." He opened the cylinder and handed a roll of parchment paper to Varney, who knew that Matthew at the moment was sitting at the bedside of his fellow constable. "Official business, y'know," said Billy.

"I'll see that he gets it. The good day has been a blessing, I hope?"

"Fine, sir. And for you and the missus?"

"Oh, yes. As always. Sure you don't want a cup to warm you on the way back?"

"I'm sure, sir. Just out and home again, I promised the folks."

"All right, then. Do give greetings to the family."

"Yes sir, I will." Billy started off with the cylinder in his hand and then turned back toward Varney before the door could close. "Oh…sir…I meant to say…a message from Sheriff Lancer to Mr. Corbett."

"What might that be?"

"Merry Christmas," said Billy, and then he went to his horse.

In the small hours of the following morning, Matthew was jarred awake by another nightmare, this one of a feeling of impending doom and the visions of indistinct faces moving in and out like dark smears against a darker background. He got up from the cotton sleeping pad on the floor at the foot of Firebaugh's bed, where Firebaugh was sleeping as peacefully as a monk who had never known a conflict in his sheltered life. As Ann Varney had most graciously offered to wash both Matthew's and Julian's clothing—yet had not offered the same for the clothes of the triple murderer Matthew was charged to guard—Matthew put on the banyan robe that had been given to him from the innkeeper's closet and quietly left the room for a breath of cold air to clear his head of phantoms.

He paused outside the room to pick up the lantern that was burning with a low wick on a nearby table and that was when he saw the open door to Julian's room. Peering in and holding the lamp up, he saw that Julian's bed was empty.

A noise alerted him. He walked into the parlor, where Julian stood with a blanket wrapped around himself, using a poker to stir embers in the hearth.

"I woke up cold," Julian said, with a quick glance at Matthew. "Drafty in that damned room. Did I miss Christmas Day?"

"By a few hours," Matthew answered.

"I always enjoyed Christmas Day." Julian continued to poke at the embers. At the back of the hearth a few small tongues of flame began to lick at a piece of charred wood. "One can enjoy the day without belief in God, you know."

"I imagine so."

Julian ceased his work with the poker, put it aside and held his palms out toward the warmth. "Are we still at the same inn?" he asked. His voice was yet somewhat slurred.

"The same."

"Because of me, I'm supposing." One hand went down to gingerly touch the wrapping that hopefully secured his ribs from moving around too much. "That doctor…had quite the strength. I remember that." He shot a severe glare at Matthew. "Why the hell didn't you go on? I would have."

"According to Fell's calculations," Matthew replied, "we are returning in the proper time. And Firebaugh has consented to give us no more trouble. In fact, I've talked him into looking forward to meeting the professor."

"Huh. You missed your calling. You should've been a politician. Or a *priest*."

"Unlikely," said Matthew.

"I need to sit down," Julian said, and he very slowly settled himself into a chair, his face still gray and pinched with pain.

"You were running a fever."

Julian put a hand up to touch his shaven scalp. "Well, now I've got the chills, so obviously I am no longer feverish. But I'm damned *hungry*. My stomach is an empty hole. Can you get me something?"

"I'll see." Matthew didn't wish to waken the Varneys, who slept in a back room off the kitchen, but he quietly followed the lamp's light into the kitchen and found on a platter two corncakes that had not been consumed at the previous meal. He took the platter to Julian, who finished them off in a matter of seconds and then asked for a drink. Back to the kitchen Matthew went, finding a clay flagon of the apple cider in the pantry. He measured out a mugful and in the parlor Julian poured the cider down his throat as if it were the golden liquid of life.

"Better," Julian said. "Not *perfect*," he amended. "But better. We should get back on the road at first light."

"I don't think you're able yet."

Julian didn't reply for a moment. Then he said, "Maybe not. I couldn't control the team."

"I'm driving the rest of the way. I think we'll probably have two more stops before we get back."

"Right." Julian closed his eyes and was silent. Matthew thought he'd gone to sleep sitting up, but at last Julian said with his eyes still closed, "I have killed many men. Many. I have lost count. Isn't that terrible?"

"Honestly? Yes."

"Some deserved to die. Others did not." His eyes opened. "Should I feel guilty?"

Matthew suspected that all of Julian's guilt was concentrated upon the boy he had crushed beneath a runaway horse on a London street. He couldn't find an answer.

"I don't," said the bad man. "In my profession—my calling—guilt leads to introspection, and introspection leads to hesitation, and hesitation leads to death. I don't fear it, but I don't wish it just yet. Does that make sense to you?"

"You didn't finish Lash off," Matthew said. "You had the chance. Why not?"

"Lash was already finished. I didn't choose to waste the shot. Oh… you're thinking I should've been merciful, and not allowed him to lie in

that snow and linger for an hour? That's all the time he had left. I didn't choose to waste the shot," he repeated. He watched the small fire burn. Then he drew a short but painful breath and slowly released it. "The truth…is that…in some way…I think I admired him. I think…for all he was…Lash *believed* in something. A vision…a plan…a *hope.* I have never had any of those. One day to me is the same as another. One job…the same. One killing…the same. Oh, of course I am *good* at what I do."

"No doubt," said Matthew.

"*Proficient* at what I do," Julian corrected. "The professional, hard at work building…what? A future? My future consists of the time I have left before someone more proficient finishes me off. A younger gun, so to speak. Though I am *not* old. I am not. Not yet. But…I wish I had *something* to believe in, Matthew. I wish I had what Lash possessed…and what I took from him, because I recognized my own lack of hope…and I burned his away. Was he a bad man, Matthew?"

"I wouldn't exactly call his methods pristine."

"But his motivations…was he bad?" Julian asked, and it seemed he wanted to hear an answer more than anything else in the world. "Really… truly…was he bad?"

Matthew had no certain reply. Samson Lash had wished to conduct the building of his airship with the auction of the book, yet the building of the airship though important to his self-worth was equally important to him to insure the military strength of England against future enemies. Of course such a thing was a mad idea, but who could say what the passage of time might bring? And Lash had given Elizabeth a chance to grow beyond the confines of the Highcliff asylum, and it was out of a strange—one might say warped—love for her that he provided an outlet for RakeHell Lizzie safe from the streets of London.

His figurehead, Matthew mused. Lash had never touched her, nor seemed to want to.

And why not?

Because Lash was still faithful in his own way to the wife who had lost her mind.

Bad or good?

Matthew thought that it was all a mix. As, perhaps, it was in every human being who walked upon the earth.

Except maybe one.

Who went by the title of Cardinal Black. Matthew could see nothing in that one but an avarice for power...demonic power, at that...and Matthew doubted very seriously that Black had any humanitarian motivations for his association with his 'master'. What Black might do if he had gotten hold of that mirror...well, the whole thing was insane, anyway. A mirror created by a sorcerer to summon up a demon from Hell?

Insane.

"Black," Matthew said. "Do you think he's still out there?"

Julian considered it. He said, "If he's not, someone like him will always be."

With Matthew's help, because Julian's strength was at a low ebb, Julian returned to his room and slept until midday, when he came hobbling out of his chamber and announced to Ann Varney that he craved something substantial to eat, and preferred beef if she had it. A bowl of beef stew served the purpose. Matthew went out walking on another sunny afternoon with Firebaugh, who maintained the act of keeping the cord around his wrists to soothe the Varneys' fears that he might attempt an escape.

On the following morning, Doctor Clark arrived to take an inspection of his patient, who at the moment was dressed in a robe and seated in the parlor involved in a game of whist with the Varneys and Matthew. Clark pronounced Julian still in precarious condition, but apparently on the road to recovery. About three hours after the doctor left, a coach pulled up out front and out of it came a well-dressed man and woman, their daughter of about fourteen years of age, and two businessmen all on their way to London from Plymouth. It was determined that this new group of travellers would need to stay the night, and therefore the time had come for goodbyes to be said to the Varneys, and for Matthew and Julian in their newly-clean clothes and that foul murderer Firebaugh in his not-very-clean and obviously ill-sized clothing to be on their way.

Matthew was able to purchase a spare coat and cap from Varney, since the innkeeper could easily buy their replacements in Whistler Green. Added to the purchase were two good woolen blankets to ease the comfort of the passengers in the semi-open-aired landship.

Thus, with bellies full, as much sleep as they had required, and the parchment of passage and the book of potions within the coach, they set out under a blue sky with Matthew at the reins. As he urged the rested team into a brisk canter away from the Flying Dragon he hoped the carnage on the road to the southeast had already been discovered by a coach travelling to the northwest, and that the lovely and charming fourteen-year-old daughter would never have to lay eyes upon such evidence of violence.

FIVE.

REVELATION

THIRTY-THREE.

The spyglass was mounted on a tripod. The glass itself was turned toward the northwest, aimed at the road taken by Matthew and Julian Devane. Behind the glass was the eye of Hudson Greathouse, and before both the glass and the eye the road remained empty across the flat plain of snow-covered Welsh landscape. Though the afternoon sky was blue and streaked only with high clouds, cold wind blew hard over the roofs of Y Beautiful Bedd from the sea beyond.

Hudson stood upon a parapet of Fell's fortress, just above and beside the wagon that still blocked the front entrance between the walls of ancient gray stones. The oaken door that had been destroyed by a gunpowder bomb in the attack nearly two weeks ago was yet in the process of being rebuilt at the carpentry shop. On either side of Hudson two guards with muskets walked the ramparts, and as Hudson peered through the spyglass one of them ambled toward him.

"Anythin'?" the man Hudson had come to recognize as Dan Gravelling asked.

"No," said Hudson. He straightened up from the glass and pulled the collar of his brown corduroy coat up higher. The fit of his black wool cap was disturbed by the width of his ears. "He'll be along, though."

"You mean the both of 'em will be along."

Hudson smiled grimly. This was a little game of words the two had begun playing in the last week. "That's what I meant, Dan."

Gravelling leaned on his musket. "I've been wonderin' for a time, and I've got to ask. A big fella like y'self," he said. "How the hell did they drag you here?"

"It was a woman's knee to the face, and three thugs with pistols to back it up," Hudson answered, referring to the hefty knee of Mother Deare that had sent him into dreamland and brought both himself and Berry Grigsby in a guarded coach to Fell's little village—a little prison for its unfortunate inhabitants—on the windswept and sea-crashed coast of Wales.

"Was she a looker?"

"Oh yes, a real beauty. Caught me sleeping." Hudson knew the man would recognize the name—and froggish face—of the hideous Mother Deare, but he hated to blight anyone's fantasy.

"Figured as such," said Gravelling, who Hudson had found was one of those salt-of-the-earth workmen who were here not because of any evil affiliation but because the accommodations were free and the protection assured. Gravelling was on the run from the law in Newport for physically assaulting a judge. He was an able watchman but honestly he didn't possess more than a thimbleful of brains.

Gravelling took a pinch of snuff from a small pouch brought out of his coat, inhaled it and offered the pouch to Hudson, who shook his head and returned his eye to the glass. "Day in and day out. Seen you up here in the night as well," Gravelling said. "Standin' out here in the cold and the snow fallin' so thick it whitewashed the world. That fella Corbett must owe you a grand sum of money."

"Thousands of pounds," said Hudson, moving the glass to scan the far distant woods.

"*Really*?"

"God's truth."

"Well, no wonder you're up here so often wishin' him back. I mean, *them* back. I ain't had a whole lot of...what would be the word?...assayin'

with Mr. Devane, but he don't seem a bad sort. Keeps to himself, though. But he'll speak back if you speak to him first."

"A real prince, from what I know."

"A *prince*? Nah, he ain't royalty. Just an ordinary bloke."

Hudson gave a noncommittal grunt and continued his surveillance of the empty road.

"You ain't the only one so interested," said Gravelling, and when Hudson looked at him with an inquiring expression Gravelling motioned with a lift of his grizzled chin toward the far realm of Y Beautiful Bedd.

Over the blackened ruins of several structures and those that were being laboriously rebuilt by the village's workforce, Hudson saw him standing on the upper floor of his castle-like lair, his eye to his own tripod-mounted spyglass aimed to the lonely road.

"I hear tell—just a whisper of it, really—that you and him has become pals," said Gravelling.

"Hardly." Hudson leaned against the rampart's wall and wished he'd thought to bring a flagon of something hot and very strong in terms of alcohol.

"I hear you supped with him."

"That was a while back."

"Well, maybe so, but still and all…I ain't never *seen* him up close. I mean, I seen him that night in the square when we put paid to them raiders, but not up close." Gravelling's eyes narrowed. "There he goes inside again. Man as slight as he is, hard to bear this cold. But he'll be out at that glass before an hour's up, and you can mark it. Maybe one of them two owes *him* money?"

Hudson realized Gravelling was asking him what was going on, since the hired help—and the guards here had their own pecking order, which Gravelling was low on the peck—didn't receive the benefit of much information. "Maybe so," Hudson said.

"I seen 'em ride out. That Corbett fella and Mr. Devane. A mismatched pair if there ever was, if you ask me."

"Agreed," said Hudson, "but I'm hoping the strengths of one will help the other survive." More like hoping Julian Devane could keep Matthew from being killed...unless Devane had already killed him, and climbing up to this parapet to sweep the canvas covering off the tripod and glass and keep watch every day for hour upon hour was a useless—

"Coach comin'!" shouted the second guard, McBray, a small slim man who had murdered his mother-in-law.

Hudson instinctively looked to the northwest, but the road to Adderlane remained empty. He turned his face toward the southeast...

...and there it was...still in the distance, over two miles away...

Hudson redirected the glass and put his eye to it.

"Coach comin'!" McBray shouted again, in case the men who manned other sections of the ramparts had failed to hear his booming bawl as it swept across the village.

Hudson made out that it was a strange-looking vehicle...huge...resembling more of a ship than a coach...pulled by four giant horses...and who was that up at the reins? Coat and cap, the face a smear, still indistinct...

"He's come to looksee again," Gravelling said, and Hudson knew he must mean Professor Fell.

Hudson kept his eye to the glass. The team was walking; obviously they had already travelled a distance today and the driver was not pushing them. A little closer, and closer still...and then Hudson could make out the driver's face.

He hadn't realized how strained he was, waiting for this moment. He hadn't realized, in his sleepless nights of reaching for a bottle in the little cottage Fell had given him, that he had thought Matthew would never return from this suicidal mission, that the boy was dead either by Devane's hand or some other equally as foul, that Berry was lost, that all was lost. He'd thought it impossible that Matthew should come back, and many times he'd entertained the idea of stealing a horse and taking out on the road to Adderlane, but the idea of leaving Berry in the clutches of Frederick and Pamela Nash prevented it.

Therefore he was unprepared for the rush of emotion that hit him like a moving brick wall.

Hudson Greathouse staggered. No blow from a human fist had ever stunned him as did the sight of Matthew Corbett driving that huge coach in toward Y Beautiful Bedd, nor had any drink of knee-dropping liquor ever burst the brilliance of a sun more brightly in his soul.

"God's truth!" Gravelling marvelled. "Is that *them*?"

"Damn right it is!" With his next shout to the men below, Hudson nearly blew Gravelling off the rampart. "*Move that wagon*! *Now*!" He didn't wait for the command to be obeyed; he went down the first four stone steps and vaulted the rest of the stairs to the ground. Hudson put his shoulder against the wagon and along with three other men shoved the thing out of the way.

The big horses came through, pulling the ship-shaped coach, and in the village's square Matthew reined the team in. "Whoa, whoa!" he called out, and had to fight the reins as the headstrong horses still didn't care much for their new driver even after all those miles.

The wheels stopped turning. With a final creak, the coach was still.

Matthew looked about himself, at the houses of Y Beautiful Bedd and the faces of the people gathering around. Who would ever have believed he would be overjoyed—a weak word to describe his feeling—to have returned to *this* place?

"You took your damned time, didn't you?" Hudson called up, standing with his hands on his hips. "Nearly two *weeks*?"

"Better late," Matthew said, "than never." He heard his voice crack. He was exhausted from this final leg of the trip, but it seemed now that the last thing in the world he wanted to do was sleep. The possible cure for Berry's condition was too close at hand. Also he was overjoyed to see that Hudson had recovered from being the cowering, terrified and drugged shell of a man he'd been when Matthew and Julian had left.

As Matthew climbed down from the driver's bench, Julian and the doctor got out of the coach. Firebaugh gazed around at this new domain,

while Julian clasped a hand to the binding around his ribcage. For a man who didn't believe in God, he was ready to fall to his knees in praise of Heaven for getting him out of that pitching rattletrap, because no matter how sturdy was the coach, the roads were shit.

"*You*," said Julian to Hudson. He smiled thinly, his mouth tight below his dark-circled eyes. "All well, I trust?"

Matthew tensed, knowing how close Julian was to having his block knocked off and then mayhem to follow.

"All well," replied Hudson dryly, who at the moment was too glad to see Matthew to lose his temper at this puffed-up buffoon. Anyway, he was certain Devane had been invaluable to Matthew in their quest, so how could he really be angry? He started to clap Matthew on the shoulder, but the young problem-solver held up a hand and said, "My bones are not properly rearranged yet for that, if you please."

"What happened to your face?"

"What *didn't* happen to my face?"

"I mean the plaster."

"Just a little gunshot wound," said Matthew.

"Yes," Julian said. "He might have another scar to go with that one from the bear cub. Someone get me a strong drink and the stronger the better!" he shouted toward the assembly. The act of shouting made him wince, but he sent out another one anyway. "Damn your eyes! Can't you see I'm needy?"

"Who is *that*?" Hudson pointed a finger at Firebaugh, who had walked out further into the square to take his bearings. "And why are his breeches about to fall down?"

"The chemist, by the name of Lazarus Firebaugh," said Matthew. "As for the breeches…a long story."

"An entertaining one, I'm sure." Hudson took the measure of Matthew's demeanor and condition and his gaze sharpened. "How was it?"

"Rough," was the reply. "How is Berry?"

"Further diminished."

Matthew didn't like the sound of that. He had to see Berry at once. "Doctor? Will you come with—"

"The professor wants to see you," said one of two men—Stalker by name—who had pushed their way forward through the twenty or so people who had gathered, most of them admiring the coach and the horses, some of them wearing blank and stupefied expressions to indicate that their own drugged conditions had not abated. "You, Julian and *him* from the coach. *Now*," Stalker added. He and the other wore pistols and knives on belts their coats had been drawn aside to reveal.

"I'm going to see Berry first," said Matthew. "Doctor, please—"

"The professor said *now* and he means now." Stalker glanced quickly at Hudson. "Not you. You're to stay—"

Without a word, Hudson hit him an uppercut to the jaw.

Stalker's whole body flew up into the air and the black cap spun off his head like a frightened crow. When he came down with a solid *thump* his body shivered but he was out like a dewicked lamp. The other man—whom Hudson knew by name as Guinnessey—drew his pistol and levelled it at Hudson.

"For God's sake, Hugh!" Hudson said with a scowl. "You're not going to shoot me! I owe you too much money at dice!"

Guinnessey's pistol dropped down. "Well, what am I supposed to do? Stand here like a droolin' fool with the professor watchin' all this from his balcony?"

"Let him watch." Hudson rubbed his scuffed knuckles. "Stalker's been asking for that, and you know it."

"A grand show, worth a half-pence at least!" Julian tipped to his mouth a clay jug someone had brought him from the village's tavern, the Question Mark. He coughed several times at the strength of the ale, which did his ribs no favor.

"I'm going to see Berry," said Matthew. "All of you can do as you please."

Before Matthew could start off for the Nashes' house on Conger Street, Hudson caught at his arm. "Matthew…listen…it may not do to see her right now. I mean to say...you should probably get some rest before you see her. Another day isn't going to make much of a difference."

"But it could make *some* difference," said Matthew, as he pulled his arm away.

"I ask you…as a friend…to delay that visit. You coming right off the road like this…I know you want to see her as soon as possible…but she won't recognize you, Matthew. It's useless to try to sit in front of her and make her remember anything. It'll just…well…it'll just tear you up all the more. Give it the rest of the day, get a meal and some sleep. What I suppose I'm telling you is to fortify yourself. And I'm telling you that as someone who cares about both of you. All right?"

No, Matthew wanted to adamantly say, but he thought there was some wisdom in what Hudson had said. *Fortify yourself.* He feared for Berry, and feared for himself as well…that when he faced her and saw her diminished condition he would crack to pieces.

Fortify yourself.

A meal and some sleep, and then to visit Berry—possibly in the company of Firebaugh—first thing in the morning. That, as much as he disliked it, sounded like a good plan.

"Yes," Matthew said. "All right." Even as he said this, he thought that to visit the professor's house at the end of Conger Street he would face the difficult challenge of walking past Mayor Nash's house also on Conger Street.

"Wise choice," said Julian.

"Button it up!" Hudson snapped. "If I didn't think you probably had saved Matthew's life a half-dozen times you'd be down on the deck with that little bastard."

"This one is a loose cannon," Julian smirked at Matthew. "His balls may be too big for his brain."

On the ground, Stalker groaned and began to stir.

"This is all well and good," said Guinnessey, "but the professor is waiting. Hudson, you're not invited."

"The hell you say. How are you going to stop me?"

"Oh, *shit*!" Guinnessey motioned them all onward with his pistol. "Come on, then!"

THIRTY-FOUR.

"Sit there," said Professor Fell.

The black leather armchair he had indicated was positioned at the center of Fell's upstairs study, before the writing desk that bore ornamental diamond shapes carved into the front. The professor, resplendent in a crimson skullcap and a crimson robe decorated with gold figures, sat behind the desk. The deep-set eyes in the mulatto face were the same smoky amber color as the liquid in the jars of marine specimens on the shelves behind him. They were fixed upon Lazarus Firebaugh, whom he had just addressed.

Matthew, Hudson, Julian and Guinnessey also stood in the room. There was one other armchair available, but no one else had been invited to sit. As Firebaugh—obviously nervous and nearly trembling in this first encounter with the professor—took the chair Fell had motioned toward, Matthew saw that the study was about the same as when he'd last been here on the occasion of Mother Deare's death by Julian's hand: shelves of the specimens and books, a black wrought-iron chandelier in the shape of an octopus hanging from the ceiling's thick rafters and holding a taper in each of its eight tentacles, the etchings of fantastic sea creatures of fable and nightmare upon the gleaming oak walls, and a door to the right leading out to the balcony that surrounded the topmost floor. Through a broad window could be seen the cloud-streaked sky and the movement of white-capped waves. The only difference in the study that Matthew could tell was that the beautiful Oriental rug with its cast of colors in sea greens and blues had been replaced by a simple dark blue rug. Matthew reasoned that Mother Deare's blood and brains upon the Oriental had finished it off, and he recalled that her brains had also splattered across the specimen shelves. He would very much have disliked that job of tidying up the professor's domain, which now smelled not of Julian's gunpowder or Mother Deare's death but a bittersweet incense that was burning in a little black cup on a table near the stairs.

Firebaugh sat down.

Fell's gaze shifted to Guinnessey. "Go tell Stalker that I forbid any retribution against Mr. Greathouse. He is a guest here and—though he does not obey my orders very well—he is to be treated with respect."

"Yes, sir," said Guinnessey, who went down the stairs and out.

"I didn't hit Stalker that hard," Hudson said. "He must have a glass jaw."

Fell ignored him and directed his attention over Firebaugh's head toward the two returned travellers. Julian had removed his cap to display the stubble of his blonde hair, and with his dark-shadowed eyes in his pallid face he hardly looked to be the same man who'd ridden out. Matthew as well appeared altered, and not just by the bullet crease beneath the plaster or the dappling of his fading bruises, but a difference in the eyes—a look that Hudson had thought was both wounded and yet harder than he remembered.

"You two," said the professor, "have experienced some difficulties. I will have you both go to the hospital for a visit with Dr. Belyard."

"Excuse me, sir." Firebaugh's voice trembled. "But...I assumed I was to be the doctor here?"

"Incorrect. You are to be the *chemist* here. *If* I choose so. Nicholas Belyard is the village's physician. You and he will share the hospital, but it is beyond his duties—and capabilities—to explore the laboratory and use the chemicals in the fashion that will fall to you. *If* I allow it."

"Ah. I see." Firebaugh shifted uneasily in his chair. "Um…I seem to recall the name of Nicholas Belyard. He—"

"Two years ago shot and killed another physician in an argument over a young woman," Fell said. "Such are the uncontrollable emotions of youths scarcely out of medical school. He escaped the clutches of the law and a year later wound up in my employ. So you as the village's chemist will not be in direct contact with patients needing such things as stitches and boils lanced. Belyard makes trips beyond the village to bring back medical supplies, ointments and instruments as needed. Those will not be your concern."

"Ah," Firebaugh repeated. "Then…basically…I will be in a position of research? A position that one might say is…solitary?"

"One might say," Fell replied. He looked at Matthew. "The book?"

It came out of Julian's cloak. Julian put the red bound volume in front of the professor, who ran a hand across it before he opened it and for a minute or two turned through the pages in silence. "I know," he said, "that you would not be here if Matthew had not decided you met the qualifications. I will hear the whole story from our travellers at a later date, but right now I want to hear from yourself why you believe you're up to this responsibility."

Responsibility, Matthew thought. He almost laughed and he knew Hudson almost did as well. Even Julian might have suppressed a guffaw that would've earned him much more than broken ribs. Fell was making the job of keeping most of Y Beautiful Bedd's inhabitants dazed with drugs sound like a task Queen Anne might have commanded. Matthew wondered what might happen if, indeed, the drugs wore off. If the people here—kept prisoner by Fell for one reason or another—began to come to their senses, as Matthew had seen a few start to resurface from their drugged depths, would the remaining contingent of guards be strong enough to hold back a revolt? Or would the whole place collapse without the power of the potions? If anything, the place would be changed, and no longer would the majority of inhabitants—prisoners—be so docile and easily contained.

He was thinking of his promise to the Italian opera star Madam Alicia Candoleri that he would get her, her manager Giancarlo Di Petri and her makeup artist Rosabella out of the village and to safety. How could that possibly be done?

As Firebaugh blabbed about his medical education, his invaluable experiences at the Royal College of Physicians under the watchful tutelage of the esteemed doctors Crippen and Jekyll, his short practice as a general physician and then his interest in chemical research that had led him to heading up the asylum at Highcliff, Matthew thought about his end of the bargain with Professor Fell.

Going to Italy and finding Brazio Valeriani, whose father Ciro had from supernatural sources fashioned a mirror that would supposedly call up a demon and put its caller in an imprecise and possibly dangerous command.

Ridiculous.

Fell was losing his mind to put such stock in a story like that.

Cardinal Black—if he still lived—was equally insane. Likely born that way.

But the fact was that Fell had already gone to great effort to try to find the mirror. He had kidnapped the opera star not for herself, but because her makeup artist Rosabella was cousin to Brazio and had some knowledge of the family.

Matthew recalled a conversation with Rosabella before he'd left for Adderlane, when she was telling him she had attended her uncle Ciro's funeral in Salerno and had spoken to Brazio there.

He asked how old I was, she had said, *and I told him thirteen. He said...I think I'm remembering this right...that thirteen was a good age, especially for Amarone.*

Amarone? What does that mean? Matthew had asked.

The answer: *It's a red wine, very strong.*

Brazio had a particular interest in wine?

She had shrugged. *I just remember he said that.*

Matthew had not been able to let this go. It seemed he was on the edge of something vital. He had asked, *Was Brazio living with his father when Ciro hanged himself?*

No, I believe he had to travel from somewhere.

Why do you say that?

He came two days late, Rosabella had replied. *The funeral was delayed until he got there.*

Did you tell that to the professor?

Yes. He asked if Brazio had been living in Salerno or had travelled there. I told him just the same as I'm saying now. Also that my mother and father had not heard from Brazio for years and they didn't know where he was living.

Let me guess what happened next, Matthew had said. *Professor Fell asked you to write down a list of the people present at Ciro's funeral?*

Correct. There were five others besides myself and my parents.

But he doesn't know Brazio mentioned the Amarone? Matthew had waited for her to answer with a shake of the head. *Why do you think your cousin might have mentioned, of all things, a variety of wine?*

I have no idea, she'd said with a shrug. *Unless...he works in a vineyard somewhere.*

Matthew had nodded. *Yes. A vineyard somewhere.*

Of course it could be that Brazio simply liked Amarone and was planning to get drunk on it after the funeral, but...thirteen years a good age for Amarone? Spoken like someone who understood and valued the aging process.

A vineyard worker? Or a vineyard *owner*?

"Those are my qualifications," said Firebaugh. "I hope they suit the purpose."

Professor Fell again slid his hand back and forth across the book, as if caressing it as Matthew had seen Julian caress the four-barrelled bastard. It was a time before he spoke. "I am going to have this taken to the hospital and locked up. You'll be given a key. You will note that there are

two differing handwritings in this: those of Jonathan Gentry and Gustav Ribbenhoff. The former created the great majority of the potions and the latter added to them. The drug that has afflicted Miss Grigsby was concocted in this fashion, therefore you can follow Ribbenhoff's scribing to decipher the formula, with the knowledge that Gentry's handwriting will be by far the predominant." The amber eyes levelled at Firebaugh. "Are you up to this task, sir?"

"I think I am."

"Not what I asked. Are you, or are you *not*?"

Firebaugh lifted the red-bearded chin. "I *am*, sir."

"Go to the tavern and get something to eat and drink. Then you also go see Belyard, make your introduction and have your injuries examined. That ear in particular looks in need of attention. I'll find a house for you and some clothes…if you don't mind wearing the clothing of someone recently dead?"

"Ribbenhoff, I presume?"

"I believe they would fit you," said Fell. "He had a very sophisticated wardrobe, as a matter of fact. The Prussians are like that."

Pah! Matthew thought.

Firebaugh stood up. "I will wear Dr. Ribbenhoff's clothing for the present, but I would like my own suits tailored for myself. Is that possible?"

"Possible," Fell answered. "Prove your worth on Miss Grigsby's behalf, and we shall proceed from that point. Now go back to the square and get a meal. I'll summon you when your house is ready. Hudson, you may escort him to—"

"He can find his own way," Hudson said.

"There it is again." Fell smiled coldly. The feral killer's gleam in his eyes had returned. "Guest or not…my patience with you is not unlimited."

"I'm going now. Thank you, sir," said Firebaugh, who suddenly was in a hurry to get out of the study, down the stairs and out of the house.

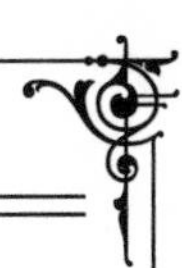

When the doctor was gone, Fell laced his blue-veined hands together atop the desk and drew a long, deep breath. "Who was behind the mortar vessel? Someone other than Black, I know."

"Vice Admiral Samson Lash of the Royal Navy," Julian replied. "Working in partnership with Black."

"And they are both dead?"

"I have no doubt Lash is dead. As for Black…" Julian shrugged.

"You mean you left him *alive*?"

"Julian shot him," Matthew said, and whether this was true or not it didn't matter because he didn't want Julian gutted by a sword or blown apart by a cannon. "At the moment we were both…um…a bit busy securing the doctor and the book to follow Black into the woods past the burning barn and—" He stopped, because Fell's eyebrows had gone up and an expression of amusement had settled upon his face. "It was freezing cold out there," Matthew continued. "Black was shot and probably froze to death." As soon as he said it, he thought that a burning barn could keep even a badly-wounded man from freezing for quite some time. Before Fell could speak, Matthew said, "I know all about Ciro Valeriani's mirror. Are you really *serious*? That you believe in such a thing?"

"Huh?" Hudson's ears had perked up. "What's *this* about?"

"Oh, this should be interesting!" said Julian, with a pained grin. "Professor, my bottom half forbids it but my top half demands that I sit down." Without waiting for permission he sank into the second leather chair, which was the nearer.

Matthew walked to the bookshelves and began searching. Where was it? Either his vision was impaired, or—

"I believe you're looking for this." Fell opened the middle drawer of his desk and brought out the copy of *The Lesser Key of Solomon*. "Take it, Hudson. Page through it, while Matthew explains the reason you are still among the living."

Hudson took the book and opened it. "What the *hell…*?" he said almost at once.

"The professor—who I think at one time in his life was sane—is searching for a mirror that he believes can raise a demon from the underworld," Matthew said, coming back to the center of the room. "Cardinal Black was after that book as well, since the professor seems to have bought up every existing copy. It's a catalogue of...well, you can see for yourself. The professor—correct me if I'm wrong—has yet to decide on which denizen of the depths he will—"

And then Matthew stopped, because he had a revelation.

The jars of marine specimens. The etchings of the frightful monsters of the sea on the walls. The huge and deadly octopus that had eaten the head of Jonathan Gentry. The professor's interest in biologics and especially marine life.

All those creatures, brought up from the depths. And in that book of demons, the descriptions of creatures even more bizarre, and dwelling at deeper depths. Matthew remembered Fell saying he had an interest in 'the creature from another world'.

"My God," said Matthew. "You're a *fisherman*. And now...you want to catch the most bizarre and deadliest creature you can bring up. Is that what it is? Just to *see* what you can land, using that mirror as a *hook*?"

Fell smiled ever so slightly. "I've never thought of it in that way. But it *does* make sense."

"It is *insane*!" Matthew had nearly shouted it. "The mirror does not exist! Even if there is a mirror that Valeriani created...it's just a mirror, and that's all! It's no damned passageway from Hell!"

The professor's expression returned to solemnity. "And you are absolutely and positively *certain* of that? So certain that you would defy the belief of centuries that there does exist the realm of Hades? You would defy the Holy Bible itself? You would attest that the descriptions of the seventy-two demons in that book amount to simple folly? Or someone's madness?"

"Someone's bad oyster, most likely," said Hudson as he continued to turn through the book.

"I'm not going to argue theology with you," Matthew replied. "I'm saying the idea of a magic mirror that can call up a demon to do the bidding of a human being is insane."

"Your opinion. My opinion is that where there is smoke there is usually fire, and where there are nets thrown down there are usually fish. Or, in this case…these bizarre—and in some ways quite beautiful—creatures of the depths. Now what has saved your life, Hudson, is the fact that in exchange for letting Matthew go with Julian to retrieve the book of potions he has agreed—*agreed,* I said—to go to Italy and find a man named Brazio Valeriani, whose father Ciro created the mirror. If at all possible, the mirror can be found as well if it still exists. And after thinking this through I have decided that not only is Matthew going to Italy to find Valeriani, but I am going with him."

"*What*?" Matthew asked. "I thought you'd be sending some of your men with me!"

"Those as well. But I wish to be present when the objects of our search are found."

"Damn, what a mug on *this* one!" Hudson said as he appraised one of the more vicious gentlemen of Hell. He closed the book and returned it to Fell's desktop. "I tend to agree with Matthew about this, but the sun of Italy will be a welcome pleasure."

"Ha!" said the professor. "You're going back to New York with Miss Grigsby. I mean to say…when she is able."

"Wrong." Hudson put his hands on the edge of Fell's desk and pushed his face toward the professor. His eyes darkened. In an instant he became a fearsome ogre. "I was on fucking pins-and-needles waiting for Matthew to come back. Thinking every day and every night he'd been killed. Couldn't sleep, had to drink myself into a stupor. And thinking about Berry over there in that house being turned into the Nashes' pretend daughter, and unable to do a thing about it. Maybe everyone has a different opinion of what Hell is, sir, but I can tell you that for me, Hell is having to sit on my hands while people I care about are out there at risk. So…you'd better load up the muskets,

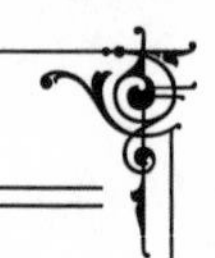

sharpen the swords, call in the sharks or whatever else you do to kill people around here, because you'll have to kill me to keep me from going with Matthew on this…*venture*," he said, finishing with a slur of sarcasm.

The professor stared into Hudson's eyes. For a few seconds Matthew thought they would come to blows right then and there. At last Fell broke the impasse and looked over at Julian.

"Not me!" Julian said, lifting his hands. "I'm not going to any damned Italy, no matter what you say!"

Professor Fell seemed to wilt in his chair. In a matter of seconds he was transformed from the master of his world to a frail old man in a crimson cap and robe that screamed too loudly of wealth and importance. He looked to Matthew as if he needed to take out his teeth and call for a hot toddy.

"I'm going," said Hudson, taking advantage of the obviously weakened moment. "That's the end of it."

Fell stared at his hands. When he spoke, his voice was quiet and in all honesty very weary. "All of you, get out. Go to the tavern and the hospital. Or do as you wish. Matthew, do you want to go see her?"

"I advised against it until he'd gotten some rest," said Hudson.

"Yes. I see. All right, Matthew. Tomorrow morning. I'll have Firebaugh meet you there, say around nine o'clock. You're still in the house on Lionfish Street. Whatever you need, ask at the tavern." Fell waved a hand for them to go. Julian stood from the chair with an arm up from Matthew. Before they reached the stairs, Fell said, "I will have you know that I believed in both of you, Matthew and Julian. I think you have done the impossible…but I believed in both of you. Good work."

They descended the stairs and left the house.

On the walk along Conger Street to the square, Matthew wondered why it was that he could feel a twinge of pity for an old man who had committed so many murders and evils, but who was in essence trapped in the creature of his own construction and had to play the part out to its bitter end.

THIRTY-FIVE.

It was as cruel and heartbreaking a sight as Hudson had warned it was going to be.

Frederick Nash, the appointed mayor of Fell's village, sat in a chair in the front room, watching the procedure in stony silence. His wife Pamela would not deign to enter the room, but stayed in her bed in the back. Matthew sat watching Lazarus Firebaugh as he perched on a stool before the shell of Berry Grigsby, she seated upon the flower-printed sofa splashed with morning sunlight that streamed through a window, and conducted his examination.

Matthew felt tears burning at his eyes. He had had a good sleep, had enjoyed a hot bath, had shaved and dressed in clean clothes and a frayed but serviceable gray jacket—likely also from one of the guards killed in Black's raid—and met Firebaugh at the Nashes' door precisely at nine o'clock. Matthew's knock at the door had had to be delivered thrice and with increasing strength, for when Nash had peered out the window and retreated Matthew figured that Pamela in her own depths of madness had begged him not to give up their daughter Mary Lynn to the possibility that she would be—as their real daughter had been—taken away from them.

But the door had been opened, Nash had allowed them in without a word, and Matthew had said in a voice that trembled more than he would've liked, "Bring her out."

The young woman who sat on the sofa amid the printed flowers was a long way from the one who had walked amid the vibrant gardens of New York. Her face was pale white and reddened with garish rouge, all the freckles and natural beauty of her skin powdered over, her copper-colored hair with its healthy hints of red covered with a brown wig of curly ringlets and childish ribbons that this morning was slightly askew and all the more false in its tilted inclination, her eyes dead…dead…deader than dead…sunken down into purple hollows, her body squeezed into a violet-hued gown with an explosion along her throat of once-pink and white ruffles that were themselves tainted with the gray of age, all wrong…all so terribly wrong.

And there was an odor from her. A scent of what Matthew could only describe as *rot*. Not overtly so, but more like an apple that has been cut open and left to shrivel in an unbearable sun.

Her entire body seemed to Matthew to have shrunken, to have withered, as if the Nashes in their will to fit Berry into the clothes and identity of their deceased daughter had actually done a witchcraft on her, reshaping her to suit a moldy mode. He could hardly stand to look at her; he felt the need to either strike at Nash or get out the door and vomit in the yard, but he did none of those things. He simply sat and endured the sight, as Firebaugh took from the pocket of his coat a small black leather pouch he'd procured from the hospital on Lionfish Street not far from Matthew's house.

Firebaugh unbuttoned the pouch and out of it brought a small brown bottle and an eyedropper. He opened the bottle, as the false Mary Lynn Nash grinned at some errant thought slipping through the dazed mind and worked her fingers together, back and forth as if trying to solve some puzzle that had no solution. Firebaugh put the eyedropper in the bottle, drew out clear liquid, and said to the young woman in the effigy of a lost child, "Open your mouth, please."

She just grinned and worked her fingers. The horrible dead eyes of the painted doll stared through him.

"Your mouth, please," Firebaugh repeated. He tapped her chin. She reached up and tapped her own as if this were the grandest game on earth.

"Mary Lynn?" Nash's voice might have issued from a tomb. "Open your mouth for the man."

She blinked, opened her mouth…closed it…opened it again, and silver threads of saliva drooled out.

At that point Matthew had to lower his head.

"Tongue out," said Firebaugh. When this was not obeyed, Firebaugh said, "Tell her, please," to the mayor.

Nash did. Her tongue flicked out and in a few times. Firebaugh was able to put upon her tongue a few drops of the liquid. Then he sat back as the white-powdered face frowned and she said, "Nassssteeee" as someone with half a brain and tied to an iron bar in a madhouse might speak it.

"The cure?" Matthew asked.

"Not yet," Firebaugh said. "A test to see what cure is needed. There are conflicting formulas in the book. I must be sure before we begin."

In the tavern yesterday, as Matthew put down a meal of vegetable stew, fried corn, turnips and biscuits washed into his belly with good strong ale, Hudson had sat across from him at the table and said, "An interesting tattoo on your hand. I think I've missed a lot."

"This tattoo saved my life. I'll tell you about it when it's no longer so pressing in my nightmares." He had paused in his copious consumption. "I met someone who knows you, by the name of Gideon Lancer."

"*Giddy*? You met him? Well, that's a shot to the head! I understood he became the sheriff in some little hamlet."

"Whistler Green."

"Ah! Yep, Giddy was quite the comrade in those days. We joined the agency at about the same time. He was the only man who ever knocked me out with one punch. Also…he stole the only woman I ever *really* loved.

Rebecca Houghton. Now there was a woman! Old Giddy!" Hudson shook his head and smiled at a memory. "I'll have to look him up sometime."

"You're not seriously thinking of going to Italy, are you?"

"No longer thinking. It's decided."

"Don't you have better things to do in New York?"

"*No*," said Hudson.

"This seems to have become a repeating refrain, but I can take care of myself."

"Of course you can!" Hudson reached for his own mug of ale and downed a swig. "No doubt about that! But…dealing with demons…that might be something you'll need help with."

"It's ridiculous!" Matthew scoffed. "Fell must be half-crazy and fully desperate! To go all that way searching for a *mirror*? Insanity!"

Hudson took another drink before he replied. "What if it's real?"

Matthew stopped with a spoonful of corn at his mouth. "I'm sorry, but I thought I heard an utterance of lunacy from somewhere near."

"No. Think on it. What if it's real? Now don't speak and don't roll your eyes like that. You and I both know there's plenty out there that can't be put into little boxes and tied up with neat little bows. You yourself have experienced some uncommon—and unsettling—things, have you not?"

Matthew knew Hudson was referring to an incident in which a wealthy dying man had hired Matthew to hold Death at bay until he could make amends with his estranged daughter. "Some things I can't explain, I grant that," he said.

"I've experienced some things I can't explain, as well. So…before we both go off talking about insanities and impossibilities, we should consider the very real fact that we don't know as much as we think we do about this world and…yes, and the world beyond. No one does, until they die. Demons coming up from Hell through an enchanted mirror? You can believe what you please, or *not* believe, but I swear I wouldn't bet my life that such a thing doesn't—"

"*Matthew*?"

The timorous voice had come from someone standing to Matthew's right side. He looked up into the face of a small, slim man nervous in appearance, dressed in a white blouse, black suit and waistcoat, all that seemed a bit grimy and in need of cleaning. He had gray hair tied back in a queue with a red ribbon, thin gray brows and the sharp blade of a nose.

"Matthew!" He grasped the younger man's shoulder as if seizing hope itself. "Thank the saints! *Alla fine*! You've come to get us out!"

"I've seen this gent around," said Hudson over the rim of his mug. "Who is he?"

"Giancarlo Di Petri, Alicia Candoleri's manager."

"*Who*?"

"Manager to a great star of the opera!" Di Petri drew himself up to his full height, which was still diminutive. "Were you not at the performance that horrid night?"

"If it was an opera performance, I can believe it was horrid," Hudson answered.

Di Petri gave Hudson a glare that would've wilted a stone rose. His attention turned back upon Matthew, his hand still clutched like a white leech to Matthew's shoulder. "Please! Please! Tell me you've come to help us! Madam Candoleri has faded to a ghost and Rosabella is hardly stronger. We've all been tortured here by these classless men! When do we escape?"

"Yes, sorcerer," Hudson said. "When do they escape?"

"Di Petri," Matthew began, "listen…I can't get you out right now. It's not in my power."

"But…before you left…you *said*—"

"I know what I said. At the moment and for the foreseeable future, I can't do anything for you. I'm sorry. Now…maybe at some point I can talk the professor into—"

"No, you cannot," Hudson interrupted. "Don't even speak it, because it will not happen." He looked up into the stricken face. "Sir, Matthew has just returned from a gruelling journey. He would help you if he could, and so would I. The truth is that neither of us can get anyone here out. This

place may have only a wagon as a front gate, but it's locked up tight. That's all I can say."

"Surely…surely there's a way to—"

"No, there's not," Hudson said flatly. "Nice to meet you. Go away." He picked up his mug and finished the ale off in two more swallows.

Matthew saw the pain and disappointment in Di Petri's face. The man looked as if he were about to burst into tears. Matthew cursed himself for ever thinking he could get anyone out of here, and double-cursed himself for saying such a thing.

"All right," Di Petri said quietly. "*Capisco. Si.* I understand."

As the man began to slink away like a wounded dog, Matthew reached out and caught at a cuff. "Wait," he said.

"Oh my God," said Hudson.

"I have a question for you," Matthew told Di Petri. "Do you know your wines?"

"My…*vino*?"

"Yes, *vino.* The Amarone wine. What region of Italy does it come from?"

"Amarone? It comes from the province of Verona. The Veneto region, near Venice. And you are asking, why?"

"Just a question," Matthew said. He kept hold of Di Petri's cuff. "If I can do anything for you, I'll try. But I can't promise, and don't go telling Madam Candoleri or Rosabella about this. Understand?"

Di Petri nodded. With great grace, he pulled his cuff free. His face was blank. "It was pleasing to see you again," he said, giving a short brisk bow. And to Hudson: "Please know that the opera makes gentlemen of barbarians. *Possa tu camminare al sole tutti i tuoi giorni.*" With that, he turned his back and departed the tavern.

"I think I just received an Italian curse," Hudson said, but Matthew figured Di Petri was too much of a gentleman himself to have stooped to curses. "What's this about the wine?"

"A place to start in Italy," Matthew replied. "Venice."

"I don't exactly understand, but I'll tell you that giving false hope to the people here is like cutting them off at the knees. I know you hate like sin to have to go back on your word, but facts are facts. No one is going anywhere anytime soon…except you, me, the professor and whoever else he pulls out of here. To Italy."

Matthew nodded. "First…there's Berry."

Was it Berry any longer? Was there any way the woman he loved could be called back from her own descent into Hell? As Matthew watched Firebaugh inspect Berry's tongue, he had to fight against a crushing feeling of despair. Had all of it been for nothing? All the deaths, all the violence…for nothing?

"Frederick?" Pamela called from the back. Her voice was ragged and hollow. "Frederick, how is our girl?"

Nash did not answer. He simply stared ahead, as Firebaugh looked at several small gray circles that had risen up on Berry's tongue.

"Ah," said Firebaugh, with an air of satisfaction. "Now I know which way to go."

THIRTY-SIX.

"Drink it all down," said Firebaugh, as he had directed for the last nine days.

"It's bitter," she answered with a scowl. "Do I have to, Father?"

In his chair by the window beyond which morning snow flurries swept past, Nash did not reply.

Matthew was seated in a chair across from the scene of Firebaugh waiting for Berry to put down the cup of dark brown liquid he had just poured from a bottle. He said, "Advise her correctly, Mayor. Otherwise the professor will be calling on you again."

Nash stirred, ran a hand across his mouth as if he wished to catch the words before they came out, but then he said, "Yes, daughter, you have to."

"Rats," she said. "That's what it must taste like. Rats, and dead ones too."

"Drink," Firebaugh repeated.

She took the liquid down and squeezed her eyes shut with the aftertaste. It had happened that way for seven days. The first day she had spit all of it up. The second day she had spit it up and Nash had gotten out of his chair, plucked the bottle of antidote from the doctor's hand and smashed it in the fireplace. That afternoon, after Matthew had reported the incident, Professor Fell had called Nash to his house. The third day,

with a newly-concocted bottle at hand, the cup of liquid—or most of it, at least—had gone down the insensate girl's throat by the aid of a funnel, while Nash had retreated to the back to console his sobbing wife.

As Matthew and Firebaugh had walked back to the hospital on that third day, after what seemed at best a partial success, Matthew had asked the doctor if it wasn't best to move Berry out of the Nashes' house and perhaps give her a bed in the hospital, as she was still so susceptible to their wiles, but Firebaugh had answered that from his experiences at the Highcliff asylum—and mark it, this was not far different from tending to a moonstruck lunatic—Berry believed herself to be the daughter and it would be more traumatic for her to be removed. So one had to trust in the power of Professor Fell over the Nashes, and there was no recourse for that.

Matthew had harbored the fear that in their delirium of what was right and what was wrong the Nashes might take up a pistol one night and kill Berry rather than see her taken away by another hand, after which they might dispatch themselves in a similar fashion, but what was there to do but to accompany the doctor at nine o'clock every morning, stop at the mayor's house at three in the afternoon, at six and at eight like clockwork as he had done since the ministrations had begun. He could move into the house, he supposed, and sleep on the floor in the front room, and he had begun to consider that as a real possibility though he considered the idea that Pamela Nash might brain him with a poker past midnight.

During the past few days he had seen Julian walking about, and had spoken briefly to him but it seemed their association was done. Julian had taken on the aura of the bad man on Fell's payroll again, and in their quick encounters Matthew caught from him the feeling that he didn't wish to be bothered any further with Matthew's situation, Berry, the sorcerer's mirror, or anything that was not about his principal interest of Julian Devane.

"If…I mean to say…*when* Berry recovers," Matthew had said to the doctor, "how might it happen? Will it be a gradual thing, or sudden?"

"I wish I could say," Firebaugh had answered. "I'm following the formula as scribed, but this is all new to me."

"I *hate* that," said Berry, as she returned the empty cup to the doctor. "Father? How long must I endure this?"

"Ah." Firebaugh smiled at her. "And how long do you believe you've been drinking it?"

"Day before yesterday," she said. "I suppose it was." Her eyes, yet dark-shadowed in the powdered face, looked past Firebaugh at Matthew. "Don't you ever speak?"

Matthew brightened. It was the first time she'd ever noted he was in the room. "When I have something to say."

"Who are you?"

Nash stood up and went to the window to stare out.

"My name is Matthew Corbett. I'm from New York, in the colonies. And what is *your* name?"

"My name is Mary Lynn Grigsby," she said. And then her eyes seemed to cloud over with confusion and her mouth worked for a moment but no sound emerged. "Mary Lynn *Nash*," she corrected. "My name. I am Mary Lynn *Nash*. Father?" In her voice there was a note of pleading.

"You gentlemen are welcome to leave at any time," said the mayor, with his back to the room.

"*Think*," Matthew said quietly to the stricken young woman on the flower-print sofa. "Are you absolutely certain that's your name?"

"Easy," Firebaugh cautioned. "We don't—"

"My *name*," said Berry. "Is...I told you my name. Why are you asking me such a question, Matthew? It makes my head...*hurt*," she said, ending on a strained near-whimper. She reached up with both hands to press against her temples, and there her fingers found the brown wig of childish curls and ribbons. With a shiver and the widening of her eyes as if she'd received a violent start she lifted the wig from her head, allowing her real hair to fall in waves about her shoulders, and there she sat on the sofa looking at the wig in her lap as if it were the carcass of a dead dog.

"Get out," said Frederick Nash. His heavily jowled face had reddened. "At once. I don't care, you can have Fell horsewhip me if you please, but get out *now*."

"Frederick? *Frederick*?" Pamela called from the back, with increasing intensity.

"We should go." Firebaugh touched Berry's arm. She was too dazed to respond and just kept staring at the wig. "Until tomorrow," he said.

Tomorrow came early.

Near midnight Matthew was awakened by a knocking at his door. When he opened it and lifted the lamp he held he saw that Firebaugh was dressed only in a banyan robe, slippers and a woolen muffler to brave the cold. "Put on a coat and hurry!" the doctor said. "She's coming out of it!"

On their quick striding to the mayor's house, Firebaugh explained that Nash had knocked at his door about ten minutes before and in distress had asked the doctor to come see 'Mary Lynn', as the 'child' was thrashing in her bed and would not be eased.

"Prepare yourself," Firebaugh said as they reached the house, but Matthew needed no further warning; he was both excited and terrified, for what if the condition was fighting the antidote and leading to Berry's death?

Nash let them in at once. By the glow of Matthew's lantern, a low fire in the hearth and two other lamps in the room, they saw Pamela in a nightgown standing with her hands to her mouth, her eyes wide as if trying to stifle a scream.

Matthew followed Firebaugh into the bedroom. There they saw Berry twisting and turning in her bed, the sheet wrapped around her and the blanket thrown to the floor, her body convulsing with such violence that Matthew feared her spine would break. Her knees came up and nearly slammed into her chin. Her arms flailed out, her head came up and fell back again, her eyes staring forth and sweat glistening on her face.

"Help me hold her," Firebaugh said.

It was a hard go. Her strength in this state of disturbance defied the two men trying to keep her from breaking her own bones. "Her mouth!"

Firebaugh said. "Get her mouth open!" He withdrew from a pocket of his robe a short length of polished wood, which with great difficulty he was able to get between her teeth to prevent her from snapping her tongue clean through. Still she fought. The two men hung on. At some point the bed collapsed. A leg came up, a foot slammed against the wall, and at last her convulsions lessened and stopped altogether.

"Dear God," said Nash at the doorway. "What have we done?"

"Go brew some tea," the doctor told him. "Strong. Stronger than strong. Go on."

Nash went. They could hear Pamela sobbing, and him trying to console her to no avail.

"Now we wait," Firebaugh said to Matthew. He offered a cautious smile. "The tea is for *me*."

The wind picked up outside. The flurries blew. Matthew tended to the hearth in the front room and listened to the ticking of a clock while the Nashes stayed out of sight and away.

Just before six, Firebaugh emerged from the bedroom. Hollow-eyed and weary, he said, "Go see her."

At once Matthew was in the bedroom. Firebaugh quietly closed the door behind him.

She was still wrapped up in the sheet, but she was sitting up and curled up, her back pressed against the wall. As Matthew approached, she blinked at him as if he were an apparition drifting toward her from a dream.

"*Matthew*," she whispered.

And then: "*My Matthew*."

Berry reached out both arms for him. Before he got to her he began to cry…to weep in wracking sobs…to feel his chest expand with overwhelming joy yet the terror remained that she had been so close…so very, very close…to being forever lost…and might still be, for was this the end of the travail, or might her condition reassert itself? He had no way of knowing, but as he pressed her against himself as to share hearts and her arms locked around his back he thought that for the moment she was returned to him, and pray God it was more than a moment.

Pray God it was a lifetime.

He kissed her full on the lips and she returned the kiss. She shivered in his arms. He kissed her again and smoothed her hair and said the thing he had been yearning to say for so long but had been so fearful of saying: "I love you."

"*I love you*," she answered, and then she began to cry as well, and did ever two souls with such joy leaping in them weep the copious amount of tears that spilled down their cheeks and further dampened the bedclothes?

Doubtful.

After a time Berry looked up at him through her bleary tear-stained eyes and she asked, "Where *are* we? Where have *you* been? Where is Hudson…he was with me, I remember. Why do I think I hear someone speaking to me, calling me a different name? And…why do I keep thinking of something that tastes like…well…like dead rats?"

Many questions and more to come, Matthew thought. But praise be to Dr. Firebaugh and praise be to the antidote, no matter how foul its taste.

"Later," he said. He held her and kissed her again. If he wasn't bound by the ropes of gentlemanly conduct he would have slipped beneath the sheet and held her body against his own in that way, as well. "You should probably get some more sleep. I'm going to sit over there and just watch you." He nodded toward a chair in the corner. "May I?"

"You may not," she said. "Get under this cover with me."

The antidote, as Berry understood what it was meant to abolish, was delivered for three more days and drunk down without hesitation in the safety and comfort of her own cottage on Redfin Street. Firebaugh informed Matthew that she should still take the antidote for a few more

days—just for the sake of completion—but to all intents and purposes the foul-tasting but vital elixir had done its job and she was most happily returned to normal.

On the third night that Berry had left the mayor's house, two shots were heard on Conger Street.

It was determined that Frederick Nash had prepared two pistols, had shot Pamela through the head at close range and then dispatched himself immediately after. Watching the bodies being brought out of the house as he stood between Hudson and Berry on the windy street, Matthew thought that the Nashes had been crushed beneath the weight of losing a second daughter, the sorrow of which they could not bear.

It was time to broach the dreaded subject. He had steeled himself for it.

"You're going back to New York," he said.

"Of course," Berry replied. "We all are."

Here was the edge of the precipice. "No," said Matthew. "Just you. I, Hudson, the professor and a few others are going to Italy."

"*What*?"

They were sitting at a table having their supper in the Question Mark, the time being around seven-thirty in the evening. Matthew had had the wisdom to order from the barkeep a mug of strong cider for himself and a cup of wine for Berry. Across the room, where other residents of Y Beautiful Bedd dined on the catch of the day, Hudson was involved in a game of dice with Hugh Guinnessey and Di Petri ate alone.

"Italy," Matthew repeated. "It's a promise I made to the professor. It has to be done."

"Then I'm going with you."

"Ohhhhhh no," was the reply, followed by a drink of cider. "No further intrigues for you."

She continued to stare at him, her lovely freckled face impassive. "I mean it," he went on. "You are going back to New York, I am going to Italy to keep my vow, and when it's done I'll come home and ask your grandfather for your hand in marriage." Would that be enough to dampen the fires?

No.

"You are absolutely *insane*," she said, "if you think I'm letting you out of my sight, Matthew Corbett! *Italy*? What's in Italy?"

"A vineyard," he answered.

"Here, have my wine." She pushed the cup toward him across the table.

He took her hand. "It won't be so very long. I'll—"

"Won't be so very *long*? It's months to get to Italy, isn't it? It could be a year before you're back!"

Matthew nodded, but to his relief Berry didn't pull her hand away. "This is something I *must* do," he said, with ample force in his voice and in his expression. "The professor has told me that in the next few days we'll be taking a coach from here to London and arranging the travel plans." He did not say that Fell had admitted he owned a townhouse in the city but they were all to be staying at an inn, as Fell did not wish that address to be known. He did not say either that Fell's first choice of a suitable inn was the Mayfair Arms, but upon Matthew's explanation of objection the choice had turned to the Emerald, which was equally grand. "A ship to take you home and a ship to take us to Italy. Venice, in fact," Matthew said. "Now...you can get mad and pout, or throw something, or whatever you'd like...but I'm getting you out of harm's way and that's that."

"Harm's way? Does that mean you're going *into* the way of harm?"

"I made a vow." Matthew glanced quickly at Di Petri, who was oblivious to everything and everyone else as he ate his grilled whitefish, and thought about how that particular vow had become tainted by circumstance. This one he had to carry through. He struck on a straw of redemption. "Hudson won't let anything happen to me."

"Who's going to keep anything from happening to him, and *then* to you?"

"It's settled," Matthew said.

Again, she just stared at him but still she didn't pull her hand away. "Oh Matthew," she said softly, "I love you so much. I have for such a long time. And I know what you went through to get the book…Dr. Firebaugh told me as much as I think he could…but…I'm frightened for you. I'm *always* frightened for you."

"This last thing, and then I'm home to stay. All right?"

"*No*," she said. "No no *no*!" And then she took a long breath and her eyes shone and she said as she knew she must, "Perhaps." Then: "If it has to be, but I hate the thought. Matthew, you're such a good man. You're too good for your own good."

"Maybe I used to be. Now I'm not so sure. But think on this: we'll likely have a week or so in London to enjoy being together. The professor's not going to put chains on us, as there's no need for any further imprisonment. We'll dine out and take in the sights. I happen to know we'll be staying at a very exclusive inn. So that's something to look forward to and be happy about, isn't it?"

Berry squeezed his hand. In her eyes there were fresh tears, but Matthew saw she had bowed before the inevitable. "I will *only* be happy when you step off a ship onto the New York dock, and I will look forward to that day," she said, with a resigned sigh. Her face softened again, as much as possible upon digesting news that tasted as bad as had the antidote. "Well," she said at last, "if I can't talk you out of this…come back to my house and I'll make tea."

On his return to his own abode an hour or so later, with the thousands of stars shining above in the night and a more gentle but still cold breeze blowing in from the sea, Matthew saw lantern light through the windows of the hospital. The doctor was still at work in his new and solitary home. Matthew felt he'd never fully thanked Firebaugh for what he'd done, so he strode past his cottage and rapped upon the hospital's door.

The doctor opened it. He was wearing his newly-acquired pair of spectacles. “Matthew!” he said. “Please come in!”

“I won’t take much of your time,” Matthew replied as he crossed the threshold. “I just wished to speak with you for a minute or two.”

“I was working. Good to take a rest, I think. Come back.” He motioned Matthew through an area where there were several beds—vacant at the moment, since Belyard had discharged a man who had suffered stomach cramps just this afternoon—and through another door into the laboratory itself. Past a writing table where sat a lantern, an inkwell and penstand and the red bound book itself was another larger table holding an array of glass tubes, many bottles of liquids, little blackened burners, two brass microscopes, glass vials containing various powders and what appeared to be botanical substances in a long rack, and a number of candleholders with tin reflectors and attached optical lenses. An assortment of various-sized and different-hued pottery jars stood on shelves around the room. Further back there was a large bellows attached to a fireplace that also held a variety of jugs and jars on hooks fixed to the bricks. A man-tall chest sported perhaps a dozen slim drawers with ivory pulls. At the back of the laboratory was a door that Matthew assumed connected to the greenhouse. It was quite the display, and Matthew knew there was much here that he probably couldn’t see.

“Isn’t she beautiful?” the doctor asked, as proudly as any father might speak it.

“*She*?”

“Oh yes.” Firebaugh put his thumbs into the lapels of his brown jacket in an attitude of pride. “*She*. As beautiful as any woman I’ve ever laid eyes upon.”

“You must be an inexpensive escort,” Matthew remarked.

“Really, though! It’s wonderful! Look at all this, here at my disposal! And I am free to work through the night…all night…every night I choose to do so…and no one bothers me.” He cast a loving gaze around at his domain. “I am free to explore, to examine, to test, to…well…it’s just wonderful, is what it is. I would offer you some tea? It's brewing in one of the burners."

"No thank you, I just had a cup. As I said, I won't take much of your time but I wanted to say thank you for what you've done."

"Thank *me*? Oh Matthew! I should thank you! This is my dream come true! The dream of any chemical researcher! And the professor says I'm to go with Belyard day after tomorrow to Swansea to the medical supply house there, so I can stock up on some elements that are in decline here. So really…my thanks to you, sir, for making this all—"

The door from the outer area suddenly opened.

Julian came in. He stopped short.

"Matthew," he said quietly. "I didn't know you were here. The front door was unlocked. Pardon me, I'll come back later."

"Hello, Mr. Devane," Firebaugh said coldly, still bearing the scars of his wounded ear and the cut down his forehead into the right eyebrow. "Now please leave, unless you'd like a taste of my latest mixture."

"What might that be?"

"It will in time be an improvement on common laudanum. At present it is poisonous enough to kill four horses. Come on, I need a test subject."

Julian smiled. Matthew was unnerved by it and didn't know exactly why. Julian wore a long gray fearnaught coat and a companion to his dark green tricorn sat rakishly upon the blonde hair growing from his scalp. The black gloves on his hands bore a slight sheen of blue.

"I trust Berry is completely herself again?" Julian asked Matthew.

"Yes, thank God. And the doctor, too, of course."

"And no chance of further complications?"

"None," huffed Firebaugh. "I know my chemicals, sir!"

"Excellent," Julian said, his voice still quiet. "Leave us, Matthew."

Now Matthew's senses were at full alarm. "Julian, what are you—"

"I thank *you*, Matthew," said Firebaugh, "for bringing me here and giving me all this bounty, but this beast deserves no appreciation! If it

hadn't been for him, Elizabeth Mulloy would still be alive! A fine young girl, dead because he wished a *hostage*!" Firebaugh turned his back on Julian and grinned at Matthew. "He's a born killer…the type to kill young girls and, I'm sure, little boys as well!"

Julian was on him in three strides.

The knife was already out.

It glinted in the lamplight.

It carved another grin from ear-to-ear below the one on the doctor's mouth.

Julian shoved the man to the floor and stood over him, his face blank, watching the runnels of blood stream across the stones.

"Christ!" Matthew cried out. "What have you *done*?"

"Wait," Julian replied.

Firebaugh's body contorted. He clutched at the gape of his throat. The blood was spraying out, nearly hitting Matthew. Firebaugh's eyes bulged from his face, the spectacles hanging by his good ear. He put a hand to the floor and tried to stand, but his hand slipped in the gore and he went down again. His chin cracked on the stones.

"Wait," Julian repeated.

Firebaugh shivered. From the gashed throat there came a noise like the wind ripping through dry reeds.

Then he was still, lying on his side like his own question mark.

Julian knelt down and wiped the blade clean on the dead doctor's shoulder.

"I knew he was ill-named," Julian said, straightening up again.

"Have you lost your *mind*?" Matthew backed away. "*Why*?"

Julian's eyes were dark and hard, but his mouth twisted in the grimace of a smile. "No one," he said, "makes me clean out their chamberpot and gets away with it." He looked toward the writing desk and walked to it. He picked up the book of potions. He slid the knife into its sheath under his coat, and he took the glass chimney off the lantern and turned the wick up high.

As Matthew watched with a mixture of terror and warped fascination, Julian began to methodically tear the pages from the book and touch them to the flame.

"This book should not be. You know that as well as I," he said as the smoke rose up and the papers curled and blackened. He dropped each one just before the flames reached his gloved fingers. The ashes fell like gray snowflakes around the doctor's corpse. "Don't speak, Matthew. Just stand there. Good boy," he said, as the pages of the book continued to crisp away.

When the last of the pages had been burned and its ashes joined with the others on the bloodied floor, Julian opened the book's empty binding and laid it down almost reverentially across Firebaugh's pallid face.

"There," Julian said. "Finished."

"You came here to kill him, didn't you," said Matthew.

"Guilty."

"The professor will cut you to pieces for this."

"Not if the professor can't find me." Julian's eyes were no longer hard but they were still cautious. "I am going to talk my way past McBray at the back gate. Easy enough. I am going to take a boat. A nice boat, not like that little splinter we took from Adderlane. I am leaving here, and soon I plan to be sailing off to Bristol." He smiled faintly. "A *plan*. How quaint. Now…as for you…you won't tell anyone where I've gone, will you?"

"No. Of course not."

"I know you won't. Because you're a good man, Matthew." Julian lifted his chin a fraction. His eyes caught shards of yellow light. "But I hope some bad has rubbed off on you. You'll need it before it's over. Good luck."

Matthew nodded. His senses were nearly overwhelmed by the carnage he'd witnessed, and perhaps he had begun to think of Firebaugh as a friend, but even though the doctor had saved Berry, the truth was that through Firebaugh the professor would've used that book to continue to keep the village's inhabitants as drug-dazed prisoners, and probably worse to come. Now…what would be the result of its permanent absence?

Julian was right. The book should not be. But whether Julian had killed the doctor and burned the book out of a sudden feeling for humanity or simply because it struck him to do so before he departed were the elements of a formula Matthew could not decipher.

"To you as well," Matthew answered.

"And if you ever happen to wonder how I'm doing," the bad man said, "be assured that I will always...*always*...start anew and afresh tomorrow."

With that Julian Devane turned and strode out the door, leaving a still-stunned Matthew standing alone in the beautiful laboratory of Y Beautiful Bedd with the ill-named Lazarus Firebaugh's blood puddling around his boots.

THIRTY-SEVEN.

"Let's go across to the Old Crock and get a brew," said Hudson.

This suggestion brought forth a groan. "I can't walk another step! You've near killed me today!"

"Nonsense! Don't you want a drink before you turn in?"

"No," Hugh Guinnessey replied from his supine position on the cow-hide sofa. "You don't need one either."

"Who said anything about *need*? Come on, man! Get up and let's go."

"I can't, Hudson. Really. I swear to God, I'm cooked."

Hudson stood before him in the sumptuous green-curtained room with his hands on his hips. "I'm going across to get a drink. You coming or not?"

"Not." Guinnessey sat up and rubbed his aching calf muscles through his white stockings. "Damn, what a set of legs you have! Well…Christ take it all…go on and get your drink. I'm stayin' right here."

"I don't think the professor would like that. Aren't you supposed to stick on me like tar-and-feathers without the feathers?"

"He's up in his room asleep by now. Anyway, where are you gonna go to? Ain't like you were wantin' to run off."

"True. Still…I like you, and I'd hate to get you in trouble with the boss."

Guinnessey scowled. "He ain't had to be tryin' to keep up with you all the damn day! Listen…go get your drink and come right back. If he don't know you're out, there's no worry."

"What about the others?" Hudson asked, with an expression of genuine concern for the man who had been tasked to not only share this room but keep watch on him so all remained in order until their ship sailed in four mornings. "I wouldn't want to run into any of them and have them tell the professor the extremely wild and dangerous Hudson Greathouse was let loose to roam around."

"They're all likely asleep by now too. Hell, I'm not used to late nights!"

"Hm," said Hudson. He glanced at Guinnessey's thin legs. The man himself was no raging bull. The scheme of the day seemed to have worked. "Then I have your permission to cross the street to the Old Crock and have one drink? After which I shall return as meekly as a little child attending the Sabbath?"

"Yes! Just go and quit jabberin'! I'm near fallin' asleep myself."

"If you insist. May I have some money?"

"How much?"

"Oh, four shillings ought to do it."

"*Four shillin's*? You gonna get a bottle and a side of beef? *Damn*!" Guinnessey hauled himself off the sofa and, wincing with every step, hobbled to the table where his pouch of money lay. He unbuttoned it and held out the coins. "Take 'em and go on."

"Thank you, sir." Hudson received the money, shrugged into the new leather coat with its fleece lining and hood he'd bought today with shillings from the same pouch—actually Professor Fell's money, but who was counting?—and he dropped his newfound fortune into a pocket. He put on the new black leather gloves he had also purchased today in their hours-long shopping trip back and forth along the fashionable streets around the Emerald Inn, the same trip that had been calculated to wear out the legs of Hugh Guinnessey and make this late-night venture possible. Hudson's watchdog had begun to howl and moan around noon, but Hudson had been adamant in finding an entire wardrobe of new clothes for the forthcoming trip to Italy. It wouldn't do to look like a common ragamuffin aboard a privately-chartered ship, would it? Anyway, what was there to do in London but eat, drink and buy clothes at the most expensive and far-flung shops that could be found, and devil take the passing cabs because exercise in this sharp, cold and bracing January air was good for a body.

Guinnessey groaned as he worked himself back on the sofa. "Bring me the change," he said.

"Surely. No need for me to take the key. I'll return in half a shake of a pig's tail."

"Listen," Guinnessey said as Hudson started out into the lamp-lit hallway. "Just to the Old Crock and no further. I mean it. If *he* knew I was lettin' you run free it would be my neck."

"Consider this," Hudson replied at the door with the nice warm hood up over his head. "If I wished to escape from you, how many times today might I have done that? Of course you were carrying your pistol—an unnecessary weight on you, I believe, that you're now paying for—and you might've shot me right there in broad daylight with a hundred thousand people as witnesses, but the truth is that I could've wrested that gun from you at any time and easily escaped. But as I told the professor...*why* would I want to escape? I'm going along to protect Matthew. It would be folly to turn my back on him, and a disgrace to me. So rest easy, Hugh... I'll get my drink and come right back. Can I bring you anything?"

"New legs," Guinnessey said.

Hudson gave a chortle, went out and closed the door.

At the end of the corridor he went down the long curving emerald-green-carpeted staircase into the realm of the rich. A huge fireplace bordered with green and white tiles burned merrily, warming a few swells and their female swellettes who lounged about in the voluptuous chairs. He looked about and saw none of the three others Fell had brought along for this jaunt: Kirby, Sanderson and Dawes, all of them somewhat brighter and harder to deal with than Guinnessey, which was why Hudson had

volunteered to share a room with him though the volunteering had to seem to be Hugh's idea. That bastard Stalker had been left in charge of the village, so God help the village.

As for the village, Hudson considered that Julian Devane had managed a neat vanishing act after putting the blade to Lazarus Firebaugh and destroying the book of potions. He understood that McBray had opened the back gate and allowed Devane to amble down to the harbor. And why wouldn't he? Devane was no prisoner there, and in fact he was a valued member of the organization. Hudson had heard that Fell took the news in gloomy silence but with the larger prospect of the Italian trip ahead, what was he to do?

Matthew had been interrogated about the incident by Stalker. Did he know anything of it? No, Matthew had said. It must've happened while he was having tea with Berry.

Having tea with Berry, Hudson thought with a suppressed grin. In his youth it was called something else.

For his money—all four shillings of it at the moment—Devane was not all bad.

Hudson lowered the hood of his coat and strode directly across the soft heaven of carpet to the clerk's desk.

"Yes sir?" asked the young man on duty.

"I need a sheet of paper, writing materials and an envelope."

"At once, sir."

When the items were presented on a green enamel tray—and Hudson thought that three more nights of everything green was all he could stand before he turned green himself—he asked where he might compose a letter and was directed to a writing desk in a well-lighted alcove.

Hudson sat down at the desk's chair. He spread the paper out on the desk's blotter—yes, green—and thought out what he was going to write. He was much more gifted at fighting than writing, but here was the moment he'd been planning for all day.

So, to the task at hand with the supplied pen and inkwell.

It took him a while.

When he was finished and had signed his name at the bottom, he folded the sheet and slid it into the envelope.

On the envelope he scribed *To Sheriff Gideon Lancer* and beneath that, *Whistler Green*. Ah…here green was a necessity rather than a bilious luxury.

Hudson took the tray of writing materials and the envelope back to the clerk. "Will you seal this with your stamp, please?"

"Of course, sir." There was a moment while the clerk fetched a candle—emerald green—and the official stamp of the Emerald Inn to seal the letter.

When it was completed, Hudson said, "Will you get this out by express mail coach as soon as possible? First thing in the morning, I hope?" He was already reaching into his pocket for the money. He brought out two shillings and laid them on the clerk's desk.

"Sir, that's far too much postage!"

"First thing in the morning," Hudson repeated, the stern notes of no nonsense and no mistakes shading his voice.

The clerk nodded, slipped the envelope into a leather pouch along with a few other letters, and it was accomplished.

Hudson pulled his hood up, walked out of the inn and into the cold night. He crossed the street to the Old Crock tavern, where he ordered an ale and sat at a back table listening to a young woman with long shining black hair playing the guitar and singing songs of lost love.

Hudson mused that she should be singing songs of newfound love, to suit the occasion. Right now Matthew was probably up in Berry's room. During the trip from Fell's village they had stayed so close to each other Hudson thought it a wonder they hadn't had to be pried apart with a crowbar. But who could fault that? Both of them had walked through their own territory of Hell, so for now let the angels sing.

There was still some difficulty ahead, and not just concerning the trip to Italy. In the morning at six o'clock Berry's ship sailed for New York.

There would be copious tears, wailings and handwringings at the dock, and Hudson figured he might have to slap Matthew to get him out of it. Berry obviously did not particularly approve of this eastward journey but she was resigned to it, and Hudson had told her he would look after the boy as best he could.

The *boy*?

No longer a moonbeam, and far from it.

The *man*.

But after Berry's ship departed in the morning, Hudson intended to get Matthew a little bit drunk, because whether Matthew knew it or not he needed to fly free out of that tight skin of his, at least for a while. He was going to get a little bit drunk too. He needed it just as much.

Hudson couldn't shake the feeling that something about Matthew had changed quite dramatically since the last time he'd seen the young man. It was in his face, in his eyes, in the way he carried himself. Of course Matthew had been through a difficult time—and difficult was not strong enough a word—but still…something about Matthew reminded him now of…

…himself?

The demonic mirror. Awaiting them in Italy?

What was awaiting them there?

Something worse than a demonic mirror?

One never knew what Fate had in store.

One never knew.

But for the moment…live for the moment, and *in* the moment.

"Another ale," Hudson told the serving girl who came to his table. "And another song from the singer." He lifted his near-empty mug in respect for her talents, and she gave him a pretty smile and a sweet chorus of notes on her guitar that sounded like birds at play in the trees of summer.

Bringing back change from the Old Crock?

The hell you say.

"I have come here as a salesman, to sell you an idea," said one man to another.

The man who sat in shadow didn't reply for a moment. Then the voice issued out: a low, sonorous voice, yet there something afflicted about it. "Go on."

"I believe you know my reputation. I of course know yours. You possess something I am in need of, and perhaps I possess knowledge that you may find invaluable."

"To the point," said the man who sat in shadow.

Cardinal Black's long thin fingers toyed with the silver skullface and satanic rings that adorned his other hand. "You possess a fast ship. I believe it is called the *Nemesis*. I need such a vessel, unencumbered by other passengers."

"And why might that be?"

Black peered into the shadow. The man before him had deliberately seated himself in this grand room, in this grand white mansion in London's Regent's Park district, so that the darkness gathered in his corner of choice enveloped him. The man sat in a white lounge chair with brass-topped nails ornamenting its curvatures. His legs were crossed. His breeches were of the finest pale gray silk, his stockings perfectly white, his ankle-length boots rich ebony and ashine with the lamplight that was directed into the cardinal's face.

"Four mornings hence," Black said, "a ship called the *Essex Triton* will depart for the port of Venice. I have employed men to gather information from the offices of passage. Some payments were made. They were worthwhile. On this *Essex Triton*, according to the ledger of the Raleigh Globe company, will be an old man who calls himself John Lamprey, a younger man by the name of Matthew Spottle, four others I care nothing about, and another man who has given his real name of Hudson Greathouse. I in particular know that name because Mother

Deare informed me he gave her some trouble in her tavern before he was taken away."

"Mother Deare," said the man who sat in shadow with the afflicted voice. "How does she abide?"

"Four fathoms deep, I imagine."

"Dead?"

"Most certainly."

"Hm," said the man who sat in shadow. "I thought that old bitch would never die."

"Sadly it is so."

"John *Lamprey*. Isn't that a fish of some sort?"

"As I understand, it is a type of eel that sucks the life from whatever it attaches upon. Which is pertinent, since John Lamprey is the alias being used by Danton Idris Fell. The young man Spottle is in actuality named Matthew Corbett. I have business with him that I wish to bring to a conclusion in my favor."

"Professor Fell," spoke the man. "Why is he sailing to Venice?"

Cardinal Black changed his position in his chair just a few inches. The movement caused his weirdly elongated face to express a wince, and his left hand went up to grasp at his right shoulder.

"An injury?"

"A near case of lead poisoning. I am still in some distress, but be assured I am strong enough to travel."

"Explain," said the man.

Cardinal Black looked about himself at the walls of the parlor, which seemed to have been constructed with sheets of gold. The ceiling was as white as a new pearl, and hanging from above was a white chandelier bearing a dozen tapers. In contrast to the golden walls were landscape paintings of dark and moody quality, depicting such things as vast lonely valleys and forests stark with ghostly moonlight, all empty of human habitation.

Black said, "Professor Fell is going to Italy to find a mirror that can call a demon up from the depths of the underworld. This mirror was created

by an Italian sorcerer and a man who though obsessed was not fully cognizant of what he was creating…or, afterward, what he possessed. From this enchanted glass can be summoned a creature to do the bidding of its caller. There is some risk involved, naturally, and a careful procedure to be followed. It would be akin to calling up a wild beast and riding upon its back…but…the benefits could be enormous. Think of it, sir. A creature that for a short time is bound to do your bidding. What would you desire? Riches? More than you possess now? Power? More than you have now? Or…beauty. That too would be within your power to command. Think of it, sir. A creature that could conceivably give you anything—*anything*—your heart or mind might desire.

"Professor Fell believes this mirror exists and can be found," Black continued. "I do, as well. Of course I do. My master has told me. It does exist, it can be found, and it can be *used.* I want the mirror as much as Fell does—even more, I believe, and I intend to get it. My master has told me it is within reach. But my master challenges me, sir. He will not tell me exactly where the mirror is. It is up to me to find it. And to find it, I need a fast ship unencumbered by other passengers to follow the *Essex Triton.*"

The man who sat in shadow did not move nor did he speak.

"I have a goodly amount of money from the recent sale of White Velvet," Black said, "but my supply is running low. I could charter a private ship, as the professor has done, but as I say I need a fast ship, and one that I know will be captained by a man of your experience who will not lose pace. Therefore I come to you, sir, to ask for the use of the *Nemesis*, in order to follow Professor Fell to the mirror. He is being led there by the young man Corbett, who has experience with the Herrald Agency. How they have come together in partnership is a mystery even my master cannot solve, but there it is. I need the *Nemesis* and I am willing to pay."

The man who sat in shadow did not speak for a time. At last he said, "You say you are selling an idea. This is it? An enchanted mirror?"

"The idea I am selling," said Black, "is that there would be two compartments aboard the *Nemesis*, and two equal partners in search of a

mirror—a well-documented item, by the way—that could give up riches, or power, or beauty beyond measure. One compartment for me, one compartment for yourself."

"A journey of considerable length," said the man. "I have businesses to guide."

"As I understand, sir, your businesses are so successful they run themselves. Also, that you don't often leave this gracious abode. I understand as well that some of your ventures are in...shall we say...competition with those of the professor. I mentioned the old man, John Lamprey. I will add to that: the *weakened* old man, John Lamprey."

"I have heard as much."

"And correctly heard. But consider why Professor Fell might be interested—desperate, possibly—to get the mirror," said Black, as he again toyed with his satanic rings. "In control of the mirror and its power, Fell might do...*what*? Destroy you and his other competitor Doctor Phibes with one breath of a desire? Bring this house down to a cinder? Wipe you out, sir, as if you had never existed? Oh...it is paramount not only to gain control of the mirror, but to prevent Fell from gaining control. And...there is one more reason a trip to Italy would be of benefit to both you and me, over and beyond the mirror."

The man who sat in shadow did not respond, but the cardinal knew he was listening.

"Professor Fell will be travelling only with a guard of four men fully loyal to him. Corbett is what I would call a wild card, and Greathouse the same," Black went on. "Fell will be far away from that army he commands...or *believes* he commands. He will be out of his element. Out of his stone walls and his protection. Out in the *open*, and thus open to being removed entirely from the scene with a minimum of effort. But first...have him lead us to the mirror, and then...a wreath of thorns for his grave?"

"He believes strongly enough in this mirror to leave his protection?" the man asked.

"Certainly so. The privately chartered *Essex Triton* sails for Venice in four mornings, at six o'clock from Dock Number Eight of the Raleigh Globe company. If the professor did *not* believe so strongly, would he be making such an effort?"

"Your information is accurate?"

"You know my reputation. That is my master's word."

The man gave a quiet grunt of consideration. Then he said, "Why don't I just kill you now and sail off to find the mirror myself?"

"Sir," Black replied with a cunning smile, "if you would take stock in the mirror, you would take stock in the anger of my master should any harm befall me from yourself. I am loyal to my Satan, sir, and he is loyal to me. He will be a benefit on this journey, I assure you. And…you would need someone with my influence over such matters to prevent yourself from being torn to pieces before the creature in the mirror could be controlled. Oh, no…you *need* me." He waited for that to sink in. "Give further thought to this, sir: it is as important for us to get the mirror as it is for us to *prevent* Fell from getting it. And as I say, every desire would be within reach. Riches, power, beauty. And certainly *renewed* beauty."

The man was silent.

In the room a grandfather clock struck eleven.

At the end of its chimings, the man said, "I do know your reputation. And you know my story, I presume. How events transpired. How I was forced to discipline a woman in my employ, after she allowed one of my possessions to escape? And there was evidence she did this injury to me with full recognition of the fact? Her name was…I forget her name. Interesting. I have her face right there in front of me, but I forget the name. And then this woman perished from the discipline inflicted, which was perfectly my right, and another of my possessions…well…you know this tale, I assume."

"I have only heard a breath of the story," Black admitted.

"Another of my possessions, being so fond of this woman," the man continued, "ambushed me with a bottle of corrosive liquid, and…therefore…her name…what was the name?"

"My idea," Black prodded. "Yourself, me and perhaps others you might wish to join our quest. Following the professor when the *Essex Triton* leaves for Venice four mornings hence, and thus to track him—and Matthew Corbett—to the mirror that will give us...*everything*."

"Riches and power," the man said. "I have all that, in abundance. But beauty...ah! I recall the traitor's name now. It was *Spanner*."

"My idea, sir?" said Black. "Your decision?"

The man leaned forward into the light.

The left side of his face was that of a man devilishly handsome, with a dark brown eye, a high aristocratic forehead, a nose carved for the statue of a god, and a chiselled chin. His abundant hair had once been fully lustrous black but now was streaked with gray at the temple.

The right side of his face was concealed by a leather mask bound to his head with straps, but upon the leather itself was sculpted a white wax image of the handsome side, the wax adorned with small sparkling moonstones along its edges, which were pressed tightly along the hairline and to the unseen ruin below. Half his mouth was covered by the leather, the lips molded in white wax.

The eye on the right side was formed of shining gold.

It bore a pupil of the deepest scarlet.

The man spoke, only the left portion of the lips able to move.

"*Sold*," said Maccabeus DeKay.